OBSESSED WITH™

MARVEL

TEST YOUR KNOWLEDGE OF THE MARVEL UNIVERSE

by Peter Sanderson and Mark Sumerak

CONTENTS

CHAPTER ONE:
Fantastic Four

1. Which of the following buildings has *not* been the headquarters of the Fantastic Four?
   A. The Baxter Building
   B. Four Freedoms Plaza
   C. Stark Tower
   D. Pier 4

2. Who is the Fantastic Four's receptionist?
   A. Mrs. Bambi Arbogast
   B. Roberta, a robot
   C. Alicia Masters
   D. Glory Grant

3. Who of the following has *not* been one of Johnny Storm's girlfriends?
   A. Ann Raymond
   B. Doris Evans
   C. Frankie Raye
   D. Crystal

4. Which of the following is *not* an alternate identity of the sinister time traveler Pharaoh Rama-Tut?
   A. Immortus
   B. Kang the Conqueror
   C. Zarrko the Tomorrow Man
   D. The Scarlet Centurion

5. Which of the following characters was *not* a member of a substitute Fantastic Four team that included Spider-Man?
   A. Ghost Rider II
   B. The Hulk
   C. The Punisher
   D. Wolverine

6. What is Fantastic Four mailman Willie Lumpkin's supposed super-power?
   A. Simultaneously patting his head and rubbing his tummy
   B. Twitching his nose
   C. Wiggling his ears
   D. Delivering the mail despite rain, sleet, hail, or snow

7. Which Fantastic Four enemy is also the blind Alicia Masters's stepfather?
   A. Doctor Doom
   B. The Mad Thinker
   C. The Wizard
   D. The Puppet Master

OPPOSITE *Fantastic Four* #90 (1978) cover

8. Which of Spider-Man's foes was a founding member of the Frightful Four?
A. Doctor Octopus **C.** Mysterio
B. Sandman **D.** Electro

9. Which of the Inhumans was a member of the original Frightful Four?
A. Gorgon **C.** Medusa
B. Karnak **D.** Triton

10.

11. At which university did Reed Richards first meet Ben Grimm and Victor von Doom?
A. Columbia University **C.** State University of New York
B. Empire State University **D.** Harvard University

12. Which of the Inhumans has elemental powers controlling air, earth, fire, and water?
A. Black Bolt **C.** Crystal
B. Karnak **D.** Triton

13. Who is responsible for creating the Inhumans from humanity's ancestors?
A. The Celestials **C.** The High Evolutionary
B. The Skrulls **D.** The Kree

14. What is the main super-power of the Inhumans' gigantic dog, Lockjaw?
A. Creates powerful sonic vibrations by barking **C.** Can teleport himself and others
B. Can discharge concussive energy from his antenna **D.** Communicates by telepathy

15. Where did Johnny Storm find Namor the Sub-Mariner in *Fantastic Four* #4 (1962)?
A. The throne room of Atlantis **C.** A flophouse in the Bowery
B. An office in a Hollywood studio **D.** The Baxter Building

16. What was the all-powerful weapon that Reed Richards threatened to use against Galactus when he first invaded Earth?
A. The Cosmic Cube **C.** The Serpent Crown
B. The Ultimate Nullifier **D.** The Infinity Gauntlet

OBSESSED WITH MARVEL

10.

The "Marvel Age of Comics" began with *Fantastic Four* #1 in 1961 (shown at right). Writer-editor Stan Lee and artist Jack Kirby together created the Fantastic Four, a team of adventurers who flew an experimental starship into outer space. There they were exposed to cosmic rays, which endowed them with superhuman powers. Mister Fantastic, Reed Richards, was already the world's most brilliant scientist, but now he could also stretch his body like rubber. His girlfriend, Susan Storm, the Invisible Girl, could not only turn invisible, but could also create force fields. Her younger brother, Johnny Storm, was the Human Torch and could burst into flame and fly. And their friend Ben Grimm became a super-strong monster called The Thing.

Before *Fantastic Four* #1, Super Heroes were one-dimensional characters in stories aimed at small children. However, with *Fantastic Four*, Lee and Kirby were intent on depicting superheroes as if they were real people, with complex personalities and emotions, and showing what might happen if they existed in the real world. Thus, *Fantastic Four* set the course for many Marvel comics that followed in its wake.

Where were the Fantastic Four originally based?

A. Cape Canaveral, Florida
B. Central City, California
C. Los Angeles, California
D. New York City, New York

17. What is the profession of Ben Grimm's longtime love Alicia Masters?

   A. Lawyer   **C.** Poet

   B. Sculptor   **D.** Musician

18. What is the Puppet Master's specialty?

   A. He turns people into actual puppets   **C.** He uses clay puppets to control the minds of people

   B. He creates human-sized puppets that obey his mental commands   **D.** He is a wooden puppet that came to life

19. Why do the alien Watchers refuse to intervene in the affairs of other inhabited worlds?

   A. Because they regret conquering worlds in the past   **C.** Because they inadvertently caused a nuclear war by giving an alien race advanced technology

   B. Because they disdain communicating with supposedly inferior beings   **D.** Because the galactic empires have forbidden them to intervene

20. What Super Hero name did Reed and Sue's daughter Valeria once use?

   A. Malice   **C.** Ms. Marvel

   B. Phoenix   **D.** Marvel Girl

21. Which of the Fantastic Four's enemies is an alchemist who has lived for centuries?

   A. Gaius Tiberius Agrippa   **C.** Nicholas Scratch

   B. Diablo   **D.** Quasimodo

22. Which heroine has *not* been a member of both the Fantastic Four and the Avengers?

   A. Crystal   **C.** She-Thing

   B. Invisible Woman   **D.** She-Hulk

23. Who stole the cosmic power of the Silver Surfer in *Fantastic Four* #57–60 (1966)?

   A. Mephisto   **C.** Doctor Doom

   B. Galactus   **D.** The Super-Adaptoid

24. Which Super Villain originally called himself Paste-Pot Pete?

   A. Chemistro   **C.** The Trapster

   B. The Painter of a Thousand Perils   **D.** The Tinkerer

Fantastic Four

25. Which of the following enemies of the Fantastic Four is *not* based in the underground realm of Subterranea?

A. Attuma

B. Kala

C. The Mole Man

D. Tyrannus

26. Which of the Inhumans can breathe underwater?

A. Gorgon

B. Triton

C. Medusa

D. Karnak

27. What is the Inhuman Medusa's super-power?

A. Like her namesake, she can also turn people to stone

B. She paralyzes people with her gaze

C. A fast healing ability that accelerates her hair growth

D. She telekinetically manipulates her long hair

28. Which of the Inhumans can create earth tremors by stamping his feet?

A. Black Bolt

B. Karnak

C. Gorgon

D. Triton

29. Which of the following is *not* one of the Mad Thinker's specialties?

A. Androids

B. Calculating the future

C. Martial arts

D. Computers

30. Whom did T'Challa, the Black Panther, marry?

A. Carrie Alexander

B. Monica Lynne

C. Monica Rambeau

D. Ororo Munroe

31. Which of the following African nations in the Marvel Universe also exists in the real world?

A. Azania

B. Rudyarda

C. Tanzania

D. Wakanda

32. Which of the following places has *not* been a site for the Inhumans' "Great Refuge," the city of Attilan?

A. The Blue Area of the Moon

B. Atlantis

C. The Andes Mountains

D. The Himalayan Mountains

33. Why doesn't Black Bolt, ruler of the Inhumans, speak?

A. He only speaks in times of political crisis

B. He was born mute

C. He communicates by telepathy, not by speech

D. His voice creates powerful vibrations that could destroy a city

OBSESSED WITH MARVEL

37.

Until *Fantastic Four* #1 (1961), the issue that introduced The Thing, comic book heroes were usually handsome men and monsters were nearly always menaces who must be defeated and destroyed. However, with The Thing, writer-editor Stan Lee and artist Jack Kirby introduced a revolutionary type of character: a monster who was a hero.

Ben Grimm piloted the fateful mission into outer space in which the Fantastic Four acquired their super-powers via cosmic radiation. But the radiation also transformed Ben Grimm into a grotesque monster, a "thing," whose thick hide looked as if it were made of orange bricks. Ben was another new concept in popular culture: a Super Hero whose powers were a curse rather than a blessing.

The Thing is a genuinely tragic figure, alienated from human society by his monsterlike appearance. Nevertheless, Ben has a strong sense of humor and an infectious joy in combat, exemplified by his battle cry, "It's clobberin' time!" (shown at left).

What is Benjamin J. Grimm's middle name?

A. Jacob
B. James
C. John
D. Joseph

34. How was the original Human Torch different from his present-day counterpart, Johnny Storm?

A. He did not have the same super-powers

B. He was not a member of a Super Hero team

C. He was an android, not a human being

D. He was a mutant

35. Where is Yancy Street, the home of the Yancy Street Gang who makes fun of The Thing?

A. The Bronx

B. Brooklyn

C. The Lower East Side of Manhattan

D. The Bowery

36. What power does the Mad Thinker's Awesome Android *not* possess?

A. Ability to expel hurricane-force winds from its mouth

B. Super-strength

C. Superhuman intelligence

D. Ability to mimic other super-powers

37.

38. What began the feud between Victor von Doom and Reed Richards when they were students?

A. Richards chose Ben Grimm rather than Doom to be his dormitory roommate

B. Richards warned him about a dangerous experiment

C. They competed for Susan Storm's attention

D. Richards got better grades than Doom did

39. Where did Reed Richards intend to go on the spaceflight that gave the Fantastic Four their super-powers?

A. To the moon

B. To the stars

C. To Mars

D. To the sun

40. Does the Impossible Man have a real name?

A. Yes, but it is a secret

B. Yes, but humans cannot pronounce it

C. No, his alien race deprived him of his name when they exiled him to Earth

D. No, he says members of his alien race do not need names: they know who they are

Fantastic Four

41. Which member of the Inhumans Royal Family has feet shaped like horse's hooves?

A. Gorgon   C. Maximus
B. Karnak   D. Triton

42. What career was Susan Storm planning before she gained super-powers?

A. Scientist   C. Pilot
B. Astronaut   D. Actress

43. What is the Human Torch's favorite place to meet with Spider-Man?

A. The Baxter Building   C. The Statue of Liberty
B. The Daily Bugle   D. The Empire State Building

44.

45. What is Johnny Storm's favorite hobby?

A. Piloting a plane   C. Race car driving
B. Photography   D. Playing guitar

46. What is the Impossible Man's primary super-power?

A. Psionic ability to rearrange the molecular structure of objects   C. Space travel by teleportation
B. Changing his own shape   D. Magic

47. Which Fantastic Four writer-artist team met the Impossible Man in the Marvel offices?

A. Tom DeFalco and Paul Ryan   C. Walter Simonson and Arthur Adams
B. Stan Lee and Jack Kirby   D. John Byrne (and himself)

48. Which one of the following Inhumans was *not* one of the evil Maximus's allies?

A. Aireo   C. Stallior
B. Leonus   D. Luna

49. How did the Molecule Man acquire his superhuman powers?

A. An experiment by an alien scientist   C. Mutation
B. A nuclear accident   D. Magic

44.

Created by Stan Lee and Jack Kirby in *Fantastic Four* #5 (1962), Doctor Doom (shown at right) has remained the Fantastic Four's leading nemesis to this day. He is a unique mix of the past and the futuristic. An orphaned gypsy boy in Eastern Europe, Victor von Doom taught himself sorcery and made himself the absolute ruler of his homeland.

But Doctor Doom is also a man of nearly super human genius in science. The metal armor he wears may look like a medieval knight's, but it's actually a high-tech battle-suit. He created technological wonders advanced far beyond modern science, like a time machine. A towering figure of nobility, ambition, and evil, Doctor Doom has devoted his life to conquering the Earth and to destroying the one man who may be his intellectual superior: Reed Richards.

What country is Doctor Doom's homeland?

A. Latveria
B. Symkaria
C. Transia
D. Wakanda

OBSESSED WITH MARVEL

50. Who became the She-Thing?

A. Lawyer turned Super Hero Jennifer Walters

B. Lady wrestler turned Super Hero Sharon Ventura

C. Ben Grimm's girlfriend, Alicia Masters

D. Ben Grimm's long-unseen Aunt Petunia

51. Which of the Sub-Mariner's relatives was briefly a substitute member of the Fantastic Four?

A. Byrrah

B. Marrina

C. Namorita

D. Namora

52. With which Marvel hero did Frankie Raye share a heroic alias?

A. Lightspeed

B. Quasar

C. Nova

D. Sunfire

53. Which villain started out fighting the Human Torch, later became one of Spider-Man's enemies, and ended up joining the Thunderbolts?

A. The Sandman

B. Paste-Pot Pete

C. The Beetle

D. The Wizard

54. Where did the Psycho-Man come from?

A. Another dimension

B. The future

C. A subatomic universe

D. Outer space

55. From where does the Puppet Master get the unusual clay from which he makes his puppets?

A. Latveria

B. The Savage Land

C. Transia

D. Wakanda

56. What is the Puppet Master's real name?

A. Alexander Masters

B. Herbert Edgar Wyndham

C. Philip Masters

D. Jacob Reiss

57. Which of the following descriptions of H.E.R.B.I.E. is incorrect?

A. A robot designed by Reed Richards

B. A toy built by Franklin Richards

C. Humanoid Experimental Robot, B-Type, Integrated Electronics

D. The host of the consciousness of the evil Doctor Sun

Fantastic Four

58. What unusual ability does Agatha Harkness's cat Ebony possess?

A. Ability to transform into a human being

B. Ability to communicate telepathically

C. Ability to transform into a ferocious black panther

D. Ability to appear and disappear by using magic

59. Which of the following sorcerers is the son of Agatha Harkness?

A. Baron Mordo

B. John Harkness

C. Nicholas Scratch

D. Master Pandemonium

60. In the *Fantastic Four*, who transferred the original Hate-Monger's consciousness into cloned bodies?

A. The High Evolutionary

B. Baron Heinrich Zemo

C. Arnim Zola

D. The Mad Thinker

61. Why does the sinister Ivan Kragoff call himself the Red Ghost?

A. Because he is dead but survives on Earth as a spirit

B. Because he can turn invisible

C. Because he can turn intangible at will

D. Because he has faked his own death

62.

63. What did Doctor Doom theorize when he encountered the time-traveling Pharaoh Rama-Tut?

A. Doom was Rama-Tut's descendant

B. Rama-Tut was Doom's descendant

C. Doom and Rama-Tut might be the same person

D. Rama-Tut was Kang the Conqueror

64. Where did the Red Ghost first battle the Fantastic Four?

A. The Baxter Building

B. The Blue Area of the Moon

C. His native Russia

D. Yancy Street

65. In the *Fantastic Four*, how did the Red Ghost and his Super Apes acquire their super-powers?

A. Laboratory experiments involving cosmic rays

B. Exposure to cosmic rays in outer space

C. Genetic engineering

D. Accidental mutation

OBSESSED WITH MARVEL

62.

In *Fantastic Four* #13 (1963), the Fantastic Four ventured into outer space and clashed with a Russian scientist called the Red Ghost and his Super Apes. Memorably, this issue contains the first appearance of writer-editor Stan Lee and artist Jack Kirby's creation of an alien called the Watcher (shown above). A gigantic figure garbed in a toga like a god of classical mythology, the Watcher is an imposing, potentially formidable figure with vast powers. But he and the rest of his alien race choose not to use their powers to intervene in the affairs of other planets' denizens. Instead, they devote their immortal existences to observing life on other worlds while never interfering, not

even to save lives. However, the Watcher, who is assigned to Earth, developed a fondness for the Fantastic Four and their planet. Hence, from time to time he makes exceptions to his oath of noninterference in order to aid the Fantastic Four, most notably in their initial confrontation with Galactus. A popular character over the years, the Watcher has starred in his own stories, *Tales of the Watcher*.

What is the real name of the alien Watcher who observes the Earth?

A. Aron
B. Ecce
C. Ikor
D. Uatu

66. Which character or characters were *not* present during at least part of the first reign of Pharaoh Rama-Tut in ancient Egypt?
A. Apocalypse
B. Spider-Man
C. The Fantastic Four
D. Doctor Strange

67. What is true about the Blue Area of the Moon, which first appeared in *Fantastic Four* #13 (1963)?
A. It has an atmosphere with enough oxygen to sustain life
B. It is the home of the Watcher
C. It was once the site of the Inhumans' city of Attilan
D. All answers are correct

68. Before he turned into a criminal, which of the following professions did the Wizard become?
A. Chess champion
B. Inventor
C. Stage magician
D. All answers are correct

69. Which alien race is an offshoot of the Skrulls?
A. The Dire Wraiths
B. The Carbon Copy Men
C. The Poppupians
D. The Reptoids

70. What is *not* true about Susan and Johnny Storm's father, Dr. Storm?
A. He spent years in prison for a crime he did not commit
B. He was once impersonated by the Super-Skrull
C. He was guilty of manslaughter for killing a loan shark's enforcer
D. He died heroically, saving the lives of the Fantastic Four

71. As a herald of Galactus, which of the four elements could Terrax the Tamer control with his cosmic power?
A. Air
B. Earth
C. Fire
D. Water

72. How did Toro acquire his flame powers?
A. He was an android
B. He was an experimental test subject
C. He was a mutant
D. The original Human Torch endowed him with his own powers

73. Who was the Fantastic Four's landlord before Reed Richards bought the Baxter Building?
A. Muggins
B. Collins
C. O'Houlihan
D. Stark

Fantastic Four

74. What happened to the man who stole the Thing's powers and identity in "This Man, This Monster" in *Fantastic Four* #51 (1966)?

A. He resumed his human form and led a reformed life

B. He died in the real Ben Grimm's arms

C. He sacrificed his life in the Negative Zone to save Reed Richards

D. He was captured by the Fantastic Four and sent to prison

75. Why did Crystal temporarily replace Susan Richards in the Fantastic Four?

A. Susan was temporarily separated from her husband, Reed

B. Susan was pregnant with her first child

C. Susan had doubts about continuing her career as a Super Hero

D. Susan was injured in combat

76. What was the "Secret Invasion"?

A. The shape-changing Dire Wraiths infiltrated Earth society by masquerading as humans

B. The Invaders (including Captain America, the original Human Torch, and Sub Mariner) battled the Nazis in Europe before D-Day

C. The Skrulls impersonated numerous Super Heroes in their plot to take over the Earth

D. The Red Skull and his agents conducted sabotage missions in the United States during World War II

77 Which member of the Fantastic Four did Doctor Doom once switch bodies with?

A. The Invisible Woman

B. Mister Fantastic

C. Human Torch

D. The Thing

78. Which of the Fantastic Four's antagonists owned a Hollywood movie studio?

A. Doctor Doom

B. Gregory Gideon

C. Namor the Sub-Mariner

D. The Monocle

79. When did the Fantastic Four first appear in costume?

A. *Fantastic Four* #3 (1962)

B. *Fantastic Four* #2 (1962)

C. *Fantastic Four* #1 (1961)

D. *Fantastic Four Annual* #1 (1963)

80. Who was the Infant Terrible?

A. Ben's nickname for Franklin Richards

B. One of the Impossible Man's Impossible Children

C. A lost child of the alien Elan race who possessed immense powers

D. Doctor Doom's protégé, Kristoff

OBSESSED WITH MARVEL

87.

Among the enormous cast of characters that writer-editor Stan Lee and artist Jack Kirby created in Fantastic Four was an entire hidden race of superhuman beings, the Inhumans (shown at left). One of the Inhumans, the long-haired Medusa, appeared as early as *Fantastic Four* #36 (1965), while the rest of the Inhumans' Royal Family debuted in a story arc that ran from *Fantastic Four* #44 to #48 (1965–1966). Their leader is the regal and silent Black Bolt, monarch of the Inhumans, who eventually made Medusa his queen. Medusa's younger sister Crystal was romantically involved with the Human Torch and even joined the Fantastic Four before eventually marrying Quicksilver of the Avengers. Other members of the Royal Family include Gorgon, Karnak, Triton, and Maximus the Mad, the cunning though insane brother of Black Bolt and his rival for the Inhumans' throne.

Although the Inhumans long lived in secrecy in their Great Refuge, the world at large ultimately became aware of their existence. Longtime inhabitants of the Marvel Universe, the Inhumans have not only appeared in *Fantastic Four* and other titles but have also starred in their own Marvel series from time to time.

What is the primary source of the Inhumans' superhuman powers?

A. Genetic engineering
B. Mutation through natural means
C. Experimentation by the Kree aliens
D. The mutagenic effects of Terrigen Mist

---

81. Why did Doctor Doom capture the Fantastic Four in their first encounter in *Fantastic Four* #5 (1962)?
A. To take revenge on Reed Richards
B. To send the Fantastic Four back in time on a mission
C. To compel the Fantastic Four to help Doom conquer the world
D. To help Doom conquer Latveria

82. What happened when Doctor Doom allied himself with the Sub-Mariner in *Fantastic Four* #6 (1962)?
A. Doom and Namor jointly took over New York City
B. Doom raised the Baxter Building into outer space
C. Namor attempted to flood New York City
D. Doom and Namor defeated the Fantastic Four in combat

83. Who was Reed Richards's most serious rival for the love of Susan Storm?
A. Ben Grimm
B. Prince Namor
C. Tony Stark
D. Victor von Doom

84. Who was the crime-fighting partner of the original Human Torch?
A. Sun Girl
B. Firelord
C. Toro
D. Firestar

85. Where did the original Human Torch first appear?
A. *Marvel Comics* #1 (1939)
B. *Human Torch* #1 (1963)
C. *Fantastic Four* #1 (1961)
D. *Fantastic Four Annual* #4 (1967)

86. Which comics professional(s) created the original Human Torch?
A. Joe Simon and Jack Kirby
B. Bill Everett
C. Carl Burgos
D. Stan Lee and Jack Kirby

87.

88. Which member of the Fantastic Four did the Frightful Four brainwash into turning evil?
A. Mister Fantastic
B. The Thing
C. Human Torch
D. The Invisible Girl

89. Which member of the Fantastic Four was brainwashed by the Mad Thinker into turning evil?
A. Mister Fantastic
B. The Thing
C. Human Torch
D. The Invisible Girl

Fantastic Four

90. Who did *not* ink any of Jack Kirby's *Fantastic Four* issues?
A. Dick Ayers
B. Mike Royer
C. Joe Sinnott
D. Chic Stone

91. Who, other than The Thing, is a regular participant in the Super Hero poker games held in New York?
A. The Beast
B. Ms. Marvel I
C. Wolverine
D. All answers are correct

92. Which of the following characters once worked as a New York City police officer?
A. T'Challa, the Black Panther
B. Jim Hammond, the original Human Torch
C. Ben Grimm, The Thing
D. Johnny Storm, the second Human Torch

93.

94. Which Marvel hero guest starred in "The Search for the Sub-Mariner" in *Fantastic Four* #27 (1964)?
A. Captain America
B. Giant-Man
C. Doctor Strange
D. Spider-Man

95. Whom did the Fantastic Four battle in "Side by Side with Sub-Mariner" in *Fantastic Four* #33 (1964)?
A. Attuma
B. Byrrah
C. Doctor Doom
D. Krang

96. Which guest star helped the powerless Fantastic Four when Doctor Doom seized control of their Baxter Building headquarters in *Fantastic Four* #39 (1965)?
A. Captain America
B. Daredevil
C. Nick Fury
D. Spider-Man

97. Which member or members of the Fantastic Four still has a living mother?
A. Ben Grimm
B. Susan Storm Richards and Johnny Storm
C. Reed Richards
D. None of these

93.

In creating Johnny Storm, the Fantastic Four's Human Torch (shown at right), writer-editor Stan Lee and artist Jack Kirby created a new version of one of Marvel's very first Super Heroes: the original Human Torch of the "Golden Age of Comics." His name was a misnomer because the original Human Torch was actually an android, a robot in human form, who was created by Professor Phineas T. Horton. Escaping from Horton, the Torch ran amuck, becoming a danger to society. But eventually the Torch settled into the role of crime-fighting Super Hero, adopting a human identity, Jim Hammond, and taking on a young human sidekick. Inevitably, Lee and Kirby had the original Torch meet and battle Johnny Storm. At the end of that encounter, the original Torch died, but he was later resurrected as a member of the West Coast Avengers.

In which year did the original Human Torch first appear?

A. 1953
B. 1942
C. 1939
D. 1966

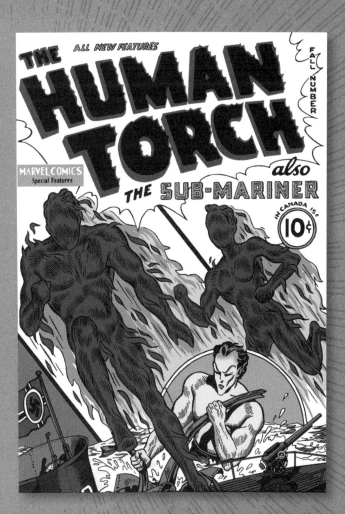

98. Which two villains simultaneously menaced the Fantastic Four in issue 63 (1967)?

A. The Mad Thinker and the Puppet Master

B. Blastaar and the Sandman

C. The Wizard and the Sandman

D. Diablo and the Dragon Man

99. Which founding member or members of the Avengers guest starred in "The Micro-World of Doctor Doom" in *Fantastic Four* #16 (1963)?

A. Iron Man

B. The Hulk

C. Ant-Man and the Wasp

D. Thor

100. Which of the following is *not* a description of the Beehive?

A. The birthplace of Adam Warlock

B. The lair of the alien insectoid Annihilus

C. The nickname for the Citadel of Science

D. The headquarters of the Enclave

101. Why did Doctor Doom abruptly call a halt to his battle with the Fantastic Four in his castle in *Fantastic Four* #87 (1969)?

A. Doom was losing badly

B. The fight threatened the lives of Doom's Latverian subjects

C. The powerful combat was wrecking the castle

D. Doom did not want his valuable art collection to be damaged

102. Which Timely Super Hero confronted and killed Adolf Hitler at the end of World War II in Europe?

A. Captain America

B. The Destroyer

C. Sub-Mariner

D. The original Human Torch

103. Why does a Skrull capture The Thing and abduct him to the planet of Kral in *Fantastic Four* #90 (1969)?

A. To have him executed as an enemy of the Skrull Empire

B. To force him to serve as a soldier in the war against the Kree

C. To compel him to reveal Reed Richards's scientific secrets

D. To turn him into a gladiator, fighting for the Skrulls' entertainment

104. When was Jack Kirby's final *Fantastic Four* story first printed in its entirety?

A. *Fantastic Four* #102 in 1970

B. *Fantastic Four: The Lost Adventure* in 2008

C. *Fantastic Four* #108 in 1971

D. None of these

Fantastic Four

105. Who was the first artist to succeed Jack Kirby in *Fantastic Four*?
- **A.** Neal Adams
- **B.** John Buscema
- **C.** Gene Colan
- **D.** John Romita Sr.

106. When Stan Lee ended his run as regular writer of *Fantastic Four*, who was his successor?
- **A.** Gerry Conway
- **B.** Archie Goodwin
- **C.** Roy Thomas
- **D.** Len Wein

107. Which of the following writers and artists did *not* appear in the Marvel offices when the Impossible Man came to visit in *Fantastic Four* #176 (1976)?
- **A.** Roy Thomas and Archie Goodwin
- **B.** Len Wein and Marv Wolfman
- **C.** Steve Englehart and Joe Sinnott
- **D.** Gerry Conway and John Romita

108. When did The Thing finally receive his own comic book series that was named after him?
- **A.** 1973
- **B.** 1974
- **C.** 1983
- **D.** 1984

109. Who was the mastermind behind the Super Villains' attack on Reed and Sue's wedding in *Fantastic Four Annual* #3 (1965)?
- **A.** Doctor Doom
- **B.** Namor the Sub-Mariner
- **C.** The Puppet Master
- **D.** The Impossible Man

110.

111. Which Marvel character or characters made their first crossover appearances into Super Hero comics at Reed and Sue's wedding in *Fantastic Four Annual* #3 (1965)?
- **A.** Kid Colt, on the cover
- **B.** Patsy Walker, in the story
- **C.** Hedy Wolfe, in the story
- **D.** All answers are correct

112. Which character did the original Human Torch battle repeatedly and spectacularly in the early 1940s?
- **A.** Captain America
- **B.** The Sub-Mariner
- **C.** The Red Skull
- **D.** All answers are correct

113. What is the name of the Thing's deceased older brother?
- **A.** Joseph
- **B.** Daniel
- **C.** Jack
- **D.** Jacob

110.

Time and again co-creators Stan Lee and Jack Kirby invented superhuman beings who represented an advanced stage of evolution, such as the mutants in X-Men and the Inhumans. Another such being was initially known only as "Him."

In *Fantastic Four* #66 (shown at right) and #67 (1967), The Thing's blind girlfriend, Alicia Masters, was taken to the Citadel of Science, the base of a cadre of scientists who would later be known as the Enclave. There the Enclave was artificially creating a superhuman being whom they intended to exploit to gain power. As she had with the Silver Surfer, Alicia succeeded in bringing out the humanity within the strange superhuman being. Him confronted his makers, looking like a godlike being as he employed his immense powers to destroy the Citadel. Lee and Kirby would use Him again, but the character's destiny lay in other creative hands under his new name of Adam Warlock.

When Alicia Masters first encountered Him in the Enclave's Citadel, what was he encased in?

- **A.** A pool of water
- **B.** A birdlike nest
- **C.** A large, human-sized cocoon
- **D.** A metal chest

114. Which of the following is *not* true about the fate of Toro after his partnership with the original Human Torch ended?

A. Toro retired and married

B. Toro was eventually revived and he joined the West Coast Avengers

C. Toro seemingly perished in an attempt to avenge the original Human Torch

D. Like his mentor, Toro fell under the mental control of the Mad Thinker

115. What color are The Thing's eyes?

A. Brown

B. Blue

C. Green

D. Grey

116. Who in recent years became engaged to marry The Thing?

A. Alicia Masters

B. Debbie Green

C. Laura Green

D. Sharon Ventura

117. What is The Thing's religious background, as revealed in *Fantastic Four* #52 (2002)?

A. Catholic

B. Protestant

C. Jewish

D. Agnostic

118. Which Marvel heroes did Ben Grimm meet when he was a pilot in the Air Force?

A. Carol Danvers, the future Ms. Marvel

B. Logan, the future Wolverine

C. Nick Fury, the future director of S.H.I.E.L.D.

D. All answers are correct

119. Which Fantastic Four members joined Captain America's Secret Avengers during the Super Heroes' Civil War?

A. Mister Fantastic and The Thing

B. The Thing and Human Torch

C. Human Torch and Invisible Woman

D. Invisible Woman and Mister Fantastic

120. What is the name for the Human Torch's maximum level of flame?

A. Solar flame

B. Plasma flame

C. Nova flame

D. Starfire

121. What profession was the Susan Storm of *Ultimate Fantastic Four* pursuing before she acquired her super-powers?

A. Actress

B. Astronaut

C. Bioengineer

D. Physicist

Fantastic Four

122. In the 2011 series *FF*, what do the letters in the title stand for?
- **A.** Fantastic Four
- **B.** Future Foundation
- **C.** Freedom Fighters
- **D.** Face Front

123. During *Secret Wars* (2015), where did the second Reed Richards, known as The Maker, come from?
- **A.** The Ultimate Universe
- **B.** Counter-Earth
- **C.** The future
- **D.** An experiment by Doctor Doom

124. Who seemingly died in the Negative Zone in *Fantastic Four* #587?
- **A.** Mr. Fantastic
- **B.** Invisible Woman
- **C.** Human Torch
- **D.** The Thing

125. Who detonated the Terrigen bomb that destroyed Attilan during *Infinity* (2013)?
- **A.** Maximus
- **B.** Black Bolt
- **C.** Medusa
- **D.** Thanos

126. Who gained god-like powers and created Battleworld in *Secret Wars* (2015)?
- **A.** Reed Richards
- **B.** Franklin Richards
- **C.** Doctor Doom
- **D.** Galactus

127.

128. Which member of Power Pack joined the Future Foundation?
- **A.** Julie
- **B.** Jack
- **C.** Katie
- **D.** Alex

129. During *Secret Wars* (2015), what was the Thing turned into?
- **A.** A monster
- **B.** A wall
- **C.** A normal man
- **D.** A mountain

OBSESSED WITH MARVEL

127.

When it came to the Fantastic Four, Marvel maintained an unbroken, continuous history from *Fantastic Four* #1 in 1961 until the present. However, as a new century approached, Marvel also began providing its readers with an alternative to the classic continuity. This was the new "Ultimate" line, in which the sagas of Marvel's celebrated Super Heroes started over from the beginning, usually with significant changes. The first series in this new line was *Ultimate Spider-Man*, which started in 2000, and was followed by *Ultimate X-Men* and *The Ultimates* (an alternative version of *The Avengers*).

Ultimate Fantastic Four (shown at right) debuted in 2004 and ran for sixty issues. Beginning with the origin story, it was radically different from the original *Fantastic Four*. For example, Reed Richards and Ben Grimm, who were adults (and World War II veterans) in the original version, were college-aged students in *Ultimate Fantastic Four* #1. The government recruited Reed into a special school for scientific prodigies, where he worked on a project that inadvertently turned the Fantastic Four into superhumans.

In *Ultimate Fantastic Four*, how did the Fantastic Four gain their super-powers?
- **A.** From traveling through a cosmic ray storm in outer space
- **B.** From being teleported through the "N-Zone"
- **C.** From being subjected to government experiments
- **D.** From being secretly mutated by the future Doctor Doom

130. Who watches over Franklin in the out-of-continuity humor series *Franklin Richards: Son of a Genius* (2005)?

A. Agatha Harkness
B. H.E.R.B.I.E. the robot
C. His sister Valeria
D. Ebony the cat

131. What super-powers has Franklin Richards manifested in *Son of a Genius*?

A. Vast reality-manipulating abilities
B. Precognition
C. Telekinesis
D. None of the answers is correct

132. Which former substitute member of the Fantastic Four also joined the Frightful Four?

A. Luke Cage
B. She-Thing
C. She-Hulk
D. Hulk

133. Which of the following statements about Lucia von Bardas is *not* true?

A. She was prime minister of Latveria
B. She served as prime minister under Doctor Doom's reign as king
C. She sold advanced technology to American Super Villains
D. She was once a teacher in the United States

134. Which member of the Frightful Four was once married to the Wizard?

A. Cole
B. Salamandra
C. Llyra
D. Thundra

135. What happens to the adult Franklin Richards in the alternate future of the *X-Men* story line "Days of Future Past"?

A. He is killed by the Sentinels
B. He is in love with Rachel Summers
C. He is imprisoned in a concentration camp for mutants
D. All answers are correct

136. What happened in *Fantastic Four Annual* #1 (1963)?

A. The Sub-Mariner is reunited with his undersea Atlantean race
B. The first modern appearance of the Sub-Mariner's future wife, Lady Dorma
C. Atlantis invades the surface world
D. All answers are correct

Fantastic Four

137. Who created the substitute Fantastic Four team that included Spider-Man?

A. Len Wein and George Perez

B. Roy Thomas and Rich Buckler

C. Walter Simonson and Arthur Adams

D. Mark Waid and Mike Wieringo

138. Which of the following Marvel characters did Jack Kirby *not* co-create?

A. The Incredible Hulk

B. Doctor Strange

C. Thor

D. The original X-Men

139. Which Marvel character did Jack Kirby co-create with his original partner Joe Simon?

A. Captain America

B. The original Angel

C. The original Human Torch

D. Sub-Mariner

140. How many young children do Reed and Susan Richards have as of 2009?

A. None

B. One

C. Two

D. Three

141. In the 2003 miniseries *Fantastic Four: Unstable Molecules*, written by James Sturm, what career does Reed Richards have?

A. World-famous Super Hero

B. Head of government space program

C. Teacher at Columbia University

D. Unemployed scientist

142.

143. What landmark story is told in *Fantastic Four Annual* #2 (1964)?

A. The origin of the Silver Surfer

B. The origin of Doctor Doom

C. The origin of the Sub-Mariner

D. The origin of the Inhumans

144. When did Reed Richards finally marry Susan Storm?

A. *Fantastic Four Special Annual* #4 (1966)

B. *Fantastic Four Annual* #3 (1965)

C. *Fantastic Four Special Annual* #5 (1967)

D. *Fantastic Four Special Annual* #6 (1968)

145. Who was the editor of Marvel's comics before Stan Lee?

A. Bill Everett

B. Joe Simon

C. Jack Kirby

D. Martin Goodman

OBSESSED WITH MARVEL

142.

Stan Lee (shown at right) presided as editor and head writer during Marvel's revolution of the comic book medium in the 1960s. In collaboration with artists such as Jack Kirby and Steve Ditko, Stan Lee co-created the characters who remain the basis of the Marvel Universe: the Fantastic Four, Spider-Man, the X-Men, the Hulk, Iron Man, and many more.

But Stan Lee's great success was decades in the making. When he first joined the Marvel staff in 1941, he was merely a gofer, an assistant who performed duties that nowadays would be given to interns. But when Marvel's editor left the still small company, it was the bright and ambitious Stan Lee who was promoted to take his place. Two decades later, he was seriously considering leaving comic books, which were then considered a children's medium. But his wife, Joan, suggested that he write the kind of comics he would like to read. The result was *Fantastic Four* #1 (1961), and history was made.

How old was Stan Lee when he first became the editor in charge of Marvel Comics?

A. Twenty-five

B. Twenty-one

C. Eighteen

D. Thirty

146. Who was Marvel's first editor in chief after Stan Lee?
- **A.** Len Wein
- **B.** Roy Thomas
- **C.** Marv Wolfman
- **D.** Gerry Conway

147. Who was the first Marvel character that Stan Lee wrote a story about?
- **A.** The original Human Torch
- **B.** Captain America
- **C.** The Fantastic Four
- **D.** Sub-Mariner

148. When did the original Human Torch and Johnny Storm first meet?
- **A.** *Fantastic Four Annual* #3 (1965)
- **B.** *Fantastic Four Special Annual* #4 (1966)
- **C.** *Fantastic Four Special Annual* #5 (1967)
- **D.** *Fantastic Four Special Annual* #6 (1968)

149. Why did Reed, Ben, and Johnny journey into the Negative Zone in *Fantastic Four Special* #6 (1968)?
- **A.** To free the Negative Zone from Annihilus's tyranny
- **B.** To find a way to save Susan and her unborn child
- **C.** To continue Reed's exploration of the dimension
- **D.** To prevent Blastaar from returning to Earth

150. How many years after first becoming Marvel's editor in chief did Stan Lee give up that position to become publisher?
- **A.** Twenty-one years
- **B.** Thirty-one years
- **C.** Forty-one years
- **D.** Stan Lee is still editor in chief as of 2017

151. In which issue of *Fantastic Four* did Stan Lee first appear?
- **A.** *Fantastic Four* #10 (1963)
- **B.** *Fantastic Four Annual* #3 (1965)
- **C.** *Fantastic Four* #11 (1963)
- **D.** *Fantastic Four* #176 (1976)

152. Which Marvel character worked as a chef in a Chinese restaurant in the Baxter Building?
- **A.** Fin Fang Foom
- **B.** Shang-Chi
- **C.** Jimmy Woo
- **D.** Leiko Wu

Fantastic Four

153. What is the Supreme Intelligence of the Kree?

A. A computer system containing the brains of the greatest Kree in history

B. A genetically engineered life-form

C. A mutated Kree with extraordinarily high intellect

D. A wholly artificial intelligence

154. Which of the following was *not* discovered by archeologist Dr. Daniel Damian?

A. The Celestials' base in the Andes

B. The Inhumans

C. The existence of the Eternals

D. Kree Sentry robot 459

155. When was Franklin Richards born?

A. *Fantastic Four Special Annual* #4 (1966)

B. *Fantastic Four Special Annual* #5 (1967)

C. *Fantastic Four Special Annual* #6 (1968)

D. *Fantastic Four* #100 (1970)

156. Who created Susan Richards's daughter Valeria?

A. Stan Lee and Jack Kirby

B. Scott Lobdell and Alan Davis

C. Chris Claremont and Salvador Larrocca

D. Carlos Pacheco and Jeph Loeb

157. Which Super Villains have taken mental control of Reed Richards's body?

A. Doctor Doom in *Fantastic Four* #10 (1963)

B. The Molecule Man in *Fantastic Four* #188 (1977)

C. The Over-Mind in *Fantastic Four* #115 (1971)

D. All answers are correct

158.

159. Where did Jack Kirby work before he started drawing comics for Marvel?

A. The Max Fleischer animation studio

B. King Features Syndicate

C. All-American Comics

D. The Terrytoons animation studio

160. Which Marvel character did Jack Kirby briefly draw in the 1950s?

A. The Black Knight

B. Captain America

C. Marvel Boy

D. The Yellow Claw

158.

In 1960 and 1961, the new trend at Marvel was monster comics, probably in response to the colossal creatures shown in the science-fiction movies of the period. Stan Lee and artists Jack Kirby and Steve Ditko turned out a succession of memorable if somewhat absurd monsters in science-fiction anthology comics like *Strange Tales* and *Tales of Suspense*. But the popular favorite still remains the gigantic Chinese dragon with the catchy name of Fin Fang Foom, who debuted in *Strange Tales* #89 (shown at right) in October 1961, only a month before the release of *Fantastic Four* #1. Stan Lee edited the story, his brother Larry Lieber scripted it, and Jack Kirby drew it. Fin Fang Foom has repeatedly returned over the decades in other series such as *Iron Man*. Recently, Fin and three other early 1960s monsters were shrunken down to human size and, having reformed, began working at the Fantastic Four's Baxter Building. They have become known as the "Fin Fang Four."

Which monster is *not* a member of the Fin Fang Four?

A. Elektro, the robot

B. Googam, Son of Goom

C. Gorgilla, the man-ape

D. Xemnu the Titan

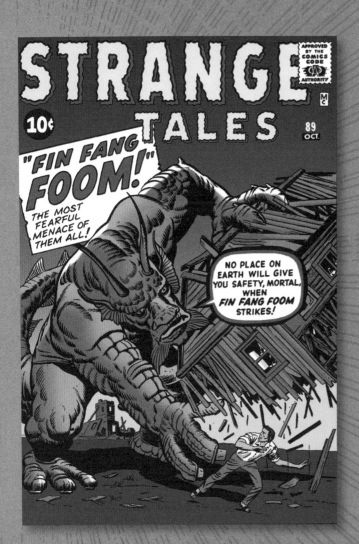

161. Bentley 23 is a clone of which longtime Fantastic Four foe?
- **A.** The Wizard
- **B.** Doctor Doom
- **C.** Mad Thinker
- **D.** Mole Man

162. Which cosmic being was murdered during the *Original Sin* crossover?
- **A.** Galactus
- **B.** Silver Surfer
- **C.** Adam Warlock
- **D.** The Watcher

163. Which member of the Future Foundation was *not* an evolved Moloid?
- **A.** Mik
- **B.** Tong
- **C.** Wu
- **D.** Korr

164. Which writer's epic three-year run on *Fantastic Four* laid the groundwork for 2015's *Secret Wars*?
- **A.** Mark Millar
- **B.** James Robinson
- **C.** Mark Waid
- **D.** Jonathan Hickman

165. Who did not help run the Future Foundation while the Fantastic Four were traveling through space and time?
- **A.** Luke Cage
- **B.** She-Hulk
- **C.** Ant-Man
- **D.** Medusa

166. The Inhuman capital city of Attilan crashed into what body of water during *Infinity*?
- **A.** East River
- **B.** Pacific Ocean
- **C.** Hudson Bay
- **D.** Lake Erie

167. What codename did musician Darla Deering use while wearing a Thing exoskeleton in *FF*?
- **A.** She-Thing
- **B.** Ms. Thing
- **C.** Lady Thing
- **D.** Rockstar

168. Who took Johnny Storm's place with the FF when he was presumed deceased?
- **A.** Spider-Man
- **B.** Iceman
- **C.** Firestar
- **D.** Wyatt Wingfoot

Fantastic Four

169. Which statement about the Doctor Doom of *Ultimate Fantastic Four* is false?

A. The accident that gave the Fantastic Four their powers gave him metallic skin

B. He is the descendant of Count Dracula

C. His face was scarred when he attempted to contact his mother's spirit

D. He has claws on his hands and goatlike legs

170. What is Doctor Doom's political position in Latveria?

A. President

B. Prime minister

C. Monarch

D. Dictator

171. How was Doctor Doom's face finally destroyed beyond repair?

A. His experimental machine blew up when he tried to contact his mother's spirit

B. He first donned his newly forged mask before the metal had cooled

C. He was disfigured by soldiers by order of King Vladimir of Latveria

D. It was ravaged by exposure to cosmic radiation

172. Who re-created "Him" as Adam Warlock in *Marvel Premiere* #1 (1972)?

A. Roy Thomas and Gil Kane

B. Stan Lee and Jack Kirby

C. Mike Friedrich and Jim Starlin

D. Steve Englehart and Frank Brunner

173. Who was *not* a member of Warlock's team, the Infinity Watch?

A. Drax the Destroyer

B. Gamora

C. Nebula

D. Pip the Troll

174. Did Jack Kirby ever return to the *Fantastic Four* comic book after leaving Marvel in 1970?

A. Yes, to draw stories

B. Yes, to write and draw his own stories

C. Yes, as a cover artist

D. No

175. Which member of the Fin Fang Four was co-created by Steve Ditko, *not* Jack Kirby?

A. Elektro the robot

B. Fin Fang Foom

C. Googam, Son of Goom

D. Gorgilla

176. Who was Adam Warlock's principal enemy on the original Counter-Earth?

A. Man-Ape
B. Man-Thing
C. Man-Beast
D. Man-Wolf

177. Who was the evil future counterpart of Adam Warlock?

A. Star Thief
B. Moondragon
C. The Magus
D. Thanos

178. What super-power does Maximus the Mad, the evil member of the Inhumans Royal Family, possess?

A. Telekinesis
B. Invisibility
C. Telepathy
D. Mind control abilities

179. Why did Black Bolt's brother Maximus go mad?

A. The effects of the Terrigen Mist
B. Maximus's own lust for power
C. The effects of Black Bolt's sonic scream
D. Insanity runs in the Royal Family

180. How was the Inhumans' Great Refuge freed from being trapped within Maximus's force barrier?

A. Reed Richards devised a means of disrupting the barrier
B. Maximus removed the barrier in exchange for gaining the throne
C. Black Bolt shattered the barrier with his powerful voice
D. The Silver Surfer destroyed the barrier with his cosmic power

181.

182. Which Inhuman discovered the mutation-inducing Terrigen Mist?

A. Agon
B. Maximus
C. Randac
D. Nadar

183. How old was Susan Storm when she first met graduate student Reed Richards?

A. Twenty-one
B. Sixteen
C. Twelve
D. Twenty-five

184. How did the Fantastick Four gain their super-powers in the alternate time-line of *Marvel 1602*?

A. From magic
B. From exposure to radiation during a balloon voyage in the upper atmosphere
C. From a wave of energy in the Sargasso Sea
D. From aliens visiting from another world

181.

Over the decades Marvel has produced various alternative versions of the Fantastic Four. In the 1990s Marvel presented *Fantastic Four 2099* and *Doom 2099*, both set in the distant future. Alex Ross, Jim Krueger, and John Paul Leon's *Earth X* series (1999–2000) portrays an alternate future in which Ben Grimm and Alicia have two sons, the Brothers Grimm, who are also Things, and Reed Richards wears the armor of the deceased Doctor Doom. Yet another Fantastic Four alternate reality came in the form of *Marvel 1602* (2003–2004). In this series, versions of Marvel's 1960s Super Heroes and Super Villains appear in Europe and America during the last year of the reign of England's Queen Elizabeth I. Among them are Sir Richard Reed and his colleagues in the "Fantastick Four."

Who wrote the miniseries *Marvel 1602: Fantastick Four* (2006, shown at left)?

A. Peter David
B. Neil Gaiman
C. Mark Millar
D. J. Michael Straczynski

Fantastic Four

185. Darla Deering had a brief romantic relationship with which fellow hero?
A. Johnny Storm
B. Scott Lang
C. Ben Grimm
D. Both A & B

186. What giant robot acted as a tutor for the children of the Future Foundation?
A. Ultimo
B. Awesome Android
C. Dragon Man
D. Cerebra

187. Who did *not* travel the world as a member of Crystal's squad in *All-New Inhumans*?
A. Flint
B. Naja
C. Grid
D. Iso

188. Which member of the Fantastic Four eventually went on to join the Guardians of the Galaxy?
A. Mr. Fantastic
B. Invisible Woman
C. Human Torch
D. The Thing

189. Who purchased the Baxter Building after the events of *Secret Wars* (2015)?
A. Tony Stark
B. Victor Von Doom
C. Peter Parker
D. King T'Challa

190. The Human Torch has *not* been a member of which group?
A. Uncanny Avengers
B. Uncanny Inhumans
C. Heralds of Galactus
D. Defenders

191. During *Fear Itself*, the Thing became the human host for the Asgardian spirit Angrir, also known as what?
A. Breaker of Stone
B. Breaker of Wills
C. Breaker of Worlds
D. Breaker of Souls

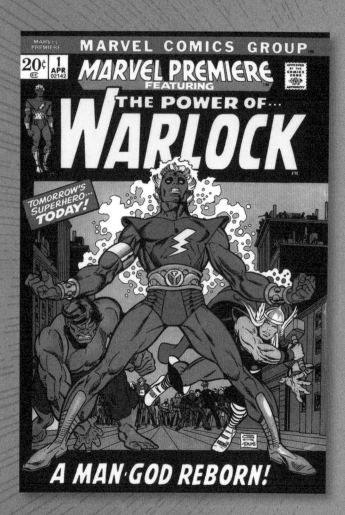

MARVEL COMICS GROUP

20¢ 1 APR 02142

MARVEL PREMIERE
FEATURING

THE POWER OF...
WARLOCK

TOMORROW'S SUPERHERO... TODAY!

A MAN·GOD REBORN!

198.

"Him," the artificially created superhuman that Stan Lee and Jack Kirby had introduced in Fantastic Four, not only lacked a name but also a purpose in life. This all changed in *Marvel Premiere* #1 (1972, shown at left), in which writer Roy Thomas and artist Gil Kane renamed him Adam Warlock in his first solo story. In it, the High Evolutionary created a duplicate of Earth, named Counter-Earth. But High Evolutionary's plans were ruined when his previous creation, the satanic Man-Beast, corrupted Counter-Earth's new human race. Adam Warlock volunteered to descend to the planet and become its savior. Thus in the original *Warlock* series, Warlock is presented as a kind of modern-day messiah. After defeating the Man-Beast, Warlock left for outer space to combat new adversaries, such as the Magus and his sinister Universal Church of Truth, and the mad Titan named Thanos.

Which writer or artist is most associated with the adventures of Adam Warlock?

A. John Byrne
B. Frank Miller
C. Walter Simonson
D. Jim Starlin

192. How does the Invisible Woman become invisible?
A. Her body literally becomes transparent
B. She telepathically creates the illusion she is invisible
C. She mentally bends light rays around her body
D. She vibrates out of sync with physical reality

193. How does the Mole Man principally compensate for his poor sight?
A. He doesn't; he is totally blind
B. He has developed a "radar sense"
C. He wears special goggles
D. His Subterranean slaves lead him like guide dogs

194. What is the real name of the Molecule Man?
A. Norton G. Fester
B. Owen Reece
C. Leonard Tippit
D. Irving Forbush

195. Which Super Villainess did the Molecule Man fall in love with during the first Secret War?
A. The Enchantress
B. Malice
C. Volcana
D. Titania

196. In which city's suburb did the Molecule Man settle down with his girlfriend after the first Secret War?
A. Boston
B. Chicago
C. Denver
D. New York

197. Who first alerted the Fantastic Four to the danger posed by the Molecule Man?
A. The Beyonder
B. The Watcher
C. The Silver Surfer
D. Doctor Strange

198.

199. Which menace did the X-Men help The Thing battle at Reed and Sue's wedding?
A. Attuma and his undersea horde
B. The Mole Man and his Subterraneans
C. The Enchantress and the Executioner
D. The Brotherhood of Evil Mutants

200. Which member of the Fantastic Four aided the X-Men in their first battle against the Juggernaut?
A. Invisible Girl
B. Human Torch
C. Mr. Fantastic
D. The Thing

Fantastic Four

201. Which villains pitted the original X-Men in combat against the Fantastic Four?

A. Magneto's Brotherhood of Evil Mutants

B. Factor Three

C. The Mad Thinker and the Puppet Master

D. The Frightful Four

202. Which emotion is *not* listed in the Psycho-Man's stimulator box?

A. Doubt

B. Despair

C. Fear

D. Hate

203. Who endowed the sentient computer Quasimodo with a mobile humanoid form?

A. Doctor Doom

B. The Mad Thinker

C. The Silver Surfer

D. Mister Fantastic

204. Who was the stepfather of Frankie Raye, who became a female Human Torch?

A. Thomas "Toro" Raymond

B. The Puppet Master

C. Professor Phineas T. Horton

D. Jim Hammond, the original Human Torch

205. Which of the Infinity Gems did Adam Warlock possess longest?

A. Mind Gem

B. Soul Gem

C. Reality Gem

D. Power Gem

206. With whom did Adam Warlock eventually fall in love?

A. Gamora

B. Alicia Masters

C. The Goddess

D. Moondragon

207. What is Adam Warlock's enemy, the Man-Beast?

A. A wolf whom the High Evolutionary endowed with human intelligence

B. A werewolf

C. A man whom the High Evolutionary endowed with animal-like attributes

D. A demon from the underworld

208.

209. How was Adam Warlock (temporarily) slain on the original Counter-Earth?

A. Asphyxiation

B. Crucifixion

C. Beheading

D. Disintegration

208.

Fantastic Four creators Stan Lee and Jack Kirby shattered comic book tradition by having their hero and heroine—Reed Richards and Susan Storm—get married in *Fantastic Four Annual #3* (1965). Two years later, Lee and Kirby took the next step and revealed in *Fantastic Four Annual #5* that Sue was expecting a baby.

But Reed discovered that because he and Sue gained their super-powers through exposure to cosmic rays, both her life and that of their unborn baby's were in danger. In a suspenseful saga in *Fantastic Four Annual #6* (1968, shown at right), Reed, Ben Grimm, and Johnny Storm venture into the mysterious Negative Zone to find a means of saving the lives of the mother and child. There they battle the creature called Annihilus and capture his control rod. Using its "anti-particles," Reed enables Sue to safely give birth to their son at the end of the issue.

But the Fantastic Four—and Lee and Kirby— were so busy with their adventures that it was another two years (in real time) before they got around to giving the new baby his name: Franklin Benjamin Richards. His middle name was in honor of Reed's best friend, Ben Grimm. But who did Reed and Susan Richards name their son Franklin after?

A. Reed's father

B. Susan's father

C. Benjamin Franklin

D. Their lawyer Franklin "Foggy" Nelson

210. Where is the Baxter Building located in New York City?
- **A.** 42nd Street and Madison Avenue
- **B.** Times Square
- **C.** Rockefeller Center
- **D.** 34th Street and Broadway

211. After who or what was the original Baxter Building named?
- **A.** Reed's former professor Noah Baxter
- **B.** The Leland Baxter Paper Company
- **C.** Colonel Robert "Buzz" Baxter
- **D.** Never revealed

212. Which of the following women has *not* been a substitute member of the Fantastic Four?
- **A.** Crystal
- **B.** Medusa
- **C.** Thundra
- **D.** Storm

213. Which of the following men has *never* been an official substitute member of the Fantastic Four?
- **A.** Ant-Man II
- **B.** The Black Panther
- **C.** Luke Cage
- **D.** Namor the Sub-Mariner

214. Who is Fantastic Four mailman Willie Lumpkin's assistant Billie Lumpkin?
- **A.** Willie Lumpkin's nephew
- **B.** Willie Lumpkin's niece
- **C.** Willie Lumpkin's son
- **D.** Willie Lumpkin's daughter

215. From which planet did the Impossible Man come?
- **A.** Poppup
- **B.** Birj
- **C.** Tribbit
- **D.** Xandar

216. Which Marvel hero has the same name as Galactus's robot enforcer?
- **A.** Colossus
- **B.** The Punisher
- **C.** Nova
- **D.** The Destroyer

217. Which *Fantastic Four* artist drew himself as present at the Trial of Galactus?
- **A.** Jack Kirby
- **B.** John Byrne
- **C.** George Perez
- **D.** Walter Simonson

218. Which Super Villain persuaded the Sub-Mariner to lead an Atlantean invasion of the surface world in the final Stan Lee/Jack Kirby *Fantastic Four* story line?
- **A.** Magneto
- **B.** Doctor Doom
- **C.** The Mandarin
- **D.** The Red Skull

Fantastic Four

219. To which American Indian tribe does the Fantastic Four's friend Wyatt Wingfoot belong?

A. Apache

B. Cheyenne

C. Keewazi

D. Wakandan

220. Where did Adam Warlock's spirit reside after he had been (temporarily) killed by Thanos?

A. In his grave

B. Within a temple of the Universal Church of Truth

C. In the dimension of Therea

D. Within "Soulworld," a realm within the Soul Gem

221. Where did Johnny and Sue Storm live in the Human Torch's *Strange Tales* series?

A. Glenview, Long Island

B. Fairfield, Connecticut

C. Brooklyn Heights, New York

D. Jackson Heights, New York

222. Who did the Fantastic Four's foe, the original Hate-Monger, turn out to be when he was unmasked?

A. Mephisto

B. Adolf Hitler in a cloned body

C. The Psycho-Man

D. The Red Skull

223. Who was Colonel Nick Fury working for when the Fantastic Four first teamed up with Fury against the Hate-Monger?

A. The United Nations

B. S.H.I.E.L.D.

C. The CIA

D. The U.S. Army

224. What was the occupation of Doctor Doom's mother, Cynthia?

A. Physician

B. Member of the royal family of Latveria

C. Sorceress

D. Scientist

225. What was Franklin Richards's Super Hero name when he was a member of Power Pack?

A. Energizer

B. Gee

C. Tattletale

D. Psi-Lord

226. Who was *not* a member of the Fantastic Force, a team led by the older Franklin Richards of an alternate future?

A. Devlor

B. Huntara

C. Vibraxas

D. Lyja the Lazerfist

A GALLERY OF THE FANTASTIC FOUR'S MOST FAMOUS FOES!

THE SKRULLS FROM OUTER SPACE!

FROM F.F. #2 JAN.

THEY CALLED THEMSELVES SKRULLS! BUT, BY ANY NAME, THEY WERE A BAND OF THE MOST DANGEROUS MENACES EARTH HAD EVER FACED! ABLE TO CHANGE THEIR APPEARANCES AT WILL, THEY TOOK THE IDENTITIES OF THE FANTASTIC FOUR, AND ALMOST SUCCEEDED IN PUTTING THE BLAME FOR THEIR OWN MISDEEDS ON THE COLORFUL QUARTET! BUT THEY LEARNED, IN TIME, THAT IT TAKES MORE THAN EXPERT MIMICRY TO TURN A GROUP OF AMAZING ALIENS INTO AMERICA'S GREATEST HEROES!

OBSESSED WITH MARVEL

230.

By their second issue (1962), the Fantastic Four were celebrities—and also outlaws, hunted by the U.S. Army. Witnesses had seen all four heroes commit crimes—or so they thought. Actually, the Fantastic Four had been impersonated and framed by members of the extraterrestrial race called the Skrulls (shown at left). (The Fantastic Four succeeded in clearing their names.)

Skrulls are reptilelike humanoids who lay eggs, though they also have certain physical characteristics of mammals, like hair. The Skrulls also have the ability to change their shape, enabling them to infiltrate Earth by posing as humans. However, they can only imitate other beings' physical appearances, not any special abilities or super-powers they may possess. The Skrulls rule one of the great interstellar empires in the Marvel Universe, and for ages have been at war with a rival empire, the Kree.

Where is the Skrull empire located?

A. The Andromeda Galaxy
B. The Greater Magellanic Cloud
C. The Milky Way Galaxy
D. The Negative Zone

227. Which job has Ben Grimm *not* held?
A. Astronaut
B. Boxer
C. Professional wrestler
D. Test pilot

228. How did the Black Panther's enemy Klaw lose his right hand?
A. The young T'Challa destroyed it with Klaw's own sonic blaster
B. It was shattered in an accident
C. The Thing crushed his hand in combat
D. It was the only part of Klaw's body he failed to convert into "living sound"

229. Whom is Reed and Sue's daughter, Valeria, named after?
A. A woman that Johnny Storm met in the "Fifth Dimension"
B. A Latverian woman whom Doctor Doom loved
C. A legendary swordswoman
D. The daughter of Doctor Doom

230.

231. Which legendary band appeared in the Human Torch's solo series in *Strange Tales*?
A. The Four Seasons
B. The Beatles
C. KISS
D. The Rolling Stones

232. What is the first name of the Black Panther's enemy Klaw?
A. Ulysses
B. Agamemnon
C. Ozymandias
D. Achilles

233. What is the first name of Reed Richards's father?
A. Franklin
B. Nathaniel
C. Noah
D. Reed

234. Who reanimated the original Human Torch and sent him to combat Johnny Storm?
A. Doctor Doom
B. The Wizard
C. The Puppet Master
D. The Mad Thinker

235. Who created the android monster called Dragon Man?
A. Diablo
B. Professor Gregson Gilbert
C. Gregory Hungerford Gideon
D. Professor Phineas T. Horton

Fantastic Four

236. What name did Susan Richards use when the Psycho-Man temporarily turned her into a Super Villain?
A. Hate-Monger
C. Malice
B. Man-Killer
D. Virago

237. Who was once married to Johnny Storm, the Human Torch?
A. Alicia Masters
C. Frankie Raye
B. Lyja, a Skrull
D. Crystal

238. Which Super Hero did the Human Torch's early foe, the Acrobat, once impersonate?
A. Daredevil
C. Iron Fist
B. Captain America
D. Spider-Man

239. Which member of X-Factor first appeared in a *Fantastic Four* story?
A. Havok
C. Madrox the Multiple Man
B. Polaris
D. Quicksilver

240. Which of the Red Ghost's "super-apes" has magnetic powers?
A. Igor the baboon
C. Mikhlo the gorilla
B. Peotor the orangutan
D. None of these

241. Which of the following villains was *not* part of Killmonger's first attempt to overthrow the Black Panther as Wakanda's ruler?
A. Baron Macabre
C. The Black Talon
B. Lord Karnaj
D. Venomm

242.

243. Vibranium, the metal found in the Black Panther's Wakanda, absorbs vibrations. What does Antarctic Vibranium do?
A. Liquefies metal
C. Absorbs vibrations
B. Emits lethal radiation
D. There is no Vibranium in Antarctica

244. Which member of the Inhumans Royal Family married someone from outside the Inhumans' race?
A. Black Bolt
C. Maximus
B. Medusa
D. Crystal

242.

Jack Kirby, the co-creator of the Fantastic Four, is considered by many to be one of the greatest artists in the history of comics, and one of the most influential artists in the Super Hero genre. Kirby originally worked at Marvel in the 1940s, where he and writer-artist Joe Simon created Captain America. There they pioneered a dynamic new style of visual storytelling that exploded with vivid action. But Kirby's prowess as a comics creator reached its summit in his partnership with editor-writer Stan Lee in the 1960s. Kirby proved to be endlessly imaginative, co-creating not only the Fantastic Four (shown at right), but the Hulk, the X-Men, Thor, the Avengers, and scores of other characters. Jack Kirby passed away in 1994, having become as much a legend in comics as Captain America himself.

How many consecutive issues of *Fantastic Four* did Stan Lee and Jack Kirby collaborate on (not counting six annuals)?

A. 55 issues
B. 123 issues
C. 102 issues
D. 77 issues

OBSESSED WITH MARVEL

245. After *Secret Wars* (2015), Victor Von Doom became an unexpected ally of which Marvel hero?

A. Iron Man   **C.** Thor

B. Captain America   **D.** Mr. Fantastic

246. Which Fantastic Four member infiltrated S.H.I.E.L.D. and the Avengers during "Time Runs Out"?

A. The Thing   **C.** Mr. Fantastic

B. Human Torch   **D.** Invisible Woman

247. Upon arriving in the mainstream Marvel Universe, Ultimate Reed Richards started what organization?

A. W.H.I.S.P.E.R.   **C.** S.H.I.E.L.D.

B. H.A.M.M.E.R.   **D.** A.I.M.

248. What was the name of the exclusive night club run by Inhuman King Black Bolt?

A. The Sounding Board   **C.** The Inhuman Condition

B. The Quiet Room   **D.** The Voice Box

249. Who accompanied the Fantastic Four to remake all of reality after *Secret Wars* (2015)?

A. Galactus   **C.** Doctor Doom

B. Molecule Man   **D.** Silver Surfer

250. The Thing was sent to prison after being framed for the murder of which villain?

A. Sandman   **C.** The Wizard

B. The Trapster   **D.** Puppet Master

251. In the 2017 series *Royals*, who accompanied the Inhumans on their voyage to the Kree Empire?

A. Ronan   **C.** The Thing

B. Noh-Varr   **D.** Human Torch

252. Which child prodigy was never a member of the Future Foundation?

A. Onome   **C.** Lunella Lafayette

B. Valeria Richards   **D.** Bentley 23

Fantastic Four

253. Whom did The Thing join forces with in the first issue of his own team-up series, *Marvel Two-in-One*?

A. Hulk

B. Human Torch

C. Spider-Man

D. Man-Thing

254. What is the principal research facility for unusual forms of alternative energy in the Marvel Universe?

A. Project: Pegasus

B. The Brand Corporation

C. Roxxon Oil

D. Stark Industries

255. The Thing befriended an alien superhuman named Wundarr, who later became the Aquarian. What was the Aquarian?

A. An ambassador from another planet

B. A soldier from another planet

C. A spiritual leader on Earth

D. A Super Hero on Earth

256. The Thing joined forces with the Inhumans to combat a menace called Maelstrom. What was Maelstrom's genetic background?

A. A Deviant

B. An Inhuman

C. A Deviant-Eternal hybrid

D. A Deviant-Inhuman hybrid

257. Who was *not* one of Maelstrom's Minions?

A. Gronk

B. Helio

C. Letha

D. Phobius

258. Who was *not* a member of the Terrible Trio that Doctor Doom organized to fight the Fantastic Four?

A. Bull Brogin

B. Thug Thatcher

C. "Handsome Harry" Phillips

D. Yogi Dakor

259. When the Fantastic Four were threatened with bankruptcy in *Fantastic Four* #9 (1962), how did they quickly raise money?

A. Selling Reed Richards's inventions

B. Becoming "heroes for hire"

C. Starring in a Hollywood movie

D. Writing their autobiography

260. What is Ben Grimm's connection to the Yancy Street Gang?

A. In his youth he led a rival gang

B. In his youth he was robbed by the Yancy Street Gang

C. He was once a policeman who arrested the Yancy Street Gang

D. In his youth he was head of the Yancy Street Gang

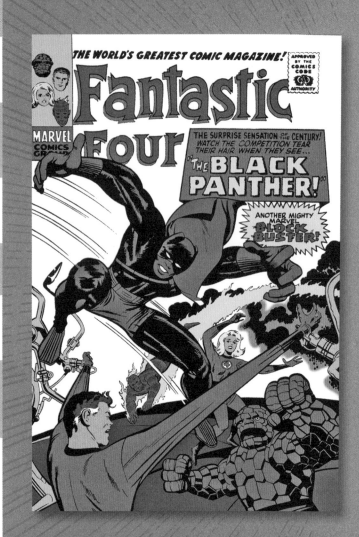

OBSESSED WITH MARVEL

262.

The first African American Super Hero in comics history to play a leading role—and not merely serve as a supporting character—is the Black Panther, whom Stan Lee and Jack Kirby created and introduced in *Fantastic Four* #52 (1966, alternate cover shown at left). He is T'Challa, the ruler of the fictional African nation of Wakanda. Chief of the Panther tribe, T'Challa not only uses the ceremonial title and costume of a black panther, but he also uses a heart-shaped herb to enhance his strength, agility, and senses. Though he adhered to ancient tribal traditions, T'Challa also presided over Wakanda's development into one of Earth's most technologically advanced nations. In *Fantastic Four* #52, T'Challa invited the Fantastic Four to Wakanda, and then surprised the team by attacking them. It turned out he was only testing them to see if they'd be powerful enough to join forces with him in a battle against his enemy Klaw. (They were worthy, as it turned out, and Klaw was defeated.)

The Panther's various solo series, starting with the "Panther's Rage" saga in *Jungle Action*, usually focus on his role as Wakanda's king and protector. Who wrote "Panther's Rage," the Black Panther's first multi-issue story arc in the 1970s?

A. Reginald Hudlin
B. Stan Lee
C. Don McGregor
D. Christopher Priest

261. Who finally destroyed the original Baxter Building?
A. Doctor Doom's chosen successor Kristoff Vernard
B. Doctor Doom
C. The Frightful Four
D. Galactus

262.

263. How did Ben Grimm first meet his longtime girlfriend Alicia?
A. When he posed for her in his studio
B. They were childhood sweethearts
C. When the Puppet Master forced her to impersonate Susan Storm
D. At a charity benefit

264. Which of the following titles was the first true continued stories in *Fantastic Four* that lasted more than one issue?
A. "The Battle of the Baxter Building"
B. "The Hulk vs. The Thing"
C. "The Brutal Betrayal of Ben Grimm"
D. "The Coming of Galactus"

265. Which story was *not* a part of Stan Lee and Jack Kirby's classic "Galactus Trilogy" in *Fantastic Four* #48–50 (1966)?
A. "The Coming of Galactus"
B. "If This Be Doomsday"
C. "The Startling Saga of the Silver Surfer"
D. "When Strikes the Silver Surfer"

266. When did The Thing first meet and fight the Incredible Hulk?
A. *The Incredible Hulk* #1 (1962)
B. *Fantastic Four* #10 (1963)
C. *Fantastic Four* #25 (1964)
D. *Fantastic Four* #12 (1963)

267. Which of the Fantastic Four's enemies claimed that he could restore The Thing to human form?
A. Kurrgo, Master of Planet X
B. Diablo
C. Maximus the Mad
D. The Monocle

268. Who brought the artificially created monster Dragon Man to life?
A. Doctor Doom
B. Diablo
C. Mad Thinker
D. Mr. Fantastic

269. Who was the villain who first masqueraded as the Invincible Man in *Fantastic Four* #32 (1964)?
A. Diablo
B. Super-Skrull
C. Miracle Man
D. Doctor Doom

Fantastic Four

270. How did the Frightful Four remove the Fantastic Four's super-powers in *Fantastic Four* #38 (1965)?

A. Bombarding them with cosmic rays

B. Tricking them into drinking the Wizard's potion

C. A device that drained their superhuman energies

D. Exposure to radiation from an atomic blast

271. How did Reed Richards finally defeat Doctor Doom after Doom stole the Silver Surfer's cosmic power?

A. Finding and freeing the Silver Surfer from captivity

B. Using Doom's own device to drain the power from him

C. Tricking Doom into flying into the energy barrier Galactus used to trap the Surfer on Earth

D. Pitting Doom against Galactus's new herald

272. Who became a father figure to "Him" when he took the new name Adam Warlock?

A. Thanos

B. The Magus

C. The High Evolutionary

D. The Watcher

273. Which Super Hero did *not* battle the *Fantastic Four* in issue 73 (1968)?

A. Daredevil

B. Thor

C. Spider-Man

D. Iron Man

274. What was Tomazooma, which the Fantastic Four battled in *Fantastic Four* #80 (1968)?

A. An American Indian deity

B. An American Indian Super Hero

C. An alien invader from outer space

D. A gigantic robot in the form of an American Indian totem

275. What was wrong with the Fantastic Four's new house in *Fantastic Four* #88 (1969)?

A. It contained a portal into the Negative Zone

B. The house was controlled by the Mole Man

C. The architect was their enemy, the Wizard

D. The neighbors didn't want Super Heroes moving onto their block

276. Whom did Agatha Harkness first combat in her new role as Franklin Richards's nanny and protectress?

A. The Frightful Four

B. The Enchantress

C. The Monster from the Lost Lagoon

D. Salem's Seven

OBSESSED WITH MARVEL

277. Whom did the Fantastic Four battle in the hundredth issue of their original series (1970)?

A. Doctor Doom

B. All of their old adversaries

C. Android replicas of themselves

D. Android replicas of their old adversaries

278.

Before the rich creative period that came to be known as the "Marvel Age of Comics," characters' lives rarely, if ever, changed. For example, readers could be certain that the hero and his leading lady would never ever get married. But only four years after *Fantastic Four* #1, co-creators Stan Lee and Jack Kirby presented "The Wedding of Sue and Reed" in the 1965 *Fantastic Four Annual* (issue 3 shown at left). It was proof that their characters and their lives could continue to evolve.

The wedding also served as an epic celebration, not just of the Super Heroes who had started the new Marvel Age, but also of the entire Marvel Universe that Lee, Kirby, and others had invented in less than half a decade. Virtually every one of the new Super Heroes was a wedding guest who ended up battling an army of party-crashing Super Villains who were out to stop the ceremony.

What happened to Fantastic Four co-creators Stan Lee and Jack Kirby at Reed and Susan Richards's wedding?

A. They were thrown out

B. They competed to be best man

C. They were guests of honor

D. Nothing; they weren't invited and didn't go

279. Who created a reality based on 1950s popular culture in "Rock around the Cosmos" in *Fantastic Four* #136 (1973)?

A. The Impossible Man

B. The Shaper of Worlds

C. The Miracle Man

D. The Skrulls

280. Which villains did *not* show up to disrupt Reed and Sue's wedding in *Fantastic Four Annual* #3 (1965)?

A. Doctor Octopus, Kraven the Hunter, Mysterio, the Sandman, and the Vulture

B. Attuma, the hordes of Hydra, the Grey Gargoyle, and the Super-Skrull

C. Kang, the Melter, the Beetle, the Red Ghost, the Wizard, and the Trapster

D. Mr. Hyde, the Cobra, The Enchantress, and the Executioner

281. Which founding member of the Fantastic Four was last to be asked to join the Avengers?

A. Human Torch

B. Invisible Woman

C. Mister Fantastic

D. The Thing

282. What is Doctor Doom's real name in *Ultimate Fantastic Four*?

A. Victor von Doom

B. Victor von Damme

C. Victor Van Damme

D. None of these

283. Which legendary figure did Ben Grimm impersonate on a time trip?

A. Count Dracula

B. Frankenstein's Monster

C. The Golem

D. Blackbeard the Pirate

284. What weapon did Abraxas intend to use to obliterate all realities?

A. The Cosmic Cube

B. The Evil Eye

C. The Ultimate Nullifier

D. The Infinity Gauntlet

Fantastic Four

285. What did the Human Torch become on Battleworld during *Secret Wars* (2015)?

A. A King
B. A Hero
C. A Slave
D. The Sun

286. Which of the following alien races was represented in the Universal Inhumans?

A. Badoon
B. Skrull
C. Shi'ar
D. Chitauri

287. Which member of the Fantastic Four traveled back in time with Wolverine during *Age of Ultron*?

A. Human Torch
B. Mr. Fantastic
C. Invisible Woman
D. The Thing

288. Who was *not* a member of the Inhuman version of the *Secret Warriors* (2017)?

A. Quake
B. Ms. Marvel
C. Moon Girl
D. Gorgon

289. During *Original Sin*, who did the Thing learn had prevented him from being cured of his powers?

A. Franklin Richards
B. Human Torch
C. Doctor Doom
D. Alicia Masters

290. Who is John Eden?

A. Quiet Man
B. Purple Man
C. Molecule Man
D. Dragon Man

291. To whom is Sue Storm married in *Secret Wars* (2015)?

A. Reed Richards
B. Ben Grimm
C. Victor Von Doom
D. Namor

292.

293. What was the name of the Inhuman whose powers of foresight began *Civil War II*?

A. Ulysses
B. Daisuke
C. Karnak
D. Eldrac

294. In the *Ultimates* (2015), Galactus took on what new role?

A. The Avatar of Death
B. Devourer of Universes
C. Lifebringer
D. The Watcher

OBSESSED WITH MARVEL

292.

Regarded as the greatest comic epic by Stan Lee and Jack Kirby, the "Galactus Trilogy" in *Fantastic Four* #48–50 was created in 1966 during the the middle of their decade-long collaboration on *Fantastic Four*. It is a story about the end of the world. Galactus (shown at right) is an armored extraterrestrial giant of seemingly omnipotent power, a god who devours the life energies of planets, caring nothing for their mortal inhabitants. Preceded by his herald, the enigmatic Silver Surfer, Galactus arrives atop the Fantastic Four's headquarters in New York City and prepares to devastate the entire Earth.

By chance, the Silver Surfer encounters The Thing's beloved Alicia Masters, who passionately argues in favor of the human race. Spiritually awakened, the Surfer rebels against his master and pays the terrible price of being exiled from the stars. Ultimately, the Fantastic Four, specifically Reed Richards, force Galactus to recognize humanity's right to exist.

What is the origin of Galactus?

A. He was originally a humanoid who existed in a dying universe
B. He was the victim of an alien experiment that transformed him into a nearly omnipotent being
C. He is a renegade member of the race of Celestials
D. He was an alien tyrant who discovered how to increase his power by consuming planets

295. Where is Doctor Doom's American castle located?
- **A.** Long Island, New York
- **B.** The Catskill Mountains
- **C.** The Adirondack Mountains
- **D.** Near Washington D.C.

296. What was the ultimate fate of Valeria, Victor von Doom's childhood sweetheart?
- **A.** Doom sacrificed her life in a ritual to gain mystical power
- **B.** She committed suicide rather than marry Doom
- **C.** She faked her own death to escape from Doom
- **D.** Doom nobly allowed her to marry someone else

297. Which artist co-created the original Willie Lumpkin with Stan Lee?
- **A.** Stan Goldberg
- **B.** Dan DeCarlo
- **C.** Al Jaffee
- **D.** Jack Kirby

298. Who were the title characters of *Fantastic Four 2099*?
- **A.** The original members of the Fantastic Four
- **B.** The descendants of the original Fantastic Four
- **C.** Clones of the original Fantastic Four
- **D.** It remains unclear if they were the originals or duplicates

299. Why were the rest of the Fantastic Four surprised when they finally met Ben's Aunt Petunia?
- **A.** She was young and beautiful
- **B.** She was related to a Super Villain
- **C.** She owned a vast fortune
- **D.** She was not really a member of his family

300. Which of Galactus's heralds died and was replaced by a robot simulacrum?
- **A.** Terrax
- **B.** Firelord
- **C.** Air-Walker
- **D.** Nova

301. The Thing belonged to the Unlimited Class Wrestling Federation. Which of the following Super Heroes did *not*?
- **A.** Demolition Man
- **B.** The Hulk
- **C.** Ikaris
- **D.** Ms. Marvel II (Sharon Ventura)

302. What relation is Karnak to his fellow Inhuman Triton?
- **A.** Brother
- **B.** Cousin
- **C.** Nephew
- **D.** No relation

Fantastic Four

303. Who was the modern-day pirate whom the Human Torch and Iceman teamed up to fight against?

A. Captain Omen
B. Captain Cyber
C. Commander Kraken
D. Captain Barracuda

304. Who is Bentley Wittman?

A. The Mad Thinker
B. The Wizard
C. The Painter of a Thousand Perils
D. The Monocle

305. Which villain was *not* a member of the Fearsome Four?

A. Devos the Devastator
B. Klaw
C. Raptor the Renegade
D. Paibok the Power Skrull

306. Which monster did the Sub-Mariner summon with the Horn of Proteus to attack New York in *Fantastic Four* #4 (1962)?

A. Giganto
B. Fin Fang Foom
C. Gigantus
D. Tricephalous

307. Who was *not* a member of the Enclave that created "Him," alias Adam Warlock?

A. Nuclear physicist Maris Moriak
B. Geneticist Wladyslav Shinski
C. Surgeon Jose Santini
D. Electronics technician Carlo Zota

308. What was the original name of the Black Panther's archenemy Erik Killmonger?

A. M'Jumbak
B. T'Chaka
C. N'Jadaka
D. W'Kabi

309. To which cult does the Black Panther's longtime enemy M'Baku belong?

A. Black Panther
B. White Gorilla
C. Lion-God
D. White Tiger

310. What was the profession of the Black Panther's former fiancée, Monica Lynne?

A. Bodyguard
B. Singer
C. Scientist
D. Diplomat

311.

In drawing the first issue of the "Galactus Trilogy," *Fantastic Four* #48 (1966), Jack Kirby gave the extraterrestrial god Galactus a herald—a messenger who would precede him to announce his arrivals and deliver proclamations. This herald was the Silver Surfer (shown at right), and he resembled a modern-day angel who instead of having wings, soared through the sky on what looked like a surfboard. Exiled to Earth because he dared to defend the human race, the Silver Surfer was both noble and melancholy, an alien who could seem deeply human. The Surfer seized readers' imaginations, and in two years he won his own comic book series.

Galactus took on a succession of heralds over the years, and they usually had elemental themes: water (the Surfer), air (Air-Walker), fire (Firelord and Nova), and earth (Terrax). Which being who derives his powers from Asgard, home of the Norse gods, has served as a herald of Galactus?

A. The Absorbing Man
B. The Destroyer
C. Heimdall
D. Surtur

OBSESSED WITH MARVEL

312. What job did the Black Panther once hold in New York City under his alias as Luke Charles?

A. Ambassador C. Scientist
B. Policeman D. Schoolteacher

313. Who was *not* a member of the Supremacists, a Super Hero team from Wakanda's enemy, the nation of Azania?

A. Captain Blaze C. White Wolf
B. Hungyr D. White Avenger

314. Which school did Reed Richards *not* attend?

A. California Institute of Technology C. Harvard University
B. Massachusetts Institute of Technology D. Columbia University

315. Which of the following menaces is *not* native to the Negative Zone?

A. Annihilus C. Stygorr
B. Terminus D. Blastaar

316. What happened to series co-creators Stan Lee and Jack Kirby the first time they appeared in the *Fantastic Four* comic?

A. They were visited by Doctor Doom C. They were victims of the Impossible Man's pranks
B. They argued with The Thing D. They got in a fight with the Yancy Street Gang

317. What was the term *Negative Zone* originally used to describe in *Fantastic Four*?

A. The antimatter universe discovered by Reed Richards C. A band of cosmic radiation near Earth
B. "Sub-space" D. The force barrier that Maximus created around the Great Refuge band of cosmic radiation near Earth

318. What happened to Reed Richards's father when he disappeared three years before the events in *Fantastic Four* #1 (1961)?

A. He was abducted by the Skrulls C. He traveled to an alternate timeline
B. He was held prisoner by Doctor Doom D. He was lost in his own expedition into outer space

Fantastic Four

319. Which of the Human Torch's old enemies is Sam Smithers?
- **A.** The Plantman
- **B.** The Asbestos Man
- **C.** The Eel
- **D.** The Acrobat

320. Who in the team Salem's Seven has the same name as an *X-Men* villain?
- **A.** Brutacus
- **B.** Vertigo
- **C.** Reptilla
- **D.** Gazelle

321. Who was the new Hate-Monger who worked with the Psycho-Man?
- **A.** A clone of a fanatical dictator
- **B.** A fanatical human follower of Psycho-Man
- **C.** A shape-shifting android
- **D.** The Psycho-Man himself

322.

323. Which fictional Latin American country did the original Hate-Monger attempt to conquer in *Fantastic Four* #21 (1963)?
- **A.** San Diablo
- **B.** Santo Marco
- **C.** San Gusto
- **D.** Santo Rico

324. What terrible accident befell the Black Panther's enemy Kiber the Cruel when he experimented with teleportation?
- **A.** He was killed outright
- **B.** Half his body was teleported to a distant location
- **C.** His body was fused to the floor
- **D.** Part of his body was disintegrated permanently

325. Which Super Hero from Marvel's early years did the insane Crusader claim to be when he battled the Fantastic Four?
- **A.** Marvel Boy
- **B.** The Blue Diamond
- **C.** Mercury
- **D.** The Mighty Destroyer

326. On which planet was Robert Grayson, alias Marvel Boy, raised by his father?
- **A.** Earth
- **B.** Mars
- **C.** Uranus
- **D.** Venus

327. Which of the following gangsters was *not* actually a Skrull from the planet Kral?
- **A.** Boss Barker
- **B.** Lippy Louie
- **C.** Caesar Cicero
- **D.** Napoleon G. Robberson

322.

In their long run with *Fantastic Four*, Stan Lee and Jack Kirby created two great galactic empires for the Marvel Universe: the Skrulls and their eternal rivals, the Kree. Unlike the Skrulls, the Kree looked human, although the original Kree had blue skin. Through interbreeding with alien humanoids, a pink-skinned race of Kree later emerged. Long ruled by the entity known as the Supreme Intelligence, Kree society is militaristic and imperialistic. The Fantastic Four and their readers first learned of the Kree in *Fantastic Four* #64 (1967), in which the four adventurers encountered a powerful robot, a Sentry (shown at right) that the Kree had stationed on Earth. In the following issue, the Supreme Intelligence dispatched an imperial official, Ronan the Accuser, to punish the Super Hero team.

Why did the Kree's Supreme Intelligence first send Ronan the Accuser to judge and punish the Fantastic Four?

- **A.** For intervening in the Kree-Skrull War
- **B.** For utilizing a spaceship of Skrull origin
- **C.** For defeating and disabling a Kree Sentry robot
- **D.** For allying themselves with the Silver Surfer

328. After debuting in *Fantastic Four* #7 (1962), when did Kurrgo, Master of Planet X, next appear in a comics story?

- **A.** Battling the Fantastic Four in their own comic
- **B.** As a villain in *The Incredible Hulk*
- **C.** As a prisoner on the Stranger's planet in *Quasar*
- **D.** Opposing The Thing and the Hulk in *Marvel Feature* #11 (1973)

329. When the Human Torch and The Thing started teaming up regularly in *Strange Tales*, whom did they fight first?

- **A.** The Terrible Trio
- **B.** The Rabble Rouser
- **C.** Paste-Pot Pete
- **D.** The Wizard

330. Who inked guest star Daredevil in *Fantastic Four* #39 and #40 (1965)?

- **A.** Vince Colletta
- **B.** Bill Everett
- **C.** Wally Wood
- **D.** Joe Sinnott

331. Who is Sam Thorne?

- **A.** A former teacher of Reed at State University
- **B.** A coach at Metro College who wanted Wyatt Wingfoot to play football
- **C.** The scientist who stole The Thing's powers and identity in *Fantastic Four* #51 (1966)
- **D.** A friend from Ben Grimm's test pilot days

332. Who was the wanderer from medieval times who carried the mystical power object called the Evil Eye?

- **A.** Prester John
- **B.** Modred the Mystic
- **C.** Murdoch Adams
- **D.** Dakimh the Enchanter

333. Where did "Him" next appear after his debut in *Fantastic Four* #66 and #67 (1967)?

- **A.** *Avengers*
- **B.** *Fantastic Four*
- **C.** *Thor*
- **D.** The first *Warlock* story in *Marvel Premiere* #1 (1972)

334. Where did the original Counter-Earth exist?

- **A.** On the opposite side of the sun from Earth
- **B.** In an alternate timeline
- **C.** In a distant solar system
- **D.** In an alternate universe

Fantastic Four

335. Which member of the original Fantastic Force was a relative of Franklin Richards?

A. Devlor   **C.** Huntara

B. Vibraxas   **D.** She-Hulk

336. Johnny Storm was once hired to play another Marvel hero in a movie. Who was that hero?

A. The original Human Torch   **C.** Spider-Man

B. The Rawhide Kid   **D.** Toro

337. Who destroyed the Fantastic Four's second headquarters, Four Freedoms Plaza?

A. Blastaar   **C.** The Thunderbolts

B. Doctor Doom   **D.** Hyperstorm

338. Which nation did the Doctor Doom of *Doom 2099* conquer?

A. Latveria   **C.** The United States

B. Myridia   **D.** All answers are correct

339. Who does Franklin Richards ultimately become in the alternate reality of *Earth X*?

A. Galactus   **C.** Eternity

B. A Celestial   **D.** A Beyonder

340. For how many issues after Jack Kirby left *Fantastic Four* did Stan Lee remain as its regular writer?

A. One   **C.** Eighteen

B. Twelve   **D.** Twenty-three

341. Where did the Willie Lumpkin character originally appear?

A. In a comic book in the 1940s   **C.** In a comic book in the 1950s

B. In a short-lived newspaper comic strip   **D.** In *Fantastic Four*

342. When Stan Lee first went to work for the company known today as Marvel, what was its name?

A. Atlas Comics   **C.** National Comics

B. Timely Comics   **D.** Marvel Comics

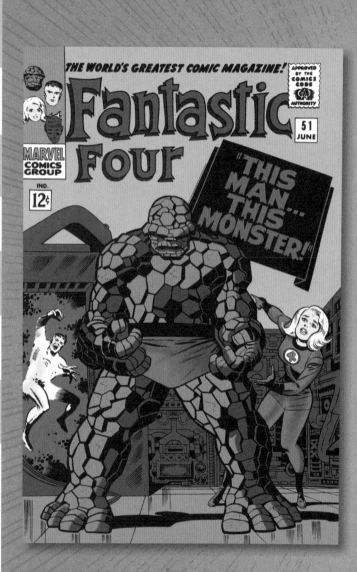

OBSESSED WITH MARVEL

345.

"This Man, This Monster" in *Fantastic Four* #51 (1966, shown at left) is regarded as co-creators Stan Lee and Jack Kirby's finest single-issue story. Though the plot initially focuses on the tragic loneliness of The Thing, Lee and Kirby shift to make a nameless scientist their central character. He steals The Thing's super-powers and physical appearance, causing Ben to revert back to human form. Envious of Mister Fantastic's fame and success, the impostor plans to kill Mister Fantastic/Reed Richards. When Richards bravely embarks on an exploration of sub-space, he enters the Negative Zone, a dangerous antimatter cosmos he has discovered, only to become trapped there, doomed to destruction. Witnessing Richards's courage, the false Thing discovers some of the real Thing's nobility within himself, and makes a fateful decision that saves Reed and redeems his life.

Who rescued Reed Richards from being trapped in the Negative Zone again in *Fantastic Four* #62 (1967)?

A. Black Bolt
B. The Human Torch
C. The Silver Surfer
D. Triton

343. Who starred in the first comics story (as opposed to prose pieces) that Stan Lee wrote at Marvel?
A. Captain America   **C.** The Whizzer
B. Headline Hunter   **D.** The Witness

344. Stan Lee attended DeWitt High School in the Bronx. Which of the following comics legends did *not* go to DeWitt?
A. Joe Simon   **C.** Bob Kane
B. Bill Finger   **D.** Will Eisner

345.

346. Which other character from the *2099* line of comics served as a member of Doom's Black Cabinet?
A. Ghost Rider 2099   **C.** Punisher 2099
B. Hulk 2099   **D.** Mr. Fantastic 2099

347. Which event in Fantastic Four-related history is *not* recreated in Kurt Busiek and Alex Ross's series *Marvels* (1994)?
A. Wedding of Reed Richards and Susan Storm   **C.** Galactus first comes to Earth
B. Atlantean invasion of New York City   **D.** Original Human Torch battles the Sub-Mariner

348. Which Marvel editor, writer, or artist was the inspiration for Mr. Mobius of the Time Variance Authority?
A. Archie Goodwin   **C.** Steve Gerber
B. Mark Gruenwald   **D.** Walter Simonson

349. Which adversary of the Fantastic Four succeeded in temporarily destroying the Savage Land in Antarctica?
A. The Dreaming Celestial   **C.** Terminus
B. Kang the Conqueror   **D.** Occulus

350. Who was the minister at Reed and Sue's wedding?
A. Reverend Jones   **C.** Reverend Smith
B. Reverend Miller   **D.** Reverend Stanley

Fantastic Four

351. In his first *Strange Tales* solo story, the Human Torch fought a saboteur called the Destroyer. What other Marvel characters or artifacts share this name?

A. An enchanted suit of Asgardian armor

B. A member of Power Pack

C. A Super Hero who battled Nazis in Europe in World War II

D. All answers are correct

352. Which omnipotent being does Reed Richards eventually become in *Earth X*'s sequel, *Universe X* (2000-2001)?

A. A Celestial

B. Galactus

C. Eternity

D. A Watcher

353. What are the names of Ben's sons, the Brothers Grimm, in *Earth X*?

A. Alex and Jim

B. Ben Jr. and Daniel

C. Buzz and Chuck

D. Reed and Johnny

354. Who becomes the Watcher's chosen successor in *Earth X*?

A. The Watcher's son

B. X-51, alias Machine Man

C. The Recorder

D. Reed Richards

355.

356. Why does the population of Earth begin to mutate in the alternate reality of *Earth X* (1999-2000)?

A. Magneto plots to turn all humans into mutants

B. As a result of the Celestials' ultimate experiment on humanity

C. The Kree Supreme Intelligence activates humanity's genetic potential

D. Black Bolt releases Terrigen Mists into Earth's atmosphere

357. Which members of the Fantastic Four are killed in the alternate reality of *Earth X* (1999-2000)?

A. Reed and Susan

B. Susan and Johnny

C. Johnny and Ben

D. Ben and Reed

358. Where is Reed Richards based in the alternate reality of *Earth X* (1999-2000)?

A. Castle Doom, Latveria

B. The Blue Area of the Moon

C. The Baxter Building, New York City

D. A space station orbiting Earth

355.

In *Fantastic Four* #4 (1962), having quit the team, Johnny Storm goes to a cheap hotel on New York City's Bowery, where he finds an old Sub-Mariner comic book. Johnny also finds a bearded derelict with amnesia. Carefully using his flame to trim the man's hair and burn off his beard, Johnny discovers that the tramp is Sub-Mariner, Prince Namor of the undersea kingdom of Atlantis (shown at right). Johnny immerses Namor in water, restoring his memory. But as a result, Namor renews his war with the human race, attacking New York City. Thus, Stan Lee and Jack Kirby revived one of Marvel's greatest characters of the Golden Age of Comics from the 1930s and 1940s. Namor made repeated appearances in *Fantastic Four*'s early years, sometimes as an adversary and sometimes as an ally, and sometimes even as Reed Richards's competitor for Susan Storm's love.

What eventually happened to the building where Johnny Storm found the Sub-Mariner?

A. It became a coffee shop

B. It was torn down to make way for a skyscraper

C. It became an off-off-Broadway theater

D. It was converted into condominiums

A GALLERY OF THE FANTASTIC FOUR'S MOST FAMOUS FOES!

PRINCE NAMOR, THE SENSATIONAL SUB-MARINER

FIRST APPEARED IN F.F. #4 MAY

SUB-MARINER! RULER OF THE SEAS! ROYAL PRINCE-OF-THE-BLOOD OF A MIGHTY, ALMOST LEGENDARY RACE! HIS STRENGTH IS THE STRENGTH OF MANY SURFACE-MEN, AND HIS FIGHTING HEART AND RAW COURAGE MAKE HIM AN INDOMITABLE FOE! ABLE TO BREATHE UNDER WATER, TO WITHSTAND THE CRUSHING PRESSURE OF THE OCEAN'S DEPTHS... ABLE TO FLY FOR SHORT DISTANCES AIDED BY HIS WINGED FEET... POSSESSING THE INCREDIBLE POWER OF ALL THE UNDERSEA CREATURES, PRINCE NAMOR, THE SUB-MARINER, IS THE MOST TALKED-ABOUT, MOST COLORFUL HERO-VILLAIN IN ALL OF COMICDOM TODAY!

359. In the role of narrator of the original *What If?* comic book series, what did the Watcher describe?

A. Possible futures for the Marvel Universe

B. Alternate timelines diverging from key moments in Marvel history

C. The lives of Marvel characters if they had lived in different times or places

D. All answers are correct

360. *What If?* #11 (1978) was titled "What if the Fantastic Four Were the Original Marvel Bullpen?" Who was *not* one of the Fantastic Four members in this story?

A. Roy Thomas as the Human Torch

B. Flo Steinberg as the Invisible Girl

C. Stan Lee as Mister Fantastic

D. Jack Kirby as The Thing

361. The "main" Earth on which Marvel stories take place is designated as Earth-616. What is the designation for the alternate Earth in *Marvel 1602*?

A. Earth-267

B. Earth-311

C. Earth-295

D. Earth-398

362. Which is the Earth that is portrayed in the 2003 limited series *Fantastic Four: Unstable Molecules*?

A. Earth-26

B. Earth-98

C. Earth-33

D. Earth-155

363. What did *not* happen on the alternate Earth called Earth-A?

A. Ben Grimm became Mister Fantastic and married Susan Storm

B. Reed Richards became The Thing

C. Susan Storm became the Invisible Girl and married Reed Richards

D. Johnny Storm became known as Vangaard

364. Who became the Brute on the High Evolutionary's Counter-Earth?

A. Victor von Doom of Counter-Earth

B. Reed Richards of Counter-Earth

C. Ben Grimm of Counter-Earth

D. Susan Storm of Counter-Earth

Fantastic Four

CHAPTER TWO:

SPIDER-MAN

365. Which Marvel Super Hero or heroes guest starred in *The Amazing Spider-Man* #1 (1963)?

A. Ant-Man
C. The Fantastic Four
B. The Human Torch
D. The Hulk

366. Who was the first Super Villain Spider-Man fought in *The Amazing Spider-Man* #1 (1963)?

A. The Chameleon
C. The Green Goblin
B. Doctor Octopus
D. The Vulture

367. What was John Jameson's occupation when he first appeared in *The Amazing Spider-Man*?

A. Soldier
C. Reporter
B. Astronaut
D. Editor

368. When did J. Jonah Jameson first appear?

A. *Amazing Fantasy* #15 (1962)
C. *The Amazing Spider-Man* #1 (1963), second story
B. *The Amazing Spider-Man* #1 (1963), first story
D. *The Amazing Spider-Man* #2 (1963), first story

369. Where did Peter Parker live with his Uncle Ben and Aunt May?

A. Upper West Side, Manhattan
C. Jackson Heights, Queens
B. Brooklyn Heights, New York
D. Forest Hills, Queens

370. Where did Peter Parker go to high school?

A. Midtown High School
C. Forest Hills High School
B. DeWitt Clinton High School
D. Kings County High School

371. Where did Peter Parker go to college?

A. Columbia University
C. Empire State University
B. Metro College
D. City College of New York

372. Where did Peter Parker attend graduate school?
- **A.** Empire State University
- **B.** City University of New York
- **C.** Columbia University
- **D.** New York University

373. Which of the following characters was *not* one of Peter Parker's high school classmates?
- **A.** Liz Allan
- **B.** Sally Avril
- **C.** Jessica Jones
- **D.** Mary Jane Watson

374.

ACCIDENTALLY ABSORBING A FANTAS-TIC AMOUNT OF RADIOACTIVITY, THE DYING INSECT, IN SUDDEN SHOCK, BITES THE NEAREST LIVING THING, AT THE SPLIT SECOND BEFORE LIFE EBBS FROM ITS RADIOACTIVE BODY!

OW!

A-A SPIDE BUT, WHY SO? WHY THA

375. Which of the following characters was *not* one of Peter Parker's college classmates?
- **A.** Harry Osborn
- **B.** Gwen Stacy
- **C.** Liz Allan
- **D.** Flash Thompson

376. Who is Dr. Curtis Connors?
- **A.** The Jackal
- **B.** Peter Parker's college biology professor
- **C.** Aunt May's physician
- **D.** The Lizard

377. Which of the following characters was *not* a member of the original Sinister Six?
- **A.** The Green Goblin
- **B.** Kraven the Hunter
- **C.** The Sandman
- **D.** Mysterio

378. Why did Curt Connors perform the experiment that turned him into the Lizard?
- **A.** To regenerate his missing arm
- **B.** To attempt to cure a fatal disease
- **C.** To become a Super Villain
- **D.** To communicate with reptiles

379. How did the Sandman acquire his ability to turn into living sand?
- **A.** An accident in an atomic laboratory
- **B.** Experimental treatment in prison
- **C.** Exposure to radiation from an atomic test
- **D.** Born with a mutant power

380. What is the original source of Mysterio's powers?
- **A.** He is a movie special-effects expert
- **B.** He is a sorcerer
- **C.** He is an alien with advanced technology
- **D.** He is a mutant

Only a year after writer-editor Stan Lee introduced a new kind of Super Hero story in *Fantastic Four* #1 (1961), *Amazing Fantasy* was on the verge of cancellation. So Lee took the opportunity to experiment further with the Super Hero concept. In *Amazing Fantasy* #15 (1962, shown above), Lee and artist Steve Ditko introduced Peter Parker, a teenage orphan and science prodigy who was a lonely outcast at his high school. During a visit to a laboratory, Peter is bitten by a spider that had been exposed to radiation. As a result, Peter discovers he has super-strength, the ability to cling to walls, and even a "spider-sense" that alerts him

OBSESSED WITH MARVEL

Speech bubbles: "...T BIT ME! BURNING **GLOWING** ...Y??"

"MY HEAD-- IT FEELS STRANGE! I-I NEED SOME AIR!"

"LOOKS AS THOUGH OUR EXPERIMENT UNNERVED YOUNG PARKER!"

"TOO BAD! HE MUST HAVE A WEAK STOMACH!"

to danger. Inspired, Peter invents web-shooters that project artificial webbing like a spider's. He creates a new masked identity for himself, Spider-Man, initially intending to exploit his new abilities to make a fortune in show business. But when tragedy strikes, the boy turned Spider-Man vows to use his powers to protect the innocent.

Who drew and inked the cover of *Amazing Fantasy* #15?

A. Jack Kirby and Steve Ditko
B. Steve Ditko
C. Steve Ditko and Dick Ayers
D. Jack Kirby and Dick Ayers

381. Which of the following is *not* a member of the Ringmaster's Circus of Crime?
- **A.** The Clown
- **B.** The Acrobat
- **C.** The Great Gambonnos
- **D.** Princess Python

382. Which villain was *not* given an alternate personality by an accident that also gave him his super-powers?
- **A.** The Sandman
- **B.** Scorpion
- **C.** The Lizard
- **D.** The Green Goblin

383. Who paid to send the original Spider-Slayer robot after Spider-Man and even worked the controls?
- **A.** The Kingpin
- **B.** Norman Osborn
- **C.** J. Jonah Jameson
- **D.** Spencer Smythe

384. In which comic did Harry Osborn and Gwen Stacy first appear?
- **A.** *The Amazing Fantasy* #15 (1962)
- **B.** *The Amazing Spider-Man* #31 (1965)
- **C.** *The Amazing Spider-Man* #1 (1963)
- **D.** *The Amazing Spider-Man* #25 (1965)

385. Which one of Spider-Man's nemeses once was a boarder at Aunt May's house?
- **A.** Doctor Octopus
- **B.** The Vulture
- **C.** Humbug
- **D.** The Black Fox

386. Why *didn't* Spider-Man turn the Green Goblin over to the police when he learned he was Norman Osborn?
- **A.** Because Osborn knew he was Peter Parker
- **B.** Because Osborn lost his memory of being the Green Goblin
- **C.** Because Osborn escaped
- **D.** Because Osborn was seemingly dead

387. Whom did Spider-Man team up with in his second annual?
- **A.** The Human Torch
- **B.** The Fantastic Four
- **C.** Doctor Strange
- **D.** Ant-Man and the Wasp

388. Who succeeded Steve Ditko as artist on *The Amazing Spider-Man*?
- **A.** John Romita Sr.
- **B.** Don Heck
- **C.** Sal Buscema
- **D.** John Buscema

Spider-Man

389. Who appeared in the fifth issues of both *The Amazing Spider-Man* and *Fantastic Four*?
- **A.** The Sub-Mariner
- **B.** Flash Thompson
- **C.** Doctor Doom
- **D.** J. Jonah Jameson

390. Which of Peter Parker's college courses did Professor Miles Warren teach?
- **A.** Biochemistry
- **B.** Physics
- **C.** Psychology
- **D.** Physiology

391.

392. Which late-night TV host had J. Jonah Jameson as his guest in *The Amazing Spider-Man* #50 (1967)?
- **A.** Johnny Carson
- **B.** Jack Paar
- **C.** Steve Allen
- **D.** David Letterman

393. Under which circumstances did Spider-Man meet President Barack Obama?
- **A.** When a Skrull impersonated Mr. Obama in "Secret Invasion"
- **B.** When the Chameleon impersonated Mr. Obama on Inauguration Day
- **C.** When the Sons of the Serpent disrupted an Obama for President rally
- **D.** When President Obama awarded a medal to Spider-Man

394. Which of the following Spider-Man foes eventually reformed (but now isn't)?
- **A.** The Sandman
- **B.** Electro
- **C.** The Shocker
- **D.** The Looter

395. Which Super Villain did Presidential candidate/comedian Stephen Colbert encounter when he met Spider-Man in *The Amazing Spider-Man* #573 (2008)?
- **A.** The Grizzly
- **B.** The Leap-Frog
- **C.** The Walrus
- **D.** The White Rabbit

396. Why did the Kingpin kidnap J. Jonah Jameson in *The Amazing Spider-Man* #51-52 (1967)?
- **A.** To hold him for ransom
- **B.** To force him to sell the *Daily Bugle*
- **C.** To retaliate for the *Daily Bugle*'s anticrime articles
- **D.** Because Jameson owed him money

391.

John Romita Sr. has created some of the most iconic *Spider-Man* imagery. With a background in romance comics, Romita was adept at drawing beautiful women and defined the look of Spider-Man's leading ladies Gwen Stacy and Mary Jane Watson. He also made Peter Parker handsomer and more robust as the character matured in his college years. One of his most notable stories is "Spider-Man No More" in *The Amazing Spider-Man* #50 (1967, shown at right), in which a despairing Peter temporarily forsakes his role as hero.

Romita collaborated with Stan Lee for years on *The Amazing Spider-Man* comic book and was the first artist on Lee's *The Amazing Spider-Man* newspaper strip as well. (His son, John Romita Jr., has long been one of the leading *Spider-Man* artists in his own right.) Spider-Man co-creator Steve Ditko first drew a well-known character's body, but John Romita Sr. first drew the character's face. Who was it?

- **A.** Gwen Stacy
- **B.** Norman Osborn
- **C.** Mary Jane Watson
- **D.** Harry Osborn

397. How did Captain George Stacy die?

A. Shot in a gun battle with criminals

B. Hit by falling debris while saving an innocent

C. Heart attack

D. Cancer

398. Why did Marvel publish *The Amazing Spider-Man* #96–98 (1971) without the Comics Code Authority seal?

A. The story showed that criminals sometimes go unpunished

B. The story featured the vampire Morbius

C. The story warned against addictive drugs

D. The story was unusually violent

399. What was Stan Lee's final issue as the regular writer of *The Amazing Spider-Man*?

A. #110 (1972)

B. #100 (1971)

C. #120 (1973)

D. #90 (1970)

400. What happened to Spider-Man in his hundredth issue?

A. He mutated so that he could shoot webs from his hands

B. He revealed his dual identity to Gwen Stacy

C. He grew four extra arms

D. He lost his super-powers

401. Who is considered to be Peter Parker's first true love?

A. Betty Brant

B. Gwen Stacy

C. Mary Jane Watson

D. Liz Allan

402. What was Betty Brant's original job at the *Daily Bugle*?

A. Reporter

B. Receptionist

C. J. Jonah Jameson's secretary

D. Joe Robertson's assistant

403. Who was the *Daily Bugle*'s editor in chief?

A. Joe "Robbie" Robertson

B. Kate Cushing

C. Ned Leeds

D. Ben Urich

404. What is true about Spider-Man's Spider-Mobile?

A. Spider-Man called it a fiasco

B. Spider-Man drove it into a river

C. The Tinkerer turned it into a weapon to attack Spider-Man

D. All answers are correct

Spider-Man

405. What is the homeland of Silver Sable?
- **A.** Latveria
- **B.** Transia
- **C.** Symkaria
- **D.** Wakanda

406. Who is Madame Web?
- **A.** A Super Heroine with spiderlike powers
- **B.** An elderly blind woman with precognitive powers
- **C.** A criminal mastermind
- **D.** An Internet blogger

407. What was the occupation of Gwen Stacy's father?
- **A.** Police captain
- **B.** Private detective
- **C.** U.S. Army captain
- **D.** U.S. Navy captain

408.

409. Who was *not* one of the writers of the original *Spider-Woman* series?
- **A.** Chris Claremont
- **B.** Steve Englehart
- **C.** Mark Gruenwald
- **D.** Marv Wolfman

410. Which great comics artist of the Golden and Silver ages of comics drew *Spider-Woman*?
- **A.** Bill Everett
- **B.** Jack Kirby
- **C.** Joe Simon
- **D.** Carmine Infantino

411. What is May "Mayday" Parker's favorite sport?
- **A.** Soccer
- **B.** Basketball
- **C.** Tennis
- **D.** Running

412. Who is the Green Goblin that Spider-Girl encounters?
- **A.** Normie Osborn
- **B.** Phil Urich
- **C.** Normie Osborn and Phil Urich
- **D.** None of these

413. What is the name of May "Spider-Girl" Parker's little brother?
- **A.** Peter Jr.
- **B.** Philip
- **C.** Benjamin
- **D.** Harry

414. Whom did the Green Goblin throw off the Queensboro Bridge in *Ultimate Spider-Man*?
- **A.** Mary Jane Watson
- **B.** Gwen Stacy
- **C.** Aunt May
- **D.** Peter Parker

408.

When Aunt May first tried to introduce Peter Parker to her friend Anna Watson's niece, he did his best to avoid Mary Jane Watson (shown at right). But when they finally met, the gorgeous redhead told Peter, "Face it, tiger, you just hit the jackpot!" And so he had.

The free-spirited, flirtatious Mary Jane was only Peter's friend at first, but after Gwen Stacy's death, things changed. Writers like Gerry Conway and Tom DeFalco showed that Mary Jane was serious and sensitive, much like Peter Parker, hiding beneath her happy-go-lucky facade as he did behind the mask of Spider-Man.

They became confidants, fell in love, and finally got married in both the comic book and comic strip. The marriage lasted two decades before coming to an end.

When did Peter Parker—and readers—first see Mary Jane's face?

- **A.** *The Amazing Spider-Man* #25 (1965)
- **B.** *The Amazing Spider-Man* #31 (1965)
- **C.** *The Amazing Spider-Man* #40 (1966)
- **D.** *The Amazing Spider-Man* #42 (1966)

OBSESSED WITH MARVEL

415. Which classic villain took over Peter Parker's brain to become the Superior Spider-Man?
- **A.** The Green Goblin
- **B.** Mysterio
- **C.** Doctor Octopus
- **D.** The Jackal

416. During which major crossover did Spider-Man join forces with versions of himself from different realities?
- **A.** *Spider Island*
- **B.** *The Clone Conspiracy*
- **C.** *Big Time*
- **D.** *Spider-Verse*

417. What was the name of Otto Octavius's romantic interest during his time as the Superior Spider-Man?
- **A.** Mary Jane Watson
- **B.** Anna Maria Marconi
- **C.** Felicia Hardy
- **D.** May Parker

418. After his tenure as the Superior Spider-Man ended, Otto Octavius uploaded his mind into which robot?
- **A.** Machine Man
- **B.** Ultron
- **C.** The Living Brain
- **D.** The Vision

419. What is the true identity of the Spider-Woman from Earth-65?
- **A.** Gwen Stacy
- **B.** Jean DeWolff
- **C.** Mattie Franklin
- **D.** Jessica Drew

420. During *The Clone Conspiracy*, what classic character was revealed to be the true identity of the Jackal?
- **A.** Miles Warren
- **B.** Ben Parker
- **C.** Ben Reilly
- **D.** Kaine Parker

421. Before he started his own company, Peter Parker worked at which cutting-edge technology firm?
- **A.** Horizon Labs
- **B.** Alchemax
- **C.** Oscorp
- **D.** Advanced Idea Mechanics

Spider-Man

422. What happened to the clone of Spider-Man at the end *of The Amazing Spider-Man* #149 (1975)?

A. Was killed by an explosion

B. Took the place of the original Spider-Man

C. Though seemingly dead, he survived and would live under an alias

D. Turned against his creator

423. Which Super Hero team has Spider-Man *never* joined?

A. Defenders

B. Fantastic Four

C. Avengers

D. New Warriors

424. How did Spider-Man acquire his original black costume?

A. He made it himself

B. On the "Battleworld" in the original *Secret Wars*

C. At the Gladiator's costume shop

D. As a gift

425. Who was the Scarlet Spider?

A. Oliver Osnick

B. Ben Reilly

C. A highly evolved arachnid

D. A Super Villain

426. Who created the clone of Spider-Man in *The Amazing Spider-Man* #149 (1975)?

A. The Jackal

B. The High Evolutionary

C. Dr. Judas Traveller

D. Dr. Seward Trainer

427. Where was Peter Parker's favorite place to go with his friends in college?

A. Coffee a Go-Go

B. The Coffee Bean

C. The Daily Grind

D. ESU Student Lounge

428. Who was Peter Parker's college roommate?

A. Flash Thompson

B. Randy Robertson

C. John Jameson

D. Harry Osborn

429. Who wrote and drew the best-selling *Spider-Man* #1 (1990)?

A. Jim Lee

B. Todd McFarlane

C. Rob Liefeld

D. John Byrne

430.

With his distinctive, quirky, and powerfully dramatic visual style, Steve Ditko is considered one of the leading cartoonists in comic book history. Ditko drew strikingly eerie and atmospheric science-fiction stories for Marvel comics such as *Amazing Fantasy,* which included his illustrations of the first *Spider-Man* story (alternate cover shown at right).

Ditko contributed greatly to *Spider-Man* stories, eventually plotting them while Stan Lee edited and scripted them. Whereas Jack Kirby drew heroic figures in a larger-than-life world in *Fantastic Four*, Ditko's Spider-Man was a believable and ordinary-looking teenager in a handmade costume, operating in a gritty, realistic city.

In sharp contrast, the other great series that Lee and Ditko co-created was *Doctor Strange*, for which Ditko devised surrealistic fantasy worlds. Though Ditko remained on *The Amazing Spider-Man* for a relatively short time, his influence on the series is indelible.

How many issues of *The Amazing Spider-Man* did Steve Ditko draw (not counting two annuals)?

A. Twenty-five

B. Thirty-one

C. Thirty-eight

D. Forty-one

431. What was *Spider-Man: Chapter One*?

A. The first Ultimate Spider-Man story arc

B. A reprint collection of Lee-Ditko *Spider-Man* stories

C. Kurt Busiek and Pat Olliffe's series about Spider-Man's early career

D. John Byrne's revised version of the the Lee-Ditko stories

432. In the divergent timeline pictured in *What If?* #1 (1977), how does Spider-Man's life change?

A. He saves Gwen Stacy from dying

B. He joins the Fantastic Four

C. He becomes a Hollywood TV star

D. He prevents Uncle Ben's death

433. Who was Ben Reilly?

A. The original Spider-Man

B. A clone of Spider-Man

C. Peter Parker's twin brother

D. An alias used by Peter Parker

434. Who was the Jackal?

A. Professor Miles Warren

B. Dr. Curt Connors

C. Dr. Morris Sloan

D. Dr. Seward Trainer

435. When did Spider-Man publicly reveal his secret identity as Peter Parker?

A. When he gave up his Super Hero career

B. During the Super Heroes' "Civil War"

C. When he joined the Avengers

D. He has never publicly revealed his dual identity

436. Who officiated at the wedding of Peter Parker and Mary Jane Watson?

A. Judge Spencer Watson

B. Stan Lee (portrayed as a justice of the peace)

C. The mayor of New York

D. Reverend Miller

437. How did the marriage of Peter and Mary Jane come to an end?

A. They were divorced

B. Mary Jane was believed dead

C. History was altered so that it never happened

D. They received an annulment

438. What happened when the crime boss Silvermane learned the ancient formula for regaining one's youth?

A. He seemingly vanished into oblivion, then returned

B. He devolved into a baby and then into nothingness

C. He immediately became forty years younger

D. Silvermane lost the formula before he could use it himself

Spider-Man

439. What is Peter Parker's middle name?
- **A.** Steven
- **B.** Benjamin
- **C.** John
- **D.** Joseph

440. How old was Peter Parker when he became Spider-Man?
- **A.** Fourteen
- **B.** Fifteen
- **C.** Sixteen
- **D.** Seventeen

441. What were the names of Peter Parker's parents?
- **A.** Jonathan and Martha
- **B.** Richard and Martha
- **C.** Richard and Mary
- **D.** Thomas and Mary

442. Who was the wrestler a disguised Peter Parker fought in his origin story?
- **A.** "Happy" Hogan
- **B.** "Crusher" Hogan
- **C.** Demolition-Man
- **D.** The Grizzly

443. What color are Peter Parker's eyes?
- **A.** Blue
- **B.** Grey
- **C.** Hazel
- **D.** Green

444. Which filmmaker wrote the comics miniseries *Spider-Man/Black Cat: The Evil That Men Do* (2002–2006)?
- **A.** Reginald Hudlin
- **B.** Sam Raimi
- **C.** Kevin Smith
- **D.** J. Michael Straczynski

445. Who is an adversary of *Spider-Man 2099?*
- **A.** The Specialist
- **B.** Tyler Stone
- **C.** Venture
- **D.** All answers are correct

446.

447. How did Gwen Stacy actually die?
- **A.** She died from the shock of the fall
- **B.** Her neck snapped when Spider-Man caught her
- **C.** She drowned in the river
- **D.** The Green Goblin strangled her before throwing her off the bridge

448. What happened to the Green Goblin after he caused Gwen Stacy's death?
- **A.** He was imprisoned for murder
- **B.** He seemingly died but recovered and went to Europe
- **C.** He was impaled by his own flying vehicle and died
- **D.** He flew from the scene, cackling in triumph

446.

When Peter Parker entered college, at first he did not get along with his new classmate Gwendolyne Stacy. But over the course of Stan Lee and John Romita's collaboration on *The Amazing Spider-Man* comic book (issue 122 shown at right), Peter and Gwen fell deeply in love. The blonde and beautiful Gwen was portrayed as the ideal girlfriend, one that Peter Parker could never forget. Her father became like a second father to Peter.

But he was doomed to lose them both. Gwen's father died first, and then, shockingly, Spider-Man was unable to stop the Green Goblin from murdering Gwen. This story, by writer Gerry Conway and artist Gil Kane, was a turning point at Marvel. Decades later, Kurt Busiek and Alex Ross's *Marvels* series pointed to Gwen's death as the moment when Super Hero stories could end in tragedy, not triumph.

Which bridge was the site of Gwen Stacy's death in *The Amazing Spider-Man* #121?

- **A.** George Washington (in the script) and Brooklyn (in the art)
- **B.** George Washington
- **C.** Queensboro
- **D.** Brooklyn

OBSESSED WITH MARVEL

449. What was the name of the scientific genius who founded Horizon Labs?

A. Curt Connors
C. Miles Warren
B. Max Modell
D. Otto Octavius

450. What was the Super Villain identity of powerful businessman Augustus Roman?

A. The Green Goblin
C. Power Broker
B. The Kingpin
D. Regent

451. What is the name of Peter Parker's hugely successful global technology firm?

A. ParCorp
C. Parker Industries
B. Spider Solutions
D. World Wide Webs

452. Which alternate reality Spider-Man was not featured in Spider-Verse?

A. Spider-Punk
C. Spider-Monkey
B. Spider-Ham
D. Spider-Skunk

453. After the Spider-Verse crossover, several alternate reality Spider-Men formed which team?

A. The Web Warriors
C. The Wall Crawlers
B. The Spider Fighters
D. The Parker Patrol

454. Who did Peter Parker hire to act as Spider-Man while he was away on Parker Industries business?

A. Scarlet Spider
C. Daredevil
B. Prowler
D. Iron Fist

455. Which member of Peter Parker's supporting cast died at the beginning of *The Clone Conspiracy* storyline?

A. Aunt May
C. Jay Jameson
B. Harry Osborn
D. Mary Jane Watson

456. Which deceased character did the new Jackal revive as a part of his master plan during *The Clone Conspiracy*?

A. Gwen Stacy
C. Prowler
B. Doctor Octopus
D. All answers are correct

457. Who became Peter Parker's S.H.I.E.L.D. liaison after Parker Industries went global?

A. Mockingbird
C. Phil Coulson
B. Nick Fury
D. Quake

Spider-Man

458. What story is told in "One More Day"?

A. Gwen Stacy's death

B. The end of Peter and Mary Jane's marriage

C. Peter Parker's death and return to life

D. Aunt May's seeming death

459. Which character from the time of King Arthur is the original Spider-Woman's archenemy?

A. Morgan Le Fey

B. Mordred

C. Modred the Mystic

D. Magnus

460. What is the super-power of the original Spider-Woman's adversary Gypsy Moth?

A. Super-strength

B. Telepathic control of insects

C. Telekinetic control over fabrics

D. Telekinetic control of flames

461. Which super-power of *Spider-Man 2099* did the present-day Spider-Man briefly possess?

A. Fast healing ability

B. Organic web-shooters

C. Retractable claws

D. Fangs that secrete poison

462. What was the Speed Demon's former alias?

A. The Whizzer

B. Quicksilver

C. Speedfreek

D. The Blue Streak

463.

The opening sequence in "The Final Chapter" in *The Amazing Spider-Man* #33 (1966, shown at right) is the dramatic peak of Stan Lee and Steve Ditko's collaboration on the series. It comes at the end of the story line in which Spider-Man tracks down the mysterious "Master Planner." Following a tremendous battle, Spider-Man is pinned beneath tons of fallen machinery, seemingly helpless. Inspired by his sense of responsibility to his Aunt May, who is seriously ill, Spider-Man fends off despair. Unwilling to surrender to his fate, Spider-Man struggles over the course of a series of increasingly large and dramatic panels to finally, triumphantly, throw off the debris, freeing himself in a full-page panel. If one sequence in all of comics history best captures the spirit of Lee and Ditko's *Spider-Man*, this is it.

Where did Spider-Man heroically lift the tons of weight pinning him down?

A. The Master Planner's undersea lair

B. A laboratory robbed by the Master Planner

C. The ruins of a skyscraper demolished in combat

D. The ruins of a building after an explosion

464. When did Professor Miles Warren first appear?

A. *Amazing Fantasy* #15 (1962)

B. *The Amazing Spider-Man* #149 (1975)

C. *The Amazing Spider-Man* #129 (1974)

D. *The Amazing Spider-Man* #31 (1965)

465. Which one of Spider-Man's foes originally pretended to be an alien from outer space?

A. The Tinkerer

B. Mysterio

C. Graviton

D. The Chameleon

466. Which name has the Sandman *not* used?

A. Sylvester Mann

B. Stephen Sanders

C. Flint Marko

D. William Baker

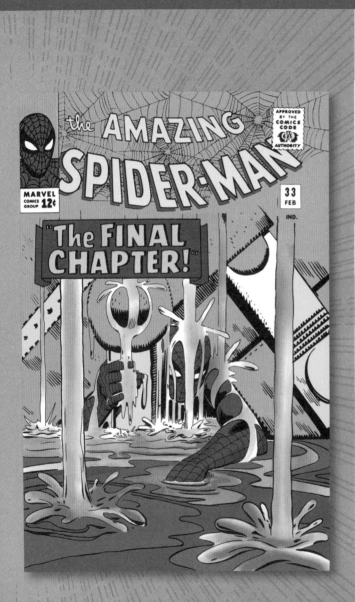

467. Where did Spider-Man first combat the Lizard?

A. The Florida Everglades
B. The Amazon jungle
C. The Bronx Zoo
D. The Central Park Zoo

468. Why did no one believe Peter Parker was Spider-Man when Doctor Octopus unmasked him in front of witnesses in *The Amazing Spider-Man* #12 (1964)?

A. Peter Parker wore makeup disguising his features
B. It was late at night and no one could see his face
C. No one recognized him
D. No witnesses believed Peter Parker was the real Spider-Man

469. Who is Max Dillon?

A. Electro
B. Boomerang
C. Slyde
D. The Schemer

470. Who is the original Mysterio?

A. Daniel Berkhart
B. Quentin Beck
C. Francis Klum
D. Bentley Wittman

471. Who was *not* a member of the original Enforcers?

A. Man-Mountain Marko
B. The Ox
C. Fancy Dan
D. Montana

472. Which of the following Spider-Man foes originally claimed to be a Super Hero?

A. The Sandman
B. Electro
C. Hydro-Man
D. Mysterio

473. Who inadvertently intruded into Spider-Man's first battle against the Green Goblin?

A. The Hulk
B. The Human Torch
C. The Crime-Master
D. The Robot-Master

474. Why did Spider-Man attempt to join the Fantastic Four in *The Amazing Spider-Man* #1 (1963)?

A. To train in using his super-powers
B. To associate with super-powered colleagues
C. To get a steady paycheck
D. To help Reed Richards in scientific research

475. Who turned out to be the masked crime boss called the Big Man?

A. Frederick Foswell
B. Wilson Fisk
C. Nick "Lucky" Lewis
D. Norman Osborn

Spider-Man

476. During *Secret Wars* (2015), what was the name of Peter and Mary Jane's daughter?

A. May
B. Annie May
C. Gwen
D. Polly

477. For a time, Venom served as a member of which spacefaring Super Hero team?

A. The Nova Corps
B. Annihilators
C. Guardians of the Galaxy
D. Alpha Flight

478. In his 2016 series, Carnage found himself in possession of what powerful ancient artifact?

A. The Eye of Agamotto
B. An Infinity Gem
C. The Darkhold
D. The Cask of Ancient Winters

479.

480. Writer Dan Slott often teamed with which co-writer during his run on *Amazing Spider-Man*?

A. Christos Gage
B. Stan Lee
C. Roy Thomas
D. Gerry Conway

481. Where did Spider-Gwen (the Spider-Woman of Earth-65) make her first appearance?

A. *Amazing Spider-Man* #31 (1965)
B. *Edge of Spider-Verse* #2 (2014)
C. *Spider-Verse* #1 (2014)
D. *Spider-Gwen* #0 (2015)

482. Who was *not* a regular member of the Web Warriors?

A. Spider-Ham
B. Spider-UK
C. Spider-Man India
D. Spider-Man J

483. Who bonded with the Venom symbiote to become its new host in 2016's *Venom* #1?

A. Mac Gargan
B. Eddie Brock
C. Lee Price
D. Flash Thompson

484. Which Super Hero gained powers from the same spider that bit Peter Parker?

A. Spider-Gwen
B. Silk
C. Scarlet Spider
D. Spider-Man 2099

485. At which Parker Industries location was the new Spider-Mobile built?

A. London
B. New York
C. Shanghai
D. San Francisco

OBSESSED WITH MARVEL

479.

Most of Spider-Man's great villains were created by Stan Lee and Steve Ditko in the earliest years of the series, including Doctor Octopus (shown at right with Spider-Man) in the third issue. Initially Ditko portrayed Dr. Otto Octavius as a bespectacled, gnomish figure with a bad haircut, hardly imposing.

An atomic scientist, Octavius had invented a metal harness with extendable arms for manipulating radioactive materials. An atomic accident fused the harness to Octavius's body and subsequently unleashed his pent-up fury. Then he was indeed a fearsome figure with four metal arms like tentacles, strong enough to overpower Spider-Man, his new perennial nemesis.

How does Doctor Octopus control his metal tentacles?

A. Mental commands
B. They are physically linked to his nervous system
C. Mechanical controls
D. They have their own artificial intelligence

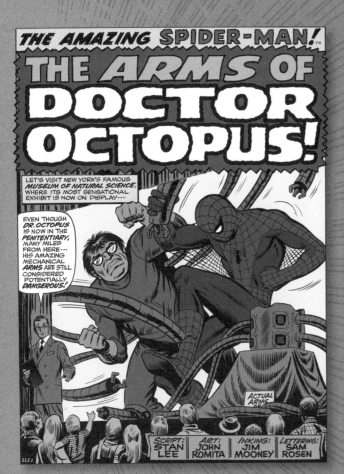

486. Who was known as the Master Planner?

A. Doctor Octopus   **C.** The Kingpin

B. The Green Goblin   **D.** The Jackal

487. Who is the Molten Man's stepsister?

A. Liz Allan   **C.** Glory Grant

B. Betty Brant   **D.** Debra Whitman

488. Who spoke at Peter Parker's high school graduation?

A. Reed Richards   **C.** J. Jonah Jameson

B. Captain George Stacy   **D.** Johnny Storm

489. Which of the following characters was *not* one of Norman Osborn's successors as the Green Goblin?

A. Roderick Kingsley   **C.** Phil Urich

B. Harry Osborn   **D.** Dr. Barton Hamilton

490. Who was "Just a Guy Named Joe"?

A. Joe "Robbie" Robertson   **C.** Marvel editor in chief Joe Quesada

B. One of Peter Parker's classmates   **D.** Joe Smith, an ordinary guy with super-strength

491. Which Super Hero or heroes did *not* make a cameo appearance in *The Amazing Spider-Man Annual* #1 (1964)?

A. The Fantastic Four   **C.** Iron Man

B. The Hulk   **D.** The X-Men

492. Where did John Romita Sr. first draw Spider-Man in a comics story?

A. *Daredevil*   **C.** *Captain America*

B. *The Amazing Spider-Man*   **D.** *Fantastic Four*

493. Who hosted the episode of *Saturday Night Live* in *Marvel Team-Up* #74 (1978), during which Spider-Man met the show's original cast?

A. Wonder Man   **C.** Captain Ultra

B. Stan Lee   **D.** Johnny Storm

494. Who did *not* appear in *Marvel Team-Up* #74 (1978), in which Spider-Man met the Not Ready for Prime Time Players on *Saturday Night Live*?

A. Dan Aykroyd   **C.** Bill Murray

B. Chevy Chase   **D.** Gilda Radner

 Spider-Man

495. Which Super Villain's identity was temporarily usurped by criminal Blackie Drago?
- **A.** The Hobgoblin
- **B.** The Green Goblin
- **C.** The Vulture
- **D.** Stilt-Man

496. Who sacrificed his life to save Jonah Jameson from the Kingpin?
- **A.** Bennet Brant
- **B.** Captain George Stacy
- **C.** Frederick Foswell
- **D.** Nick Katzenberg

497. Who is Adrian Toomes?
- **A.** Tombstone
- **B.** Carrion
- **C.** The Vulture
- **D.** The Black Fox

498.

499. Who is Herman Schultz?
- **A.** The Rhino
- **B.** The Shocker
- **C.** The Gibbon
- **D.** The Grizzly

500. What is *not* an identity that has been used by the Kingpin's son, Richard?
- **A.** The Rose
- **B.** The Schemer
- **C.** The Crime-Master
- **D.** Supreme Hydra

501. What is the name of Gwen Stacy's uncle who lived in England?
- **A.** Alan
- **B.** Ian
- **C.** Arthur
- **D.** Richard

502. Who first succeeded Stan Lee as regular writer of *The Amazing Spider-Man*?
- **A.** Len Wein
- **B.** Gerry Conway
- **C.** Archie Goodwin
- **D.** Marv Wolfman

503. What were the occupations of Peter Parker's parents when they died?
- **A.** Police officers
- **B.** Scientists
- **C.** Secret agents
- **D.** Schoolteachers

504. Who teamed up against Spider-Man and the Human Torch in Hollywood in *The Amazing Spider-Man Special* #4 (1967)?
- **A.** Mysterio and the Wizard
- **B.** The Green Goblin and the Enforcers
- **C.** The Wizard, Sandman, and Trapster
- **D.** Doctor Octopus and the Wizard

498.

In the 1980s, Spider-Man gave up his familiar red-and-blue costume for a new black uniform. But this new costume turned out to be alive and intelligent—an alien symbiote that sought to bond mentally and physically with its human host. When Spider-Man rid himself of the living costume, the creature felt rejected and instead bonded with news photographer Eddie Brock, a man with a grudge against the web-slinger. Brock and the symbiote fused into the being called Venom (shown above), who looked like a huge, powerful, evil version of Spider-Man, complete with sharp fangs.

Initially Venom was Spider-Man's implacable enemy, but Venom eventually became the un-

OBSESSED WITH MARVEL

505. Which of Spider-Man's adversaries nearly became his uncle?
A. Doctor Octopus
B. The Green Goblin
C. The Vulture
D. The Black Fox

506. Who was the ally of the Jackal when he first appeared in *The Amazing Spider-Man* #129 (1974)?
A. Kaine
B. The Punisher
C. Spidercide
D. Bullseye

507. Who teamed up with Spider-Man in *Marvel Team-Up* #1 (1972)?
A. Captain America
B. The Hulk
C. The Human Torch
D. The Silver Surfer

508. Who drew the story in *Marvel Team-Up* #100 (1980) in which Spider-Man teamed up with the Fantastic Four?
A. John Byrne
B. Frank Miller
C. George Perez
D. John Romita Jr.

509. What is the name of the Kingpin's wife?
A. Diana
B. Miranda
C. Samantha
D. Vanessa

510. What is the origin of Stegron the Dinosaur Man?
A. Dinosaur that used evolved human intelligence
B. Scientist who genetically engineered dinosaurs
C. Scientist who injected himself with dinosaur DNA
D. Savage Land native who trained dinosaurs

511. What is the name of Curt Connors's son?
A. Billy
B. Bobby
C. Curt Jr.
D. Tommy

512. Where is the Daily Bugle building located?
A. 39th Street and 2nd Avenue
B. 42nd Street and Broadway
C. 57th Street and Madison Avenue
D. 27th Street and Park Avenue South

513. Who did *not* work at the *Daily Bugle*?
A. Amber Grant
B. Eddie Brock
C. Lance Bannon
D. Jessica Jones

likely star of his own comics, striving in his own way to protect the innocent. Brock finally got free of the symbiote, but later while he was sharing a cell on Ryker's Island with serial killer Cletus Kasady, the symbiote comes back to bond with Brock. It left behind the symbiote's offspring, which bonded with Kasady, creating a new fusion of man and symbiote—Carnage— who proved to be an even worse menace.

Why did Eddie Brock originally hate Spider-Man?

A. Spider-Man proved Brock plagiarized a news photo
B. Spider-Man sent his brother to prison
C. He envied Spider-Man's super-powers
D. Spider-Man proved Brock's news story was wrong

Spider-Man

514. Who edited *Woman* magazine for J. Jonah Jameson?
- **A.** Joy Mercado
- **B.** Kate Cushing
- **C.** Carol Danvers
- **D.** Irene Merryweather

515. Who was a classmate of Joe Robertson?
- **A.** Ben Urich
- **B.** Frederick Foswell
- **C.** Tombstone
- **D.** Norman Osborn

516. Who is Anti-Venom?
- **A.** Nickname for Spider-Man
- **B.** Eddie Brock, whose body repels the symbiote
- **C.** New identity for Carnage
- **D.** An alien who hunts symbiotes now

517. Who is the Black Fox?
- **A.** An elderly jewel thief
- **B.** A Super Hero in the 2000–2001 series *Marvel: The Lost Generation*
- **C.** Both characters
- **D.** Neither character

518. What was Kraven the Hunter's nationality?
- **A.** German
- **B.** Serbian
- **C.** South African
- **D.** Russian

519. Who is Cletus Kasady?
- **A.** Carnage
- **B.** The Foreigner
- **C.** Jack O'Lantern
- **D.** The Owl

520. Which villains did Spider-Man and the X-Men face in *Marvel Team-Up* #150 (1985)?
- **A.** The Hellfire Club
- **B.** Magneto and his Brotherhood of Mutants
- **C.** The Sinister Six
- **D.** The Juggernaut and Black Tom Cassidy

521. Which Spider-Man villain eventually became the new Venom?
- **A.** The Shocker
- **B.** Tombstone
- **C.** A Guy Named Joe
- **D.** The Scorpion

522. What is the Rocket Racer's mode of transportation?
- **A.** Rocket-powered skateboard
- **B.** Rocket-powered backpack
- **C.** Rocket-powered skates
- **D.** A rocket

OBSESSED WITH MARVEL

523. What is the origin of Carnage?
A. Bonded with an alien symbiote that came to Earth
B. Bonded with an alien symbiote in outer space
C. Offspring of alien symbiote
D. Scientist who cloned Venom's symbiote

524.

Since Spider-Man was such a tremendously successful character, it was inevitable that Marvel would introduce his female counterpart, Spider-Woman. In fact, over the decades there have been three Super Heroines known as Spider-Woman.

The first and best known is Jessica Drew, who was introduced in *Marvel Premiere* #32 in February 1977 and starred in her own fifty-issue *Spider-Woman* comic book (issue 1 shown at left). She was originally depicted as a spider whom the High Evolutionary had turned into a super-powered human, but Stan Lee instead decided to have her revealed to be a human who had been endowed with spiderlike powers.

The next Spider-Woman, Julia Carpenter, was introduced in the landmark limited series *Marvel Super-Heroes Secret Wars* in 1984. The third, Mattie Franklin, debuted as Spider-Woman in *Amazing Spider-Man* #5 in 1999 and starred in her own short-lived series.

Recently, Jessica Drew resumed her costumed career and joined the New Avengers. Which of the following places was among Jessica Drew's base of operations?

A. Berlin
B. Madripoor
C. Cairo
D. Beirut

525. Who was *not* a member of the Outlaws?
A. Prowler
B. Rocket Racer
C. The Black Cat
D. Sandman

526. What kind of organization is Silver Sable International?
A. Mercenary soldiers
B. Charity foundation
C. High-tech manufacturer
D. Fashion design

527. What is *not* true about Kaine?
A. He is an imperfect clone of Spider-Man
B. He was destroyed by another clone, Spidercide
C. His body and face are covered with scars
D. He can burn the "Mark of Kaine" onto a victim

528. Whom did Flash Thompson once marry in the *Spider-Girl* timeline?
A. Liz Allan
B. Betty Brant
C. Felicia Hardy
D. Glory Grant

529. Which of the following Spider-Man adversaries once owned the *Daily Bugle*?
A. Norman Osborn
B. Thomas Fireheart
C. J. Jonah Jameson
D. All answers are correct

530. Who was once a heroic version of the Green Goblin?
A. Dr. Barton Hamilton
B. Phil Urich
C. Ned Leeds
D. Jason Macendale

531. In *Marvel 1602* (2003-2004), to whom is Peter Parker's counterpart, Peter Parquagh, apprenticed?
A. Sir Richard Reed
B. Dr. Stephen Strange
C. Sir Nicholas Fury
D. Matthew Murdoch

Spider-Man

532. Whom did Peter Parker marry in the alternate timeline of *House of M* (2005-2006)?

A. Mary Jane Watson

B. Gwen Stacy

C. Jessica Drew

D. Nobody

533. Who was the original Tarantula?

A. A Marvel Super Hero of the 1940s

B. The previous host of the "spider totem" powers

C. An unlawful copper miner

D. One of the Jackal's Spider-Man clones

534. How did J. Jonah Jameson first meet his future wife, Marla Madison?

A. He hired her to build a Spider-Slayer Robot

B. She was a *Daily Bugle* employee

C. She worked at NASA with his son John

D. She was his childhood sweetheart

535. How did John Jameson gain superhuman powers in *The Amazing Spider-Man* #42?

A. From Dr. Stillwell's experiments

B. From wearing a costume that boosted his strength

C. From a strange gem he found on the moon

D. He was infected with alien spores on a space mission

536. What is the name of Mary Jane Watson's cousin?

A. Kristy

B. Kitty

C. Katie

D. Chrissie

537. Why was the gangster introduced in *The Amazing Spider-Man* #113 (1972) named Hammerhead?

A. Because he resembles a shark

B. Due to the metal plate in his head

C. Because he wears a helmet resembling a hammer

D. His real last name is Hammer

538. What is *not* true about Thomas Fireheart?

A. He is known as the Puma

B. He was a puma mystically transformed into a human

C. He is an American Indian superhuman

D. He is a member of the Outlaws

539. Who removed the Black Cat's bad luck power?

A. Doctor Strange

B. The Kingpin

C. Dr. Jonas Harrow

D. The Jackal

OBSESSED WITH MARVEL

548.

The Marvel Universe is actually a multiverse that includes a potentially infinite number of alternate Earths, each in which history takes a different path. The world of *Spider-Girl* is set in the future of one of these alternate Earths. Here Peter Parker and Mary Jane remain married and have a daughter, whom they named after his beloved Aunt May. At the age of fifteen, young May "Mayday" Parker discovers that she has inherited her father's spider-powers. Peter has retired as a Super Hero, and inevitably, May becomes his successor as the amazing Spider-Girl (shown at left), complete with her own large cast of allies, adversaries, and supporting characters.

Created by writer Tom DeFalco and artist Ron Frenz, *Spider-Girl* was part of the short-lived *MC2* line of comics set in this alternate future of the Marvel Universe. *Spider-Girl* outlasted the other *MC2* books, ran one hundred issues, and continues today as the web comic (no pun intended) *Spectacular Spider-Girl*.

In which series did Spider-Girl first appear?

- **A.** *The Amazing Spider-Man*
- **B.** *What If?*
- **C.** *Spider-Girl*
- **D.** *Marvel Fanfare*

540. Which of the following did Spider-Woman (Jessica Drew) have in her 2015 series?
- **A.** Her own TV talk show
- **C.** A nervous breakdown
- **B.** A son named Gerry
- **D.** A Skrull imposter

541. During 2016's *Civil War II*, the Inhuman Ulysses had a vision of Miles Morales killing which hero?
- **A.** The Hulk
- **C.** Iron Man
- **B.** Captain America
- **D.** Captain Marvel

542. What is true about Peter Parker and Mary Jane Watson in the series *Amazing Spider-Man: Renew Your Vows*?
- **A.** They are still married
- **C.** They all fight crime
- **B.** They have a daughter
- **D.** All answers are correct

543. Who was not a member of the Superior Foes of Spider-Man?
- **A.** Boomerang
- **C.** Speed Demon
- **B.** The Beetle
- **D.** The Rhino

544. After the defeat of his family of Inheritors, who became the new Master Weaver on Loomworld?
- **A.** Karn
- **C.** Jennix
- **B.** Morlun
- **D.** Solus

545. What former Super Villain now occasionally babysits for Spider-Woman?
- **A.** Sandman
- **C.** Purple Man
- **B.** The Mandrill
- **D.** The Porcupine

546. Spider-Man teamed up with which popular X-Men character for a 2016 ongoing series?
- **A.** Wolverine
- **C.** Storm
- **B.** Cyclops
- **D.** Deadpool

547. Who is Clayton Cole?
- **A.** Clash
- **C.** Spider-UK
- **B.** Prowler
- **D.** Carnage

548.

Spider-Man

549. What was the name of Dr. Curt Connors's late wife?

A. Mary
B. Maggie
C. Martha
D. Dorothy

550. Who is Dr. Edward Lansky?

A. Lightmaster
B. Peter Parker's biology professor
C. Aunt May's heart surgeon
D. Cardiac

551. Which writer and artist first depicted Venom?

A. Jim Shooter and Mike Zeck
B. David Michelinie and Todd McFarlane
C. Roger Stern and John Romita Jr.
D. Tom DeFalco and Ron Frenz

552. What happened in Spider-Man's final battle with the Green Goblin in the alternate timeline of *Spider-Girl*?

A. Spider-Man survived intact
B. Spider-Man lost an eye
C. Spider-Man lost his arm
D. Spider-Man lost his leg

553. Which of the following characters made his or her debut, unnamed, in *Marvel Team-Up* #1 (1972)?

A. Colleen Wing
B. Misty Knight
C. Eddie Brock
D. Hector Ayala

554. Who was the Brainwasher?

A. Doctor Octopus
B. A scientist serving the Kingpin
C. The Kingpin
D. An operative of the Foreigner

555. Which foe of the Punisher debuted in *The Amazing Spider-Man* #161 (1976)?

A. Jigsaw
B. Bullseye
C. The Kingpin
D. Bushwacker

556.

557. Who is Morris Bench?

A. The Sandman
B. Boomerang
C. Master of Vengeance
D. Hydro-Man

558. Who was *not* once believed or suspected to be the original Hobgoblin?

A. Harry Osborn
B. Ned Leeds
C. Flash Thompson
D. Lefty Donovan

556.

With the dawn of a new century, Marvel launched an alternative version of its Super Hero universe, starting with *Ultimate Spider-Man* #1 in 2000. By then the classic *Spider-Man* continuity was nearly forty years old. *Ultimate Spider-Man* (shown at right) started the story of Spider-Man over from the beginning, updating it to the early twenty-first century and making changes large and small along the way. In the new version, for example, Mary Jane Watson was Peter Parker's high school classmate, whereas in the original he did not meet her until he was in college.

Writer Brian Michael Bendis and artist Mark Bagley not only created the new series but also collaborated on it for one hundred eleven consecutive issues, setting a new Marvel record. The success of *Ultimate Spider-Man* led to an entire *Ultimate* line of comics with revamped versions of other familiar Marvel heroes.

How did Peter Parker acquire his super-powers in *Ultimate Spider-Man*?

A. He was bitten by an irradiated spider
B. He was bitten by a genetically altered spider
C. He injected himself with spider DNA
D. He was secretly subjected to an experiment by scientist

OBSESSED WITH MARVEL

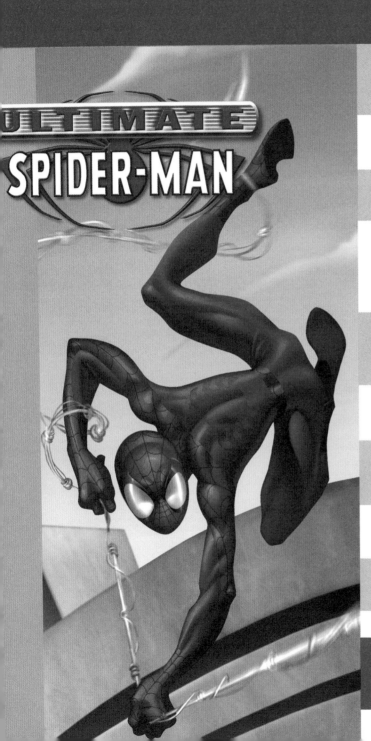

559. Who is Jason Philip Macendale Jr.?
- **A.** One of the Hobgoblins
- **B.** Original Jack O'Lantern
- **C.** Both A and B
- **D.** None of these

560. Which time period is the gangster Hammerhead obsessed with?
- **A.** 1920s
- **B.** 1930s
- **C.** 1940s
- **D.** 1950s

561. Which villain was vice-chancellor of Empire State University?
- **A.** The Jackal
- **B.** Lightmaster
- **C.** Humbug
- **D.** Spencer Smythe

562. What happened when Hydro-Man first encountered Sandman in *The Amazing Spider-Man* #217–218 (1981)?
- **A.** Sandman bested Hydro-Man in battle
- **B.** They merged into a mud-man
- **C.** They became best friends
- **D.** Hydro-Man washed Sandman away

563. Why did Doctor Octopus want to marry Aunt May?
- **A.** She had inherited a nuclear power facility
- **B.** She had inherited a fortune in stocks
- **C.** She had inherited land that contained oil
- **D.** She had inherited land that contained uranium

564. How tall is Peter Parker?
- **A.** 6'
- **B.** 5'11"
- **C.** 5'10"
- **D.** 5'9"

565. Which villain named after a Lewis Carroll character debuted in *Marvel Team-Up* #131 (1983)?
- **A.** Mad Hatter
- **B.** White Rabbit
- **C.** March Hare
- **D.** The Walrus

566. What is the name of Mary Jane Watson's father?
- **A.** Philip
- **B.** Spencer
- **C.** Martin
- **D.** William

567. What is the name of Mary Jane Watson's previously married sister?
- **A.** Christine
- **B.** Janet
- **C.** Gayle
- **D.** Susan

Spider-Man

568. Where did Spider-Man battle his clone in *The Amazing Spider-Man* #149 (1975)?
- **A.** Yankee Stadium
- **B.** Shea Stadium
- **C.** Madison Square Garden
- **D.** Radio City Music Hall

569. Which member of the New Mutants first appeared in the Spider-Man story in *Marvel Team-Up* #100 (1980)?
- **A.** Cannonball
- **B.** Sunspot
- **C.** Karma
- **D.** Wolfsbane

570. Whom did Spider-Man and Wolverine encounter in *Spider-Man* #8–12 (1991)?
- **A.** A Wendigo
- **B.** Sabretooth
- **C.** The Hulk
- **D.** Arcade

571. Who was *not* a member of the Misfits?
- **A.** Spider-Kid
- **B.** Frog-Man
- **C.** Batwing
- **D.** The Toad

572. Who is Phineas Mason?
- **A.** One of Aunt May's boarders
- **B.** The Tinkerer
- **C.** Chance
- **D.** The Black Fox

573.

574. What happened to Mary Jane in the Kulan Gath story in *Marvel Team-Up* #79 (1979)?
- **A.** Held captive by Kulan Gath
- **B.** Transformed into legendary swordswoman
- **C.** Possessed by the spirit of a princess
- **D.** Fled in terror from Kulan Gath

575. What is Flash Thompson's real first name?
- **A.** Fred
- **B.** Thomas
- **C.** Eugene
- **D.** Horace

576. Under what circumstances did Spider-Man first meet the Green Goblin?
- **A.** The Goblin invited Spider-Man to star in a movie
- **B.** The Goblin invited Spider-Man to be his partner in crime
- **C.** The Goblin challenged Spider-Man to a public duel
- **D.** Spider-Man found the Goblin robbing a bank

THE YOUTH OF THIS NATION MUST LEARN TO RESPECT **REAL** HEROES -- MEN SUCH AS MY SON, JOHN JAMESON, THE TEST PILOT! NOT SELFISH FREAKS SUCH AS SPIDER-MAN -- A MASKED MENACE WHO REFUSES TO EVEN LET US KNOW HIS TRUE IDENTITY!

573.

Daily Bugle publisher J. Jonah Jameson (shown above, left panel) likes to say that his son John is a true hero, whereas Spider-Man only pretends to be one. John Jameson first appeared as early as *The Amazing Spider-Man* #1 (1963). John ultimately transformed into a savage werewolflike creature called the Man-Wolf. He starred in his own *Man-Wolf* series in *Creatures on the Loose* and *Marvel Premiere*. Eventually, he traveled to another dimension, the Other Realm. There the Man-Wolf regained

his human intellect and became the immensely powerful champion Stargod.

John Jameson continues to play supporting roles in comics series like *Spider–Man* and *Captain America*, sometimes in human form and other times as the Man–Wolf or Stargod.

How did John Jameson become the Man–Wolf?

A. Bitten by a werewolf
B. Put under a supernatural curse
C. Result of a government experiment
D. A mystical gem he found on the moon

577. Which of Spider-Man's enemies pretended to be Dr. Ludwig Rinehart, his psychiatrist?
A. The Jackal   C. The Chameleon
B. Mysterio   D. Doctor Faustus

578. Who was Nick "Lucky" Lewis?
A. The Big Man   C. The Blood Rose
B. The Crime-Master   D. The Schemer

579. Who was Patch?
A. Peter Parker's puppy   C. An alias used by Kaine
B. Gwen's pet kitten   D. Fred Foswell's undercover identity

580. Who is Mark Raxton?
A. The Molten Man   C. Electro
B. Slyde   D. The Blood Rose

581. Who was once Norman Osborn's business partner?
A. Wilson Fisk   C. Professor Mendel Stromm
B. Thomas Fireheart   D. Justin Hammer

582. Who was the musical guest on *Saturday Night Live* in *Marvel Team-Up* #74 (1978), in which Spider-Man visited the show?
A. The Dazzler   C. The Hypno-Hustler
B. Rick Jones   D. Lila Cheney

583. Who did John Belushi battle in *Marvel Team-Up* #74 (1978), in which Spider-Man met the original cast of *Saturday Night Live*?
A. The Jester   C. Doctor Bong
B. The Silver Samurai   D. The Impossible Man

584. At which New York landmark did the sorcerer Kulan Gath battle Spider-Man in *Marvel Team-Up* #79 (1979)?
A. The Statue of Liberty   C. The Empire State Building
B. The American Museum of Natural History   D. The Metropolitan Museum of Art

585. Where did J. Jonah Jameson, Peter Parker, and Gwen Stacy travel on an expedition in *The Amazing Spider-Man* #103 (1971)?
A. Wakanda   C. An uncharted island
B. The Savage Land   D. The jungles of the Congo

Spider-Man

586. Who is Silvermane's son?
A. The Kingpin
B. The Rose
C. Hammerhead
D. Blackwing

587. Who is Michael Morbius?
A. A supernatural vampire
B. A scientist with vampirelike superhuman attributes
C. An expert in black magic
D. A secret agent from Europe

588. Which of Spider-Man's nemeses was converted into a cyborg?
A. Silvermane
B. The Vulture
C. Kaine
D. Meteor Man

589. Who owned the *Daily Bugle* as of 2009?
A. J. Jonah Jameson
B. Rupert Dockery
C. Dexter Bennett
D. K. J. Clayton

590. How was the Wraith related to Jean DeWolff?
A. Brother
B. Father
C. Son
D. His killer

591.

In 1990, the first issue of a new *Spider-Man* comic book became one of the top-selling comic books of all time. With its various editions with different covers, *Spider-Man* #1 (shown at right) sold at least 2.5 million copies. This series was nicknamed the "adjectiveless" *Spider-Man* to distinguish it from the original series, *The Amazing Spider-Man* and *The Spectacular Spider-Man*.

Artist Todd McFarlane had already made a name for himself collaborating with writer David Michelinie on *The Amazing Spider-Man*. Editor Jim Salicrup gave McFarlane the opportunity to write and draw this new *Spider-Man* series himself. Through modifying Spider-Man's costume and putting the character in unusual poses, McFarlane recaptured and updated the essence of the look that co-creator Steve Ditko had given the wall-crawling hero in the early years. Except for issue #15, McFarlane wrote and drew the first sixteen issues of the new series.

Which classic *Spider-Man* villain appeared in *Spider-Man* #1 (1990)?

A. The Lizard
B. The Vulture
C. The Green Goblin
D. Doctor Octopus

592. Which vigilante or vigilantes debuted in *Peter Parker, the Spectacular Spider-Man* #64 (1982)?
A. The Punisher
B. Cloak and Dagger
C. Solo
D. Silver Sable

593. Which of Peter's classmates was portrayed in the 1960s as serving in the Vietnam War?
A. Jason Ionello
B. Harry Osborn
C. Randy Robertson
D. Flash Thompson

594. Who was Harry Osborn's wife?
A. Betty Brant
B. Liz Allan
C. Joy Mercado
D. Mary Jane Watson

595. Who killed Nathan Lubensky?
A. Carnage
B. Kaine
C. The Jackal
D. The Vulture

OBSESSED WITH MARVEL

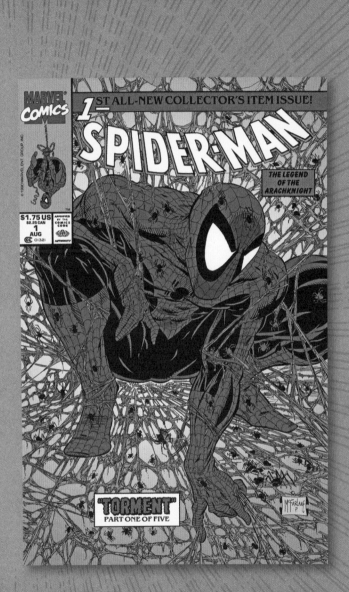

596. To which team did Spider-Woman (Julia Carpenter) belong?

A. Freedom Force   **C.** West Coast Avengers

B. Omega Flight   **D.** All answers are correct

597. Which super-power did Julia Carpenter have as Spider-Woman that Jessica Drew didn't?

A. Creating webs of psionic energy   **C.** Ability to stick to walls

B. Bioelectric "venom" blasts   **D.** Super-strength

598. What is the name of Spider-Woman's (Julia Carpenter's) daughter?

A. Cassie   **C.** Rachel

B. Alice   **D.** Juliet

599. Who killed police Captain Jean De Wolff?

A. The Foreigner   **C.** Kaine

B. The Sin-Eater   **D.** The Kingpin

600. Who was Gregory Bestman?

A. The Vulture's ex-partner   **C.** Uncle Ben's rival for Aunt May

B. A *Daily Bugle* staffer   **D.** One of Norman Osborn's executives

601. Who was Johnny Jerome?

A. A criminal who dated Aunt May before she married Ben Parker   **C.** The Steel Spider

B. Editor of *The Daily Globe*   **D.** Spider-Man's agent during his early show business career

602. Who guest starred in *Giant-Size Spider-Man* #1 (1974) without meeting Spider-Man?

A. Shang-Chi   **C.** Dracula

B. Howard the Duck   **D.** Millie the Model

603. Whom did Aunt May marry in *Amazing Spider-Man* #600 (2009)?

A. J. Jonah Jameson   **C.** Otto Octavius

B. J. Jonah Jameson Sr.   **D.** Nathan Lubensky

604. What was the title of Peter Parker's book of photographs of Spider-Man?

A. "Marvels"   **C.** "Webspinners"

B. "Webs"   **D.** "The Sensational Spider-Man"

Spider-Man

605. What was the true identity of the original villain known as the Hobgoblin?
A. Daniel Kingsley
B. Roderick Kingsley
C. Ned Leeds
D. Jacob Conover

606. When did *The Amazing Spider-Man* newspaper strip begin?
A. 1977
B. 1967
C. 1987
D. 1971

607.

608. What is the name of Gwen Stacy's cousin?
A. Nancy
B. Jill
C. Sarah
D. Howard

609. Who was Mamie Muggins?
A. A neighbor of Aunt May
B. Peter Parker's landlady
C. The Sandman's girlfriend
D. The *Daily Bugle* cleaning lady

610. Who was Dr. Elias Wirtham?
A. One of Aunt May's heart doctors
B. One of Peter Parker's ESU professors
C. A Super Villain called Cardiac
D. A Super Hero called Cardiac

611. Where did the alien symbiote first attach itself to Eddie Brock, turning him into Venom?
A. A church
B. Battleworld
C. Central Park
D. Prison

612. Who endowed the Black Cat with the super-power to induce bad luck?
A. Baron Mordo
B. The Foreigner
C. The Kingpin
D. The Scarlet Witch

613. Where did Miguel O'Hara work in the first issue of *Spider-Man 2099* (1992)?
A. Empire State University
B. Alchemax
C. Baintronics
D. Psionex

614. How did Spider-Man become Captain Universe?
A. He was posing as the hero of a kids' TV show
B. He temporarily gained vast powers from the Enigma Force
C. He was dreaming about gaining cosmic powers
D. This only happened in a *What If?* story

607.

Introduced in 1992, Marvel's 2099 line of comics presented futuristic versions of classic Marvel heroes living on the verge of the twenty-second century. These series were influenced by cyberpunk fiction, a form of science fiction depicting a dystopian society with highly advanced technology—most notably, computers.

Artist Rick Leonardi and writer Peter David created Miguel O'Hara, the Spider-Man of 2099 (shown above). A brilliant young geneticist, O'Hara inadvertently gained strange, spiderlike powers. Adopting a costumed identity, O'Hara opposed corrupt corporations and new versions of classic *Spider-Man* villains such as the Vulture,

OBSESSED WITH MARVEL

615. Which artist created Captain Universe with writer Bill Mantlo?

A. Michael Golden
B. Steve Ditko
C. Jack Kirby
D. Sal Buscema

616. Where did Peter and Mary Jane move to when Ben Reilly took over as Spider-Man?

A. Portland, Oregon
B. Cambridge, Massachusetts
C. San Diego, California
D. Cresskill, New Jersey

617. Where did Peter, Mary Jane, and Aunt May live after May's house was destroyed?

A. Stark Tower
B. Avengers Mansion
C. The Baxter Building
D. Anna Watson's house

618. Which of the following characters did *not* first appear in *Untold Tales of Spider-Man*?

A. Supercharger
B. Batwing
C. Commanda
D. The Scorcher

619. Which of Spider-Man's enemies is a master of sumo wrestling?

A. Kraven the Hunter
B. Kaine
C. The Kingpin
D. Morlun

620. Which writer and artist created the Black Cat?

A. Roger Stern and John Romita Jr.
B. Stan Lee and John Romita Sr.
C. Gerry Conway and Ross Andru
D. Marv Wolfman and Keith Pollard

621. Which writer and artist collaborated on "Kraven's Last Hunt"?

A. J. Michael Straczynski and John Romita Jr.
B. Kevin Smith and Joe Quesada
C. J. Marc DeMatteis and Mike Zeck
D. Tom DeFalco and Ron Frenz

622. Who was *not* one of the writers of the story line "The Other"?

A. Peter David
B. Dan Slott
C. Reginald Hudlin
D. J. Michael Straczynski

623. Which supernatural being made his first appearance clashing with Spider-Man and Man-Thing in *Marvel Team-Up*?

A. D'Spayre
B. The Dweller in Darkness
C. Thog the Nether-Spawn
D. Death-Stalker

Green Goblin, and Venom, as well as brand-new adversaries, such as Thanatos.

In the aptly titled 1995 special *Spider-Man 2099 Meets Spider-Man*, O'Hara joined forces with the original web-slinger against a future version of the Hobgoblin. Although the 2099 line ended in 1998, Spider-Man 2099 continues to make guest appearances in Marvel comics from time to time.

How did Miguel O'Hara acquire his super-powers as Spider-Man 2099?

A. Bitten by an irradiated spider
B. Bitten by a genetically modified spider
C. Through genetic restructuring of his body
D. Through injecting himself with spider DNA

Spider-Man

624. What was *not* one of Carrion's powers?
- **A.** Near-intangibility
- **B.** Reanimating the dead
- **C.** Turning organic matter to ash
- **D.** Self-teleportation

625. Where was Jessica Drew born?
- **A.** Wundagore Mountain, Transia
- **B.** Los Angeles
- **C.** San Francisco
- **D.** London

626.

627. Which of Spider-Man's enemies gouged out his eye (which later regenerated)?
- **A.** Kraven the Hunter
- **B.** Venom
- **C.** Morlun
- **D.** Carnage

628. Who hired the gunman who shot Aunt May?
- **A.** The Kingpin
- **B.** Silvermane
- **C.** Norman Osborn
- **D.** Mister Negative

629. Who is Solo?
- **A.** A secret agent
- **B.** An assassin for hire
- **C.** A member of Silver Sable's Wild Pack
- **D.** A costumed counterterrorist

630. Who is Jonathan Caesar?
- **A.** Billionaire who bought the *Daily Bugle*
- **B.** Millionaire who stalked and blacklisted Mary Jane Watson-Parker
- **C.** An alias used by the Hobgoblin
- **D.** The Rose

631. Who was *not* one of the pretty girls who sunbathed on the roof of the rooming house where Peter Parker once lived?
- **A.** Bambi
- **B.** Candi
- **C.** Randi
- **D.** Cyndi

632. Who is Nicholas Powell?
- **A.** Chance, a criminal for hire
- **B.** The Blood Rose, a criminal mastermind
- **C.** A columnist at the *Daily Bugle*
- **D.** A candidate for mayor of New York

626.

Sergei Kravinoff, alias Kraven the Hunter (shown at right with Spider-Man), was no ordinary big game hunter. Rather than use guns, he grappled with wild animals using his bare hands. A potion he concocted from jungle herbs endowed him with enough super-human strength to overpower an elephant—or a Super Hero.

Created by Stan Lee and Steve Ditko, Kraven first appeared in *The Amazing Spider-Man* #15 (1964), when he was invited to America to test his prowess by stalking and defeating a new kind of prey: Spider-Man. Over the years, Kraven clashed repeatedly with Spider-Man, but finally triumphed in the 1987 story line "Kraven's Last Hunt," in which he not only buried Spider-Man alive but also usurped his costumed identity. At the end of this remarkable look into a Super Villain's psyche, Kraven was dead, but three of his heirs have since followed in his path.

How did Kraven the Hunter meet his end?

- **A.** Died in combat
- **B.** Assassinated by Scourge
- **C.** Suicide
- **D.** Killed by wild beasts

OBSESSED WITH MARVEL

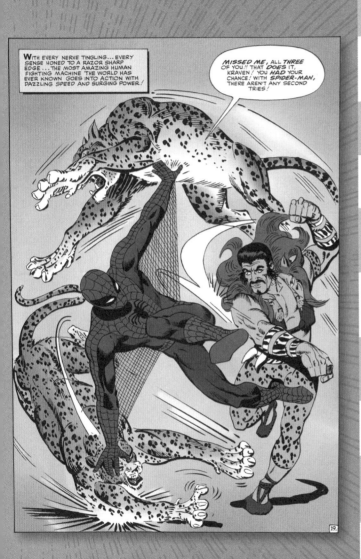

633. Who was Vernon Jacobs?

A. The Zodiac villain, Scorpio
B. Grandson of Jake Fury
C. A Parker Industries investor
D. All answers are correct

634. Which spider-themed hero was a member of the Secret Avengers alongside Spider-Woman (Jessica Drew)?

A. Spider-Man
B. Scarlet Spider
C. Black Widow
D. Spider-Girl

635. Which alternate Earth is the home base of the spider-hunting Inheritors?

A. Earth-616
B. Earth-65
C. Earth-001
D. Earth-1610

636. Who became the spider-powered Super Heroine called Silk?

A. Cindy Moon
B. Jessica Carpenter
C. Jessica Drew
D. Mattie Franklin

637. J. Jonah Jameson went on to work as an on-screen personality for what TV network?

A. MNN
B. The Fact Channel
C. TruthNet
D. Daily Bugle TV

638. Ezekiel locked Silk in captivity for over a decade to keep her safe from which villain?

A. Morlun
B. The Vulture
C. Doctor Octopus
D. Mephisto

639. After *Secret Wars* (2015), which spider-hero made their home in the mainstream Marvel Universe?

A. Spider-Gwen
B. Spider-Punk
C. Spider-UK
D. Spider-Man (Miles Morales)

640. Which team of Avengers has *not* had a Spider-Man on its roster?

A. New Avengers
B. All-New, All-Different Avengers
C. Secret Avengers
D. Mighty Avengers

641. Which two spider-heroes shared a kiss when their series crossed-over in early 2017?

A. Miles Morales and Gwen Stacy
B. Peter Parker and Jessica Drew
C. Miguel O'Hara and Cindy Moon
D. Ben Reilly and Mary Jane Watson

Spider-Man

642. Which future member of the Avengers first appeared in her costumed identity in *Marvel Team-Up* #95 (1980)?
A. Black Widow
B. Mockingbird
C. Spider-Woman (Julia Carpenter)
D. Firestar

643. Which of the following women did *not* date Peter Parker?
A. Marcy Kane
B. Betty Brant
C. Cissy Ironwood
D. Debra Whitman

644. How did the enigmatic Ezekiel utilize his spider-powers?
A. To become a Super Villain
B. To become a Super Hero
C. To become a wealthy businessman
D. To become the ultimate warrior

645. Which costumed heroine did Peter's high school classmate Sally Avril become?
A. Bluebird
B. Commanda
C. Songbird
D. Marvel Girl

646. How did Spider-Man return to life after apparently being killed by Morlun?
A. Magic conjured by Ezekiel
B. Top doctors hired by Tony Stark
C. The spirit of Anansi
D. Regenerated a new body within a cocoon

647. Which *X-Men* villain first appeared in Spider-Man's series *Marvel Team-Up*?
A. Arcade
B. Mister Sinister
C. Black Tom Cassidy
D. Proteus

648. Which criminal disrupted the wedding of Betty Brant and Ned Leeds?
A. The Cyclone
B. The Molten Man
C. The Hobgoblin
D. Mirage

649. Who is Buford Hollis?
A. A country singer who lived next door to Peter Parker
B. The Super Hero Frog-Man
C. The Super Hero Razorback
D. Flash Thompson's cousin from the South

650.

651. How much does Peter Parker weigh?
A. 165 lbs.
B. 170 lbs.
C. 160 lbs.
D. 155 lbs.

OBSESSED WITH MARVEL

650.

In creating the Vulture in *The Amazing Spider-Man* #2 (1963), Stan Lee and Steve Ditko provided the wall-crawler with one of his most memorable foes. It was a war of youth against age: the inexperienced young hero in his mid-teens against a wizened elderly criminal wearing a winged costume that enabled him to fly. As his name suggests, the Vulture (shown above with Spider-Man) is a predator, swooping down on the victims he robs. He is also like a bird of death, and Spider-Man risks his life fighting him in the air high above the streets of Manhattan.

As early as issue #48 (1967), the Vulture appeared to be on his deathbed, and a fellow convict usurped his name and costume. But the original Vulture returned and bested his impostor in aerial battle a year later. Although there has since been a third Vulture, it is the original who keeps returning to plague Spider-Man.

How does the Vulture manage to fly?

A. Antigravity device
B. Electromagnetic harness
C. Mutant power
D. Levitation by telekinesis

652. Where was the Vulture born?
A. New Jersey   **C.** Brooklyn
B. Staten Island   **D.** The Bronx

653. Who is Sha Shan?
A. A graduate student at Empire State University
B. A ninja assassin serving the Kingpin
C. Flash Thompson's Vietnamese ex-girlfriend
D. A waitress at the Coffee Bean

654. Who draws "Petey," the adventures of Peter Parker as a young boy?
A. John Romita Sr.   **C.** June Brigman
B. Fred Hembeck   **D.** Ron Frenz

655. Who writes the "Petey" stories?
A. Fred Hembeck   **C.** Jim Sallicrup
B. Danny Fingeroth   **D.** Howard Mackie

656. Who originally employed the arsonist called the Scorcher?
A. Norman Osborn   **C.** The Crime-Master
B. The Big Man   **D.** He was self-employed

657. What was one way Aunt May survived her apparent death?
A. She went into a coma and was later revived
B. It was really an impostor who died
C. She had been drugged to feign death
D. History was altered so that she never died

658. Who was Nathan Lubensky?
A. Uncle Ben's rival for Aunt May in their youth
B. Head of the biology department at Empire State University
C. Aunt May's former boyfriend in her senior years
D. The Vulture's former business partner

659. Why did the burglar break into Ben Parker's home?
A. To search for a hidden treasure
B. He picked the house by sheer chance
C. To steal Aunt May's jewelry
D. He thought the elderly couple would not put up a fight

Spider-Man

660. Who has the criminal surgeon Dr. Jonas Harrow endowed with superhuman attributes?
- **A.** The Scorpion
- **B.** The Black Cat
- **C.** The Scorpion and the Black Cat
- **D.** Hammerhead and the Kangaroo

661. Who was Frank Oliver?
- **A.** One of Peter's high school classmates
- **B.** The Kangaroo
- **C.** Mirage
- **D.** The Big Wheel

662. Who employed the Finisher to assassinate Peter Parker's parents?
- **A.** Baron Strucker
- **B.** Silvermane
- **C.** The Nazi Red Skull of the 1940s
- **D.** The Communist Red Skull of the 1950s

663. Who was *not* an original member of the Sinister Syndicate?
- **A.** Rhino
- **B.** Blacklash
- **C.** Boomerang
- **D.** Speed Demon

664. Who was *not* a member of the Sinister Twelve?
- **A.** The Lizard
- **B.** Tombstone
- **C.** Doctor Octopus
- **D.** Venom (Mac Gargan)

665. Who is Anne Weying?
- **A.** Eddie Brock's ex-wife
- **B.** Harry Osborn's girlfriend
- **C.** A *Daily Bugle* reporter
- **D.** Owner of the Daily Grind

666. Who is Martin Li?
- **A.** One of Peter's graduate school classmates
- **B.** Mister Negative
- **C.** A *Daily Bugle* staffer
- **D.** The Foreigner

667. Who was *not* one of Peter Parker's graduate school classmates?
- **A.** Philip Chang
- **B.** Debra Whitman
- **C.** Steve Hopkins
- **D.** Marcy Kane

668. Who was Thanatos in *Spider-Man 2099*?
- **A.** An alternate version of Rick Jones
- **B.** An alternate version of Peter Parker
- **C.** The descendant of Thanos
- **D.** A human incarnation of Death

OBSESSED WITH MARVEL

669. Who is Spider-Girl's ally, the Buzz?
- **A.** The son of Flash Thompson and the Wasp
- **B.** The nephew of Phil Urich
- **C.** The son of Henry Pym
- **D.** J. Jonah Jameson's grandson

670. Who is Spider-Girl's former enemy, Raptor?
- **A.** Granddaughter of the original Vulture
- **B.** Daughter of former Vulture Blackie Drago
- **C.** Daughter of the Super Hero Nighthawk
- **D.** Granddaughter of the Owl

671. Who is Charlotte Witter?
- **A.** Commanda
- **B.** Scorpia
- **C.** Gypsy Moth
- **D.** Super Villain called Spider-Woman

672. Who was introduced in "Kraven's First Hunt"?
- **A.** The original Kraven the Hunter
- **B.** Kraven's alleged daughter, Ana Kravinoff
- **C.** Kraven's son
- **D.** The Grim Hunter

673. What is Peter Parker's role in the alternate timeline of *Earth X* (1999–2000)?
- **A.** Active Super Hero
- **B.** Research scientist, retired as Super Hero
- **C.** Policeman, retired as Super Hero
- **D.** Staff photographer, *Daily Bugle*

674. Which villain is the Chameleon's half-brother?
- **A.** The Foreigner
- **B.** The Spymaster
- **C.** The Scorpion
- **D.** Kraven the Hunter

675.

There is a long comic book tradition of using funny animal characters to parody Super Heroes. In the 1940s when Super Heroes were still a new phenomenon, one of Marvel's biggest stars was Super Rabbit, a parody of rival DC Comics' Superman. The tradition was carried on with Peter Porker, the Spectacular Spider-Ham (shown at left), who debuted in the 1980s. He starred in his own comic book, which was published by Marvel's children's imprint, Star Comics, and subsequently appeared as a backup feature in *Marvel Tales*. Supporting cast members included Mary Jane Waterbuffalo and J. Jonah Jackal. Among his many fellow heroes are Captain Americat, Croctor Strange, Deerdevil, Goose Rider, the Fantastic Fur, Hulk-Bunny, and Iron Mouse. Their enemies include Ducktor Doom, Kang Aroo, and Magsquito. Recently Peter Porker was revealed to have a daughter, Swiney-Girl, his answer to Spider-Girl!

What is Spider-Ham's origin?

- **A.** Pig bitten by radioactive spider
- **B.** Pig who tries to imitate his hero Spider-Man
- **C.** Spider bitten by an irradiated pig
- **D.** Pig who ate an irradiated spider

676. Which writer co-created the funny animal hero Peter Porker, the Spectacular Spider-Ham, with artist Mark Armstrong?
- **A.** Jim Salicrup
- **B.** Steve Gerber
- **C.** Tom DeFalco
- **D.** Fred Hembeck

677. Who was Martin Blank?
- **A.** The Gibbon
- **B.** The Looter
- **C.** The burglar who killed Uncle Ben
- **D.** Mister Nobody

Spider-Man

678. Which Marvel UK character made his or her first U.S. appearance in *Marvel Team-Up*?

A. Meggan

B. Death's Head

C. Night Raven

D. Captain Britain

679. Who helped Spider-Man combat the Lords of Light and Darkness in *Marvel Team-Up Annual* #1 (1976)?

A. Thor

B. The X-Men

C. Doctor Strange

D. Adam Warlock

680. Who is Lindsay McCabe?

A. Jessica Drew's partner in her detective agency

B. Julia Carpenter's best friend

C. May "Mayday" Parker's classmate

D. Mattie Franklin's cousin

681. Who or what is Swarm?

A. A Super Villain who mentally controls all insects

B. A swarm of bees controlled by a human consciousness

C. A Super Villain with wasplike powers

D. An army of costumed mercenaries

682. Which of the following statements about Humbug is *not* correct?

A. He is an unreformed Super Villain

B. He was an entomology professor at ESU

C. He was a member of Heroes for Hire

D. His real name is Buck Mitty

683. Who was Hector Ayala?

A. The Tarantula

B. The White Tiger

C. El Tigre

D. El Aguila

684. Who is Carolyn Trainer?

A. Doctor Octopus II

B. Otto Octavius's student

C. Lady Octopus

D. All answers are correct

685. Who were Carlos and Eduardo Lobo?

A. Werewolves

B. Criminal brothers who own a pack of wolves

C. Members of the Circus of Crime

D. Mutants with werewolflike powers

686.

686.

The glamorous Silver Sablinova is better known as the formidable Silver Sable (shown at right with Spider-Man), leader of the Wild Pack of world-class mercenary soldiers. Her father, Ernst, funded the Wild Pack decades ago to hunt down Nazi war criminals. Under Silver Sable's leadership, the Wild Pack also takes paying assignments to capture dangerous criminals or to recover stolen property. Silver Sable's track record is so successful that her operations provide a major source of income for her small Eastern European homeland.

Writer Tom DeFalco and artist Ron Frenz introduced Silver Sable in *The Amazing Spider-Man* #265 (1985), and the web-slinger has since allied with her on numerous occasions. His former foe, the Sandman, even became a paid member of the Wild Pack. She won her own comic book series, *Silver Sable and the Wild Pack*, written by Gregory Wright and drawn by Steve Butler, in 1992.

Who else once led a team known as the Wild Pack?

A. Wolverine

B. Stryfe

C. Cable

D. Kraven the Hunter

687. With which head of state does Silver Sable have dinner once every year?
- **A.** Doctor Doom
- **B.** The Black Panther
- **C.** The Sub-Mariner
- **D.** The Queen of England

688. Which villain tried to fly the S.H.I.E.L.D. Heli-Carrier into the U.S. Capitol building in *Marvel Team-Up* in the 1980s?
- **A.** The Viper
- **B.** The Red Skull
- **C.** Flag-Smasher
- **D.** Baron Strucker

689. Who was *not* one of Spider-Man's allies in foiling the plot to wreck the U.S. Capitol in *Marvel Team-Up*?
- **A.** Captain America
- **B.** Black Widow
- **C.** Nick Fury
- **D.** Shang-Chi

690. Who teamed up with Spider-Man against Arcade in *Marvel Team-Up* #65 (1978)?
- **A.** The X-Men
- **B.** The Human Torch
- **C.** Captain Britain
- **D.** Daredevil

691. Who is Steven Hudak?
- **A.** Boomerang
- **B.** The Scorcher
- **C.** Sin-Eater
- **D.** Supercharger

692. Where did the story in *The Amazing Spider-Man* #116–118 (1973) appear in somewhat different form?
- **A.** *The Amazing Spider-Man Special* #4 (1967)
- **B.** *Spectacular Spider-Man Magazine* #1 (1968)
- **C.** *The Amazing Spider-Man Special* #3 (1966)
- **D.** *Giant-Size Spider-Man* #1 (1974)

693. Why didn't Spider-Man join the Avengers when he was offered membership in *The Amazing Spider-Man Annual* #3 (1966)?
- **A.** He was not interested in joining a team
- **B.** He failed his assignment to locate the Hulk
- **C.** He refused to capture the Hulk
- **D.** He would have had to reveal his own secret identity

694. Who is Darkdevil in *Spider-Girl*?
- **A.** Ben Reilly's son Reilly Tyne
- **B.** Daredevil
- **C.** The host of Zarathos
- **D.** All three characters in one body

Spider-Man

695. Who was Maxwell Markham?
- **A.** Will-o'-the-Wisp
- **B.** The Grizzly
- **C.** Humbug
- **D.** The Hypno-Hustler

696. Who was Dr. Clifton Shallot?
- **A.** The third Vulture
- **B.** Lightmaster
- **C.** Harry Osborn's psychiatrist
- **D.** The Spot

697. Who was once married to John Jameson?
- **A.** Rachel Leighton
- **B.** Kristine Saunders
- **C.** Jennifer Walters
- **D.** Dr. Ashley Kafka

698. Into which series did the Richard Raleigh story line in *The Spectacular Spider-Man Magazine* #1 (1968) cross over?
- **A.** *Daredevil*
- **B.** *The Amazing Spider-Man*
- **C.** *Marvel Team-Up*
- **D.** *Captain America*

699.

700. Which team of villains starred in *Deadly Foes of Spider-Man* (1991)?
- **A.** Sinister Syndicate
- **B.** Sinister Six
- **C.** Sinister Twelve
- **D.** Squadron Sinister

701. Where did Gwen Stacy go to high school?
- **A.** Midtown High
- **B.** Standard High School
- **C.** Massachusetts Academy
- **D.** School for Gifted Youngsters

702. What ultimately happened to Peter's classmate Sally Avril?
- **A.** Married and had children
- **B.** She is an active Super Hero
- **C.** Killed in an auto accident
- **D.** Killed in combat

703. Who was the bodyguard, and murderer, of crime lord Don Rigoletto?
- **A.** The Kingpin
- **B.** Tombstone
- **C.** Silvermane
- **D.** Hammerhead

704. Which of the immortal Elders of the Universe first appeared in *Marvel Team-Up*?
- **A.** The Grandmaster
- **B.** The Collector
- **C.** The Gardener
- **D.** The Contemplator

699.

Who is Spider-Man's most persistent and implacable adversary? You could argue it is J. Jonah Jameson, longtime publisher of the *Daily Bugle,* who has been attacking Spider-Man in the media almost from the very beginning (shown above). Moreover, since Peter Parker is a freelance photographer for the *Bugle,* he has to put up with JJJ's temper tantrums in *both* of his identities.

Jameson is a man of contradictions. He accuses Spider-Man of being a fraud, a glory hound, and a criminal. He also knows that running news photos of Spider-Man sells newspapers.

BUT, NOT SATISFIED WITH MERELY WRITING EDITORIALS, J. JONAH JAMESON, PUBLISHER OF THE POWERFUL "DAILY BUGLE" DELIVERS LECTURES ALL OVER TOWN...

WE CANNOT ALLOW THAT MASKED MENACE TO TAKE THE LAW INTO HIS OWN HANDS! HE IS A BAD INFLUENCE ON OUR YOUNGSTERS!

However obsessed and irrational he can be about Super Heroes, Jameson is a courageous crusader for civil rights and against crime. Beneath his bluster he can even show fatherly feelings towards Peter. Once in *The Amazing Spider-Man*, Jameson admitted to himself that he was actually jealous of Spider-Man. But that moment of self-awareness soon passed, and he went back to his usual attitude of asking, "Spider-Man: Threat or Menace?"

What is the original name of the Daily Bugle Building?

A. The Lieber Building
B. The Goodman Building
C. The Jameson Building
D. The Timely Publications Building

705. Which villains warred on each other in *Marvel Team-Up* #9–11?
A. Doctor Doom and the Red Skull   **C.** The Mandarin and the Yellow Claw
B. Doctor Octopus and the Kingpin   **D.** Kang and the Tomorrow Man

706. Which real-life historical figure did Spider-Man and Doctor Doom encounter in *Marvel Team-Up* #41–45 (1976)?
A. Cagliostro   **C.** Benjamin Franklin
B. Cotton Mather   **D.** Queen Elizabeth I

707. Which villains' son and daughter appeared in *Marvel Team-Up* #39–40 (1975)?
A. Green Goblin and   **C.** Big Man and Crime-Master
Mendel Stromm
B. Green Goblin and   **D.** Vulture I and Vulture II
Crime-Master

708. Who are Hammer Harrison and Snake Marston?
A. Two of the Kingpin's henchmen   **C.** Members of the Circus of Crime
B. Members of the Enforcers   **D.** Adversaries of Kid Colt

709. Who is Max Shiffman?
A. *Daily Bugle* photographer   **C.** Spider-Man's show business agent
B. The Painter of a Thousand Perils **D.** Humbug

710. Where did Sally Avril first appear?
A. *Amazing Fantasy* #15 (1962)   **C.** *Spider-Man: Chapter One* #1 (1998)
B. *The Amazing Spider-Man* #1 (1963)   **D.** *Untold Tales of Spider-Man* #1 (1995)

711. Who was Norman Osborn's father?
A. Charles F. Osborn   **C.** Oswald Osborn
B. Amberson Osborn   **D.** Robert Norman Osborn

712. Who is Dmitri Smerdyakov?
A. The Rhino   **C.** The Foreigner
B. The Chameleon   **D.** Kraven the Hunter

Spider-Man

713. What is the parody version of the X-Men in *Peter Porker*?
- **A.** X-Bugs
- **B.** X-Cats
- **C.** X-Dogs
- **D.** X-Babies

714. Who or what is Batwing?
- **A.** A highly evolved bat
- **B.** A teenager with batlike wings
- **C.** A vampire
- **D.** The Green Goblin's flying vehicle

715. How was the Grim Hunter related to Kraven?
- **A.** Half-brother
- **B.** Daughter
- **C.** Son-in-law
- **D.** Son

716.

717. Who was *not* one of the villains in the original *Spider-Woman* series?
- **A.** The Mandrill
- **B.** The Hangman
- **C.** The Needle
- **D.** Nekra

718. When was the *Daily Bugle* founded?
- **A.** 1963
- **B.** 1948
- **C.** 1923
- **D.** 1897

719. Where was Peter Parker bitten by the radioactive spider?
- **A.** Osborn Industries
- **B.** Midtown High
- **C.** General Techtronics
- **D.** Empire State University

720. Who destroyed the Parker home?
- **A.** Norman Osborn
- **B.** The Kingpin
- **C.** Eddie Brock
- **D.** Charlie Weiderman

721. What was the address of the house where Peter Parker grew up?
- **A.** 20 Northern Boulevard
- **B.** 20 Ingram Street
- **C.** 20 Queens Boulevard
- **D.** 20 Steinway Street

716.

Wilson Fisk (shown at right with Spider-Man) long claimed in public to be merely a humble dealer in spices. In fact, he was the Kingpin of Crime, the absolute ruler of the New York City underworld. At first glance, he looks morbidly obese, but much of that massiveness is solid muscle. As an impoverished, overweight child, he was the victim of bullies. Fisk trained himself to become stronger and fight back. He formed a small gang and began his rise to power.

When Stan Lee and John Romita Sr. introduced him in *The Amazing Spider-Man* #50 (1967), Fisk succeeded in organizing and taking control of a coalition of the New York City criminal gangs. Starting with Frank Miller's work on the series, the Kingpin has been featured more prominently as an archenemy of Daredevil. But it was in *The Amazing Spider-Man* that Fisk first appeared, and he remains one of the web-slinger's greatest foes.

What happened to the Kingpin after his hit man shot Aunt May?

- **A.** Spider-Man beat him up in prison
- **B.** He was arrested and sent to prison
- **C.** He fled the country to avoid capture
- **D.** He avoided being blamed for the attack

722. Who was Kwaku Anansi?

A. Ambassador from Wakanda

B. ESU graduate student

C. "Spider-Man" in an African language

D. The first to bear the spider totem powers

723. Who was Dr. Judas Traveller?

A. A sorcerer with vast mystical powers

B. An alien wanderer who visited Earth

C. A psychologist with mutant powers

D. A Super Villain with advanced technology

724. Who is the first costumed villain Spider-Man ever fought (though the story was published many years after the event's occurrence)?

A. The Vulture

B. The Chameleon

C. The Scorcher

D. Supercharger

725. Which Manhattan precinct was Jean De Wolff police captain of?

A. 35th

B. 36th

C. 37th

D. 38th

726. Who is Aleksei Mikhailovich Sytsevich?

A. Kraven the Hunter

B. The Rhino

C. The Chameleon

D. The Foreigner

727. Who is Jessica Carradine?

A. The daughter of the burglar who killed Uncle Ben in "Brand New Day"

B. The wife of the burglar who killed Uncle Ben

C. The girlfriend of Harry Osborn

D. The Super Heroine Jackpot

728. Where did characters called Uncle Ben and Aunt May appear before the first *Spider-Man* story?

A. As relatives of Kid Colt in his origin story

B. As relatives of Patsy Walker in the 1940s story of the Rawhide Kid

C. Stan Lee and Steve Ditko's story about mermaid Linda Brown in *Strange Tales* #97 (1962)

D. Stan Lee and Jack Kirby's origin

Spider-Man

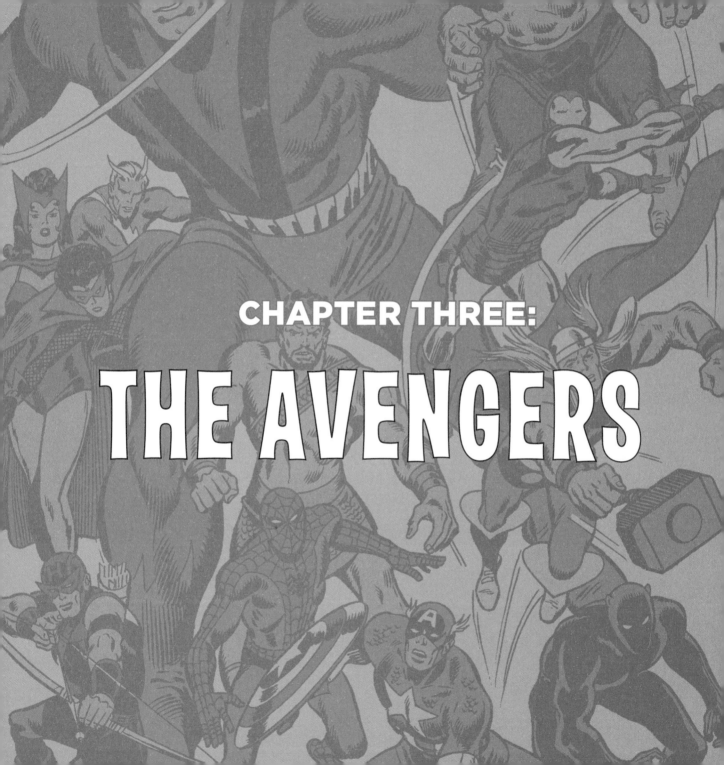

CHAPTER THREE:
THE AVENGERS

729. What is Jarvis the butler's first name?
- **A.** Edward
- **B.** Edgar
- **C.** Edwin
- **D.** Edmund

730. What was the name of the project that created Captain America?
- **A.** Project Super-Soldier
- **B.** The Manhattan Project
- **C.** Operation: Rebirth
- **D.** The Reinstein Project

731. Where was Tony Stark originally depicted as suffering his heart injury in *Tales of Suspense* #39 (1963)?
- **A.** Afghanistan
- **B.** Vietnam
- **C.** China
- **D.** The Middle East

732. Which future Avenger first appeared as a Communist agent in *Tales of Suspense* #52 (1964)?
- **A.** The Black Widow
- **B.** Hawkeye
- **C.** Wonder Man
- **D.** The Swordsman

733. Where is Avengers Mansion located?
- **A.** Fifth Avenue at 86th Street
- **B.** Fifth Avenue at 70th Street
- **C.** Park Avenue at 59th Street
- **D.** Madison Avenue at 75th Street

734. What identity did Henry Pym adopt in *The Avengers* #28 (1966)?
- **A.** Giant-Man
- **B.** Yellowjacket
- **C.** Goliath
- **D.** Colossus

735. Which Marvel character became Hellcat in *The Avengers* #144 (1976)?
- **A.** Felicia Hardy
- **B.** Hedy Wolfe
- **C.** Millie the Model
- **D.** Patsy Walker

736. Who was the Scarlet Witch's instructor in sorcery?
- **A.** Dakimh the Enchanter
- **B.** Agatha Harkness
- **C.** Doctor Strange
- **D.** The Ancient One

737. What happened to Captain America at the end of World War II?
- **A.** Continued to be active but did not age due to super-soldier serum
- **B.** Put into suspended animation by experimental gas
- **C.** Was in suspended animation in ice
- **D.** Was kept in suspended animation by the U.S. government

738.

739. What was Avengers Mansion originally?
- **A.** An art museum
- **B.** Tony Stark's town house
- **C.** The mayor's residence
- **D.** The Liberty Legion's headquarters in World War II

740. Who drew *Captain America* #100 (1968)?
- **A.** Jack Kirby
- **B.** John Romita Sr.
- **C.** Gil Kane
- **D.** Gene Colan

741. How long did the Hulk stay with the Avengers?
- **A.** Three issues
- **B.** One issue
- **C.** Two issues
- **D.** He never accepted membership

742. Who first succeeded Jack Kirby as *The Avengers* artist?
- **A.** Rich Buckler
- **B.** Sal Buscema
- **C.** Don Heck
- **D.** John Buscema

743. Which artist first drew *The Avengers* #93 (1971)?
- **A.** Sal Buscema
- **B.** Neal Adams
- **C.** John Buscema
- **D.** George Perez

744. Who first found Captain America in suspended animation?
- **A.** Sub-Mariner
- **B.** Thor
- **C.** Iron Man
- **D.** Giant-Man and the Wasp

745. Who alerted the future Avengers about the Hulk in *The Avengers* #1 (1963)?
- **A.** The news media
- **B.** The Teen Brigade
- **C.** General "Thunderbolt" Ross
- **D.** Loki

738.

In 1963, only two years after *Fantastic Four* #1 debuted, Stan Lee and Jack Kirby had introduced enough new Super Heroes to combine them into another team: the Avengers.

In *The Avengers* #1 (shown at right), the Asgardian god of evil, Loki, manipulated the incredible Hulk into wrecking a railroad track, intending to lure his foster brother, Thor, into battling a creature who rivaled Thor's vast strength. What Loki did not expect was that new Super Heroes Iron Man, the original Ant-Man, and the Wasp would also respond to the emergency. Not only did Thor end up capturing Loki, but the five heroes also decided to band together to combat menaces that were too great for any one hero to fight. Thus, Loki was inadvertently responsible for the creation of the team of Earth's mightiest heroes.

Who came up with the name "Avengers"?
- **A.** Iron Man
- **B.** Ant-Man
- **C.** The Wasp
- **D.** Thor

746. How does Thor use his hammer to create rain, thunder, or lightning?
- **A.** Stamps the hammer once
- **B.** Stamps the hammer twice
- **C.** Stamps the hammer three times
- **D.** Whirls the hammer in a circle

747. Who impersonated the Hulk in *The Avengers* #2 (1963)?
- **A.** Loki
- **B.** A Space Phantom
- **C.** A Skrull
- **D.** One of the Carbon Copy Men

748. What was Jane Foster's profession?
- **A.** Surgeon
- **B.** Reporter
- **C.** Nurse
- **D.** Receptionist

749. Whom does Avenger member Quicksilver marry in *Fantastic Four* #150 (1974)?
- **A.** Medusa
- **B.** Crystal
- **C.** The Scarlet Witch
- **D.** Nobody because the wedding is interrupted

750. Where did Iron Man battle Super Villains in *Iron Man* #72 (1974)?
- **A.** The offices of Marvel Comics
- **B.** The San Diego Comic Convention
- **C.** The set of a Hollywood movie
- **D.** The New York Comic Convention

751. Who is Sam Wilson?
- **A.** The Falcon
- **B.** War Machine
- **C.** U.S. Agent
- **D.** Hawkeye

752. Who was *not* one of the new Avengers in *The Avengers* #16 (1965)?
- **A.** Quicksilver
- **B.** The Scarlet Witch
- **C.** Hawkeye
- **D.** The Swordsman

753. What was the first *Avengers* issue written by Roy Thomas?
- **A.** #16 (1965)
- **B.** #35 (1966)
- **C.** #34 (1966)
- **D.** #28 (1966)

754. What has *not* been one of Steve Rogers's jobs?
- **A.** Policeman
- **B.** Sailor
- **C.** Soldier
- **D.** Comic book artist

755. Who is Mrs. Arbogast?
- **A.** Tony Stark's secretary
- **B.** Steve Rogers's high school teacher
- **C.** Dr. Don Blake's nurse
- **D.** None of these

The Avengers

756. Who was Madame MacEvil in *Iron Man* #54 (1973)?
- **A.** Moondragon
- **B.** The Black Widow
- **C.** Madame Masque
- **D.** Sunset Bain

757. Who or what is Redwing?
- **A.** The Falcon's falcon
- **B.** A Soviet Super Villain
- **C.** An American Indian Super Hero
- **D.** Aircraft designed by Tony Stark

758. Who succeeded Henry Pym as the second Ant-Man?
- **A.** Bill Foster
- **B.** Erik Josten
- **C.** Scott Lang
- **D.** Clint Barton

759. Who created Ultron?
- **A.** Tony Stark
- **B.** Henry Pym
- **C.** Prof. Phineas T. Horton
- **D.** The Mad Thinker

760. When did Henry Pym first appear as Ant-Man?
- **A.** *Tales to Astonish* #35 (1962)
- **B.** *Tales to Astonish* #27 (1962)
- **C.** *Strange Tales* #75 (1960)
- **D.** *Tales to Astonish* #44 (1963)

761. In which identity did Henry Pym marry Janet Van Dyne?
- **A.** Ant-Man
- **B.** Goliath
- **C.** Yellowjacket
- **D.** Dr. Henry Pym

762. Who gave Wonder Man his powers?
- **A.** Baron Heinrich Zemo
- **B.** Professor Reinstein
- **C.** The Enchantress
- **D.** Himself

763. What was the cover date of *Captain America Comics #1*
- **A.** March 1941
- **B.** December 1940
- **C.** December 1941
- **D.** January 1941

764. Who was the new Black Knight in *The Avengers* #48 (1968)?
- **A.** Professor Nathan Garrett
- **B.** Sir Percy of Scandia
- **C.** Dane Whitman
- **D.** Bram Velsing

765. Whose body was the Vision constructed from?
- **A.** Ultron-1
- **B.** The original Vision of the 1940s
- **C.** Human Torch I
- **D.** Mad Thinker's Awesome Android

766. What is Mrs. Arbogast's first name?
- **A.** Holly
- **B.** Bambi
- **C.** Candi
- **D.** Randi

OBSESSED WITH MARVEL

772.

Anthony Stark (shown at left with his alter ego Iron Man) was a man who seemed to have everything. This handsome, wealthy, celebrated playboy was also one of the world's most brilliant inventors and the head of Stark Industries, which manufactured munitions and pioneered advanced technologies. But during a government mission in Asia, Stark was mortally injured by the explosion of a bomb. He found himself the captive of a warlord, Wong-Chu, who demanded that Stark create a super-weapon for him. With the aid of a fellow captive, Professor Yinsen, Stark created an armored battle-suit that not only kept his injured heart beating, but also enabled him to overpower his captors and escape.

Returning to America, Stark began a new career as the armored avenger Iron Man. Stan Lee plotted Iron Man's origin story in *Tales of Suspense* #39 (1963); Larry Lieber scripted it, and Don Heck drew it.

When did Iron Man's own comic book begin?

- **A.** 1963
- **B.** 1968
- **C.** 1970
- **D.** 1972

767. Who was not a member of the All-New, All-Different Avengers?
- **A.** Nova
- **B.** Ms. Marvel
- **C.** Spider-Man
- **D.** The Hulk

768. When Steve Rogers rapidly aged after losing his super-soldier serum, who inherited Captain America's shield?
- **A.** Sharon Carter
- **B.** Sam Wilson
- **C.** Bucky Barnes
- **D.** Rick Jones

769. Who is the Infamous Iron Man?
- **A.** Victor Von Doom
- **B.** Otto Octavius
- **C.** Ezekiel Stane
- **D.** Justin Hammer

770. What is the name of Hawkeye's pizza-loving dog?
- **A.** Arrow
- **B.** Chance
- **C.** Lucky
- **D.** Trickshot

771. Which woman was worthy enough to lift Mjolnir and become the new Thor?
- **A.** Sif
- **B.** Roz Solomon
- **C.** Valkyrie
- **D.** Jane Foster

772.

773. What organization was Captain America (Steve Rogers) secretly working for during his 2016 series?
- **A.** S.H.I.E.L.D.
- **B.** Avengers
- **C.** Hydra
- **D.** A.I.M.

774. After *Civil War II*, to whom was the mantle of Iron Man was passed?
- **A.** James Rhodes
- **B.** Riri Williams
- **C.** Carol Danvers
- **D.** Steve Rogers

775. Who was known as the Unworthy Thor?
- **A.** Beta Ray Bill
- **B.** Jane Foster
- **C.** Thor Odinson
- **D.** Dargo Ktor

776. Redwing gained vampiric abilities after being bitten by what villain?
- **A.** Morbius
- **B.** Dracula
- **C.** Baron Blood
- **D.** Deacon Frost

777. Which of the following has *not* been a subtitle of a series starring Angela?
- **A.** Asgard's Assassin
- **B.** Queen of Hel
- **C.** Heven's Warrior
- **D.** Witch Hunter

The Avengers

778. What was a previous identity of Kang before *The Avengers* #8 (1964)?
- **A.** The Time-Master
- **B.** Doctor Doom
- **C.** The Tomorrow Man
- **D.** Pharaoh Rama-Tut

779. Why did Janet Van Dyne become the Wasp?
- **A.** She was in love with Ant-Man
- **B.** For excitement
- **C.** For publicity
- **D.** To avenge her father's death

780. Which historical figure regularly appeared in Iron Man stories in *Tales of Suspense* #41–64 (1963–1965)?
- **A.** President John F. Kennedy
- **B.** Nikita Khrushchev
- **C.** Mao Tse-Tung
- **D.** President Lyndon Johnson

781. Who is Agent 13 of S.H.I.E.L.D.?
- **A.** Jasper Sitwell
- **B.** Sharon Carter
- **C.** Countess Valentina de la Fontaine
- **D.** Nick Fury

782. To whom was Pepper Potts once married?
- **A.** Morgan Stark
- **B.** Alex von Tilburg
- **C.** Happy Hogan
- **D.** Tony Stark

783. Who teamed up with the Hulk in *The Avengers* #3 (1964)?
- **A.** The other founding members of the Avengers
- **B.** The Sub-Mariner
- **C.** The Leader
- **D.** The Space Phantom

784. Who is Dr. Myron MacLain?
- **A.** Don Blake's mentor in medical school
- **B.** Tony Stark's college professor
- **C.** Inventor of Adamantium
- **D.** Creator of the Super-Soldier serum

785. Who is Johann Shmidt?
- **A.** Agent Axis
- **B.** Zeitgeist
- **C.** The Red Skull
- **D.** Hauptmann Deutschland

786. Who was the original Scarlet Centurion?
- **A.** Master Menace
- **B.** A member of Kang's Anachronauts
- **C.** Kang's son
- **D.** Kang the Conqueror

787. What is Batroc the Leaper's nationality?
- **A.** Belgian
- **B.** Italian
- **C.** French
- **D.** Spanish

OBSESSED WITH MARVEL

788. Whose brain patterns were the Vision's based on?
A. The original Human Torch
B. Wonder Man
C. Professor Phineas T. Horton
D. Dr. Henry Pym

789. What is Bethany Cabe's profession?
A. Industrial espionage agent
B. Fashion model
C. Corporate executive
D. Bodyguard

790. What organization was behind the attempted government takeover in *Captain America* #175 (1974)?
A. The Secret Empire
B. Advanced Idea Mechanics
C. The National Force
D. The Royalists

791. Who is *not* a member of Odin's family?
A. Buri
B. Laufey
C. Vili
D. Ve

792. Who is Owayodata?
A. The Lion God from *The Avengers* #112 (1973)
B. Deity of the Keewazi tribe
C. The Wolf Spirit who gave super-powers to the hero Red Wolf
D. Mother of Snowbird of Alpha Flight

793. Who is Doctor Faustus?
A. An evil sorcerer
B. A criminal inventor
C. A Nazi agent in World War II
D. Criminal and psychologist

794.

On a vacation in Norway, the crippled surgeon Donald Blake found himself trapped within a cave, where he found a gnarled wooden cane. Trying to free himself, he struck the cane against a cave wall. Suddenly, Blake was transformed into Thor, the thunder god of Norse mythology (shown at left), and the cane had become his enchanted hammer. Thor possessed vast superhuman strength and could use the hammer to fly and command the weather around him.

With "The Mighty Thor," which began in *Journey Into Mystery* #83, co-creators Stan Lee and Jack Kirby fused ancient mythology with the modern Super Hero story. In subsequent issues they would present Asgard, the other-dimensional home of the Norse gods; Thor's father, Odin, as its ruler; and Thor's archfoe, Loki, the god of evil.

Who scripted the first *Thor* story?

A. Larry Lieber
B. Jack Kirby
C. Stan Lee
D. Robert Bernstein

795. According to Odin's spell, what kind of person can lift Thor's hammer?
A. Only he who is worthy
B. Anyone with super-strength
C. Only an Asgardian god
D. Anyone

796. With whom did Thor battle in his first appearance?
A. Stone Men from Saturn
B. Loki
C. The Mad Merlin
D. The Carbon Copy Men

797. Whose identity did Madame Hydra usurp in *Captain America* #180 (1974)?
A. The Cobra
B. The Viper
C. The Asp
D. Black Mamba

798. Who calls himself the "Lion of Asgard" due to his courage?
A. Thor
B. Volstagg
C. Hogun
D. Balder

The Avengers

799. What was the Red Skull's job when he first met Adolf Hitler?
A. Soldier
B. Bellboy
C. Nazi political activist
D. Taxicab driver

800. Who took over Manhattan in *The Avengers* #72 (1970)?
A. The Kree
B. The Secret Empire
C. Hydra
D. Zodiac

801. Where did Captain America see Number One of the Secret Empire unmasked?
A. The U.S. Capitol Building
B. Oval Office of the White House
C. The Committee to Regain America's Principles
D. Front lawn of the White House

802. What body part does Arnim Zola lack?
A. Hand
B. Leg
C. Arm
D. Head

803. Who was the Falcon before becoming a Super Hero?
A. Policeman
B. Teacher
C. Criminal
D. Professional bird trainer

804. Who was the first substitute Iron Man?
A. Kevin O'Brian
B. Eddie March
C. Happy Hogan
D. James Rhodes

805. Which of the following characters has proved able to lift Thor's hammer?
A. Captain America
B. The Destroyer
C. Beta Ray Bill
D. All answers are correct

806. Who killed Vernon Van Dyne?
A. Kulla
B. The Time-Master
C. Creature from Kosmos
D. Egghead

807.

During the early 1960s, Marvel shifted from science-fiction stories to Super Hero adventures. In *Tales to Astonish* #27 (1962, shown at right) Stan Lee and Jack Kirby introduced "The Man in the Ant Hill." That man was Dr. Henry Pym. He discovered the subatomic "Pym particles" that enabled him to shrink himself to the size of an ant. Thus Pym became one of Marvel's new Super Heroes, the original Ant-Man. Soon he gained a partner, his future wife, Janet Van Dyne, alias the Wasp. She not only shrunk to insect size, but also grew wings.

Later, Lee and Kirby made Pym more formidable by enabling him to also increase in size and strength to become Giant-Man. Since then Pym has taken on other Super Heroic identities as well.

Over the years Pym suffered a nervous breakdown, was jailed, and divorced from his wife. But Pym redeemed himself, resumed his heroic career, and was eventually reunited with Jan.

When did Janet Van Dyne become the Wasp?

A. *Tales to Astonish* #44 (1963)
B. *Tales to Astonish* #49 (1963)
C. *Tales to Astonish* #35 (1962)
D. *Tales to Astonish* #51 (1964)

808. What is Modok?
A. Mental Organism Designed Only for Computation
B. Mental Organism Designed Only for Killing
C. Master Organism Designated Only for Killing
D. Mobile Organism Devised Only for Killing

OBSESSED WITH MARVEL

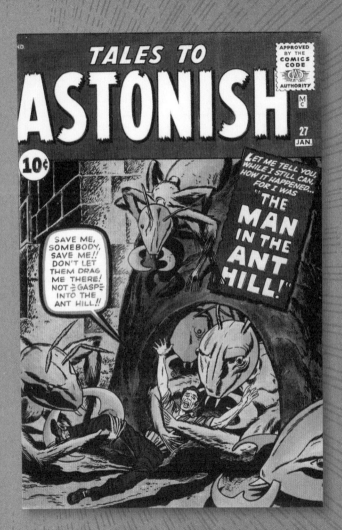

809. Who is Arnim Zola?
- **A.** Nazi robot builder
- **B.** Former Nazi general
- **C.** Nazi genetic engineer
- **D.** Former Nazi terrorist

810. What is Batroc the Leaper's specialty?
- **A.** Savate
- **B.** Jujitsu
- **C.** Karate
- **D.** Tae Kwan Do

811. Where does Heimdall stand guard?
- **A.** The gates of Asgard
- **B.** The throne room of Odin
- **C.** The Rainbow Bridge
- **D.** The Odinsword

812. Who was *not* one of Ant-Man/Giant-Man's foes?
- **A.** The Porcupine
- **B.** The Living Eraser
- **C.** Mr. Doll
- **D.** The Human Top

813. What is Mjolnir?
- **A.** One of Odin's ravens
- **B.** Beta Ray Bill's hammer
- **C.** Thor's belt of strength
- **D.** Thor's hammer

814. Whom does Karnilla the Norn Queen love?
- **A.** Balder
- **B.** Volstagg
- **C.** Loki
- **D.** Thor

815. Which of the following foes of Thor became a continuing team?
- **A.** Karnilla and the Enchantress
- **B.** Mr. Hyde and the Cobra
- **C.** Loki and the Absorbing Man
- **D.** Surtur and Ymir

816. What is Thor's hammer made of?
- **A.** Adamantium
- **B.** Asgardian stone
- **C.** Asgardian steel
- **D.** Uru metal

817. Who is "Crusher" Creel?
- **A.** The Growing Man
- **B.** The Absorbing Man
- **C.** The Thermal Man
- **D.** The Destroyer

818. What are the Sleepers?
- **A.** Secret Nazi agents
- **B.** Nazi robot war machines
- **C.** Superhumans kept in a trancelike state
- **D.** Special S.H.I.E.L.D. agents

The Avengers

819. Who became Captain America's writer and artist in *Captain America* #193?

A. Roger Stern and John Byrne

B. Mark Gruenwald and Kieron Dwyer

C. Jack Kirby

D. Steve Englehart and Sal Buscema

820. What weapon did the Red Skull first acquire in *Tales of Suspense* #79-81 (1966)?

A. The Ultimate Nullifier

B. The Serpent Crown

C. The Cosmic Cube

D. The Evil Eye

821. Who or what are the Cotati?

A. Alien race of lizardlike beings

B. Alien race of sentient plants

C. Alien race of humanoids

D. Alien race of birdlike beings

822. What is Bifrost?

A. Realm of the Ice Giants

B. The Rainbow Bridge of Asgard

C. Whitney Frost's company

D. The Blizzard's device for creating intense cold

823. Who is Madame Masque?

A. Big M of the Maggia

B. Whitney Frost

C. Countess Giulietta Nefaria

D. All answers are correct

824. Who is Ymir?

A. Dragon

B. Warrior troll

C. Ice giant

D. Storm giant

825. Who is Surtur?

A. Skrull Emperor

B. Fire demon

C. Military officer of the Kree

D. Vizier of Arkon the Imperion

826. Who took over Stark Industries in *Iron Man* #103 (1977)?

A. Obadiah Stane

B. Justin Hammer

C. Morgan Stark

D. Mordecai Midas

827.

828. Who is ruler of the Olympian underworld of Hades?

A. Cerberus

B. Mephisto

C. Hela

D. Pluto

827.

The greatest foe of the Avengers, Kang the Conqueror (shown at right) is a time traveler who was born on an alternate future Earth in the thirty-first century. Using a time machine, he traveled back to ancient Egypt, where he ruled as the tyrant Pharaoh Rama-Tut. After clashing with the time-traveling Fantastic Four, Rama-Tut traveled forward in time to the fortieth century AD, where he became the warlord Kang the Conqueror.

As Kang he built a vast empire through time and space. But Kang repeatedly returns to the present age of Super Heroes to pit himself against the Avengers.

In his constant travels, alternate versions of Kang have arisen in divergent timelines. Tiring of conquest, one such alternate Kang resumed his role of Rama-Tut, this time to rule benevolently, and ultimately to become the enigmatic time lord, Immortus.

Which major city did Kang once destroy?

A. New York City

B. Washington D.C.

C. London

D. Paris

829. Who is the High Evolutionary?
- **A.** A human geneticist who later achieved godlike power
- **B.** A member of the Celestials' First Host
- **C.** An Elder of the Universe
- **D.** The Inhumans' head geneticist

830. What happens if the Odinsword is drawn from its sheath?
- **A.** The holder of the sword gains Odin's powers
- **B.** The world comes to an end
- **C.** The holder of the sword becomes ruler of Asgard
- **D.** Alarms go off

831. Which Avenger underwent a court-martial by the team?
- **A.** Simon Williams
- **B.** Henry Pym
- **C.** Clint Barton
- **D.** Natasha Romanova

832. What is the Teen Brigade?
- **A.** Rick Jones and friends using ham radios
- **B.** Rick Jones's Internet friends
- **C.** A team of young Super Heroes
- **D.** The Avengers' first fan club

833. What is the Destroyer in *Thor*?
- **A.** The partner of the Executioner
- **B.** What Thor is called when he has berserker madness
- **C.** Another name for Surtur
- **D.** Enchanted suit of nearly indestructible armor

834. What happened to the Red Skull at the end of World War II?
- **A.** He went into suspended animation
- **B.** He was killed and then cloned by Arnim Zola
- **C.** He was put on trial for war crimes
- **D.** He went to work for the Soviets

835. How did Pluto get Hercules to sign an unbreakable "Olympian contract" in *Thor* #127–130 (1966)?
- **A.** By threatening the life of his father, Zeus
- **B.** Hercules thought he was signing a movie contract
- **C.** By holding Thor hostage
- **D.** By promising to make Hercules the new ruler of Olympus

836. What did Odin once lose to gain knowledge from Mimir?
- **A.** A vast treasure
- **B.** Rulership of Asgard
- **C.** An eye
- **D.** His brothers' lives

The Avengers

837. Who led the Masters of Evil in taking over Avengers Mansion in *The Avengers* #273-277 (1986-1987)?

A. Baron Helmut Zemo

B. The Crimson Cowl

C. Ultron

D. Baron Heinrich Zemo

838. What is Ego?

A. Odin's evil other self

B. A living planet

C. A sentient computer devised by Stark Industries

D. A disembodied alien consciousness

839. Who became the new Bucky in *Captain America* #110 (1969)?

A. Hawkeye

B. Peter Parker

C. Rick Jones

D. Jack Monroe

840. What must Odin regularly do to renew his immortality?

A. Hang from Yggdrasil the World-Tree for days

B. Draw the Odinsword from its sheath

C. Renew his past romance with the Earth goddess

D. The Odinsleep

841. Where is Wundagore Mountain?

A. Serbia

B. Germany

C. Transia

D. Symkaria

842. Which major villain was introduced in *Iron Man* #55 (1973)?

A. Justin Hammer

B. The Controller

C. Firebrand

D. Thanos

843. What character was named Ragnarok?

A. The Asgardian Destroyer

B. The Mangog

C. A clone of Thor

D. One of the Frost Giants

844. Who is Sif's brother?

A. Harokin

B. Fandral

C. Heimdall

D. Balder

845. What are the Knights of Wundagore?

A. Semi-humanoid animals evolved by the High Evolutionary

B. Warriors led by Val-Larr of Luminia

C. Members of the Einherjar

D. Followers of Modred the Mystic

851.

The first team to spin off from the original Avengers was the West Coast Avengers, who debuted in 1985 (issue 1 shown at left). Since the Avengers were based in New York, it made sense for the organization to have a West Coast hub as well.

Second-generation Avenger Hawkeye and his new bride, the costumed Super Heroine Mockingbird, went to Southern California to organize the West Coast team, which initially included Iron Man, Tigra, and Wonder Man. Among the many other Avengers, old and new, who joined the West Coast division were the Vision and the Scarlet Witch, Henry Pym and the Wasp, Moon Knight, the second Spider-Woman, the U.S. Agent, a Latino hero called the Living Lightning, and the resurrected original Human Torch.

Classic *Avengers* writers Roger Stern, Steve Englehart, and Roy Thomas all contributed to the new series, as did writer-artist John Byrne. Originally known as *West Coast Avengers,* the series later changed its title to *Avengers West Coast.*

What was the name of the Avengers' West Coast base?

A. Avengers Mansion West
B. Avengers Compound
C. Avengers Tower
D. The Triskelion

846. What is the Wrecker's enchanted weapon?
A. A mace
B. A crowbar
C. A hammer
D. A ball and chain

847. What is the Absorbing Man's enchanted weapon?
A. A mace
B. A crowbar
C. A hammer
D. A ball and chain

848. Who switched bodies with Captain America in *Captain America* #115?
A. The Red Skull
B. The Falcon
C. Doctor Doom
D. Batroc the Leaper

849. Who is Madame Masque's father?
A. Mordecai Midas
B. Silvermane
C. Byron Frost
D. Count Nefaria

850. What is Ragnarok?
A. The Trial of the Gods
B. End of the Norse gods
C. The home of the honored Asgardian dead
D. Hela's realm of the dead

851.

852. Whose brain did Arnim Zola attempt to transplant in *Captain America* #210-212 (1977)?
A. Bucky Barnes
B. Baron Heinrich Zemo
C. The Red Skull
D. Adolf Hitler

853. Who is Zarrko?
A. The Tomorrow Man
B. The Man with the Voice of Doom
C. The Living Eraser
D. One of the Lava Men

854. Who is Thunderstrike?
A. Kevin Masterson
B. Jake Olsen
C. Eric Masterson
D. Keith Kincaid

855. Who is War Machine?
A. James Rhodes
B. Michael O'Brien
C. Frank Castle
D. Basil Sandhurst

856. Which S.H.I.E.L.D. agent was assigned to Tony Stark in *Tales of Suspense* #93-95 (1966)?
A. Gabe Jones
B. Jasper Sitwell
C. Clay Quartermain
D. Dum Dum Dugan

The Avengers

857. When the youngest members of the Avengers quit after *Civil War II*, what group did they form?

A. Defenders   **C.** Runaways

B. New Warriors   **D.** Champions

858. Which group focused primarily on community service and fighting street level crime in their 2013 series?

A. The Ultimates   **C.** A-Force

B. Mighty Avengers   **D.** Avengers Academy

859. Who is the new Wasp that was introduced in *All-New, All-Different Avengers*?

A. Nadia Pym   **C.** Cassie Lang

B. Katie Summers   **D.** Hope Van Dyne

860. Who was secretly the S.H.I.E.L.D. whistleblower known as The Whisperer?

A. Rick Jones   **C.** Phil Coulson

B. Sam Wilson   **D.** Daisy Johnson

861.

862. Angela was co-created by which writer and artist team?

A. Stan Lee and Jack Kirby   **C.** Neil Gaiman and Todd McFarlane

B. Roy Thomas and John Buscema   **D.** Jason Aaron and Simone Bianchi

863. Cannonball had a child with which fellow Avengers team member?

A. Captain Universe   **C.** Spider-Woman

B. Smasher   **D.** Abyss

864. Which member of the Avengers was also a hero in Marvel's *New Universe*?

A. Captain Universe   **C.** Starbrand

B. Nightmask   **D.** Both B & C

865. What idyllic Connecticut town was secretly a Super Villain prison?

A. Peaceful Grove   **C.** Silent Cove

B. Pleasant Hill   **D.** Shady Lake

866. Who was not a member of Thanos's Black Order?

A. Corvus Glaive   **C.** Nebula

B. Proxima Midnight   **D.** Black Dwarf

861.

From the series' early stories, the Avengers' sinister counterparts were a team of Super Villains known as the Masters of Evil. Baron Heinrich Zemo founded the original Masters, and his son Helmut later took over leadership.

Helmut conceived a plan whereby he and his new Masters of Evil would pose as Super Heroes in order to win the public's trust. Thus, the Masters of Evil became the Thunderbolts (*Avenger/Thunderbolts* #1, 2004, shown at right), and the notorious Super Villains the Beetle, the Fixer, Goliath, Moonstone, and Screaming Mimi became, respectively, MACH-1, Techno, Atlas, Meteorite, and Songbird.

Writer Kurt Busiek and artist Mark Bagley, who created the series, would later have Avenger Hawkeye take over as leader, guiding the members toward becoming genuine heroes. The Thunderbolts have nonetheless usually been at odds with the law. Another version of the team was later organized by the outwardly reformed Norman Osborn, alias the Green Goblin.

Which Golden Age hero's identity did Helmut Zemo assume in *Thunderbolts*?

A. The Destroyer

B. Citizen V

C. The Witness

D. The Black Marvel

867. What is the Mangog?

   A. A gigantic demon

   B. A renegade Asgardian god

   C. A giant who transformed into a monster to guard treasure

   D. Physical embodiment of a billion beings

868. Who has been known as Ronin?

   A. The Silver Samurai

   B. Sunfire

   C. Hawkeye

   D. Wolverine

869. Whom did the Committee for Regaining America's Principles frame Captain America for murdering?

   A. The Planner

   B. The Tumbler

   C. The Acrobat

   D. Moonstone I

870. Which member of the Egyptian pantheon of gods is Thor's enemy?

   A. Osiris

   B. Isis

   C. Seth

   D. Horus

871. Who are *not* members of the Illuminati?

   A. Mister Fantastic and Prince Namor

   B. Doctor Strange and Professor X

   C. Black Bolt and Black Panther

   D. Captain America and Zuras

872. Which high government position has Tony Stark held?

   A. Secretary of Commerce

   B. National Security Advisor

   C. Secretary of Defense

   D. Vice President

873. Which of the following is *not* one of Thor's past human identities?

   A. Jake Olson

   B. Dr. Keith Kincaid

   C. Siegmund

   D. Eric Masterson

874. Where on Earth was Asgard re-created?

   A. California

   B. Oklahoma

   C. New Mexico

   D. Arizona

875. Who seized control of Stark International after manipulating Stark into succumbing to alcoholism?

   A. Justin Hammer

   B. Morgan Stark

   C. Obadiah Stane

   D. Mordecai Midas

The Avengers

876. Which member of Power Pack joined Avengers-Next?
- **A.** Alex
- **B.** Julie
- **C.** Katie
- **D.** Jack

877. What is Count Nefaria's first name?
- **A.** Federico
- **B.** Luchino
- **C.** Michelangelo
- **D.** Roberto

878. What is Captain America's shield made of?
- **A.** Vibranium and an alloy resembling Adamantium
- **B.** Vibranium
- **C.** Adamantium
- **D.** Vibranium and steel

879. What shape was Captain America's original shield?
- **A.** Triangular
- **B.** Square
- **C.** Circular
- **D.** Rectangular

880. Who presented Captain America with his indestructible shield?
- **A.** Dr. Myron MacLain
- **B.** Professor Reinstein
- **C.** Franklin D. Roosevelt
- **D.** General Dwight D. Eisenhower

881. What is the Asgardian name for Earth?
- **A.** Midgard
- **B.** Alfheim
- **C.** Vanaheim
- **D.** Nidavellir

882. What was Obadiah Stane's armored identity?
- **A.** Firepower
- **B.** The Mauler
- **C.** Titanium Man
- **D.** Iron Monger

883. Which Super Villainess was Captain America's girlfriend?
- **A.** Superia
- **B.** Diamondback
- **C.** Mother Night
- **D.** Black Mamba

884.

885. How is Morgan Stark related to Tony Stark?
- **A.** Ne'er-do-well cousin
- **B.** Younger brother
- **C.** Young son
- **D.** Sister

886. What does the Red Skull's "dust of death" do?
- **A.** Turns victim to dust
- **B.** Kills victim and turns his head into a red skull
- **C.** Causes victim to suffocate
- **D.** Poisons victim

OBSESSED WITH MARVEL

884.

A-Next (1998–1999), short for Avengers-Next, was part of the *MC2* line of comics, which presented an alternate future for the Marvel Universe. The best-known *MC2* character is Spider-Man's daughter, Spider-Girl. Her creators, writer Tom DeFalco and artist Ron Frenz, also conceived *A-Next* (issue 1 shown at right).

This series was about the Avengers one generation from present day, mainly the children of the team's present-day Super Heroes. Among them were Stinger (Cassie Lang, daughter of the second Ant-Man), Thunderstrike (Kevin Masterson, the son of the original Thunderstrike), reservists Argo (the son of Hercules) and Coal Tiger (the son of the Black Panther), and J2 (the son of the X-Men's old enemy, the Juggernaut). Other members include Jubilee and Speedball as adults, as well as American Dream, Bluestreak, Crimson Curse, Freebooter, Mainframe, and more.

Who was related to the heroine American Dream?

- **A.** Sharon Carter
- **B.** Steve Rogers
- **C.** Nick Fury
- **D.** John Walker

887. Which terrorist group was purchased by Roberto Da Costa and turned into an Avengers team?

A. Hydra

B. The Hand

C. H.A.M.M.E.R.

D. A.I.M.

888. During the *Avengers vs. X-Men* event, the nation of Wakanda was flooded by which former Avenger?

A. Stingray

B. Crystal

C. Namor

D. Scarlet Witch

889. The brilliant scientific heroes who starred in *New Avengers* (2013) were also known by what name?

A. The Illuminati

B. The Cabal

C. The Infinity Watch

D. The Ultimates

890. Who was *not* a student at the Avengers Academy?

A. White Tiger

B. Lightspeed

C. Machine Teen

D. Skaar

891. Who was the lead character in the 2016 *Hawkeye* series?

A. Clint Barton

B. Barney Barton

C. Kate Bishop

D. Lucky the Pizza Dog

892. Which classic Avenger has never been a member of the Uncanny Avengers?

A. Thor

B. Black Widow

C. Captain America

D. Wonder Man

893. After the *AXIS* storyline, which original Avenger maintained a more sinister personality for a time?

A. Iron Man

B. Thor

C. Ant-Man

D. Hulk

894. With which Secret Avenger did Valkyrie share a brief romantic relationship?

A. Captain Britain

B. Beast

C. Venom

D. Ant-Man

895. At the beginning of *Civil War II*, which longtime Avenger is killed by Thanos?

A. Captain Marvel

B. Iron Man

C. She-Hulk

D. War Machine

896. After *Secret Wars*, who was *not* a regular member of A-Force?

A. Medusa

B. She-Hulk

C. Ms. Marvel

D. Dazzler

The Avengers

897. Who is Lorelei's sister?
- **A.** The Enchantress
- **B.** Karnilla the Norn Queen
- **C.** Sif
- **D.** Sigyn

898. Who killed the original Swordsman?
- **A.** Pharaoh Rama-Tut
- **B.** Kang the Conqueror
- **C.** Mantis
- **D.** Hawkeye

899. Where were Quicksilver and the Scarlet Witch born?
- **A.** Hungary
- **B.** Germany
- **C.** Transia
- **D.** Latveria

900. Whose TV talk show did the Avengers appear on in *The Avengers* #239 (1984)?
- **A.** Johnny Carson
- **B.** Dick Cavett
- **C.** David Letterman
- **D.** Regis Philbin

901. Which villain attacked the Avengers on a talk show in *The Avengers* #239 (1984)?
- **A.** The Impossible Man
- **B.** Fabian Stankowitz
- **C.** The Jester
- **D.** The Grim Reaper

902.

903. Which *Captain America* character was *not* created by Jack Kirby?
- **A.** Demolition-Man
- **B.** Cheer Chadwick
- **C.** General Argyle Fist
- **D.** William Taurey

904. Who was *not* one of the Night People of Zero Street?
- **A.** Brother Inquisitor
- **B.** Brother Powerful
- **C.** Brother Nature
- **D.** Brother Wonderful

905. What name was *not* used by the original Power Man (Erik Josten)?
- **A.** Atlas
- **B.** Goliath
- **C.** Giant-Man
- **D.** The Smuggler

906. When did Erik Josten give up the name Power Man?
- **A.** When he gained the power to grow to giant size
- **B.** When he lost it in a fight to Luke Cage
- **C.** When he lost his super-powers
- **D.** When he joined the Thunderbolts

902.

Created by writer Allan Heinberg and artist Jim Cheung, the Young Avengers are a team of young Super Heroes who model themselves after members of the classic Avengers. At a point when the Avengers had disbanded, a young Iron Lad (shown above), who wore an armored battle-suit, founded the Young Avengers by locating and recruiting Hulkling (Teddy Altman); the new Patriot (Eli Bradley); and Wiccan (Billy Kaplan), who possesses magical powers. Other members who subsequently have joined

the team are the new Hawkeye (Kate Bishop); Speed (Thomas Shepherd), who can move at super-speed; Stature (Cassie Lang, daughter of Ant-Man II), who can change size; and a new version of the Vision, consisting of the original's operating system within Iron Lad's armored battle-suit.

Whom did Iron Lad of the Young Avengers eventually become?

A. Iron Man 2020
B. Kang the Conqueror
C. Tony Stark's heir
D. Obadiah Stane's heir

907. Who is Princess Ravonna?
A. The woman Kang loved
B. Princess of the Skrulls
C. Princess of the Norns
D. Wife of Arkon the Imperion

908. Which Elder of the Universe first appeared in *The Avengers* #28 (1966)?
A. The Runner
B. The Collector
C. The Grandmaster
D. The Trader

909. What was the location of the Halloween parade in *The Avengers* #83 (1970)?
A. New York, New York
B. Cambridge, Massachusetts
C. Rutland, Vermont
D. San Francisco, California

910. Which member of the Inhumans was also a member of the Avengers?
A. Crystal
B. Medusa
C. Karnak
D. Triton

911. What was Bill Foster's profession when he debuted in *The Avengers* #32 (1966)?
A. An engineer working for Tony Stark
B. Dr. Henry Pym's assistant
C. Agent of S.H.I.E.L.D.
D. Reporter investigating the Sons of the Serpents

912. Which Eternals have been members of the Avengers?
A. Sersi
B. Gilgamesh and Sersi
C. The Forgotten One
D. Makkari and Sersi

913. Which Super Villain had a crush on Janet Van Dyne?
A. The Human Top
B. Egghead
C. The Porcupine
D. The Living Laser

914. Who is the Red Guardian in *The Avengers* #43-44 (1967)?
A. The Black Widow's husband
B. The Black Widow's brother
C. Dr. Tanya Belinskaya
D. A Soviet Super Hero of World War I

915. Where were the New Warriors killed?
A. Philadelphia, Pennsylvania
B. Newark, New Jersey
C. Stamford, Connecticut
D. New York City

916. Which Elder of the Universe first appeared in *The Avengers* #69 (1969)?
A. The Collector
B. The Grandmaster
C. The Gardener
D. The Contemplator

The Avengers

917. Who is the Grim Reaper's brother?
- **A.** Wonder Man
- **B.** Hawkeye
- **C.** The Swordsman
- **D.** The Black Widow

918. What other career did Wonder Man pursue after rejoining the Avengers?
- **A.** Engineer
- **B.** Movie star
- **C.** Scientist
- **D.** Business executive

919. Who joined the Avengers in *The Avengers* #38 (1967)?
- **A.** The Vision
- **B.** The Black Knight
- **C.** Hercules
- **D.** The Black Panther

920. Which form of energy gives Wonder Man his powers?
- **A.** Electromagnetic
- **B.** Ionic
- **C.** Gamma
- **D.** Cosmic

921. Which Iron Man foe in *Tales of Suspense* #41 (1963) had the same name as a later hero?
- **A.** Doctor Strange
- **B.** Warlock
- **C.** The Punisher
- **D.** Colossus

922. Who is *not* a member of the Squadron Sinister?
- **A.** Hyperion
- **B.** Nighthawk
- **C.** Power Princess
- **D.** Doctor Spectrum

923. Who were the parents of the mutant Nuklo?
- **A.** Magneto and his late wife
- **B.** Professor Xavier and Gabrielle Haller
- **C.** The Blue Diamond and Spitfire
- **D.** The Whizzer and Miss America

924. Who was engaged to marry Tony Stark?
- **A.** Marianne Rodgers
- **B.** Janice Cord
- **C.** Rae LaCoste
- **D.** Roxanne Gilbert

925.

926. What country is Mantis from?
- **A.** China
- **B.** Japan
- **C.** Vietnam
- **D.** Thailand

927. Which Iron Man villain debuted in *Tales of Suspense* #50 (1964)?
- **A.** The Mandarin
- **B.** The Melter
- **C.** Kala, Queen of the Netherworld
- **D.** The Titanium Man

OBSESSED WITH MARVEL

Following the conclusion of the Civil War, the U.S. government launched the Fifty State Initiative, a plan that was conceived by Reed Richards (Mister Fantastic), Anthony Stark (Iron Man), and Dr. Henry Pym (Yellowjacket). Through the Initiative, the federal government organized all registered Super Heroes into a national security task force. Specific Super Heroes were assigned to each of the fifty states. The Mighty Avengers, the post–Civil War version of the Avengers, for example, were based in New York.

A rival team of Avengers, the New Avengers (which included Luke Cage, Doctor Strange, Iron Fist, Ronin, Spider-Man, Spider-Woman I, and

928. Who became Goliath in *The Avengers* #63 (1969)?
- **A.** Eric Josten
- **B.** Henry Pym
- **C.** Bill Foster
- **D.** Clint Barton

929. Who is the Celestial Madonna?
- **A.** The Scarlet Witch
- **B.** Mantis
- **C.** Sersi
- **D.** Moondragon

930. Who is Boris Bullski?
- **A.** The Unicorn
- **B.** The Titanium Man
- **C.** The Crimson Dynamo
- **D.** The Spymaster

931. Whom did Kang bargain with to resurrect Princess Ravonna?
- **A.** Eternity
- **B.** Mephisto
- **C.** The Grandmaster
- **D.** Mistress Death

932. Who was *not* introduced in *Tales of Suspense* #45 (1963)?
- **A.** Pepper Potts
- **B.** Senator Harrington Byrd
- **C.** The Super Villain Jack Frost
- **D.** Happy Hogan

933. Which of Thor's adversaries commanded Satan's Forty Horsemen and the Jinni Devil?
- **A.** Mogul of the Mystic Mountain
- **B.** Malekith
- **C.** Mephisto
- **D.** Loki

934. Who invaded Yellowjacket's wedding to the Wasp?
- **A.** The Masters of Evil
- **B.** The Lethal Legion
- **C.** The Ringmaster's Circus of Crime
- **D.** Zodiac

935. Who was Sgt. Mike Duffy?
- **A.** A policeman who became the Cowled Commander
- **B.** A veteran who welcomed Captain America back in *The Avengers* #4 (1964)
- **C.** A security guard at Stark Industries who fell under Lucifer's control
- **D.** Steve Rogers's sergeant during World War II

936. Which villains brought about the Avengers-Defenders War?
- **A.** Baron Mordo and Count Nefaria
- **B.** Doctor Doom and Kang
- **C.** Dormammu and Loki
- **D.** Kang and Ultron

Wolverine) refused to register and hence operated illegally.

Newly registered superhumans first had to undergo training at Camp Hammond, a "Super Hero boot camp." The series *Avengers: The Initiative* (issue 8 shown above), originally written by Dan Slott and Christos Gage, deals with both Camp Hammond trainees and Initiative teams in different states.

Where did Camp Hammond get its name?

- **A.** The town where the camp is located
- **B.** The original Human Torch's secret identity
- **C.** The name of one of the victims of Nitro's massacre
- **D.** The head of the original Super-Soldier program

The Avengers

937. Which future Avenger first appeared as a villain in *Tales of Suspense* #57 (1964)?

A. Hawkeye

B. The Black Widow

C. The Swordsman

D. The Falcon

938. Which X-Men member joined the Avengers in *The Avengers* #137 (1975)?

A. The Angel

B. Marvel Girl

C. The Beast

D. Iceman

939. Which of Iron Man's foes was *not* a Communist agent?

A. The Crimson Dynamo

B. The Titanium Man

C. The Unicorn

D. The Melter

940. Who was Heinz Kruger?

A. An alias used by the Red Skull

B. The German agent who killed the Super-Soldier serum's creator

C. The Super Hero Hauptmann Deutschland

D. One of the Nazi agents who reactivated the Sleepers

941. Where did *The Avengers* #100 (1972) take place?

A. New York City

B. The Kree homeworld

C. Olympus

D. Asgard

942. Who drew *The Avengers* #100 (1972)?

A. Barry Windsor-Smith

B. Neal Adams

C. Gil Kane

D. John Buscema

943. Who is the Ghost?

A. A spirit of a Nazi who haunted Captain America

B. The original name of the 1940s Vision

C. A Giant-Man foe who could become invisible and intangible

D. A costumed high-tech saboteur who combats Iron Man

944. What was Jack Kirby's last issue as *Avengers* artist?

A. #12 (1965)

B. #16 (1965)

C. #15 (1965)

D. #20 (1965)

945. How did the Scarlet Centurion change history in *The Avengers Special* #2 (1968)?

A. The original Avengers conquer the world

B. He prevents the formation of the Avengers

C. He kills the original Avengers

D. He prevents the original Avengers from gaining their super-powers

OBSESSED WITH MARVEL

946. Where did the Mandarin obtain his power rings?
- **A.** From the ruins of an ancient civilization
- **B.** From an alien spacecraft
- **C.** From aliens from another dimension
- **D.** He made them himself

947. Which of the following is *not* one of the Mandarin's power rings?
- **A.** Ice Blast Ring
- **B.** Teleportation Ring
- **C.** Disintegrator Ring
- **D.** Matter Rearranger Ring

948.

The *Dark Avengers* series was created by writer Brian Michael Bendis and artist Mike Deodato as part of Marvel's "Dark Reign" story line in 2009.

In the aftermath of the alien Skrulls' Secret Invasion of Earth, the U.S. government disbanded the Avengers and assigned a surprising candidate to reorganize the team: Norman Osborn. Although Osborn was the original Green Goblin, he had redeemed himself in the public eye by his role in thwarting the Skrull invasion. He was even appointed as the new head of S.H.I.E.L.D., which he renamed H.A.M.M.E.R.

But Osborn had not truly reformed, and he organized a new version of the Avengers that would serve him and H.A.M.M.E.R. Among the members of Osborn's Dark Avengers (shown at left) were Ares, the Olympian god of war; the new Captain Marvel (Noh-Varr); and the Sentry. Other members were actually Super Villains disguised as familiar Super Heroes, including Bullseye as Hawkeye, Moonstone as Ms. Marvel, and Daken as his own father, Wolverine.

Who is the Iron Patriot in the Dark Avengers?

- **A.** Flag-Smasher
- **B.** Crossbones
- **C.** Norman Osborn
- **D.** The U.S. Agent

949. Who was Bruno Horgan?
- **A.** Firebrand
- **B.** The Melter
- **C.** Radioactive Man
- **D.** The Ghost

950. Who was the woman Captain America loved during World War II?
- **A.** Peggy Carter
- **B.** Miss America
- **C.** Spitfire
- **D.** Sharon Carter

951. Who is the master villain in *The Avengers Special* #1 (1967)?
- **A.** The Mandarin
- **B.** Kang the Conqueror
- **C.** Baron Zemo
- **D.** The Red Skull

952. Who was Dr. Abraham Erskine?
- **A.** Creator of the Super-Soldier serum
- **B.** Tony Stark's former college professor
- **C.** Inventor of Adamantium
- **D.** Creator of the original Human Torch

953. Who employed the Swordsman as a secret agent in *The Avengers* #20 (1965)?
- **A.** The Mandarin
- **B.** Count Nefaria
- **C.** Doctor Doom
- **D.** The Black Widow

954. Which of the following men has *not* substituted as Iron Man?
- **A.** Jack Hart
- **B.** Michael O'Brien
- **C.** Happy Hogan
- **D.** Eddie March

955. Who was the first person to transform into the Freak?
- **A.** Eddie March
- **B.** Happy Hogan
- **C.** Kevin O'Brien
- **D.** Michael O'Brian

The Avengers

956. Who was the villain in *Captain America* #100 (1968)?
- **A.** The Red Skull
- **B.** An impostor posing as Baron Heinrich Zemo
- **C.** Baron Heinrich Zemo
- **D.** Baron Helmut Zemo

957. Where did Iron Man and Titanium Man battle in *Tales of Suspense* #81-83 (1966)?
- **A.** Manhattan
- **B.** Washington D.C.
- **C.** Moscow
- **D.** Stark Industries, Long Island

958. Who is Odin's wife?
- **A.** Sigyn
- **B.** Freya
- **C.** Frigga
- **D.** Gaea

959. Who or what is Ultimo?
- **A.** A gigantic robot that serves the Mandarin
- **B.** The Red Skull's Fourth Sleeper
- **C.** An alien robot also known as the Colossus
- **D.** An evil robot created by Henry Pym

960. Who is Amora?
- **A.** One of the Norns
- **B.** Loki's wife
- **C.** Mother Night
- **D.** The Enchantress

961. Who is Skurge?
- **A.** The Executioner
- **B.** A warrior Rock Troll
- **C.** An assassin of Super Villains
- **D.** An immense dragon

962. What did the Red Skull do to Manhattan in *Tales of Suspense* #90 (1967)?
- **A.** Invaded with his army of Exiles
- **B.** Used the Cosmic Cube to seal it off from the world
- **C.** Destroyed buildings in a terror attack
- **D.** Captured and levitated the island into the sky

963. Who was Irma Kruhl in *Tales of Suspense* #97-100 (1968)?
- **A.** Mother Night
- **B.** An agent of Baron Zemo
- **C.** Sharon Carter in disguise
- **D.** An elderly Nazi from World War II

964.

965. Which member of Zodiac was Cornelius Van Lunt?
- **A.** Aries
- **B.** Leo
- **C.** Scorpio
- **D.** Taurus

OBSESSED WITH MARVEL

964.

The Red Skull (shown at right) is Captain America's absolute opposite and eternal nemesis. Where Captain America embodies liberty and democracy, the Red Skull personifies totalitarian tyranny.

Joe Simon and Jack Kirby put a version of the Red Skull in *Captain America Comics* #1 back in the 1940s, and Kirby and Stan Lee reintroduced the Red Skull in the mid-1960s. According to his origin story, the Red Skull was an obscure malcontent who happened to encounter Adolf Hitler. Recognizing the hatred in his eyes, Hitler personally trained him to be his foremost agent of terror. Indeed, Hitler was so successful that he too came to fear the Red Skull. Captain America battled the Red Skull throughout World War II, and both hero and villain miraculously returned in the 1960s. Time and again the Red Skull has survived seeming death—and even actual death—to plague Captain America and the world yet again.

What is the Red Skull's theme music?

- **A.** The Third Reich's national anthem
- **B.** Wagner's "Ride of the Valkyries"
- **C.** Chopin's "Funeral March"
- **D.** Beethoven's "Fifth Symphony"

966. Why did Steve Rogers quit being Captain America in *Captain America* #175 (1974)?

A. He was fired by the U.S. government

B. He was disillusioned with the government

C. He was injured

D. He was framed as a criminal

967. Which new identity did Steve Rogers adopt after quitting being Captain America in *Captain America* #175 (1974)?

A. Flag-Smasher

B. Nomad

C. The Patriot

D. Vagabond

968. Who substituted for Steve Rogers as Captain America in *Captain America* #181–183 (1975)?

A. The 1950s Bucky

B. The 1950s Captain America

C. A boy named Roscoe

D. Rick Jones

969. What was the fate of the Captain America substitute from *Captain America* #181–183 (1975)?

A. Killed by the Red Skull

B. Crippled in combat

C. Became the new Bucky

D. Retired when Steve Rogers resumed being Captain America

970. Why did Steve Rogers resign as Captain America in *Captain America* #332 (1987)?

A. Refused to take orders from the Commission on Superhuman Activities

B. Refused to join Freedom Force

C. Felt he had failed in a mission

D. Wanted to try leading a normal life

971. Which new identity did Steve Rogers adopt after resigning as Captain America in *Captain America* #332 (1987)?

A. Yankee Clipper

B. Spirit of '76

C. U.S. Agent

D. The Captain

972. Whom did the U.S. government appoint Captain America after Steve Rogers resigned in 1987?

A. John Walker, alias Super-Patriot

B. Jack Monroe, alias Nomad

C. Jack Flag

D. Lemar Hoskins, alias Battle Star

973. Which of the following characters has *not* substituted as Captain America during a period when Steve Rogers was believed to be dead?

A. Bucky Barnes

B. The Patriot (Jeff Mace)

C. The Spirit of '76

D. The U.S. Agent

The Avengers

974. Who wrote the first two years of Iron Man's own comic book?

A. Stan Lee

B. Mike Friedrich

C. Gerry Conway

D. Archie Goodwin

975. Who did the 1950s Bucky later become?

A. Flag-Smasher

B. Winter Soldier

C. Grand Director of the National Force

D. The new Nomad

976.

977. Who plotted and drew *Iron Man* #55 (1973)?

A. Jack Kirby

B. Steve Englehart and Jim Starlin

C. Jim Starlin

D. Steve Gerber and George Tuska

978. Who is the Scarlet Beetle?

A. An insect-themed Super Hero

B. An insect-themed Super Villain

C. A genius insect seeking world conquest

D. Henry Pym's flying vehicle

979. Who was the Black Knight who first appeared in *Tales to Astonish* #52 (1964)?

A. Sir Percy of Scandia

B. Professor Nathan Garrett

C. Dane Whitman

D. Bram Velsing

980. Who scripted the *Iron Man* stories in *Tales of Suspense* #40–46 (1963)?

A. Stan Lee

B. Denny O'Neil

C. Robert Bernstein

D. Larry Lieber

981. Who is ruler of the Trolls?

A. Ulik

B. Geirrodur

C. Orikal

D. Eitri

982. When did Henry Pym first become Giant-Man?

A. *Tales to Astonish* #49 (1963)

B. *The Avengers* #2 (1963)

C. *The Avengers* #28 (1966)

D. *Tales to Astonish* #35 (1962)

983. Which member of the S.H.I.E.L.D. Super-Agents in *Captain America* later got his or her own series?

A. The Blue Streak

B. Marvel Man (alias Quasar)

C. The Vamp

D. Texas Twister

976.

At the end of Stan Lee and Jack Kirby's collaboration on *The Avengers*, Captain America battled Baron Heinrich Zemo (shown at right) to the death in South America, while the other Avengers battled the Masters of Evil in New York City. Thor soon left for Asgard, and Iron Man, Giant-Man, and the Wasp all decided to leave the Avengers for their own reasons.

Filling their places were three new recruits, each of them a Super Villain who now wanted to be a Super Hero. One was Hawkeye the Archer, a former foe of Iron Man. The other two were the mutant siblings Quicksilver and the Scarlet Witch, who, feeling a debt of gratitude to Magneto, had served as members of his Brotherhood of Evil Mutants. When Captain America returned, he discovered he was now leader of these new Avengers, dubbed "Cap's Kooky Quartet." Giant-Man would later rejoin as Goliath. Ever since the days of the quartet, the membership of the Avengers has been in a continual state of change.

Under which identity did Giant-Man rejoin the Avengers in *The Avengers* #28 (1966)?

A. Giant-Man

B. Goliath

C. Yellowjacket

D. The Wasp

984. What is the Grey Gargoyle's power?
- **A.** Turns flesh to stone
- **B.** Brings statues to life
- **C.** Wields magic
- **D.** Hypnotically paralyzes victims

985. Who is Tana Nile?
- **A.** The Scarlet Scarab
- **B.** The Asp
- **C.** One of the Colonizers of Rigel
- **D.** Former girlfriend of Tony Stark

986. Who is Thor's mother?
- **A.** Gaea
- **B.** Frigga
- **C.** Thena
- **D.** Brunnhilda

987. Who gave the Wrecker his super-strength?
- **A.** Karnilla the Norn Queen
- **B.** Loki
- **C.** The Norn Stones
- **D.** No one; he is a mutant

988. Who is *not* a member of the Wrecking Crew?
- **A.** Bulldozer
- **B.** Piledriver
- **C.** Thunderboot
- **D.** Thunderball

989. Which monument came to life and fought Captain America in *Captain America* #222 (1978)?
- **A.** The Statue of Liberty
- **B.** The Lincoln Memorial statue
- **C.** A statue of Captain America
- **D.** The Washington Monument

990. In the 1940s, to which team did Bucky belong?
- **A.** The Liberty Legion
- **B.** Young Allies
- **C.** Kid Commandos
- **D.** The Invaders

991. Which future Super Hero provoked Thor into madness in *Thor* #165–166 (1969)?
- **A.** The Silver Surfer
- **B.** Adam Warlock
- **C.** Ares
- **D.** Wolverine

992. With which issue was *Tales of Suspense* rechristened *Captain America*?
- **A.** #58 (1964)
- **B.** #100 (1968)
- **C.** #59 (1964)
- **D.** #99 (1968)

993. With which issue did *Journey into Mystery* change its name to *The Mighty Thor*?
- **A.** #83 (1962)
- **B.** #100 (1964)
- **C.** #125 (1966)
- **D.** #126 (1966)

The Avengers

994. Whom did Thor first meet in "When Titans Clash" in *Journey into Mystery/Thor Annual* #1 (1965)?
- **A.** The Destroyer
- **B.** The Absorbing Man
- **C.** Hercules
- **D.** Mr. Hyde

995. Which former Spider-Man enemy joined the Avengers?
- **A.** Sandman
- **B.** Electro
- **C.** Boomerang
- **D.** The Puma

996. Who was the Avengers' first government liaison?
- **A.** Nick Fury
- **B.** Derek Freeman
- **C.** Raymond Sikorski
- **D.** Henry Peter Gyrich

997. Who is Adam Austin?
- **A.** Texas Twister
- **B.** Phantom Rider
- **C.** Inker on *The Avengers*
- **D.** Alias initially used by artist Gene Colan on *Iron Man*

998. Which New Warriors joined the Avengers?
- **A.** Night Thrasher and Firestar
- **B.** Firestar and Justice
- **C.** Justice and Namorita
- **D.** Namorita and Night Thrasher

999. Who framed Iron Man for killing the Carnelian ambassador?
- **A.** The Mandarin
- **B.** Mordecai Midas
- **C.** Obadiah Stane
- **D.** Justin Hammer

1000. Why did Tony Stark fight the Armor Wars?
- **A.** To prove his armor's superiority to other battle-suits
- **B.** To destroy battle-suits based on his stolen designs
- **C.** To destroy stolen suits of his own armor
- **D.** As a mission for the U.S. government

1001. What was Thor's civilian profession when he had his secret identity of Sigurd Jarlson?
- **A.** Paramedic
- **B.** Architect
- **C.** Surgeon
- **D.** Construction worker

1002. Which dragon did Thor battle and slay in *Thor* #341–343 (1984)?
- **A.** Fin Fang Foom
- **B.** Fafnir of Nostrond
- **C.** The Midgard Serpent
- **D.** Fasolt

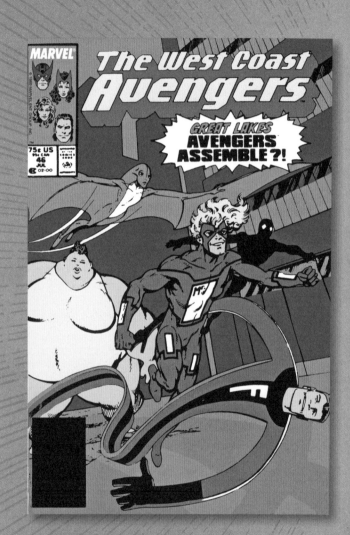

OBSESSED WITH MARVEL

1006.

In *West Coast Avengers* #46 (1989, shown at left), writer-artist John Byrne introduced the Great Lakes Avengers, a team of Super Hero wannabes who operated in the Midwest. On discovering that he could not be killed, mutant Craig Hollis became the crime fighter Mr. Immortal and placed a newspaper ad to recruit teammates. He soon recruited Big Bertha, Dinah Soar, Doorman, and Flatman, and they named themselves the Great Lakes Avengers.

However, they had failed to ask the permission of the real Avengers. But when West Coast Avengers Hawkeye and Mockingbird investigated, they ended up becoming the newbies' mentors. The Great Lakes Avengers eventually had to change their name, and have done so repeatedly over the years. They have also taken in new members, including Grasshopper and the infamous Squirrel Girl. Once they registered with the Initiative, they became the Great Lakes Initiative, based in Wisconsin.

Which name have the Great Lakes Avengers *not* used?

A. Lightning Rods
B. Great Lakes Champions
C. Great Lakes X-Men
D. Great Lakes Defenders

1003. Where did the Avengers regroup after Wakanda's destruction during *Avengers vs. X-Men*?
A. The Dark Dimension
B. The Blue Area of the Moon
C. K'un Lun
D. Attilan

1004. Which classic Avengers villain amplified his power by stealing the deceased Professor X's brain?
A. Kang
B. The Red Skull
C. Baron Zemo
D. Ultron

1005. What group of Avengers was also known as the Unity Squad?
A. Mighty Avengers
B. Secret Avengers
C. All-New, All-Different Avengers
D. Uncanny Avengers

1006.

1007. Who created Dimension Z, where Captain America was seemingly trapped for years?
A. Baron Zemo
B. Arnim Zola
C. Zuras
D. The Zodiac

1008. Which Captain America did *not* play a major role *in Avengers: Standoff*?
A. Steve Rogers
B. Sam Wilson
C. Bucky Barnes
D. John Walker

1009. During which Marvel event series did Thor lose the ability to lift Mjolnir?
A. *Fear Itself*
B. *AXIS*
C. *Original Sin*
D. *Civil War II*

1010. What underground Super Villain nation was first introduced in *Secret Avengers*?
A. Madripoor
B. Bagalia
C. Latveria
D. Symkaria

1011. Where did the Uncanny Avengers have their headquarters in their 2015 series?
A. Avengers Island
B. Avengers Mansion
C. The Triskelion
D. The Schaefer Theater

1012. Which villain trapped several young Avengers on an island and forced them to fight to the death?
A. Arcade
B. Baron Zemo
C. Enchantress
D. Grandmaster

The Avengers

1013. During *Fear Itself*, what powerful weapons were wielded by The Worthy?
- **A.** Asgardian Hammers
- **B.** Infinity Gems
- **C.** Replusor Cannons
- **D.** Vibranium Shields

1014. Which member of Avengers Academy was *not* abducted as part of the *Avengers Arena* series?
- **A.** Hazmat
- **B.** Mettle
- **C.** Reptil
- **D.** Striker

1015. What did all of the members of A-Force have in common?
- **A.** All mutants
- **B.** All women
- **C.** All Inhumans
- **D.** All teenagers

1016. Which Avenger returned from the dead during *Avengers: The Children's Crusade*?
- **A.** Scarlet Witch
- **B.** Thunderstrike
- **C.** The Wasp
- **D.** Ant-Man (Scott Lang)

1017. Which classic Avenger did *not* star in the *Avengers Prime* limited series (2010)?
- **A.** Captain America
- **B.** The Hulk
- **C.** Thor
- **D.** Iron Man

1018. During the *Original Sin* crossover, whom did Angela discover to be her father?
- **A.** Thor
- **B.** Loki
- **C.** Surtur
- **D.** Odin

1019. The young heroes from *Avengers Arena* continued their story in which series?
- **A.** *Avengers Undercover*
- **B.** *Avengers Unplugged*
- **C.** *Avengers Assemble*
- **D.** *A-Force*

1020. Who is Kamala Khan?
- **A.** Captain Marvel
- **B.** Marvel Girl
- **C.** Ms. Marvel
- **D.** Ms. America

1021. What is the real name of the new Falcon?
- **A.** Dennis Dunphy
- **B.** Joaquin Torres
- **C.** Kamala Khan
- **D.** Sam Alexander

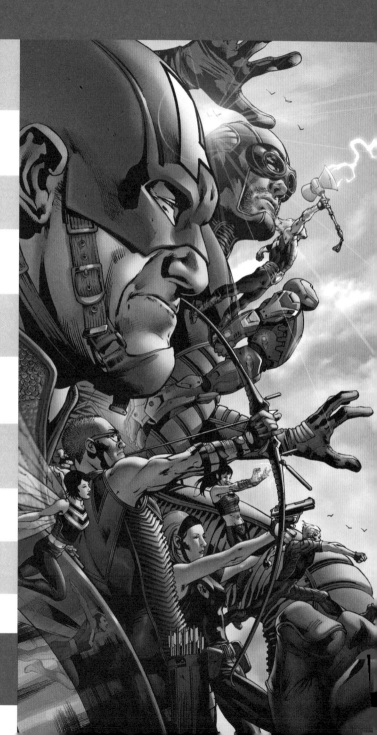

OBSESSED WITH MARVEL

1022. Who is Jormungand?

A. The Midgard Serpent

B. An immense wolf

C. The dwarf who forged Thor's hammer

D. One of the Frost Giants

1023.

In 2000, Marvel launched its *Ultimate* line of comics, presenting an alternative version of its classic heroes, starting their stories over from the beginning. *The Ultimates* (shown at left), created by writer Mark Millar and artist Bryan Hitch, is the Ultimate Universe's version of *The Avengers*. In the classic continuity, the founding members of the Avengers banded together on their own, whereas in *The Ultimates*, it is General Nick Fury of S.H.I.E.L.D. who organized the team. They were headquartered on S.H.I.E.L.D.'s high-tech base, supported by military troops and black-ops agents. As before, the founding members were Thor, Iron Man, Henry Pym and the Wasp, the Hulk, and Captain America. Soon they were joined by intelligence agents Hawkeye and the Black Widow and former terrorists Quicksilver and the Scarlet Witch. In time the Ultimates decided to operate independently of the government, and were instead financed by Tony Stark—just as the original Avengers were. Who was the Ultimates' Director of Communications?

A. Edwin Jarvis

B. Pepper Potts

C. Rick Jones

D. Betty Ross

1024. Who originally led the Serpent Society?

A. The original Viper

B. Sidewinder

C. King Cobra

D. The second Viper

1025. Which Golden Age villain did *not* appear in *Captain America* #112 (1969)?

A. Asbestos Man

B. The Plundering Butterfly

C. The Ringmaster of Death

D. The Unholy Legion of Beggars

1026. To which branch of the Armed Services did James Rhodes belong?

A. Army

B. Navy

C. Air Force

D. Marines

1027. Who was *not* a member of the Red Skull's Skeleton Crew?

A. Crossbones

B. The Man with the Voice of Doom

C. Flag-Smasher

D. Machinesmith

1028. Who was *not* one of the original Captain America's protégés?

A. Free Spirit

B. Jack Flag

C. Battle Star

D. Demolition-Man

1029. Who was Django Maximoff?

A. Quicksilver and the Scarlet Witch's foster father

B. Mr. Doll

C. The Spymaster

D. Quicksilver and the Scarlet Witch's father

1030. From which Super Villain did Count Nefaria *not* steal his super-powers?

A. Living Laser

B. Graviton

C. Power Man

D. Whirlwind

The Avengers

1031. Which Super Hero team debuted in *Thor* #411 (1989)?

A. Earth Force
B. The Young Gods
C. Avengers-Next
D. The New Warriors

1032. Which villains were *not* killed by Scourge?

A. Cyclone and the Melter
B. Turner D. Century and the Soviet Red Skull
C. The Porcupine and the original Eel
D. Letha and the Vamp

1033. Which Golden Age hero was the mastermind behind Scourge's assassinations of Super Villains?

A. The Destroyer
B. The original Angel
C. Father Time
D. The original Black Widow

1034. Who was the original Crimson Cowl?

A. Ultron
B. Justine Hammer
C. Edwin Jarvis
D. Dallas Riordan

1035. What was the true identity of the all-powerful being called Michael who battled the Avengers?

A. The Molecule Man
B. Leonard Tippit
C. Michael Korvac, cyborg from the future
D. The Beyonder

1036. Who was the father of Michael's girlfriend, Carina Walters?

A. Morris Walters
B. The Stranger
C. The Watcher
D. The Collector

1037. Who was *not* one of the Exiles allied with the Red Skull in *Captain America* #102–104 (1968)?

A. Cadavus
B. Arnim Zola
C. Iron-Hand Hauptmann
D. General Ching

1038. Who was the Terminatrix?

A. Nebula
B. Princess Ravonna
C. Titania
D. Stellaris

1039.

1039.

One of the most unlikely couples in the history of Marvel Comics was the Vision and the Scarlet Witch, both longtime members of the Avengers. The Vision was a "synthezoid," an android with various super-powers, including the ability to alter his body's density to become intangible or diamond-hard. The sinister robot Ultron created the Vision, intending to use him as a weapon against the Avengers, but the Vision joined the team instead.

Wanda Maximoff, the Scarlet Witch, had the mutant "hex" power to manipulate probability as well as a talent for wielding "chaos magic." The outwardly emotionless android fell in love with the mutant Witch, they married, and, through magic, even had children (or so it seemed). Their married life was chronicled in two separate limited series called *Vision and the Scarlet Witch* (issue 1 shown at right), but subsequent writers ended the marriage and even revealed the children to be demonic entities.

Where did the title characters live in the *Vision and the Scarlet Witch*?

A. Leonia, New Jersey
B. Cresskill, New Jersey
C. Stamford, Connecticut
D. Cambridge, Massachusetts

1031D 1032C 1033B 1034A 1035C 1036D 1037B 1038B 1039A

1040. Who was *not* a member of the team Heavy Metal?

    A. Super-Adaptoid

    B. TESS-One

    C. Kree Sentry 459

    D. Ultron

1041. Who or what is Kubik?

    A. The Beyonder in a new form

    B. The Molecule Man in a new form

    C. The Cosmic Cube evolved into a sentient humanoid being

    D. The Shaper of Worlds

1042. Which heroes have *never* (as of 2016) been members of the Avengers?

    A. Mister Fantastic and the Invisible Woman

    B. Cyclops and Phoenix

    C. The Sub-Mariner and the Black Panther

    D. Jack of Hearts and Triathlon

1043. Who was Tony Stark's boyhood sweetheart?

    A. Janice Cord

    B. Meredith McCall

    C. Marianne Rodgers

    D. Pepper Potts

1044. Who aided Captain America in thwarting Mr. Hyde's attempt to destroy Manhattan in *Captain America* #251–252 (1980)?

    A. The Cobra

    B. Daredevil

    C. The Falcon

    D. Batroc the Leaper

1045. Which Super Villain did Jarvis once feel forced to serve?

    A. Ultron

    B. The Grim Reaper

    C. Graviton

    D. Baron Helmut Zemo

1046. Who is Victor Timely?

    A. Alias for the original Human Torch

    B. Head of Operation: Rebirth

    C. Kang in his 1901 identity

    D. Original publisher of the *Daily Bugle*

1047. When did Spider-Man first join the Avengers?

    A. *The Amazing Spider-Man Special* #3 (1966)

    B. *The Avengers* #329 (1991)

    C. *The Avengers* #235 (1983)

    D. *New Avengers* #3 (2005)

The Avengers

1048. Who is Kang's ancestor and namesake?

A. Unknown
B. Victor von Doom
C. Reed Richards
D. Nathaniel Richards

1049. Who was Utgard-Loki?

A. Loki's true father
B. King of the Frost Giants
C. Loki's son
D. King of the Storm Giants

1050.

1051. Who was Tony Stark's longtime girlfriend?

A. Clytemnestra Erwin
B. Ling MacPherson
C. Bethany Cabe
D. Marcy Pearson

1052. Who once shot Tony Stark in the spine, paralyzing him?

A. Kathy Dare
B. Sunset Bain
C. Madame Masque
D. Clytemnestra Erwin

1053. Who is Red Norvell?

A. Co-worker of Sigurd Jarlson (Thor)
B. Mortal who became a red-haired version of Thor
C. Head of security at Stark Industries
D. Bloodaxe the Executioner

1054. Who is Harris Hobbs?

A. Tony Stark's communications director
B. Steve Rogers's boyhood friend
C. Television reporter who filmed a documentary on Asgard
D. U.S. Senator who investigated Tony Stark

1055. Where did the talking frogs that Thor met live?

A. The Everglades
B. The Bronx Zoo
C. The New York subway tunnels
D. Central Park

1056. Who were the Death Throws?

A. Team of assassins
B. Criminal team of jugglers
C. Performers in the Circus of Crime
D. Rick Jones's rock band

1050.

Next to Stan Lee and Jack Kirby's original collaboration on the series, perhaps the most brilliantly creative period on *Thor* consisted of writer-artist Walter Simonson's stories in the 1980s. With his first issue, *Thor* #337 (1983, shown at right), Simonson shook up the status quo by revealing that another person was worthy of wielding the magical hammer of Thor. Thus it was that Beta Ray Bill, a cyborg warrior champion of an alien race, gained the powers of Thor, while the real Thor's alter ego, Dr. Don Blake, was seemingly left helpless on Earth.

In time, Thor regained his godly persona and hammer, and he and Beta Ray Bill became allies. But Simonson had surprises in store for readers: Thor would abandon his mortal Don Blake form and adopt a new secret identity; there was a climactic battle between Thor's father, Odin, and Surtur the fire demon; and Thor's brother, Loki, even temporarily transformed Thor into a talking animal! What animal did Loki turn Thor into?

A. A frog
B. A goat
C. A mouse
D. A horse

1048D 1049B 1050A 1051C 1052A 1053B 1054C 1055D 1056B

1057. Who is *not* a member of the most recent Champions team?
- **A.** Viv Vision
- **B.** Cyclops
- **C.** Ghost Rider
- **D.** The Hulk

1058. Which Secret Avenger was killed and replaced by an evil robotic duplicate?
- **A.** Captain Britain
- **B.** Hawkeye
- **C.** Ant-Man (Eric O'Grady)
- **D.** Valkyrie

1059. Bucky Barnes, the Winter Soldier, inherited what important title after *Original Sin*?
- **A.** Sorcerer Supreme
- **B.** Director of S.H.I.E.L.D.
- **C.** The Man on the Wall
- **D.** Captain America

1060. Tony Stark's actual birth mother, Amanda Armstrong, was revealed to have what profession?
- **A.** Musician
- **B.** Hydra Agent
- **C.** Engineer
- **D.** Professor

1061. In *Avengers: Standoff*, Steve Rogers was returned to his youthful state by what powerful artifact?
- **A.** A sentient Cosmic Cube
- **B.** The Time Gem
- **C.** The Darkhold
- **D.** The Serpent Crown

1062. Who served as the leader of the Thunderbolts in their 2016 series?
- **A.** Baron Zemo
- **B.** Moonstone
- **C.** Luke Cage
- **D.** Winter Soldier

1063. Who originally masqueraded as both Spider Hero and Ronin in the pages of *Mighty Avengers*?
- **A.** Blue Marvel
- **B.** Spectrum
- **C.** Power Man
- **D.** Blade

The Avengers

1064. What physical handicap has Hawkeye experienced?
- **A.** Partial deafness
- **B.** Partial blindness
- **C.** Paralyzed arm
- **D.** None of these

1065. Which alien race created the Mandarin's rings?
- **A.** The Cotati
- **B.** Sneepers
- **C.** Prosilicans
- **D.** Makluans

1066. Who was *not* a member of Force Works?
- **A.** Iron Man
- **B.** Spider-Woman II (Julia Carpenter)
- **C.** The Vision
- **D.** The Scarlet Witch

1067. Who is Sabreclaw?
- **A.** Wolverine's son in *Avengers-Next*
- **B.** Wolverine's son in the *Dark Avengers*
- **C.** Sabretooth's son in *Avengers-Next*
- **D.** Brother of Avengers reservist Silverclaw

1068. Who is *not* a member of Code: Blue?
- **A.** Fireworks Fielstein
- **B.** Mother Majowski
- **C.** Mad Dog Rassitano
- **D.** Thug Thatcher

1069. Who is Thor Girl?
- **A.** A member of the Young Avengers
- **B.** Jane Foster's name in a *What If?* story in which she became a goddess
- **C.** Tarene, The Designate
- **D.** Thor's daughter Thena in *Avengers-Next*

1070. Who is Dargo Ktor?
- **A.** Thor of the twenty-second century AD
- **B.** Thor of the twenty-sixth century AD
- **C.** Thor's counterpart in an extraterrestrial race
- **D.** Beta Ray Bill's real name

1071. Who has *not* been one of Captain America's girlfriends?
- **A.** Sally Floyd
- **B.** Betsy Ross
- **C.** Rachel Leighton
- **D.** Bernadette Rosenthal

1072. Who is *not* a member of Earth Force?
- **A.** Earth-Lord
- **B.** Skyhawk
- **C.** Water Wizard
- **D.** Wind Warrior

1073.

Inspired by the great Marvel comics of the 1960s, a new generation of writers and artists came to Marvel in the late 1960s and early 1970s. The first major writer in this new wave of talent was Roy Thomas, who followed Stan Lee on *The Avengers*, *The X-Men*, *Daredevil*, and *Doctor Strange*. When Stan Lee became publisher in 1972, it was Roy Thomas who succeeded him as editor in chief. Thomas saw the great potential in the characters and concepts that Lee and his artists had created and took them still further. One of Thomas's great triumphs was the Kree-Skrull War in *The Avengers* #89–97 (1971–1972), pitting the two great galactic empires that Stan Lee and Jack Kirby had created against each other. This epic saga included the Avengers' founding members Captain America, Iron Man, and Thor; Captain Marvel; Nick Fury; the Inhumans; and even, in the concluding issue, doppelgangers of Super Heroes from Marvel's Golden Age of the 1940s.

Which Golden Age hero did not appear in *The Avengers* #97 (1972, shown at left)?

- **A.** The original Angel
- **B.** The Fin
- **C.** The original Vision
- **D.** Major Liberty

1074. How did Asgard's rule of Earth come to an end during the "Reigning" storyline?
- **A.** Revolution by the people of Earth
- **B.** Time was altered so the conquest never took place
- **C.** The Asgardians overthrew Thor
- **D.** Thor led the Asgardians from Earth back to Asgard

1075. Who is ultimately responsible for decreeing that Asgard must undergo Ragnarok?
- **A.** The pantheons of Earth's gods
- **B.** The Norns
- **C.** The Celestials
- **D.** Those Who Sit Above in Shadow

1076. Who was *not* a member of the Mad Thinker's Triumvirate of Terror in *The Avengers* #39 (1967)?
- **A.** Hammerhead I
- **B.** Bulldozer
- **C.** Piledriver I
- **D.** Thunderboot

1077. What were the names of the Vision and Scarlet Witch's "children"?
- **A.** Thomas and William
- **B.** William and Steven
- **C.** Steven and Richard
- **D.** Richard and Thomas

1078. What were the Vision and Scarlet Witch's children revealed to be?
- **A.** Illusions created by the Scarlet Witch
- **B.** Demons conjured by Master Pandemonium
- **C.** Spirits summoned by Agatha Harkness
- **D.** Portions of the demon Mephisto

The Avengers

1079. Who was allied with the Credit Card Soldiers in *Thor*?
- **A.** Kronin Krask
- **B.** The Thermal Man
- **C.** Titanium Man
- **D.** General Sam Sawyer

1080. What happened to Captain America in *Captain America* #405 (1992)?
- **A.** Went into suspended animation again
- **B.** Transformed into a werewolf
- **C.** Aged to his actual chronological age
- **D.** Transformed into a vampire

1081. What was Eric Masterson's profession?
- **A.** Construction worker
- **B.** Paramedic
- **C.** Doctor
- **D.** Architect

1082. Where did the Wrecking Crew battle Thor in *Thor* #304 (1981)?
- **A.** Times Square
- **B.** Rockefeller Center
- **C.** Lincoln Center for the Performing Arts
- **D.** The United Nations complex

1083. Which legendary figures did Captain America *not* encounter in *Captain America* #383 (1991)?
- **A.** Davy Crockett and Daniel Boone
- **B.** John Henry and Paul Bunyan
- **C.** Johnny Appleseed and Pecos Bill
- **D.** Uncle Sam and Father Time

1084. Who were the parents of the Young Avenger Hulkling?
- **A.** Bruce and Betty Banner
- **B.** Captain Mar-Vell and Princess Anelle
- **C.** Jennifer Walters and Wyatt Wingfoot
- **D.** The Super-Skrull and Princess Anelle

1085. In which of Thor's identities did he fall in love with Brunnhilda the Valkyrie?
- **A.** Siegmund
- **B.** Don Blake
- **C.** Siegfried
- **D.** Thor

OBSESSED WITH MARVEL

1090.

As soon as Steve Rogers was transformed by the Super-Soldier serum into Captain America, a Nazi agent shot and killed the scientist who had created the formula. With his death, the formula was lost. According to the 2003 limited series *The Truth: Red, White, and Black* (shown at left), written by Robert Morales and illustrated by Kyle Baker, the U.S. government secretly experimented on African American soldiers in an attempt to recreate the Super-Soldier serum. Only five of them survived. One of them, Isaiah Bradley, dressed as Captain America when he went on a suicide mission to destroy the Nazis' own Super-Soldier serum program. Bradley survived, although the imperfect formula used on him eventually damaged his mind and body. Not until 2003 did Steve Rogers learn about the "black Captain America," who had already become a legend among African Americans in the Marvel Universe.

Which contemporary Super Hero is related to Isaiah Bradley?

A. Luke Cage
B. Patriot (Young Avengers)
C. Night Thrasher
D. Triathlon

1086. Who was *not* one of the Enchanters?
    A. Forsung   **C.** Brona
    B. Magnir   **D.** Tiwaz

1087. Who is Ebeneezer Wallaby in *The Avengers* #43 (1967)?
    A. A representative of the U.S. State Department   **C.** A butler who substitutes for Jarvis
    B. Janet Van Dyne's attorney   **D.** Henry Pym's new assistant

1088. Which historical figure was *not* a member of the Hangman's Lethal Legion in *Avengers West Coast* #98–100 (1993)?
    A. Adolf Hitler   **C.** Lucrezia Borgia
    B. Joseph Stalin   **D.** Lizzie Borden

1089. Which Spider-Man adversary first returned in *Captain America* #246 (1980)?
    A. The Meteor Man   **C.** Joe Smith
    B. The Living Brain   **D.** Professor Mendel Stromm

1090.

1091. Who is Virginia Dare?
    A. The secret identity of Mockingbird   **C.** Captain America's costumed protégée Free Spirit
    B. Tony Stark's bodyguard and girlfriend   **D.** The young woman whom Captain America protects in *Marvel 1602*

1092. Which political party asked Captain America to run for President in *Captain America* #250 (1980)?
    A. The Democratic Party   **C.** The Republican Party
    B. The New Populist Party   **D.** The All-Night Party

The Avengers

CHAPTER FOUR:
X-MEN

1093. Which Marvel hero debuted in *The X-Men* #10 (1965)?
- **A.** The Mimic
- **B.** Quicksilver
- **C.** The Scarlet Witch
- **D.** Ka-Zar

1094. Who created the Sentinels?
- **A.** Dr. Steven Lang
- **B.** Judge Chalmers
- **C.** Dr. Bolivar Trask
- **D.** Larry Trask

1095. To whom was Charles Xavier once engaged?
- **A.** Gabrielle Haller
- **B.** Emma Frost
- **C.** Raven Darkholme
- **D.** Moira MacTaggert

1096. How did the Juggernaut get his powers?
- **A.** From a magic ruby
- **B.** Mutation
- **C.** Genetic engineering
- **D.** From a magic spell

1097. Who or what is Zabu?
- **A.** A Warskrull
- **B.** One of the Morlocks
- **C.** A saber-toothed tiger
- **D.** Member of a Savage Land tribe

1098. Who was *not* an original member of the first Brotherhood of Evil Mutants?
- **A.** The Toad
- **B.** The Blob
- **C.** The Scarlet Witch
- **D.** Mastermind

1099. What is the Master Mold?
- **A.** An enormous mutant fungus
- **B.** A master roboticist
- **C.** Magneto's device for creating artificial mutants
- **D.** An enormous Sentinel

1100. Who is one of Cyclops's brothers?
- **A.** Havok
- **B.** Corsair
- **C.** The Angel
- **D.** Erik the Red

1101. Who was Lilandra?
- **A.** Princess of a Savage Land tribe
- **B.** A Brood Queen
- **C.** Real name of Deathbird
- **D.** Empress of the Shi'ar

1102.

1103. Near which town is Professor Xavier's school located?
- **A.** Fairfield, Connecticut
- **B.** Scarsdale, New York
- **C.** Salem Center, New York
- **D.** White Plains, New York

1104. Whom did Storm marry?
- **A.** Forge
- **B.** Black Panther
- **C.** Arkon the Imperion
- **D.** No one

1105. Who was Jason Wyngarde?
- **A.** Mastermind
- **B.** The Black King
- **C.** Mister Sinister
- **D.** Gambit

1106. Who is Proteus?
- **A.** A living island
- **B.** Member of the Imperial Guard
- **C.** Mutant son of Moira MacTaggert
- **D.** Mutant son of Charles Xavier

1107. Off which coast is Muir Isle?
- **A.** Wales
- **B.** Long Island
- **C.** Maine
- **D.** Scotland

1108. Where was Magneto imprisoned as a boy?
- **A.** Auschwitz
- **B.** Dachau
- **C.** Buchenwald
- **D.** Birkenau

1109. What makes Wolverine's bones unbreakable?
- **A.** Organic steel
- **B.** Adamantium
- **C.** Mutation that affects his skeleton
- **D.** Force field

OBSESSED WITH MARVEL

1102.

Created by Stan Lee and Jack Kirby, the original *The X-Men* #1, published in 1963, opens at Professor Xavier's School for Gifted Youngsters. Charles Xavier (shown at right), known as Professor X, is confined to a wheelchair, but he has immense telepathic powers. He calls his students the X-Men because, like himself, they are mutants, born with "x-tra" powers. Within the story, it's established that people fear and resent super-powered mutants, but Xavier has a dream that mutants and non-mutant humans can co-exist in peace.

His original students include Scott Summers, alias Cyclops, who projects force beams from his eyes; Jean Grey, aka Marvel Girl, who has telekinetic abilities; Warren Worthington, the winged Angel; Henry McCoy, the Beast, who has apelike agility; and Bobby Drake, alias Iceman, who generates intense cold.

Xavier's goal is to teach his teenage students how to control their newly emerged powers and to direct them in using those powers to combat evil mutants, like their archfoe Magneto, who debuts in the first issue.

Who among the initial five students joins the X-Men in the original *The X-Men* #1?

- **A.** Scott Summers
- **B.** Jean Grey
- **C.** Bobby Drake
- **D.** Warren Worthington

1110. Which form of music was the mutant Dazzler's original specialty?
- **A.** New Wave
- **B.** Classic Rock
- **C.** Disco
- **D.** Heavy Metal

1111. To whom is Black Tom Cassidy related?
- **A.** Siryn
- **B.** The Banshee
- **C.** Both A and B
- **D.** The Juggernaut

1112. Who is Charles Xavier's step-brother?
- **A.** The Juggernaut
- **B.** Magneto
- **C.** Mister Sinister
- **D.** Lucifer

1113. Who found the feral Wolverine in the Canadian wilderness?
- **A.** Charles Xavier
- **B.** James and Heather Hudson
- **C.** Weapon X Project operatives
- **D.** Professor X and Cyclops

1114. Which future version of an X-Man went back in time in "Days of Future Past" in *The Uncanny X-Men* #141–142 (1981)?
- **A.** Wolverine
- **B.** Ororo Munroe
- **C.** Rachel Summers
- **D.** Kate Pryde

1115. Which classic comics artist collaborated with Roy Thomas on *The X-Men* #56–63 and #65 (1969–1970)?
- **A.** Werner Roth
- **B.** Don Heck
- **C.** Neal Adams
- **D.** Jim Steranko

1116. Where did Cain Marko first become the Juggernaut?
- **A.** Korea
- **B.** Vietnam
- **C.** Cambodia
- **D.** China

1117. What does Sauron resemble?
- **A.** A crocodile
- **B.** A pterodactyl
- **C.** A velociraptor
- **D.** A tyrannosaur

X-Men

1118. Which name was *not* used by the mutant Tabitha Smith?
A. Boom Boom
B. Boomer
C. General Meltdown
D. Meltdown

1119. Who is Ka-Zar's criminal brother?
A. The Mandrill
B. The Plunderer
C. Captain Barracuda
D. Kraven the Hunter

1120. Whom did Ka-Zar marry?
A. Shanna the She-Devil
B. Zaladane
C. Ororo
D. Calypso

1121.

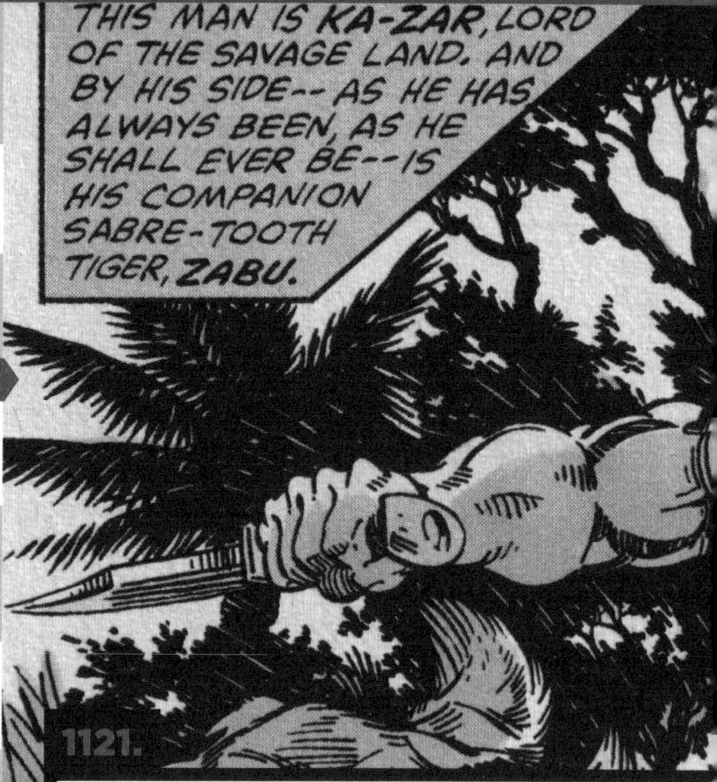

1122. Who was Black Tom Cassidy's partner in crime?
A. The Juggernaut
B. The Banshee
C. Warhawk
D. Mesmero

1123. Who were Generation X's teachers?
A. Charles Xavier and Moira MacTaggert
B. Banshee and White Queen
C. Charles Xavier and Emma Frost
D. Scott Summers and Jean Grey

1124. Who caused Charles Xavier to lose the use of his legs?
A. The Juggernaut
B. Lucifer
C. The Shadow King
D. Both B and C

1125. Which mystical entity empowered the Juggernaut?
A. Margali of the Winding Way
B. Xorak the Outcast
C. Cyttorak
D. Kukulcan

1126. Who is Dr. Karl Lykos?
A. Dominus
B. The Cobalt Man
C. Sauron
D. The Mimic's father

THIS MAN IS KA-ZAR, LORD OF THE SAVAGE LAND. AND BY HIS SIDE-- AS HE HAS ALWAYS BEEN, AS HE SHALL EVER BE-- IS HIS COMPANION SABRE-TOOTH TIGER, ZABU.

1121.

Ka-Zar (shown above) is Marvel's contribution to the long fictional tradition of telling stories about "lords of the jungle." The original Ka-Zar first appeared in a prose story in the pulp magazine *Ka-Zar* #1, published in 1937 by Martin Goodman. When Goodman published his first comic book, *Marvel Comics* #1, in 1939, Ka-Zar appeared in comics form.

In *The X-Men* #10 in 1965, Stan Lee and Jack Kirby devised a new version of Ka-Zar: he was Lord Kevin Plunder, a British nobleman who had grown up as an orphan in the Savage Land, a tropical jungle where prehistoric animals,

1127. Who was the first evil mutant Charles Xavier met?

A. Amahl Farouk

B. Magneto

C. Apocalypse

D. Lucifer

1128. What happened in *The X-Men* #67–93 in the 1970s?

A. They featured stories by Len Wein about the "new" X-Men

B. There were reprint issues

C. They featured new stories by Roy Thomas about the original X-Men

D. There were no such issues

1129. Who finally defeated and captured Magneto in *The X-Men* #11 (1965)?

A. The Sentinels

B. The Stranger

C. The U.S. Army

D. The X-Men

1130. Who or what is Garokk the Petrified Man?

A. A mutant who has lived for centuries

B. A petrified caveman brought back to life

C. A sailor who gained immortality

D. A statue that was infused with life

1131. To whom was Mariko Yashida related?

A. Sunfire

B. The Silver Samurai

C. Sunpyre

D. All answers are correct

1132. Where did Storm work as a pickpocket as a child?

A. Cairo, Egypt

B. New York City

C. Wakanda

D. Nairobi, Kenya

1133. Who is Corsair of the Starjammers?

A. Scott Summers's brother Gabriel

B. D'Ken Neramani

C. Cyclops's father Christopher Summers

D. Davan Shakari

1134. Who was Cyclops's first wife?

A. Jean Grey

B. Madelyne Pryor

C. Emma Frost

D. Aleytis Forrester

including dinosaurs, still existed. Ka-Zar's loyal companion was a saber-toothed tiger, Zabu, who raised the boy to manhood.

After guest appearances in *The X-Men* and *Daredevil*, Ka-Zar won his own series in *Astonishing Tales*, and subsequently starred in his own comic books, notably the 1980s series *Ka-Zar the Savage* by writer Bruce Jones and artist Brent Anderson.

Where is the Savage Land?

A. Africa

B. Antarctica

C. South America

D. Australia

1135. Who or what is Lockheed?

A. A large super-powered dog

B. The name of the X-Men's jet

C. A member of the Acolytes

D. A small alien dragon

1136.

1137. What happened to Thunderbird in *The X-Men* #95 (1975)?

A. He died in an explosion

B. He quit the X-Men

C. He changed his name to Warpath

D. He was murdered by Count Nefaria

1138. Who did the "new" X-Men battle in *The X-Men* #100 (1976)?

A. Magneto

B. The Imperial Guard

C. The original X-Men

D. Sentinels resembling the original X-Men

1139. Which mutant hero comes from New Orleans?

A. Gambit

B. Rogue

C. Cannonball

D. Razorback

1140. Who was Candy Southern?

A. Henry McCoy's girlfriend

B. Warren Worthington's girlfriend

C. Bobby Drake's girlfriend

D. Scott Summers's girlfriend

1141. Which classic comics artist drew *The X-Men* #50 and #51 (1968)?

A. Jack Kirby

B. Don Heck

C. Werner Roth

D. Jim Steranko

1142. Who is *not* a member of the Starjammers?

A. Hepzibah

B. Raza

C. D'Ken

D. Ch'od

1143. Who was the "Professor X" who died in *The X-Men* #42 (1968)?

A. The Changeling

B. Cassandra Nova

C. The Mimic

D. A Warskrull

1144. Who became Cyclops's girlfriend after his estrangement from Jean Grey?

A. Ororo Munroe

B. Emma Frost

C. Madelyne Pryor

D. Aleytis Forrester

OBSESSED WITH MARVEL

1136.

Strange as it may seem, the original *The X-Men* of the 1960s was never a top-selling series and was canceled. In the 1970s, editor in chief Roy Thomas came up with the idea of a new international team of X-Men. Writer Len Wein and artist Dave Cockrum created the "new" X-Men, who debuted in *Giant-Size X-Men* #1 in 1975 (shown at right).

When most of the original X-Men were captured by Krakoa the Living Island, Charles Xavier and Cyclops recruited a new team of mutants to rescue them. Among them were the Banshee, an Irish mutant who created powerful sonic vibrations; Colossus, a Russian who could turn his body to "organic steel"; Nightcrawler, a German who looked like a demon and could teleport; Storm, an African woman who could control the weather; the super-strong American Indian Thunderbird; and a Canadian called Wolverine, whose bones and retractable claws were infused with unbreakable adamantium. This new team became the stars of the newly revived *The X-Men* comic.

What was Chris Claremont's first issue as *The X-Men* scripter?

A. *Giant-Size X-Men* #1 (1975)

B. *The X-Men* #94 (1975)

C. *The X-Men* #96 (1975)

D. *The X-Men* #95 (1975)

1145. What is the country of Sunfire's origin?
- **A.** Korea
- **B.** Vietnam
- **C.** Japan
- **D.** China

1146. When was Chris Claremont's original run as *X-Men* scripter?
- **A.** 1975–1989
- **B.** 1976–1990
- **C.** 1975–present
- **D.** 1975–1991

1147. What was Roy Thomas's first issue as *The X-Men* writer?
- **A.** #19 (1966)
- **B.** #20 (1966)
- **C.** #27 (1966)
- **D.** #55 (1969)

1148. Where in Manhattan is the Hellfire Club mansion located?
- **A.** Park Avenue
- **B.** Madison Avenue
- **C.** Fifth Avenue
- **D.** Gramercy Park

1149. Which name was *not* used by James MacDonald Hudson?
- **A.** Weapon X
- **B.** Guardian
- **C.** Weapon Alpha
- **D.** Vindicator

1150. Which member of the Hellfire Club's Inner Circle is *not* a mutant?
- **A.** Emma Frost
- **B.** Harry Leland
- **C.** Sebastian Shaw
- **D.** Donald Pierce

1151. Which hero did Scott Summers and Jean Grey raise in *The Adventures of Cyclops and Phoenix* (1994)?
- **A.** Legion
- **B.** X-Man
- **C.** Cable
- **D.** Rachel Summers

1152. What is Nightcrawler's last name?
- **A.** Strauss
- **B.** Liszt
- **C.** Schubert
- **D.** Wagner

1153. What does Apocalypse's name "En Sabah Nur" mean?
- **A.** The Mighty One
- **B.** The First One
- **C.** The Conqueror
- **D.** The Eternal One

X-Men

1154. What is Colossus's first name (in English)?
A. Alexander
C. Peter
B. Nicholas
D. Joseph

1155. Who is Cable's father?
A. Apocalypse
C. Charles Xavier
B. Cyclops
D. Wolverine

1156. Who brainwashed Jean Grey/Phoenix into becoming the Hellfire Club's Black Queen?
A. Sebastian Shaw
C. Mastermind
B. The White Queen
D. Mesmero

1157. Where did the Jean Grey version of Phoenix first appear?
A. *The X-Men* #100 (1976)
C. *The Uncanny X-Men* #134 (1980)
B. *The Uncanny X-Men* #129 (1980)
D. *The X-Men* #101 (1976)

1158. Which of the following was *not* a product of the Weapon X program?
A. John Wraith
C. Deadpool
B. Cable
D. Maverick

1159. Where did Phoenix commit suicide?
A. Central Park, Manhattan
C. The Blue Area of the Moon
B. Professor Xavier's estate
D. The Shi'ar Throneworld

1160. How did the Beast gain his furry form?
A. Exposure to radiation
C. Experiment by Dr. Carl Maddicks
B. Delayed mutation in reaching adulthood
D. Drank his own mutagenic serum

1161. How is Sabretooth related to Wolverine?
A. Former CIA partner
C. Father
B. Brother
D. Killed his father

OBSESSED WITH MARVEL

1167.

In 1975, Chris Claremont scripted the first issue of the newly revived *The X-Men* comic, and he wrote the series—which was eventually retitled *The Uncanny X-Men*—continuously into the start of the 1990s. With his skills in characterization and drama, Claremont molded *The X-Men* into a highly successful series. Along with artist Dave Cockrum, Claremont also created a new identity for Jean Grey, the Phoenix, who possessed vast cosmic powers. Claremont and artist/co-plotter John Byrne (who succeeded Cockrum) would later create "The Dark Phoenix Saga," in issues 129 through 138 (1980, issue 135 shown at left), which is considered one of the greatest epics in Super Hero comics.

The saga begins when an old enemy of the X-Men tampers with Jean Grey's mind, releasing the dark side of Jean Grey's personality. She becomes the insane Dark Phoenix, whose seemingly limitless power poses a threat to the universe. Though Jean regains her sanity, the X-Men must wage a trial by combat to prevent the alien Shi'ar from executing her. In the end, Jean saves the cosmos by tragically committing suicide to prevent herself from reverting to Dark Phoenix.

Who or what really was the Phoenix in *The Uncanny X-Men* #100–137 (1976–1980)?

A. Jean Grey
B. The Phoenix Force using a duplicate of Jean Grey's body and part of her psyche
C. The Phoenix Force inhabiting a duplicate of Jean Grey's body
D. Madelyne Pryor

1162. What did Mystique's Brotherhood become when they went to work for the government?
A. X-Factor   **C.** Liberty Legion
B. Freedom Force   **D.** S.H.I.E.L.D. Super Agents

1163. Who drew the first *Wolverine* comics series?
A. John Buscema   **C.** Dave Cockrum
B. John Byrne   **D.** Frank Miller

1164. Where is Madripoor located?
A. Off the west coast of Africa   **C.** Southeast Asia
B. South Pacific   **D.** Caribbean

1165. Who is Magik's brother?
A. Nightcrawler   **C.** Belasco
B. Doctor Strange   **D.** Colossus

1166. Which state did Cannonball come from?
A. Kentucky   **C.** West Virginia
B. Arkansas   **D.** South Carolina

1167.

1168. What does Jubilee call her energy powers?
A. Power bursts   **C.** Fireworks
B. Explosives   **D.** Sparklers

1169. What is Nathan Summers's middle name?
A. Christopher   **C.** Scott
B. Charles   **D.** Alexander

1170. Where did the Morlocks get their name?
A. A novel by Jules Verne   **C.** A novel by Robert Heinlein
B. A short story by H. P. Lovecraft   **D.** A novel by H. G. Wells

X-Men

1171. Who brought younger versions of the original five X-Men into the present day in *All-New X-Men*?

A. Cable **C.** Cyclops
B. Forge **D.** Beast

1172. The Extraordinary X-Men moved the Xavier Institute to which alternate dimension?

A. Limbo **C.** Dark Dimension
B. Weirdworld **D.** Otherworld

1173. Which X-Man was actually a teenage clone of Apocalypse?

A. Fantomex **C.** Genesis
B. Archangel **D.** Cable

1174.

1175. Which former New Mutant became a disciple of Doctor Strange?

A. Karma **C.** Magik
B. Mirage **D.** Warlock

1176. Which mutant hero was never a member of the Uncanny Avengers?

A. Havok **C.** Sunfire
B. Cyclops **D.** Cable

1177. Which All-New X-Man was physically transformed by the Black Vortex?

A. Beast **C.** Cyclops
B. Iceman **D.** Angel

1178. Which alien race abducted young Jean Grey during 2014's "Trial of Jean Grey" storyline?

A. Kree **C.** Shi'ar
B. Skrull **D.** Chitauri

1179. The Extraordinary X-Men moved their base to another dimension to avoid what imminent threat?

A. Humans **C.** Apocalypse
B. Sentinels **D.** Terrigen Mist

1180. Which mutant had a romantic relationship and a child with the Wasp in a future timeline?

A. Havok **C.** Wolverine
B. Quicksilver **D.** Beast

1174.

By far the most popular of the X-Men is the man known as Logan, alias Wolverine (shown at right), the short but deadly Canadian mutant who has starred in many of his own comic book series. His mutant powers include retractable bone claws that emerge from the backs of his hands; acute, animal-like senses; and the ability to heal quickly and completely from virtually any injury. The healing ability combined with the unbreakable adamantium that has been bonded to his skeleton makes Wolverine virtually unkillable.

Len Wein wrote and Herb Trimpe drew the story arc in which Wolverine debuted in *The Incredible Hulk* #180–182 (1974). Chris Claremont, Dave Cockrum, and John Byrne further developed the character in *The Uncanny X-Men*.

It was in the first Wolverine limited series (1982) that Claremont and Frank Miller truly defined the character's personality: a man who continually and heroically struggles to tame the beast within and his capacity for animalistic rage and violence—a quest in which he will never fully succeed.

Who wrote and drew the "Weapon X" story showing how Wolverine was infused with adamantium?

A. Paul Jenkins and Adam Kubert
B. Chris Claremont and John Byrne
C. Barry Windsor-Smith
D. Chris Claremont and Frank Miller

1171D 1172A 1173C 1174C 1175C 1176B 1177D 1178C 1179D 1180A

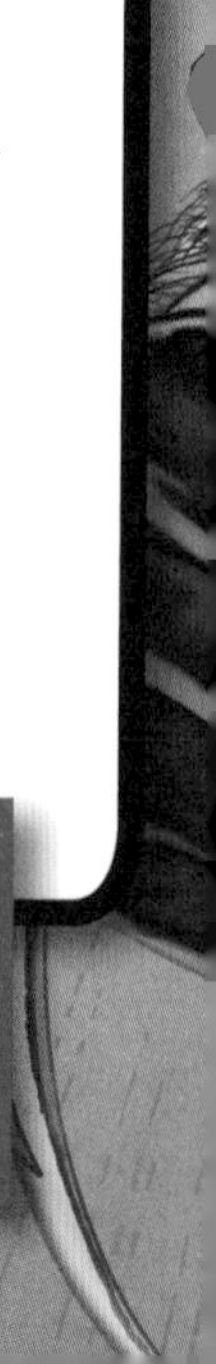

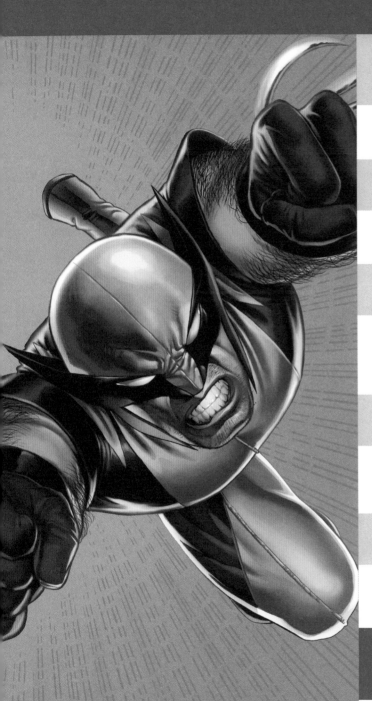

1181. Which of Wolverine's foes has *not* had Adamantium?
- **A.** Sabretooth
- **B.** Lady Deathstrike
- **C.** Roughouse
- **D.** Cyber

1182. Which alien race once turned Charles Xavier into one of them?
- **A.** The Shi'ar
- **B.** The Skrulls
- **C.** The Phalanx
- **D.** The Brood

1183. Which Super Hero's powers did Rogue absorb seemingly permanently?
- **A.** Captain Mar-Vell
- **B.** Ms. Marvel
- **C.** Spider-Woman I
- **D.** The Mimic

1184. Who is responsible for the Mutant Registration Act?
- **A.** Senator Robert Kelly
- **B.** Dr. Bolivar Trask
- **C.** Senator Harrington Byrd
- **D.** Graydon Creed

1185. Which member of the X-Men served as Apocalypse's Horseman Death?
- **A.** Gambit
- **B.** Archangel
- **C.** Wolverine
- **D.** All answers are correct

1186. Who killed Wolverine's ex-fiancée Mariko?
- **A.** Matsu'o Tsurayaba, who had her poisoned
- **B.** Wolverine because she was dying painfully from poison
- **C.** Reiko, who poisoned her
- **D.** Sabretooth, seeking revenge

1187. Who raised Rogue?
- **A.** Margali Szardos
- **B.** Charles Xavier
- **C.** Mystique
- **D.** Her mother, Priscilla

1188. Who is Akiko?
- **A.** A female Japanese ninja
- **B.** Sunpyre
- **C.** Daken's mother
- **D.** Japanese orphan under Wolverine's protection

1189. Who killed Scott Summers's mother?
- **A.** Apocalypse
- **B.** Magneto
- **C.** Mister Sinister
- **D.** Emperor D'Ken Neramani

X-Men

1190. Which alias has *not* been used by Kitty Pryde?

A. Ariel
B. Catseye
C. Sprite
D. Shadowcat

1191. Who was Madelyne Pryor?

A. Jean Grey's twin sister
B. Jean Grey under an alias
C. Duplicate of Jean Grey created by Phoenix Force
D. Jean Grey clone created by Mister Sinister

1192. Where did the X-Men first battle Alpha Flight?

A. Toronto, Ontario
B. Ottawa, Ontario
C. Calgary, Alberta
D. Montreal, Quebec

1193. Who succeeded James MacDonald Hudson as the Guardian?

A. Wolverine
B. Jerome Jaxon
C. Delphine Courtney
D. His wife Heather

1194. Who is Psylocke's sibling?

A. Brian Braddock
B. Revanche
C. Emma Frost
D. Jean Grey

1195.

1196. Which identity did Carol Danvers adopt after undergoing Brood experiments?

A. Ms. Marvel
B. Binary
C. Warbird
D. Phoenix

1197. Where is Genosha located?

A. Off the west coast of Africa
B. South Africa
C. The East Indies
D. Off the east coast of Africa

1198. What is the real first name of M in *Generation X*?

A. Monet
B. Massenet
C. Manet
D. Matisse

1195.

Born in the United Kingdom, writer-artist John Byrne grew up in Canada and did his early work for Marvel there, including *The Uncanny X-Men*, before moving to the United States. As a Canadian, Byrne took an interest in his countryman Wolverine and created an entire team of Canadian Super Heroes called Alpha Flight in *The Uncanny X-Men* #120–121 (1979). Byrne was the original writer and artist for Alpha Flight's own series, which debuted in 1983 (issue 1 shown at right).

The team was organized for the Canadian government and led by James MacDonald Hudson, alias Guardian, who had originally intended for Wolverine to lead Alpha Flight. But Wolverine had quit serving the Canadian government to join the X-Men.

Who was *not* a member of Alpha Flight when the team first appeared?

A. Shaman
B. Snowbird
C. Sasquatch
D. Puck

1190B 1191D 1192C 1193D 1194A 1195D 1196B 1197D 1198A

1199. Who drew the original *Longshot* miniseries?
- **A.** Bill Sienkiewicz
- **B.** John Romita Jr.
- **C.** Arthur Adams
- **D.** Walter Simonson

1200. Who is Longshot?
- **A.** A mutant with good-luck powers
- **B.** An alien humanoid from another planet
- **C.** Artificially created humanoid from another dimension
- **D.** A stunt man who gained super-powers

1201. Who is Deathbird?
- **A.** Lilandra's sister
- **B.** Lilandra's mother
- **C.** One of Apocalypse's Horsemen
- **D.** One of Count Nefaria's Ani-Men

1202. With which Earth creatures besides humans do the Shi'ar share physical attributes?
- **A.** Insects
- **B.** Cats
- **C.** Reptiles
- **D.** Birds

1203. Who ordered the Marauders to massacre the Morlocks?
- **A.** Apocalypse
- **B.** Mister Sinister
- **C.** Bastion
- **D.** Magneto

1204. Who is *not* one of the Marauders?
- **A.** Arclight
- **B.** Scalphunter
- **C.** Harpoon
- **D.** Warhawk

1205. Which member of the X-Men has an *M* tattooed on his or her face?
- **A.** Bishop
- **B.** Marrow
- **C.** Maggott
- **D.** Thunderbird III

1206. What is Bamf?
- **A.** A town in Canada
- **B.** One of the Warskrulls
- **C.** The sound Nightcrawler makes when teleporting
- **D.** One of the M'Kraan Crystal's guards

X-Men

1207. Which artist co-created *Excalibur* and created *Clandestine*?

A. Alan Davis
B. Dale Keown
C. John Cassaday
D. Bryan Hitch

1208. Where did Mystique work while in her Raven Darkholme identity?

A. S.H.I.E.L.D.
B. The State Department
C. The Pentagon
D. The White House

1209. Which member of the X-Men first appeared in "Days of Future Past"?

A. Kitty Pryde
B. Mystique
C. Emma Frost
D. Rachel Summers

1210.

1211. Which famed movie and TV writer collaborated on *Astonishing X-Men* with artist John Cassaday?

A. J. Michael Straczynski
B. Joss Whedon
C. Reginald Hudlin
D. Kevin Smith

1212. Who publicly exposed Charles Xavier as a mutant?

A. Bolivar Trask
B. William Stryker
C. Charles Xavier himself
D. Cassandra Nova, after taking possession of Xavier's body

1213. Who once forcibly removed the Adamantium from Wolverine's skeleton?

A. Magneto
B. Apocalypse
C. The Weapon X Project
D. Romulus

1214. In which series did Rogue debut?

A. *Ms. Marvel* (1977–1978)
B. *The X-Men Annual* (1970–present)
C. *The Avengers Annual* (1967–1994)
D. *The Uncanny X-Men* (1963–present)

1210.

Besides "The Dark Phoenix Saga," Chris Claremont and John Byrne's other great triumph in their collaboration on *The Uncanny X-Men* was "Days of Future Past" in issues #141 (shown at right) and #142 (1981).

The overall theme of X-Men has always been the battle against bigotry. Mutants serve as a metaphor for any group or individual who has been the object of prejudice. "Days of Future Past" presented an alternate future in which the mutant-hunting Sentinel robots have either exterminated mutants or confined them to prison camps. The spirit of the middle-aged mutant Kate Pryde travels back to the present, into the body of her teenage self, the X-Men's Kitty Pryde. She then joins the alternate future X-Men team in an attempt to change history by preventing the event that led to the dystopian future: the assassination of a U.S. Senator by Mystique's Brotherhood of Evil Mutants. Which member of Mystique's Brotherhood also served in Magneto's Brotherhood of Evil Mutants?

A. The Blob
B. Avalanche
C. Pyro
D. Mystique

1215. Whom did the young Charles Xavier and Magneto once fight in order to rescue Gabrielle Haller?

A. Amahl Farouk
B. Baron Strucker
C. Apocalypse
D. The Red Skull

1216. What is the Blackbird?

A. A member of X-Statix
B. A student at the Xavier Institute
C. A winged member of the Morlocks
D. The X-Men's jet

1217. Who deprived most of Earth's mutants of their super-powers?

A. Bastion
B. The Sentinels
C. The Scarlet Witch
D. The Stranger

1218. Which member of Alpha Flight was the Marvel Universe's first openly gay Super Hero?

A. Aurora
B. Northstar
C. Talisman
D. Box

1219. Where did Firestar first appear?

A. The "Spider-Man and His Amazing Friends" TV show
B. *Firestar* #1 (1986)
C. *The New Warriors* #1 (1990)
D. *The Uncanny X-Men* #193 (1985)

1220. What realms do the Exiles visit?

A. Other planets
B. Other countries
C. Other time periods
D. Alternate realities

1221. Which member of Alpha Flight has multiple personality disorder?

A. Sasquatch
B. Northstar
C. Aurora
D. Wild Child

1222. Whom did Marrina of Alpha Flight marry?

A. Sub-Mariner
B. Karthon the Quester
C. Puck
D. No one

X-Men

1223. Where did Charles Xavier and Magneto first meet?
- **A.** Egypt
- **B.** Genosha
- **C.** United States
- **D.** Israel

1224. Which state is Rogue from?
- **A.** Louisiana
- **B.** Mississippi
- **C.** Alabama
- **D.** Georgia

1225. Which member of the X-Men was once a hound who hunted other mutants?
- **A.** Bishop
- **B.** Gambit
- **C.** Rachel Summers
- **D.** Wolverine

1226. Who founded the X-Men in the Age of Apocalypse?
- **A.** Apocalypse
- **B.** Magneto
- **C.** Charles Xavier
- **D.** Cyclops

1227. What is Bishop's mutant power?
- **A.** Super-strength
- **B.** Time travel
- **C.** Generates energy blasts
- **D.** Absorbing and redirecting energy

1228. What does X.S.E. stand for?
- **A.** X-Men Superhuman Elite
- **B.** X-Men Security & Education
- **C.** Xavier School Enforcers
- **D.** Xavier Security Enforcers

1229. Who or what is Onslaught?
- **A.** A member of the Mutant Liberation Front
- **B.** The combination of the dark side of Xavier's psyche with Magneto's psyche
- **C.** One of the Dark Riders
- **D.** A highly advanced Sentinel

1230. Who is Sage?
- **A.** Tessa of the Hellfire Club
- **B.** Lilandra's prime minister
- **C.** Member of the Imperial Guard
- **D.** Leader of the Askani

OBSESSED WITH MARVEL

IT'S STILL HIS COUNTRY.

1233.

By the 1970s, Marvel Comics was producing comics for the United Kingdom, reprinting stories originally published in America. Marvel decided to create new material specifically for the British market; thus *Captain Britain Weekly* debuted with the cover date of October 13, 1976.

In his origin story, Brian Braddock is a physics student working at the Darkmoor Nuclear Research Center when it is attacked by a villain called the Reaver. Escaping on a motorcycle, Braddock suffers a near-fatal crash. The figures of Merlyn the Magician and Roma appear to him and ask him to choose between the mystic Amulet of Right and

1231. How does the Juggernaut resist psychic attacks?

A. He cannot

B. The spell of Cyttorak

C. His force field

D. His helmet

1232. What happened in the *X-Men* story arc "Inferno"?

A. The X-Men rescued Nightcrawler from a re-creation of hell

B. Magik and her allies fought Belasco in Limbo

C. Demons invaded Manhattan

D. The X-Men invaded the dimension of the N'Garai

1233.

1234. Which British-born writer wrote *Captain Britain* for Marvel UK in the early 1980s?

A. Alan Moore

B. Grant Morrison

C. Neil Gaiman

D. Chris Claremont

1235. What mutant power does Emma Frost have besides telepathy?

A. Telekinesis

B. Hyper smell sense

C. Astral projection

D. Able to make her body diamond-hard

1236. What is unusual about Chamber's appearance?

A. The left side of his body is scarred

B. The right side of his head is missing

C. The lower half of his face and part of his chest are missing

D. Half his body is organic metal

1237. Which artist co-created Gambit with writer Chris Claremont?

A. Jim Lee

B. Marc Silvestri

C. Paul Smith

D. John Romita Jr.

1238. What is Gambit's mutant power?

A. Has ability to alter probability

B. Charges objects with kinetic energy

C. Projects explosive force

D. Has psionic powers

the Sword of Might. Braddock chooses the Amulet and is transformed into the superhuman Captain Britain (shown above). Captain Britain later co-starred in the X-Men spin-off series *Excalibur*.

He was the British counterpart of Captain America, the Super Heroic champion of the United Kingdom. Who created Captain Britain for Marvel UK?

A. Chris Claremont and Alan Davis

B. Chris Claremont and Herb Trimpe

C. Stan Lee and John Buscema

D. Roy Thomas and Barry Windsor-Smith

X-Men

1239. Who infected the infant Cable with a techno-organic virus?
- **A.** The Phalanx
- **B.** Warlock
- **C.** Stryfe
- **D.** Apocalypse

1240. Whose guiding philosophy is "survival of the fittest"?
- **A.** Magneto
- **B.** Mister Sinister
- **C.** Apocalypse
- **D.** Wolverine

1241. What is the lens of Cyclops's visor made of?
- **A.** Adamantium-infused glass
- **B.** Ruby quartz
- **C.** Vibranium
- **D.** Unstable molecules

1242. Whom did Banshee once work for?
- **A.** Interpol
- **B.** FBI
- **C.** Irish Revolutionary Army
- **D.** Government of Ireland

1243. Who is James Howlett?
- **A.** Sabretooth
- **B.** Sasquatch
- **C.** Wild Child
- **D.** Wolverine

1244. In which series did Wolverine first appear?
- **A.** *Giant-Size X-Men*
- **B.** *Alpha Flight*
- **C.** *The Incredible Hulk*
- **D.** *The X-Men*

1245. What was Henry McCoy's claim to fame before he joined the X-Men as the Beast?
- **A.** A teenage scientific genius
- **B.** High school football star
- **C.** College football star
- **D.** A supposed freak with huge hands and feet

1246. Who is Victor Creed?
- **A.** Sabretooth
- **B.** Maverick
- **C.** Leader of the Friends of Humanity
- **D.** Minister who opposed mutants

1247. Where did Bobby Drake (Iceman) grow up before joining the X-Men?
- **A.** New Jersey
- **B.** Long Island, New York
- **C.** Westchester County, New York
- **D.** Connecticut

1248.

When Charles Xavier's original X-Men were introduced, they were all teenage students at his school. But the new X-Men introduced in the 1970s were mostly adults. In an attempt to recapture the original concept of the X-Men, writer Chris Claremont and artist Bob McLeod created *The New Mutants* in 1982, which started in one of Marvel's first graphic novels (shown at right) and would continue in their own monthly comic book.

Among Xavier's class of New Mutants were Sam Guthrie, aka Cannonball, who could shoot through the air; Karma, who could take mental possession of other people; the American Indian Dani Moonstar, alias Psyche, who could manifest images from other people's minds; Sunspot, who drew super-strength from solar energy; and the mutant werewolf called Wolfsbane. They were soon joined by Illyana Rasputin, the mutant sorceress called Magik; Magma, who controlled molten lava; and a strange alien entity known as Warlock.

What team did the original New Mutants later become?

- **A.** X-Terminators
- **B.** Team X
- **C.** X-Factor
- **D.** X-Force

1239D 1240C 1241B 1242A 1243D 1244C 1245B 1246A 1247B 1248D

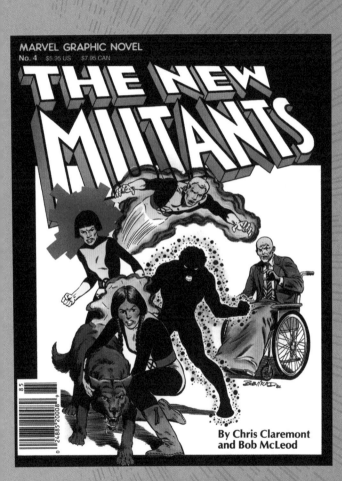

MARVEL GRAPHIC NOVEL
No. 4 $5.95 US $7.95 CAN

THE NEW MUTANTS

By Chris Claremont
and Bob McLeod

1249. Which character did Chris Claremont *not* co-create?
A. Sabretooth
C. Mystique
B. Longshot
D. Rogue

1250. What was Scott Summers's nickname in *The X-Men* #1 (1963)?
A. Specs
C. Slim
B. Scotty
D. None of these

1251. Which X-Men team member is subject to berserker rages?
A. Dark Phoenix
C. The Beast
B. Wolverine
D. Cable

1252. Which team did Angel and Iceman co-found right after leaving the X-Men?
A. X-Factor
C. Mutant Force
B. The Champions of Los Angeles
D. The Defenders

1253. Where did Magneto first battle the X-Men in *The X-Men* #1 (1963)?
A. Cape Citadel
C. Valhalla Mountain
B. Cape Canaveral
D. United Nations headquarters

1254. Who is Daken?
A. Wolverine's brother
C. Wolverine's son
B. Sabretooth's son
D. A clone of Wolverine

1255. Who is the father of the Fenris siblings?
A. Sabretooth
C. Baron Strucker
B. The Red Skull
D. Magneto

1256. Who is Telford Porter?
A. Avalanche
C. The Vanisher
B. Cypher
D. Pyro

X-Men

1257. How did Cyclops ultimately meet his end in the *Death of X* series?
- **A.** Killed by Black Bolt
- **B.** Infected by Terrigen Mist
- **C.** Terminated by Sentinels
- **D.** Assassinated by Wolverine

1258. Which of the original X-Men came out as gay?
- **A.** Jean Grey
- **B.** Beast
- **C.** Cyclops
- **D.** Iceman

1259. Old Man Logan comes from a future where the X-Men were killed by whom?
- **A.** Red Skull
- **B.** The Hulk
- **C.** Logan himself
- **D.** Sentinels

1260. *Uncanny X-Men* (2016) featured a strike force of the X-Men's most dangerous members led by whom?
- **A.** Mystique
- **B.** Magneto
- **C.** Deadpool
- **D.** Cable

1261. Which clawed mutant became the new Wolverine after Logan's death?
- **A.** X-23
- **B.** Sabretooth
- **C.** Lady Deathstrike
- **D.** Daken

1262. Who was *not* trained at the New Charles Xavier School for Mutants by Cyclops and Emma Frost?
- **A.** Goldballs
- **B.** Tempus
- **C.** Triage
- **D.** Genesis

1263. The mercenary called Fantomex had a tumultuous romantic relationship with which X-Man?
- **A.** Psylocke
- **B.** Storm
- **C.** Jean Grey
- **D.** Rogue

1266.

The man called Cable (shown at left) has perhaps the most complicated backstory of any Marvel hero. He first appeared as the infant Nathan Summers, the son of Scott Summers (Cyclops) and Madelyne Pryor. The baby was infected with a techno-organic virus that began transforming his body into organic metal.

In order to save him, a member of a sister-hood called the Clan Askani transported the baby into her far future time period. Half of his body was now like a machine, but he also possessed great telepathic and telekinetic abili-ties. Nathan grew up to become the Askani's son, the leader of the freedom fighters of his future era. But eventually he chose to travel to the X-Men's time to battle the near-immortal tyrant Apocalypse.

As Cable, he took over the New Mutants and reorganized them into the mutant strike force X-Force. Among its original members were Boom Boom, Cannonball, Feral, Shatterstar, and Warpath. Cable has since joined the X-Men and starred in various comics series of his own.

What relation does Cable have to his enemy Stryfe?

A. Stryfe is Cable's son
B. Stryfe is Cable's brother
C. Stryfe is Cable's clone
D. They have no relation

1264. Who is Fred J. Dukes?
A. Cannonball
B. Synch
C. The Blob
D. Tusk

1265. Who is Fred Duncan?
A. Micromax
B. Agent of Black Air
C. FBI liaison with Professor Xavier
D. National Public Radio reporter in *X-Men* stories

1266.

1267. What did Cable originally call his team of mercenaries?
A. Mutant Liberation Front
B. Wild Pack
C. Six Pack
D. Dark Riders

1268. Who first took over from Charles Xavier as headmaster of the New Mutants?
A. White Queen
B. Cable
C. Magneto
D. Moira MacTaggert

1269. How many issues did *The New Mutants* run before being replaced by *X-Force*?
A. 50
B. 75
C. 100
D. 150

1270. Which Latin American country did Magneto's Brotherhood take over in *The X-Men* #4 (1964)?
A. San Diablo
B. Santo Marco
C. San Gusto
D. Santo Rico

1271. Which X-Man is Nightcrawler's foster sister?
A. Rogue
B. Rogue and Daytripper
C. Nocturne
D. Daytripper

1272. What is Kitty Pryde's hometown in Illinois?
A. Chicago
B. Deerfield
C. Elgin
D. Springfield

X-Men

1273. Whose parents are John and Elaine?

    A. Bobby Drake   **C.** Jean Grey

    B. Scott Summers   **D.** Henry P. McCoy

1274. Who performed for the X-Men at the Coffee-a-Go-Go?

    A. The Dazzler   **C.** Rock musician Rick Jones

    B. Bernard the poet   **D.** Go-go dancer Mary Jane Watson

1275. Whom did Magneto attempt to recruit into the Brotherhood in *The X-Men* #6 (1964)?

    A. The Blob   **C.** Sub-Mariner

    B. Unus the Untouchable   **D.** Ka-Zar

1276. Who is Warlock of the New Mutants?

    A. The Maha Yogi   **C.** Adam Warlock

    B. A mutant sorcerer   **D.** A techno-organic alien

1277. Who collaborated with Jack Kirby on the art for *The X-Men* #12 (1965)?

    A. Werner Roth   **C.** Alex Toth

    B. Jay Gavin   **D.** Chic Stone

1278. What was the job of the Beast's girlfriend Vera?

    A. Waitress at the Coffee-a-Go-Go   **C.** Scientist

    B. Librarian   **D.** Model

1279. Who are Edna and Norton?

    A. Kitty Pryde's parents   **C.** Bobby Drake's parents

    B. Henry McCoy's parents   **D.** Jean Grey's nephew and niece

1280. Who is *not* a member of the Crazy Gang?

    A. Tweedledee   **C.** Knave

    B. Red Queen   **D.** Tweedledope

1281. Who did Brian Braddock's girlfriend, Courtney Ross, resemble?

    A. Meggan   **C.** Saturnyne

    B. Captain UK   **D.** Roma

OBSESSED WITH MARVEL

1290.

In 1986, Chris Claremont and British artist Alan Davis created Excalibur, a new British-based Super Hero team featuring Captain Britain, the hero that Claremont had co-created a decade before. Debuting in the first *Excalibur Special Edition*, the team immediately moved to its own monthly comic book. Whereas *Captain Britain* had been published in the United Kingdom, *Excalibur* was published for Marvel's American audience. Other original members included the shape-shifting mutant Meggan, from Marvel UK's *Captain Britain* series, and three veteran members of the *X-Men*: Nightcrawler; Kitty Pryde, alias Shadowcat; and Rachel Summers, the new Phoenix.

Claremont and Davis also used *Excalibur* to introduce other characters from *Captain Britain* to American readers, like the Technet and Saturnyne. Captain Britain organized a new British-based team in *New Excalibur* in 2005, which included the formerly villainous Juggernaut and the Dazzler (both shown at left), Sage, British agent Peter Wisdom, and Nocturne of the Exiles.

Who led the Technet in *Excalibur* #1 (1988)?

A. Bodybag
B. Gatecrasher
C. Joyboy
D. Scatterbrain

1282. The All-New X-Factor was funded by which corporation?
A. Worthington Industries **C.** Trask Industries
B. Serval Industries **D.** Stark Industries

1283. Which member of the All-New X-Men shared a romantic relationship with Wolverine (X-23)?
A. Cyclops **C.** Beast
B. Iceman **D.** Angel

1284. Which mutant did *not* die as a direct result of Terrigen Mist exposure?
A. Jamie Madrox **C.** Wolverine
B. Alchemy **D.** Cyclops

1285. Who was a team member through both volumes of *Uncanny X-Force*?
A. Storm **C.** Psylocke
B. Puck **D.** Deadpool

1286. Who was prophesized as the next host of the Phoenix Force in *Avengers Vs. X-Men*?
A. Jean Grey **C.** Rachel Summers
B. Emma Frost **D.** Hope Summers

1287. What was the name of the island nation off the coast of San Francisco that the X-Men once inhabited?
A. Utopia **C.** Xavier Bay
B. X-Isle **D.** Genosha

1288. What was *not* a new ongoing series included as part of the 2017 *RessurXion* relaunch?
A. *Cable* **C.** *Generation X*
B. *Weapon X* **D.** *X-Force*

1289. Who was *not* one of the Phoenix Five in the *Avengers Vs. X-Men* crossover?
A. Cyclops **C.** Namor
B. Jean Grey **D.** Emma Frost

1290.

X-Men

1291. Who claimed to be Lorna Dane's father in *The X-Men* #50–52 (1968–1969)?

A. Magneto
B. Mesmero
C. A Magneto robot
D. Erik the Red

1292. Which classic monster did the alien robot in *The X-Men* #40 (1968) resemble?

A. Dracula
B. The Mummy
C. Frankenstein's Monster
D. The Wolf Man

1293. Where did Sunfire battle the X-Men in *The X-Men* #64 (1970)?

A. Tokyo, Japan
B. New York City
C. Washington D.C.
D. Boston, Massachusetts

1294. Where did the X-Men battle the Hulk in *The X-Men* #66 (1970)?

A. Denver, Colorado
B. Phoenix, Arizona
C. Las Vegas, Nevada
D. Los Angeles, California

1295. Which alien race did the X-Men combat in *The X-Men* #65 (1970)?

A. The N'garai
B. Sidrian Hunters
C. The Z'nox
D. The Arcane

1296. Which artist designed Warlock of the New Mutants?

A. Gil Kane
B. Bill Sienkiewicz
C. Sal Buscema
D. Jim Starlin

1297. Who is Jean Grey's sister?

A. Jill
B. Karen
C. Sara
D. Susan

1298. What is Forge's mutant power?

A. Tekekinesis
B. Enhanced physical strength
C. Intuitive skill at invention
D. Psionic ability to manipulate metal

1299. Which mutant is Charles Xavier's son?

A. Proteus
B. Legion
C. Tattletale
D. J2

Everyone thought that Jean Grey had died during "The Dark Phoenix Saga." But when Jean made her surprising return to the world of the living, she reunited with the other original X-Men: the Angel, the Beast, Iceman, and Cyclops, the man who loved her. Together they formed a new team, X-Factor, which debuted in *X-Factor* #1 in February 1986.

In their everyday civilian identities, X-Factor posed as hunters of dangerous mutants. This was merely a front for finding new mutants and then secretly training them to cope with their powers, continuing Charles Xavier's work. Ultimately, the members of X-Factor rejoined the X-Men, and the U.S. government

organized a new X-Factor to combat mutant men-aces. Among the members of the new X-Factor were Havok and Polaris, Forge, Madrox the Multiple Man, Quicksilver, Strong Guy, Wolfsbane, and even the shape-shifting mutant Mystique.

How did Jean Grey return after Cyclops saw her commit suicide (shown above) at the end of "The Dark Phoenix Saga"?

A. The Phoenix Force brought her back to life
B. Phoenix had duplicated Jean's body, and Jean's original body healed within a cocoon
C. Phoenix/Jean had faked her own death
D. The Jean who returned was from a parallel Earth

1300. Where was Storm born?
- **A.** Wakanda
- **B.** Cairo, Egypt
- **C.** Harlem, New York
- **D.** Serengeti Plain, Kenya

1301. When and where did the beginning of *The X-Men* #98 (1978) take place?
- **A.** Rockefeller Center on Christmas Eve
- **B.** Times Square on New Year's Eve
- **C.** A birthday party at the Coffee-a-Go-Go, Greenwich Village
- **D.** Christmas party at Charles Xavier's mansion

1302. Who is leader of the Shi'ar Imperial Guard?
- **A.** Oracle
- **B.** Mentor
- **C.** Gladiator
- **D.** Tempest

1303.

1304. Which member of the X-Men wears a Mohawk?
- **A.** Wolverine
- **B.** Rogue
- **C.** Storm
- **D.** Bishop

1305. With which issue was the original *X-Men* comic canceled?
- **A.** #65 (1970)
- **B.** #66 (1970)
- **C.** #93 (1975)
- **D.** #94 (1975)

1306. Who was Erik the Red in *The X-Men* #52 (1969)?
- **A.** Davan Shakari
- **B.** Cyclops
- **C.** D'Ken Neramani
- **D.** Gabriel Summers

1307. Who leads *Marvel 1602*'s version of the X-Men?
- **A.** Sir Charles Xavier
- **B.** Carlos Javier
- **C.** Grand Inquisitor Enrique
- **D.** Rojahz

1308. Which Earth hero joined the Starjammers?
- **A.** Alex Summers
- **B.** Charles Xavier
- **C.** Carol Danvers
- **D.** All answers are correct

X-Men

1309. Who switched bodies with Storm in *The Uncanny X-Men* #151 (1981)?

A. Deathbird

B. Mystique

C. The White Queen

D. The Shadow King

1310. Who was Nate Grey, the X-Man?

A. Cable's son

B. Jean Grey's son in an alternate reality

C. A genetically engineered clone of Cable

D. Cable's counterpart from the Age of Apocalypse

1311. What is the country of Sunspot's origin?

A. Mexico

B. Colombia

C. Brazil

D. Argentina

1312. Which nation did the United Nations grant to Magneto to rule?

A. Genosha

B. Santo Marco

C. Transia

D. Magneto's island in the Bermuda Triangle

1313. What is the name of Cannonball's sister who became Husk, a member of Generation X?

A. Joelle

B. Sharon

C. Paige

D. Peg

1314. Where did Jubilee first encounter members of the X-Men?

A. The Australian Outback

B. The Shi'ar Throneworld

C. A California shopping mall

D. A Manhattan department store

1315. Which member of X-Force first appeared in *Secret Wars II* (1985–1986)?

A. Warpath

B. Feral

C. Boomer

D. Shatterstar

1316. Who is Legion's mother?

A. Emma Frost

B. Gabrielle Haller

C. Moira MacTaggert

D. Cassandra Nova

1323.

The original X-Men starred in a series aptly titled *X-Men: First Class*. The new X-Men of 1975 were Charles Xavier's second class at his school, and the New Mutants were his third class.

Inevitably, yet another generation of new mutant students was created in *Generation X* #1 (1994, shown at left), created by writer Scott Lobdell and artist Chris Bachalo. However, this time Xavier was not the teacher. His School for Gifted Youngsters was now the Xavier Institute, where he supervised the large team of adult X-Men. He appointed two other mutants to teach the new students: Sean Cassidy, the Banshee and veteran member of the X-Men, and Emma Frost, who had once been the X-Men's enemy as the White Queen of the Hellfire Club. On the initial roster of students were Chamber; Husk; Jubilee, a young Asian-American girl who had already been serving with the X-Men; Synch; and the mysterious M and Skin.

Where was Generation X based?

A. The Massachusetts Academy
B. The Sanctuary
C. Angel Island
D. Muir Island

1317. Which team of mutants included a reprogrammed Sentinel named Cerebra?
A. Ultimate X-Men
B. Amazing X-Men
C. All-New X-Men
D. Extraordinary X-Men

1318. What classic member of the X-Men was resurrected in the pages of *Amazing X-Men* (2013)?
A. Colossus
B. Banshee
C. Nightcrawler
D. Jean Grey

1319. Which member of the Stepford Cuckoos is currently deceased?
A. Celeste
B. Sophie
C. Phoebe
D. Irma

1320. Which young member of the X-Men went on to be the school roommate of Miles Morales (Spider-Man)?
A. Goldballs
B. Benjamin Deeds
C. Triage
D. Hijack

1321. Who was the leader of the squad featured in 2017's *X-Men: Gold* series?
A. Kitty Pryde
B. Colossus
C. Storm
D. Nightcrawler

1322. Who did Deadpool marry?
A. Domino
B. Copycat
C. Shiklah
D. Bea Arthur

1323.

1324. Which member of the original Generation X was also featured regularly in the 2017 series?
A. Husk
B. Skin
C. Synch
D. Jubilee

1325. In the *Death of Wolverine* series, how was Logan killed?
A. Disintegrated by Cyclops
B. Murdered by Sabretooth
C. Encased in Adamantium
D. Dissected by Weapon X

X-Men

1326. Who transformed Manhattan into an ancient city from before recorded history?

- **A.** Morgan Le Fey
- **B.** Kulan Gath
- **C.** Arkon the Imperion
- **D.** Apocalypse

1327. Who was Bastion?

- **A.** The Master Mold in human form
- **B.** A human who led Operation: Zero Tolerance
- **C.** A fusion of the Master Mold and Nimrod
- **D.** The advanced Sentinel called Nimrod

1328.

1329. What disease did Deadpool's healing factor suppress in his body?

- **A.** Ebola
- **B.** Heart disease
- **C.** AIDS
- **D.** Cancer

1330. What is Deadpool's pet Deuce?

- **A.** A cat
- **B.** A bat
- **C.** A dog
- **D.** A rat

1331. Who was *not* one of the original Exiles?

- **A.** The Mimic
- **B.** Morph
- **C.** Nocturne
- **D.** Havok

1332. Who was put on trial in *The Uncanny X-Men* #200 (1985)?

- **A.** Professor Charles Xavier
- **B.** Magneto
- **C.** The X-Men
- **D.** Mystique

1333. Who were Slym and Redd?

- **A.** Cable's children
- **B.** Scott Summers and Jean Grey in the far future
- **C.** A pair of Morlocks
- **D.** Scott Summers and Jean Grey in "The Age of Apocalypse"

1328.

The unlikeliest hero—or antihero—to emerge from the *X-Men* family of comics is Deadpool (shown at right with Wolverine). He is a mercenary, he is an assassin, he can be mentally unstable—and yet he has his own moral code.

After discovering he was dying, mercenary Wade Wilson joined the Weapon X program. Its scientists endowed him with a healing factor that saved his life but horribly scarred his face and body and adversely affected his sanity. As the superhuman Deadpool, Wilson resumed his mercenary career.

Created by Rob Liefeld and Fabian Nicieza, Deadpool was originally presented as a villain, battling X-Force and Wolverine. But Deadpool has also allied himself with Cable and other heroes and has acted heroically himself. What is most appealing about this "Merc with a Mouth" is his sharp, irreverent sense of humor. Like the She-Hulk, Deadpool knows he is in a comic book and will even talk directly to the readers!

How did Deadpool get his name?

- **A.** He nearly died before joining Weapon X
- **B.** He participated in a "dead pool" game to bet on who would die first
- **C.** He has killed so many people
- **D.** He was named after the movie of the same name

1334. Who was the Mutant Master who headed Factor Three?

A. A previously unknown mutant   **C.** An extraterrestrial

B. A human scientist manipulating mutants   **D.** Magneto

1335. Who is Roma?

A. Empress of Nova Roma   **C.** Daughter of Merlyn

B. The Lady of the Northern Skies   **D.** Both B and C

1336. Which Morlock terrorist from Gene Nation joined the X-Men?

A. Mikhail Rasputin   **C.** Marrow

B. Vessel   **D.** Callisto

1337. What was Nova Roma?

A. Colony resembling ancient Rome in Amazon jungle   **C.** Full name of the Omniversal Guardian

B. Name of Manhattan transformed into ancient city   **D.** Capital city of Genosha

1338. What is different about the Storm of the alternate reality of *Mutant X*?

A. She is a vampire   **C.** She has devolved into a child

B. She has no super-powers   **D.** She has gone insane

1339. Which of the following is a hero in the alternate reality of *Mutant X*?

A. Doctor Doom   **C.** Nick Fury

B. Mister Fantastic   **D.** Professor X

X-Men

1340. How is Carmen Pryde related to Kitty?
- **A.** Mother
- **B.** Father
- **C.** Sister
- **D.** Daughter in an alternate timeline

1341. Who is the Timebroker?
- **A.** An incarnation of Kang the Conqueror
- **B.** A member of the Time Variance Authority
- **C.** A humanoid being who employs the Exiles
- **D.** Construct by insectlike aliens

1342. What is Blink's mutant power?
- **A.** Super-speed
- **B.** Projects intense light
- **C.** Teleportation
- **D.** Invisibility

1343. Who are the parents of Nocturne of the Exiles?
- **A.** Nightcrawler and Storm
- **B.** Gambit and Rogue
- **C.** Forge and Mystique
- **D.** Nightcrawler and Scarlet Witch

1344. Where did Jean Grey go to school after she briefly dropped out of Professor Xavier's school?
- **A.** Empire State University
- **B.** New York University
- **C.** Metro College
- **D.** City College of New York

1345.

1346. Which is *not* one of Legion's personalities but another person's consciousness in his mind?
- **A.** Jack Wayne
- **B.** Jemail Karami
- **C.** Cyndi
- **D.** David Haller

1347. Who was *not* a member of Factor Three?
- **A.** Unus the Untouchable
- **B.** The Blob
- **C.** Lucifer
- **D.** Mastermind

1345.

The Marvel Universe is really a "multiverse," an infinite collection of dimensions, parallel universes, and alternate timelines. Most of the adventures chronicled in Marvel comics take place in the universe containing the world known as Earth-616. But, for example, the stories in Marvel's line of *Ultimate* comics take place on their own Earth in a parallel universe.

The heroes of *Exiles* (shown at right), created in 2001 by writer Judd Winick and artist Mike McKone, travel among the alternate realities in order to repair and save realities that have somehow become "broken." The Exiles themselves come from different alternate realities. For example, Blink comes from the divergent timeline known as the Age of Apocalypse. Other members have been alternate versions of familiar characters like the Mimic and Sabretooth and Thunderbird I, or original characters like Nocturne, and even characters from Earth-616, such as Beak, Longshot, Psylocke, and Sage.

What is the Panoptichron?

- **A.** Mystical path favored by Nocturne
- **B.** The headquarters of the Exiles at the Nexus of All Realities
- **C.** A palace made of slate
- **D.** Final resting place for broken realities

1348. Which Nazi villain appeared in Archie Goodwin and John Byrne's collaboration on *Wolverine*?

- **A.** Baron Strucker
- **B.** Geist
- **C.** The Red Skull
- **D.** Baron Blood

1349. Who was Tyger Tiger before she became queen of Madripoor's underworld?

- **A.** A barmaid
- **B.** A banker
- **C.** A policewoman
- **D.** A corporate executive

1350. Who is Elsie Dee?

- **A.** One of the Morlocks
- **B.** A small girl who befriended Wolverine
- **C.** A robot resembling a little girl
- **D.** A mutant student at the Xavier Institute

1351. Who recruited the Marauders for Mister Sinister?

- **A.** Taskmaster
- **B.** Sabretooth
- **C.** Gambit
- **D.** Scalphunter

1352. Who is *not* one of the Reavers?

- **A.** Skullbuster
- **B.** Riptide
- **C.** Pretty Boy
- **D.** Bonebreaker

1353. What profession did William Stryker hold in the graphic novel *X-Men: God Loves, Man Kills* (1982)?

- **A.** Military officer
- **B.** Scientist
- **C.** Minister
- **D.** Politician

1354. Who teamed up with Wolverine against the Hand in Madripoor in 1941?

- **A.** Nick Fury
- **B.** Sub-Mariner
- **C.** Captain America
- **D.** Dominic Fortune

X-Men

1355. Who is Halloween Jack?
- **A.** A member of the Morlocks
- **B.** A shape-shifter previously called Loki
- **C.** A supernatural demon
- **D.** A mutant in AD 2099

1356. What is the relationship between Lifeguard and Slipstream in *X-Treme X-Men*?
- **A.** Sister and brother
- **B.** Cousins
- **C.** Colleagues
- **D.** Wife and husband

1357.

1358. Who is the Witness whom Bishop knew in an alternate future?
- **A.** Gambit
- **B.** Wolverine
- **C.** Callisto
- **D.** Cable

1359. What is the name of the first mutant baby born after M-Day?
- **A.** Faith
- **B.** Charity
- **C.** Hope
- **D.** Charles

1360. Who or what triggered the Beast's change into a leonine appearance?
- **A.** Infectia
- **B.** Sage
- **C.** Mister Sinister
- **D.** Another mutagenic serum concocted by Henry McCoy

1361. What was District X?
- **A.** Area of Genosha populated by mutant slaves
- **B.** "Mutant Town" ghetto in Manhattan
- **C.** Property owned by Charles Xavier in Westchester County
- **D.** None of these

1362. Which antimutant group did William Stryker lead?
- **A.** Friends of Humanity
- **B.** Purifiers
- **C.** Humanity's Last Stand
- **D.** The U-Men

1357.

The *Marvel 2099* line of comics also introduced an AD 2099 version of the X-Men, set on an alternate future Earth. Created by writer John Francis Moore and writer Ron Lim, *X-Men 2099* (shown at right) was founded by Xi'an Chi Xan, a former mutant criminal. Even in AD 2099, mutants were still an oppressed group. Following the example of Charles Xavier, Xi'an intended to help bring about peaceful co-existence between mutants and other humans. Among the other members of X-Men 2099 were the winged Bloodhawk, Cerebra, Krystalin, La Lunatica, Meanstreak, and Skullfire.

The *2099* line also introduced another mutant team and comic book: *X-Nation 2099*, created by writer Tom Peyer and artist Humberto Ramos. Its premise was that Cerebra gathered a group of young mutants together, one of whom might prove to be a prophesied leader for mutant-kind. Among the members were Clarion, December, Metalsmith, Nostromo, Twilight, Uproar, Willow, and Wulff.

What is the alias of X-Men 2099's leader Xi'an Chi Xan?

- **A.** The Foolkiller
- **B.** Controller X
- **C.** Desert Ghost
- **D.** Brimstone Love

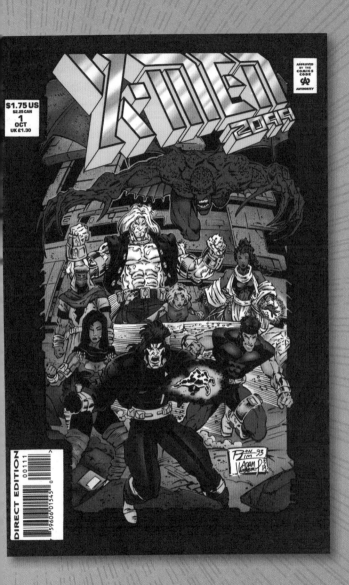

1363. Which group did Gambit *not* belong to?
- **A.** Assassins Guild
- **B.** X-Ternals
- **C.** Horsemen of Apocalypse
- **D.** Thieves Guild

1364. Who was Mother Askani?
- **A.** Jean Grey
- **B.** Rachel Summers
- **C.** Cable's wife
- **D.** None of these

1365. Who was Nathaniel Essex?
- **A.** Mesmero
- **B.** Mister Sinister
- **C.** Albion
- **D.** Britannic

1366. Who successfully succeeded Brian Braddock as Captain Britain?
- **A.** Elisabeth Braddock
- **B.** Kelsey Leigh, alias Lionheart
- **C.** Linda McQuillan
- **D.** Jamie Braddock

1367. What is Peter Wisdom's super-power?
- **A.** Telepathy
- **B.** Creates flames
- **C.** Creates "hot knives" of energy
- **D.** Projects laser blasts

1368. Who is *not* a member of New Excalibur?
- **A.** Sage
- **B.** Dazzler
- **C.** Rachel Summers
- **D.** The Juggernaut

1369. What was Dr. Cecilia Reyes's mutant power?
- **A.** Generates force field
- **B.** Heals others rapidly
- **C.** Heals herself rapidly
- **D.** She had no super-powers

1370. What is the designation of the alternate Earth of "The Age of Apocalypse"?
- **A.** Earth-33
- **B.** Earth-295
- **C.** Earth-300
- **D.** Earth-395

X-Men

1371. Who was *not* a member of Deadpool's Mercs for Money team?
A. Solo
B. Slapstick
C. Silver Sable
D. Stingray

1372. The time-displaced original X-Men went on to star in which 2017 series?
A. *X-Men: Blue*
B. *Generation X*
C. *X-Men: Gold*
D. *Weapon X*

1373. During the "Apocalypse Wars" storyline, which team of X-Men found themselves in a future timeline?
A. Extraordinary X-Men
B. Uncanny X-Men
C. All-New X-Men
D. Amazing X-Men

1374. Old Man Logan came to the present-day Marvel Universe during which major event?
A. *Avengers Vs. X-Men*
B. *Inhumans Vs. X-Men*
C. *Civil War II*
D. *Secret Wars* (2015)

1375. Which X-Man also attended Avengers Academy?
A. Anole
B. Rockslide
C. X-23
D. Goldballs

1376. Which X-Man briefly served as a S.H.I.E.L.D. liaison to the team?
A. Dazzler
B. Emma Frost
C. Forge
D. Bishop

1377. Who was the powerful mutant that Tempus and Professor X erased from existence?
A. Benjamin Deeds
B. Evan Sabahnur
C. Fabio Medina
D. Matthew Malloy

1378. Which X-Man married Kyle Jinadu in *Astonishing X-Men* #51 (2012)?
A. Northstar
B. Karma
C. Iceman
D. Warbird

1379. Which of the original X-Men lost his powers by subconsciously blocking them in the Decimation following *House of M* (2005-2006)?

A. Cyclops   **C.** Iceman

B. The Angel   **D.** The Beast

1380. Who is Dr. Peter Corbeau?

A. The Genegineer in Genosha   **C.** Head of Project Starcore

B. Physician at Weapon X Project   **D.** Roboticist at Operation Wideawake

1381. Which member of the X-Men worked as an FBI agent in "District X"?

A. Bishop   **C.** Cyclops

B. Wolverine   **D.** Banshee

1382. Who has *not* been known as Marvel Girl?

A. Jean Grey   **C.** Jubilation Lee

B. Rachel Summers   **D.** Valeria Richards

1383. Who is Captain UK?

A. Betsy Braddock   **C.** Kelsey Leigh

B. Linda McQuillan   **D.** Alysande Stuart

1384. What was the Council of the Chosen?

A. Ruling circle of Factor Three   **C.** Cabinet of Magneto's government in Genosha

B. Former name of Hellfire Club's Inner Circle   **D.** Inner circle of Magneto's government in *House of M*

1385. In which series did Deadpool first appear?

A. *Deadpool* miniseries   **C.** *X-Force*

B. *The New Mutants*   **D.** *Cable*

1386. Who helped Wolverine regain his long-lost memories?

A. Professor X through his telepathic powers   **C.** Scarlet Witch, in *House of M*

B. Himself: he found his memories stored at Weapon X facility   **D.** No one; he has not recovered his full memories

1387.

1387.

The reality of the X-Men's world radically altered with the eight-issue limited series *House of M* (issue 1 shown at left), which ran from 2005 to 2006.

In this saga, written by Brian Michael Bendis and drawn by Olivier Coipel, the Scarlet Witch suffers a mental breakdown over the loss of her twin sons. Her brother, Quicksilver, manipulates the distraught Scarlet Witch into using her mutant power to alter probability to its fullest extent. As a result, history is altered, and mutants dominate the Earth.

Magneto and his family—including the Scarlet Witch's sons, now alive—are Earth's royal family, the House of M, rulers of the planet. Of all Earth's Super Heroes, only Wolverine remembers the way the world used to be.

In the end the Scarlet Witch not only restores history to its proper course, but—declaring "No more mutants!"—strips Magneto and most other mutants of their super-powers.

To whom is Cyclops married in *House of M*?

A. Lorna Dane

B. Madelyne Pryor

C. Emma Frost

D. Jean Grey

X-Men

1388. Who is Amanda Sefton?
- **A.** Nightcrawler's girlfriend
- **B.** Sorceress
- **C.** Stewardess
- **D.** All answers are correct

1389. When was M-Day?
- **A.** April 25th
- **B.** November 2nd
- **C.** November 30th
- **D.** December 28th

1390. Where was Professor Xavier a visiting lecturer in *The Uncanny X-Men* #196 (1985)?
- **A.** Columbia University
- **B.** Harvard University
- **C.** Princeton University
- **D.** Yale University

1391. Which city did Count Nefaria capture in *The X-Men* #22–23 (1966)?
- **A.** Washington D.C.
- **B.** New York City
- **C.** London, England
- **D.** Rome, Italy

1392. Who was *not* one of Count Nefaria's minions in *The X-Men* #22–23 (1966)?
- **A.** The Human Top
- **B.** The Plantman
- **C.** The Unicorn
- **D.** The Porcupine

1393. Who first designed the visual appearance of Wolverine?
- **A.** John Byrne
- **B.** John Romita Sr.
- **C.** Herb Trimpe
- **D.** Dave Cockrum

1394. Who are Modt and Jahf?
- **A.** The two beings making up Warstar
- **B.** Guardians of the M'Krann Crystal
- **C.** Members of the Shi'ar Imperial Guard
- **D.** Demons serving N'astirh

1395. Who was Ted Roberts?
- **A.** The Mimic
- **B.** Morph
- **C.** The Cobalt Man
- **D.** Metro College student Jean Grey dated

1403.

For decades, Wolverine's origins were a mystery, even to himself. His own memory was a patchwork of false implants and gaps. The "Weapon X" story line in *Marvel Comics Presents* first revealed how the scientists of the Weapon X project bonded adamantium to Wolverine's skeleton. But it wasn't until the 2001–2002 miniseries *Origin* (shown at left), drawn by Andy Kubert, that the story of Wolverine's youth was at last revealed.

His original name was James Howlett, and he was born in Canada in the nineteenth century. It was when Thomas Logan (who bore a resemblance to the adult Wolverine) murdered James's father, John, that the claws first emerged from James's hands. James killed Thomas Logan in furious retaliation, whereupon James's mother killed herself. James fled, taking "Logan" as his alias.

Later, in a battle with Thomas Logan's son "Dog," James inadvertently kills the woman he loves. He flees again into the wilderness, his mind having blocked out the traumatic memories of his past.

Who was *not* one of the writers of the original *Wolverine: Origin* series?

A. Paul Jenkins
B. Bill Jemas
C. Chris Claremont
D. Joe Quesada

1396. Who is Vulcan?
A. Scott Summers's brother, Gabriel
B. Nightcrawler's foster brother, Stefan
C. Peter Rasputin's brother, Mikhail
D. Scott Summers's brother, Alex

1397. Who is *not* one of Emma Frost's siblings?
A. Christian
B. Winston
C. Adrienne
D. Cordelia

1398. Where was Emma Frost born?
A. Chicago
B. London
C. Boston
D. New York

1399. Which of these members of the second X-Force survived their first issue?
A. Zeitgeist
B. Anarchist
C. Gin Genie
D. Battering Ram

1400. Who was Dr. August Hopper?
A. The Genegineer
B. Mekano
C. The Porcupine
D. The Locust

1401. Which famous TV news person(s) appeared in *The X-Men* #58 (1969) and #65 (1970)?
A. Dan Rather
B. Chet Huntley and David Brinkley
C. Barbara Walters
D. Walter Cronkite

1402. When did Nathan Summers, alias Cable, first appear in any form?
A. *The New Mutants* #86 (1990)
B. *The New Mutants* #100 (1991)
C. *X-Force* #1 (1991)
D. *The Uncanny X-Men* #201 (1986)

1403.

1404. What is the name of Wolverine's mother?
A. Jean
B. Elizabeth
C. Rebecca
D. Rose

X-Men

1405. Which member of the X-Men was turned into a vampire by Xarus?
- **A.** Nightcrawler
- **B.** Magik
- **C.** Jubilee
- **D.** Marrow

1406. Who was not one of the "Five Lights" in *Generation Hope*?
- **A.** Velocidad
- **B.** Transonic
- **C.** Primal
- **D.** Anole

1407. Who was the star of the 2012 *X-Men Legacy* series?
- **A.** Hope Summers
- **B.** Legion
- **C.** Cable
- **D.** Legacy

1408. Which All-New X-Man traveled back in time to ancient Egypt with Genesis during "Apocalypse Wars"?
- **A.** Angel
- **B.** Cyclops
- **C.** Beast
- **D.** Iceman

1409. What codename did Rachel Summers use in 2017's *X-Men: Gold*?
- **A.** Marvel Girl
- **B.** Phoenix
- **C.** Prestige
- **D.** Revenant

1410. Young Cyclops left the All-New X-Men for a time to travel through space with whom?
- **A.** Guardians of the Galaxy
- **B.** Shi'ar Imperial Guard
- **C.** His father, Corsair
- **D.** His brother, Vulcan

1411.

1412. Which X-Man was once engaged to the Guardians of the Galaxy's Star-Lord?
- **A.** Jean Grey
- **B.** Kitty Pryde
- **C.** Storm
- **D.** Rachel Summers

1411.

The most unusual of Marvel's mutant teams, X-Statix, debuted in *X-Force* #116 (2001), usurping the name of a previous group. Traditionally, Super Heroes are selflessly motivated to fight for justice without expecting any financial reward. Created by writer Peter Milligan and artist Mike Allred, the members of X-Statix became costumed crime fighters in order to become media celebrities, to exploit their notoriety, and to make themselves rich.

But it was a dangerous path to take to fame and fortune. Most of the team were killed in the first

1413. How did Magneto survive decapitation by Wolverine?

A. The Scarlet Witch altered probability

B. History was altered to prevent his death

C. It was the impostor Xorn who was beheaded

D. It was a clone that was beheaded

1414. Who killed the Juggernaut's friend Sammy Pare?

A. Arcade

B. The Friends of Humanity

C. The Juggernaut

D. Black Tom Cassidy

1415. What was the source of Anarchist's energy bolts?

A. Absorption of kinetic energy

B. Electromagnetic energy from nervous system

C. Psionic energy

D. Acidic sweat

1416. What is U-Go Girl's mutant power?

A. Super-speed

B. Self-teleportation

C. Superhuman agility

D. Flight via self-levitation

1417. Who is Reverend Craig?

A. Minister who officiated at Scott and Jean's wedding

B. Minister who persecuted Wolfsbane

C. Minister who advocated mutant rights

D. Member of William Stryker's Purifiers

1418. Which of the following is *not* true about Ricochet Rita?

A. She was a Hollywood stuntwoman

B. She is a mutant with four extra arms

C. She had an original identity of Spiral

D. She was once Longshot's ally

1419. Who is the only nonmutant to die from the Legacy Virus?

A. Senator Robert Kelly

B. Dr. Valerie Cooper

C. Moira MacTaggert

D. Reverend William Conover

1420. Which mutant seemingly sacrificed his or her life to provide a cure for the Legacy Virus?

A. Illyana Rasputin

B. Colossus

C. Pyro

D. Mastermind

issue, but X-Force/X-Statix seemed to have no trouble recruiting young replacements. Among the many unusual members of the team were its leader, the Orphan aka Mister Sensitive; Anarchist; Bloke; Dead Girl (shown above), who was literally dead; Doop, a strange, seemingly nonhuman creature; El Guapo; Phat; Saint Anna; Spike; U-Go Girl; Venus Dee Milo, whose body was made of pure energy; and Vivisector.

Who was X-Statix's cameraman?

A. Dead Girl
B. Bloke
C. Phat
D. Doop

X-Men

1421. Who is Grand Inquisitor Enrique in *Marvel 1602*?
- **A.** Charles Xavier's counterpart
- **B.** Magneto's counterpart
- **C.** The Toad's counterpart
- **D.** None of these

1422. Who is Jonothon Starsmore?
- **A.** Skin
- **B.** Synch
- **C.** Chamber
- **D.** Emplate

1423. Who was the original Penance?
- **A.** Nicole St. Croix
- **B.** Nicole and Claudette St. Croix
- **C.** Monet St. Croix
- **D.** Robbie Baldwin

1424. Which X-Men adversary has *not* been ruler of the Shi'ar?
- **A.** Deathbird
- **B.** The Brood Empress
- **C.** D'ken Neramani
- **D.** Vulcan

1425. Who was *not* a member of Stryfe's Mutant Liberation Front?
- **A.** Thumbelina
- **B.** Strobe
- **C.** Forearm
- **D.** Bodybag

1426. Who is the Magus in *New Mutants* #18 (1984)?
- **A.** Adam Warlock's evil other self
- **B.** The Maha Yogi
- **C.** Warlock's alien father
- **D.** The Mad Merlin

1427. Who did *not* belong to the Acolytes?
- **A.** Amelia Voght
- **B.** Kleinstock Brothers
- **C.** Fabian Cortez
- **D.** Shinobi Shaw

1428. Whom did Kitty Pryde date in the *Ultimate X-Men* universe?
- **A.** Johnny Storm
- **B.** Peter Parker
- **C.** Peter Rasputin
- **D.** Bobby Drake

1429. What was the relationship of Charles Xavier and Moira MacTaggart in *Ultimate X-Men*?
- **A.** Formerly engaged
- **B.** Ex-spouses
- **C.** Husband and wife
- **D.** Platonic friends

1430. What is Kitty's role in "Kitty's Fairy Tale" in *The Uncanny X-Men* #153 (1982)?
- **A.** Knight
- **B.** Magician
- **C.** Pirate
- **D.** Princess

OBSESSED WITH MARVEL

1434.

Following *Ultimate Spider-Man*, the second series introduced in Marvel's *Ultimate* line of comics was *Ultimate X-Men* in 2001, originally written by Mark Millar and drawn by Adam Kubert. Like all of the *Ultimate* titles, *Ultimate X-Men* (shown at left) starts the saga of its characters over from the beginning, presenting an alternate version of traditional Marvel continuity. For example, *Ultimate X-Men*'s original lineup combines X-counterparts of characters from both the original X-Men (Cyclops, Jean Grey, Beast, and Iceman) and the new X-Men (Colossus and Storm).

In the initial story arc, "The Tomorrow People," Wolverine joins the X-Men, secretly planning to assassinate team founder Charles Xavier on behalf of Magneto, but then switches sides. Other changes in the *Ultimate* continuity are still more radical: the "Ultimate" Cable turns out to be Wolverine's future self.

Over the course of its one hundred—issue run, *Ultimate X-Men* devised its own variations on classic X-Men concepts and story lines, such as "The Dark Phoenix Saga."

Which writer did *not* work on *Ultimate X-Men*?

A. Brian K. Vaughan
B. Brian Azzarello
C. Brian Michael Bendis
D. Robert Kirkman

1431. Who is the Genie in "Kitty's Fairy Tale" in *The Uncanny X-Men* #153 (1982)?
A. Charles Xavier   **C.** Phoenix
B. Storm   **D.** Nightcrawler

1432. Who created the X-Babies?
A. Mister Sinister   **C.** Mojo
B. The Impossible Man   **D.** Nanny and Orphan-Maker

1433. What is *not* true about Margali of the Winding Way?
A. She is a powerful sorceress   **C.** She is Nightcrawler's foster mother
B. She is Nightcrawler's mother   **D.** Her last name is Szardos

1434.

1435. Who originally led Japan's Big Hero 6?
A. Hiro Takachiho   **C.** Sunfire
B. The Silver Samurai   **D.** Sunpyre

1436. Which World War II Super Hero did *not* battle Storm and Wolverine in *The Uncanny X-Men* #215–216 (1987)?
A. Crimson Commando   **C.** Stonewall
B. Black Marvel   **D.** Super Sabre

1437. Who was *not* an original member of Japan's Big Hero 6?
A. Baymax   **C.** Honey Lemon
B. The Ebon Samurai   **D.** GoGo Tomago

1438. Who was the Goblin Queen?
A. Cassandra Nova   **C.** Selene
B. Madelyne Pryor   **D.** Margali of the Winding Way

1439. Who are Scott Summers's grandparents?
A. Owen and Priscilla   **C.** Robert and Beatrice
B. Philip and Deborah   **D.** Brian and Sharon

1440. What job is Bobby Drake (Iceman) trained for?
A. Librarian   **C.** Dentist
B. Lawyer   **D.** Certified Public Accountant

X-Men

1441. In Old Man Logan's future timeline, what was the name of his daughter?

A. Jeannie   C. Jade

B. Stormy   D. Kitty

1442. Which title was not a part of the 2013 *X-Termination* crossover?

A. *Age of Apocalypse*   C. *Astonishing X-Men*

B. *Amazing X-Men*   D. *X-Treme X-Men*

1443. In the future timeline seen in 2016's "Apocalypse Wars," which X-Man becomes a Horseman of Apocalypse?

A. Colossus   C. Old Man Logan

B. Nightcrawler   D. Magik

1444.

1445. What is the name of the orphaned boy that Jubilee adopts in the 2013 *X-Men* series?

A. Logan   C. Nathan

B. Shogo   D. Charlie

1446. Which X-Men villain's personality remained "inverted" after the events of the *AXIS* crossover?

A. Mystique   C. Sabretooth

B. Apocalypse   D. Red Onslaught

1447. Which classic X-Men storyline was not revisited during 2015's *Secret Wars*?

A. "Inferno"   C. "Days of Future Past"

B. "X-Tinction Agenda"   D. "X-Cutioner's Song"

1448. Which former Avenger became an X-Man for the first time in *Amazing X-Men* (2013)?

A. Firestar   C. Scarlet Witch

B. Justice   D. Quicksilver

1444.

Introduced as the X-Men's arch-villain in *The X-Men* #1 (1963) by co-creators Stan Lee and Jack Kirby, Magneto (shown at right) has become one of the most complex figures in the X-Men cast of characters. Magneto has been depicted as a ruthless, fanatical tyrant, willing to slaughter all humans who are not mutants. But at other times he has worked alongside Charles Xavier and the X-Men in the interests of mutant-kind.

Lee and Kirby established early on that Xavier and Magneto disagreed on how best to ensure the freedom of mutants. Writer Chris Claremont revealed that Magneto and Xavier were friends in their youth, and that Magneto had been a prisoner in a Nazi death camp. Having witnessed the Holocaust, Magneto was determined to do whatever he deemed necessary to prevent his fellow mutants from falling victim to a similar fate. That has led to Magneto's repeated attempts at world conquest, thwarted time and again by Xavier and his X-Men.

What is Magneto's real name?

A. Erik Lehnsherr

B. Max Eisenhardt

C. Magnus (last name unrevealed)

D. True name never revealed

1449. Who is John Grey in *Marvel 1602*?

A. Jean Grey's father

B. Jean Grey masquerading as a boy

C. Jean Grey's male counterpart

D. Nate Grey's counterpart

1450. Who is Ismael Ortega?

A. The Super Villain Kukulcan

B. Policeman who is Bishop's partner in District X

C. Sunspot

D. Man who found Kulan Gath's amulet

1451. What is Rogue's real name in the main *X-Men* continuity?

A. Carrie

B. Anna Raven

C. Anna Marie

D. Marie

1452. Who is the first mutant to appear in a Marvel comic?

A. Charles Xavier

B. Magneto

C. Toro

D. Sub-Mariner

1453. Who is *not* one of Hardcase's Harriers in *The Uncanny X-Men* #261 (1990)?

A. Lifeline

B. Arclight

C. Piston

D. Longbow

1454. In *The Uncanny X-Men* #135 (1980), Dark Phoenix destroyed a member of the alien D'Bari race; where did the D'Bari first appear?

A. *The Uncanny X-Men* #101 (1976)

B. *Fantastic Four* #7 (1962)

C. *Journey into Mystery* #83 (1962)

D. *The Avengers* #4 (1964)

1455. What is *not* true about the comics series *X-Men Forever*, which debuted in 2009?

A. It is part of the main X-Men continuity

B. It is set in an alternate timeline following *X-Men* #3 (1991)

C. It was written by Chris Claremont

D. It was published as a biweekly comic book

1456. Who is elected President of the United States in the alternate future of *X-Men: The End* (2004–2006)?

A. Kitty Pryde

B. Charles Xavier

C. Henry McCoy

D. Scott Summers

X-Men

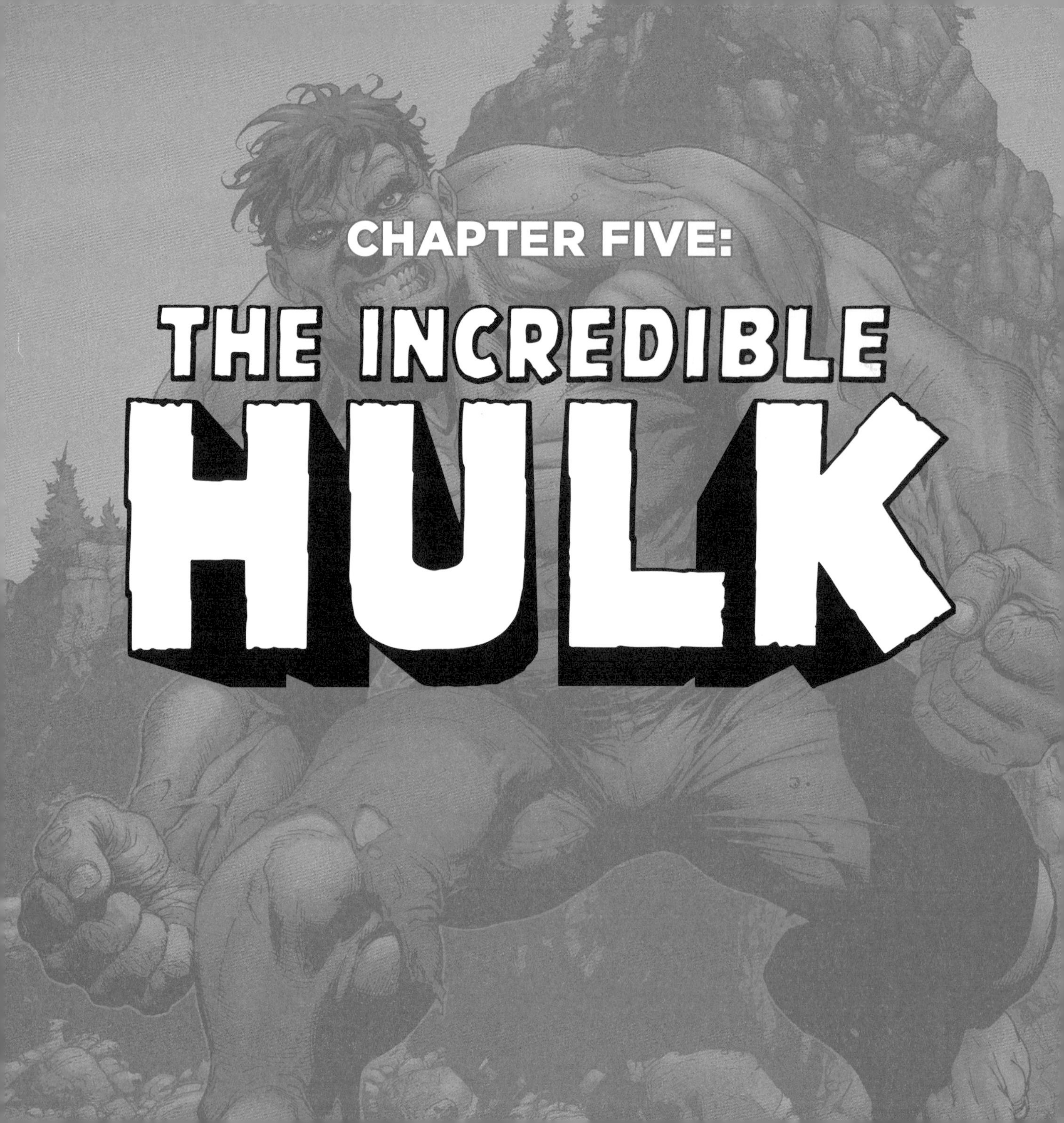

CHAPTER FIVE:

THE INCREDIBLE

HULK

1457. What is Bruce Banner's full name?
- **A.** Bruce Banner
- **B.** Robert Bruce Banner
- **C.** Bruce Robert Banner
- **D.** Bruce David Banner

1458. Who dubbed Bruce Banner's monstrous self "the Hulk"?
- **A.** Rick Jones
- **B.** An unidentified soldier
- **C.** General "Thunderbolt" Ross
- **D.** Bruce Banner

1459. After the gamma explosion, when does Bruce Banner first change into the Hulk?
- **A.** When he is reunited with Betty Ross
- **B.** When he grows angry in a quarrel with General Ross
- **C.** When night falls the evening of the explosion
- **D.** When he is attacked by enemy agents

1460. Who sought to kill Bruce Banner the second time he tried to marry Betty Ross?
- **A.** The Hulk
- **B.** Glenn Talbot
- **C.** The Leader
- **D.** General "Thunderbolt" Ross

1461. What does the Ringmaster use to hypnotize his victims?
- **A.** Telepathic power
- **B.** A spinning disc on his hat
- **C.** Eye contact
- **D.** His voice

1462. Who is Tyrannus?
- **A.** An ancient wizard
- **B.** The last emperor of ancient Rome
- **C.** A Deviant warlord
- **D.** An alien monarch

1463. Who is Tyrannus's archrival in Subterranea?
- **A.** Queen Kala of the Netherworld
- **B.** Grotesk
- **C.** The Mole Man
- **D.** The Lava Men

1464. How has Tyrannus maintained his youth over the centuries?

A. Mutation
B. Magic
C. A fountain of youth
D. Deviant technology

1465. Who was the Soviet spy responsible for turning Bruce Banner into the Hulk?

A. Igor Drenkov
B. Anton Vanko
C. Igor Sklar
D. Emil Blonsky

1466.

1467. How many issues did the original *Hulk* series run?

A. Ten
B. Six
C. Twelve
D. Five

1468. Who were the aliens whose invasion of Earth was thwarted by the Hulk in *The Incredible Hulk* #2 (1962)?

A. The Toad Men
B. The Tribbitites
C. Both A and B
D. Neither A nor B

1469. Which Communist villain appeared in *The Incredible Hulk* #1 (1962)?

A. The Chameleon
B. The Gargoyle
C. The Gremlin
D. The Devastator

1470. How many issues of the original *The Incredible Hulk* series did Jack Kirby draw?

A. Six
B. Four
C. Five
D. Three

1471. Who drew the final issue of the original *The Incredible Hulk* series?

A. Jack Kirby
B. Steve Ditko
C. Bob Powell
D. Dick Ayers

1472. Who is Sam Sterns?

A. Speedfreek
B. Madman
C. The Leader
D. The Abomination

1466.

With *The Incredible Hulk* #1 in 1962 (shown at right), Stan Lee and Jack Kirby combined the world of the Super Hero with the world of the monster by creating a character who was both. Lee has said that the Hulk was partly inspired by Dr. Jekyll and Mr. Hyde.

In the origin story, scientist Bruce Banner was testing his latest creation, the gamma bomb. When teenager Rick Jones accidentally drove onto the test site, Banner raced out to save him. An enemy spy disobeyed the order to stop the bomb countdown and Banner was inundated with gamma radiation. He did not die, but later he changed into a superhumanly strong monster with a brutish personality—and grey skin. (Not until later did he turn into his familiar color of green.) From then on Banner was cursed to change back and forth between his human self and the monster known as the Hulk.

In which issue did the Hulk become green?

A. #3 (1962)
B. #2 (1962)
C. #4 (1962)
D. #6 (1963)

1464C 1465A 1466B 1467B 1468C 1469B 1470C 1471B 1472C

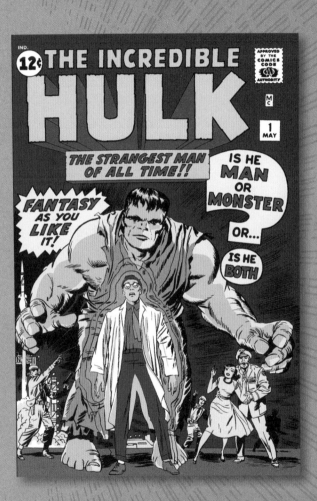

1473. Who was Betty Ross's first husband?

A. Bruce Banner

B. Leonard Samson

C. Major Glenn Talbot

D. Major Matt Talbot

1474. Who sought to kill Bruce Banner the first time he tried to marry Betty Ross?

A. The Rhino

B. The Leader and the Rhino

C. The Leader

D. Major Glenn Talbot

1475. What traditionally triggered Banner's transformations into the Hulk?

A. Exposure to gamma radiation

B. Fear

C. Nightfall

D. Becoming angry or excited

1476. How did the Leader gain his superhuman intellect?

A. He was born a mutant

B. He was exposed to gamma radiation

C. He was exposed to nuclear radiation

D. He was involved in genetic experiments

1477. Which U.S. president appeared in a Hulk story in *Tales to Astonish* #64 (1965) and #88 (1967)?

A. John F. Kennedy

B. Lyndon B. Johnson

C. Richard M. Nixon

D. Gerald R. Ford

1478. Who was General Ross's principal aide in *Tales to Astonish*?

A. Spad McCracken

B. Glenn Talbot

C. Jack Armbruster

D. Clay Quartermain

1479. Which of the following was the first to learn that Bruce Banner was the Hulk?

A. Betty Ross

B. Reed Richards

C. Glenn Talbot

D. General "Thunderbolt" Ross

The Incredible Hulk

1480. Which Spider-Man foe first appeared in a Hulk story in *Tales to Astonish* #81 (1966)?

- **A.** The Sandman
- **B.** Boomerang
- **C.** The Rhino
- **D.** Speed Demon

1481. Where did the Inedible Bulk first appear?

- **A.** *What Th--!?*
- **B.** *Not Brand ECCH*
- **C.** *Crazy*
- **D.** *The Incredible Hulk*

1482. Which artist first drew the Abomination?

- **A.** Steve Ditko
- **B.** Herb Trimpe
- **C.** Jack Kirby
- **D.** Gil Kane

1483. Who drew the first issue of the second *The Incredible Hulk* series?

- **A.** Gil Kane
- **B.** Marie Severin
- **C.** Jack Kirby
- **D.** Herb Trimpe

1484. When the Hulk first appeared in *Tales to Astonish*, who starred in the book's other series?

- **A.** Doctor Strange
- **B.** Giant-Man and the Wasp
- **C.** Sub-Mariner
- **D.** Iron Man

1485. Which statement is true about the Red Hulk?

- **A.** He is Bruce Banner
- **B.** As he gets angrier, he becomes even stronger
- **C.** As he gets angrier, he emits more intense heat
- **D.** He lacks human intelligence

1486. Who drew the Hulk's first eight *Tales to Astonish* installments?

- **A.** Dick Ayers
- **B.** Steve Ditko
- **C.** Jack Kirby
- **D.** Bill Everett

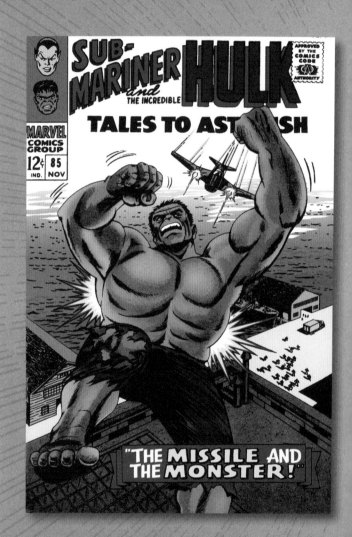

1487. Who drew or did layouts for the Hulk in *Tales to Astonish* #68–83 (1965–1966)?

A. Bob Powell   **C.** Jack Kirby
B. Steve Ditko   **D.** John Buscema

1488. Which future Defender did the Hulk battle in *Tales to Astonish* #93 (1967)?

A. Hawkeye   **C.** Doctor Strange
B. The Sub-Mariner   **D.** The Silver Surfer

1489. With which issue was *Tales to Astonish* retitled *The Incredible Hulk*?

A. #99 (1968)   **C.** #102 (1968)
B. #101 (1968)   **D.** #100 (1968)

1490.

1491. Which Spider-Man foe first fought the Hulk in *The Incredible Hulk* #104 (1968)?

A. The Green Goblin   **C.** The Rhino
B. The Speed Demon   **D.** The Sandman

1492. Whom did the Hulk and Sub-Mariner battle in *Tales to Astonish* #100 (1968)?

A. The Secret Empire   **C.** The Puppet Master
B. Each other   **D.** The Legion of the Living Lightning

1493. What was Boomerang's former occupation?

A. Mercenary assassin   **C.** Baseball player
B. Boomerang maker   **D.** Children's TV show host

1494. What is the Abomination's native country?

A. Hungary   **C.** The Soviet Union
B. The United States   **D.** Yugoslavia

1490.

The original *The Incredible Hulk* series may have been a little ahead of its time: it was canceled soon after it began. But Marvel continued to feature the Hulk as a guest star in other series, and finally awarded him half of the *Tales to Astonish* comic book (issue 85 shown at left).

Where Stan Lee had tried different approaches to the Hulk in the original series, it was in *Tales to Astonish* that the traditional portrayal of the Hulk was established. In contrast to the brilliant Bruce Banner he changes from, the Hulk has the intellect and emotions of a small child prone to terrible temper tantrums. The Hulk's vast strength makes him incredibly dangerous and destructive, and the angrier he gets, the greater his strength becomes. Yet the Hulk does not seek out conflict and highly values the few people he considers his friends. Indeed, the Hulk is a solitary soul who prefers to be left alone.

What was the first issue of *Tales to Astonish* in which the Hulk appeared?

A. #58 (1964)
B. #59 (1964)
C. #60 (1964)
D. #61 (1964)

The Incredible Hulk

1495. What guise was used by the spy who became the Abomination when he first appeared?
- **A.** Scientist
- **B.** Soldier
- **C.** U.S. government agent
- **D.** S.H.I.E.L.D. agent

1496. In which series did Attuma first appear?
- **A.** *Iron Man*
- **B.** *Sub-Mariner*
- **C.** *Giant-Man*
- **D.** *Fantastic Four*

1497. Who is Lord Vashti?
- **A.** Priest
- **B.** Scientist
- **C.** Namor's vizier
- **D.** Philosopher

1498. Who is the god of the Atlanteans?
- **A.** Kamuu
- **B.** Oceanus
- **C.** Poseidon
- **D.** Father Neptune

1499. Who was Namor's first wife?
- **A.** Dorma
- **B.** Namora
- **C.** Marrina
- **D.** Namorita

1500.

1501. How was the Sub-Mariner story different when it was reprinted in *Marvel Comics* #1 (1939)?
- **A.** There was no difference
- **B.** It had additional pages
- **C.** It was in color
- **D.** Both B and C

1502. Who was the original artist of the *Sub-Mariner* series in *Tales to Astonish*?
- **A.** Jack Kirby
- **B.** John Buscema
- **C.** Gene Colan
- **D.** Bill Everett

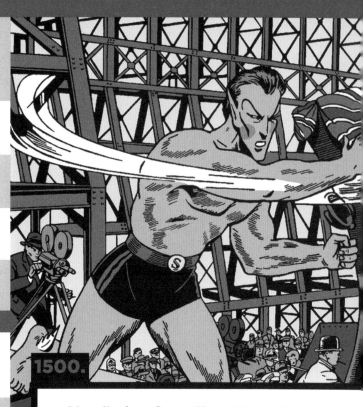

1500.

Marvel's first Super Hero, Prince Namor the Sub-Mariner (shown above) debuted in a story in *Motion Picture Comics Weekly* #1 (1939) that was then reprinted in the landmark *Marvel Comics* #1 in 1939. The Super Hero genre was then only a year old. But Namor, the creation of writer-artist "Wild" Bill Everett, was radically different from the other early Super Heroes who were beginning to appear.

Namor was the son of sea captain Leonard MacKenzie and Fen, the princess of a water-breathing race of humanoids known as submariners. Possessing vast strength, Namor could breathe air or water and had tiny wings in his feet that enabled him to fly. When his grandfather, Emperor Thakorr, decided

...as he prepared to launch the warship!

1503. What relation is Namora to Namor?
- **A.** Sister
- **B.** Cousin
- **C.** Daughter
- **D.** Wife

1504. Who or what is Namorita?
- **A.** Namora's clone
- **B.** Namora's daughter
- **C.** Namor's cousin
- **D.** All answers are correct

1505. Who murdered Lady Dorma?
- **A.** Attuma
- **B.** Llyra
- **C.** Krang
- **D.** Byrrah

1506. Who created Namorita?
- **A.** Bill Everett
- **B.** John Byrne
- **C.** Roy Thomas and John Buscema
- **D.** Stan Lee and Gene Colan

1507. To which team did Namorita belong?
- **A.** Thunderbolts
- **B.** The New Mutants
- **C.** The New Warriors
- **D.** S.U.R.F.

1508. Who destroyed the Atlantean city beneath the Antarctic Ocean?
- **A.** Destiny
- **B.** Surface dwellers with atomic tests
- **C.** Naga
- **D.** The U.S. Navy

1509. How does the Sub-Mariner breathe underwater?
- **A.** His lungs are adapted for breathing underwater
- **B.** He has gills
- **C.** He absorbs oxygen through his skin
- **D.** He doesn't; he can hold his breath indefinitely

1510. What is Oracle?
- **A.** Namor's corporation
- **B.** Member of the Shi'ar Imperial Guard
- **C.** Captain MacKenzie's ship
- **D.** All answers are correct

that the people of the surface world posed a threat to their undersea kingdom, Namor began a one-man war against America. He battled the original Human Torch and even unleashed a tidal wave against Manhattan. Despite Namor's attacks against humans, Everett allowed readers to understand and sympathize with Namor's point of view. Namor was the first super-antihero, and thus foreshadowed the Marvel Super Heroes of the 1960s.

Which other major Marvel Super Hero did Bill Everett co-create?

- **A.** Iron Man
- **B.** Ant-Man
- **C.** Ka-Zar
- **D.** Daredevil

The Incredible Hulk

1511. To which Super Hero team did Namor belong in 1940s comics?
- **A.** The Invaders
- **B.** Young Allies
- **C.** All Winners Squad
- **D.** Liberty Legion

1512. Which of Ka-Zar's foes did Namor battle in *Tales to Astonish* #95–98 (1967)?
- **A.** Zaladane
- **B.** Belasco
- **C.** Garokk the Petrified Man
- **D.** The Plunderer

1513. What other race besides the water-breathing Lemurians dwells in undersea Lemuria?
- **A.** The Deviants
- **B.** Molian Subterraneans
- **C.** Red Raven's people
- **D.** Tyrannian Subterraneans

1514. Which villain was the brother of Diane Arliss?
- **A.** Orka
- **B.** Tiger Shark
- **C.** Dr. Hydro
- **D.** The Plantman

1515. Who was the principal cover artist for *Sub-Mariner Comics* in the first half of the 1940s?
- **A.** Joe Maneely
- **B.** Alex Schomberg
- **C.** Bill Everett
- **D.** Syd Shores

1516. Who were the original writer and artist on the 1960s *Sub-Mariner* comic book?
- **A.** Stan Lee and John Buscema
- **B.** Roy Thomas and John Buscema
- **C.** Roy Thomas and Bill Everett
- **D.** Stan Lee and Gene Colan

1517. Which Golden Age character reappeared in *Sub-Mariner* #8 (1968)?
- **A.** Princess Fen
- **B.** The Fin
- **C.** Betty Dean
- **D.** Venus

1518. Which old ally or foe did Namor battle in *Sub-Mariner* #14 (1969)?
- **A.** Captain America
- **B.** Byrrah
- **C.** Toro
- **D.** The original Human Torch

1522.

In the fourth issue of *Fantastic Four* (1962), the new Human Torch found a bearded, amnesiac derelict in a flophouse on New York City's Bowery. The mysterious tramp turned out to be Namor, the long-missing Sub-Mariner (shown at left). Once his memory was restored, Namor resumed his war against the surface world, unleashing a whalelike monster against Manhattan.

Namor's undersea kingdom was Atlantis, and he would eventually lead the Atlanteans in an invasion of the surface world in *Fantastic Four Annual* #1 (1963). Collaborators Stan Lee and Jack Kirby emphasized Namor's heroism and sense of honor, making him a competitor of Reed Richards for Susan Storm's love.

Marvel gave the Sub-Mariner his own series in *Tales to Astonish*, a monthly comic he shared with the Hulk. There, Stan Lee depicted Namor as a regal figure, speaking in eloquent, elevated language, as if he were a Shakespearean monarch. Within several years Namor again starred in his own *Sub-Mariner* comic book as he had in the 1940s. In which issue of *Tales to Astonish* did Namor's series begin?

A. #70 (1965)
B. #72 (1965)
C. #71 (1965)
D. #73 (1965)

1519. On which creature are Orka's super-powers based?
A. Killer whale
B. Tiger shark
C. Great white shark
D. Sperm whale

1520. Which Golden Age hero fought Namor in *Sub-Mariner* #26 (1970)?
A. Red Raven
B. The Blue Diamond
C. The Blazing Skull
D. The Whizzer

1521. Who killed Leonard MacKenzie?
A. Llyra
B. Emperor Thakorr's soldiers
C. Tiger Shark
D. Paul Destine

1522.

1523. What is Llyra's parentage?
A. Human father, Lemurian mother
B. Atlantean father, human mother
C. Lemurian father, human mother
D. Human father, Atlantean mother

1524. Which 1940s Marvel heroine returned in *Sub-Mariner* #57 (1973)?
A. Sun Girl
B. Venus
C. Namora
D. Miss America

1525. Which Super Hero team used Hydrobase as its headquarters?
A. The Avengers
B. Fantastic Four
C. Defenders
D. X-Force

1526. When did Namorita debut?
A. *Tales to Astonish* #100 (1968)
B. *Sub-Mariner* #51 (1972)
C. *Sub-Mariner* #50 (1972)
D. *Sub-Mariner* #67 (1973)

1527. Who acted as the bride at Namor's wedding ceremony in *Sub-Mariner* #36 (1971)?
A. Dorma
B. Llyra
C. Susan Storm
D. Diane Arliss

The Incredible Hulk

1528. Who became the Red She-Hulk?
- **A.** Betty Ross
- **B.** Thundra
- **C.** Jennifer Walters
- **D.** Lyra

1529. When Hulk's intelligence was enhanced by the Extremis virus, what name did he use?
- **A.** Joe Fixit
- **B.** The Professor
- **C.** Dr. Banner
- **D.** Doc Green

1530. Who became the hero known as the Totally Awesome Hulk?
- **A.** Skaar
- **B.** Amadeus Cho
- **C.** Rick Jones
- **D.** Thunderbolt Ross

1531. What weapon did Red She-Hulk carry as a member of the Defenders?
- **A.** An enchanted sword
- **B.** An Uru hammer
- **C.** A laser pistol
- **D.** A flame thrower

1532. Who killed Bruce Banner during *Civil War II*?
- **A.** Iron Man
- **B.** Spider-Man
- **C.** Hawkeye
- **D.** Captain Marvel

1533. After his death, which criminal organization stole and reanimated the Hulk's remains?
- **A.** The Hand
- **B.** A.I.M.
- **C.** Hydra
- **D.** The Intelligentsia

1534. Who was the title character in the 2016 *Hulk* series?
- **A.** Bruce Banner
- **B.** Jennifer Walters
- **C.** Thunderbolt Ross
- **D.** Amadeus Cho

1535. Which team of heroes did not have a Hulk on its roster?
- **A.** A-Force
- **B.** All-New, All-Different Avengers
- **C.** Champions
- **D.** U.S.Avengers

1536. Who is *not* one of the Vishanti?
- **A.** Agamotto
- **B.** Hoggoth
- **C.** Raggadorr
- **D.** Oshtur

1537. Where in Manhattan is Doctor Strange's Sanctum Sanctorum located?
- **A.** East Village
- **B.** Greenwich Village
- **C.** Soho
- **D.** Tribeca

1538.

1538.

Standing apart from the other classic 1960s Marvel Super Heroes is Doctor Strange, Master of the Mystic Arts (shown at left), who debuted in *Strange Tales* #110 (1963). Stan Lee and Steve Ditko created both Doctor Strange and Spider-Man, yet Peter Parker's gritty, realistic city could not be more different from the surreal, occult realms that Doctor Strange traverses. In his origin story, Stephen Strange is an arrogant, wealthy surgeon—until his hands are injured in an automobile accident. Unable to operate, Strange loses everything, becoming a derelict. Hoping for a miraculous cure, he journeys to Tibet, where he meets the mystic master called the Ancient One. Strange finds a new selfless purpose in life as the Ancient One's student. Eventually, Doctor Strange becomes Earth's Sorcerer Supreme, its guardian against occult menaces from beyond.

What is Doctor Strange's address?

- **A.** 152C Prince Street
- **B.** 177A Bleecker Street
- **C.** 153B Houston Street
- **D.** 207A Lafayette Street

1539. Who scripted Steve Ditko's final *Doctor Strange* story?
- **A.** Roy Thomas
- **B.** Stan Lee
- **C.** Denny O'Neil
- **D.** Steve Ditko

1540. Who first succeeded Steve Ditko as *Doctor Strange* artist?
- **A.** Bill Everett
- **B.** Dan Adkins
- **C.** Jim Lawrence
- **D.** Marie Severin

1541. What does Eternity *not* embody?
- **A.** Death
- **B.** Life
- **C.** Time
- **D.** The universe

1542. What do the Mindless Ones lack besides minds?
- **A.** Legs
- **B.** Arms
- **C.** Faces
- **D.** Heads

1543. With which issue did *Strange Tales* become *Doctor Strange*?
- **A.** #160 (1967)
- **B.** #165 (1968)
- **C.** #169 (1968)
- **D.** #170 (1968)

1544. When Doctor Strange won his own *Dr. Strange* comic book in the late 1960s, who was the series' first creative team?
- **A.** Roy Thomas and Dan Adkins
- **B.** Roy Thomas and Gene Colan
- **C.** Stan Lee and Steve Ditko
- **D.** Roy Thomas and Marie Severin

The Incredible Hulk

1545. Whom did Doctor Strange and Spider-Man combat in *The Amazing Spider-Man Annual* #2 (1965)?
A. Baron Mordo
B. Mysterio
C. Xandu
D. Mister Rasputin

1546. What was the biggest change in Doctor Strange's costume in *Doctor Strange* #177 (1969)?
A. No Cloak of Levitation
B. Face mask
C. Different colors
D. No Amulet of Agamotto

1547. In which form did Agamotto appear to Doctor Strange?
A. A talking white rabbit
B. A grinning cat
C. A griffin
D. A giant talking caterpillar

1548. Which historical figure did Doctor Strange and Clea meet in *Doctor Strange* #18 (1976)?
A. Benjamin Franklin
B. George Washington
C. Thomas Jefferson
D. John Adams

1549. Who wrote the first issue of the new *Incredible Hulk* series in 1968?
A. Stan Lee
B. Roy Thomas
C. Gary Friedrich
D. Archie Goodwin

1550. Who wrote *The Incredible Hulk* from issue #109 to #120 (1968–1969)?
A. Stan Lee
B. Roy Thomas
C. Gary Friedrich
D. Archie Goodwin

1551.

1552. Where did the first issue of the second *The Incredible Hulk* series (1968) take place?
A. Asgard
B. Olympus
C. Atlantis
D. The Great Refuge

1553. Which Spider-Man foe first fought the Hulk in *The Incredible Hulk* #113–114 (1969)?
A. Medusa
B. Quicksilver
C. The Chameleon
D. The Sandman

1551.

When he first appeared in The *Incredible Hulk* #1 (1962), Rick Jones appeared to be in the mold of a hip teenager commonly shown in movies and TV shows of the 1950s and early 1960s. He drove his jalopy onto a gamma bomb test site on a dare, unaware of the danger. In pushing the boy into a protective trench just before the explosion, Banner exposed himself to the bomb's intense radiation. That night, the grateful Rick witnessed Banner's first transformation into the Incredible Hulk (shown at right). From then on, Rick was Banner's loyal friend and confidant, and the Hulk's, although sometimes the raging Hulk has rejected him.

Over the years Rick became a sidekick to the Avengers and other heroes and even tried being a Super Hero himself, wearing Bucky Barnes's uniform. For a time he was bonded with Captain Mar-Vell, exchanging places with him between Earth and the Negative Zone. Ultimately, however, Rick always returns to the *Hulk* series.

Which hero has Rick Jones *not* been a sidekick of?

A. Captain America
B. Daredevil
C. Rom
D. Captain Marvel's son Genis-Vell

OBSESSED WITH MARVEL

1554. Who succeeded Stan Lee as *The Incredible Hulk* writer in 1969?
- **A.** Gerry Conway
- **B.** Roy Thomas
- **C.** Gary Friedrich
- **D.** Archie Goodwin

1555. What was Herb Trimpe's first issue as *Hulk* artist?
- **A.** *The Incredible Hulk* #102 (1968)
- **B.** *The Incredible Hulk* #107 (1968)
- **C.** *The Incredible Hulk* #109 (1968)
- **D.** *The Incredible Hulk* #110 (1968)

1556. What is the Teen Brigade?
- **A.** Rick Jones's friends who communicate over ham radios
- **B.** Rick Jones's friends in New Mexico
- **C.** Rick Jones's rock band
- **D.** Rick Jones's friends who communicate over the Internet

1557. Whom did Rick Jones marry?
- **A.** April Sommers
- **B.** Brandy Clark
- **C.** Marlo Chandler
- **D.** Lou-Ann Savannah

1558. How many siblings does Bruce Banner have?
- **A.** None
- **B.** One
- **C.** Two
- **D.** Three

1559. Which Iron Man foe first menaced the Hulk in *The Incredible Hulk* #107 (1968)?
- **A.** The Titanium Man
- **B.** The Crusher
- **C.** Ultimo
- **D.** The Mandarin

1560. Which of Thor's nemeses did the Hulk first battle in *The Incredible Hulk* #125 (1970)?
- **A.** The Absorbing Man
- **B.** The Grey Gargoyle
- **C.** Loki
- **D.** Mr. Hyde

The Incredible Hulk

1561. Which future member of the Defenders appeared in *The Incredible Hulk* #126 (1970)?
- **A.** Patsy Walker
- **B.** Barbara Norriss
- **C.** Kyle Richmond
- **D.** Tania Belinskaya

1562. Who is the son of the original Gargoyle?
- **A.** The Abomination
- **B.** The Grey Gargoyle
- **C.** The Gremlin
- **D.** The Gargoyle of the Defenders

1563. Where did the Hulk's friend Jim Wilson live when he first met the Hulk?
- **A.** Washington D.C.
- **B.** Chicago, Illinois
- **C.** Watts, Los Angeles
- **D.** Harlem, New York City

1564. How did Jim Wilson die?
- **A.** Accidentally killed by the Hulk
- **B.** Sacrificed his life to save Bruce Banner
- **C.** Cancer
- **D.** AIDS

1565. Which famous writer from outside comics co-created Jarella?
- **A.** Orson Scott Card
- **B.** Stephen King
- **C.** Michael Moorcock
- **D.** Harlan Ellison

1566. Which TV writer-producer wrote an *Ultimate Wolverine vs. Hulk* limited series (2005–2009)?
- **A.** Joss Whedon
- **B.** Damon Lindelof
- **C.** Carlton Cuse
- **D.** Allen Heinberg

1567. Which Marvel character died the same way as Jarella?
- **A.** Dark Phoenix
- **B.** Ben Parker
- **C.** Captain George Stacy
- **D.** Gwen Stacy

1568. Which future member of the Defenders appeared in The *Incredible Hulk* #142 (1971)?
- **A.** The Valkyrie
- **B.** Doctor Strange
- **C.** The Silver Surfer
- **D.** Nighthawk

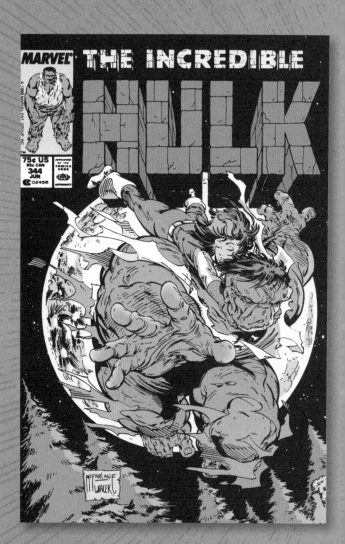

1569. What is Doc Samson's profession apart from being a Super Hero?
- **A.** Psychiatrist
- **B.** Physician
- **C.** Nuclear physicist
- **D.** Surgeon

1570. Which monster first appeared in *The Incredible Hulk* #162 (1973)?
- **A.** Zzzax
- **B.** The Space Parasite
- **C.** The Wendigo
- **D.** The Crawling Unknown

1571.

Along with Bruce Banner and Rick Jones, *The Incredible Hulk* #1 (1962) introduced two other key members of the series' cast: General T. E. "Thunderbolt" Ross and his daughter, Betty (shown at left with the Hulk). In charge of the military side of the gamma bomb project, General Ross despised the scholarly Bruce Banner for not living up to his stereotypical standards of masculinity. In fact, Banner and Ross's daughter, Betty, were in love with each other. In the 1960s, Betty was originally portrayed as rather subdued and introverted, like Banner, though decades later she would be depicted as an "army brat" with a forceful personality. As Captain Ahab is to Moby Dick, so "Thunderbolt" Ross has been to the Hulk, as Ross is obsessed with capturing and destroying the Hulk. As for Betty, though she once wed another man, she ultimately proved loyal to Bruce and finally, bravely married him. Once believed dead, Betty has since turned up alive.

What is "Thunderbolt" Ross's real first name?

- **A.** Theodore
- **B.** Thaddeus
- **C.** Tiberius
- **D.** Thomas

1572. What gamma-irradiated creature did Betty Ross once become?
- **A.** Ogress
- **B.** The Harpy
- **C.** She-Hulk
- **D.** Man-Killer

1573. How was Betty Ross Banner believed to have perished?
- **A.** Hit by car
- **B.** Pushed off building
- **C.** Gamma radiation poisoning
- **D.** Beaten to death

1574. Who was responsible for the seeming death of Betty Ross Banner?
- **A.** The Abomination
- **B.** The Maestro
- **C.** The Leader
- **D.** Bruce Banner/The Hulk

1575. Which political figures appeared in *The Incredible Hulk* #146 and #152 (1971–1972)?
- **A.** Mao Tse-Tung and Leonid Brezhnev
- **B.** Richard Nixon and Henry Kissinger
- **C.** Richard Nixon and Leonid Brezhnev
- **D.** Richard Nixon and Spiro Agnew

1576. Which 1940s character was also known as Betty Ross?
- **A.** Captain America's girlfriend
- **B.** Golden Girl
- **C.** Both A and B
- **D.** Policewoman in *Sub-Mariner*

1577. Which member of the *X-Men* cast seemingly died in *The Incredible Hulk* #161 (1973)?
- **A.** The Juggernaut
- **B.** The Beast
- **C.** The Beast's girlfriend, Vera
- **D.** The Mimic

The Incredible Hulk

1578. Which hero debuted in *The Incredible Hulk* #180 (1974)?
- **A.** Wolverine
- **B.** The Phantom Eagle
- **C.** Sabra
- **D.** Doc Samson

1579. Who or what is Zzzax?
- **A.** Giant mutated insect
- **B.** Monster that discharges electrical bolts
- **C.** Creature composed of electromagnetic/psionic energy
- **D.** Alien from another world

1580. Who were the aliens who menaced Earth in the 1970s *The Rampaging Hulk* series?
- **A.** The Krylorians
- **B.** The Sagittarians
- **C.** The Skrulls
- **D.** The Toad Men

1581. Who drew the initial three issues of the original *The Rampaging Hulk* (1977)?
- **A.** Howard Chaykin
- **B.** Walter Simonson
- **C.** Tom Sutton
- **D.** Tony DeZuniga

1582.

1583. What was the profession of the alien woman Bereet?
- **A.** Technician
- **B.** Techno-artist
- **C.** Diplomat
- **D.** Actress

1584. With which issue was *The Rampaging Hulk* retitled *The Hulk!*?
- **A.** #15 (1979)
- **B.** #8 (1978)
- **C.** #10 (1978)
- **D.** #12 (1978)

1585. What is the name of Bruce Banner's mother?
- **A.** Rebecca
- **B.** Elizabeth
- **C.** Mary
- **D.** Jennifer

1586. Where did Bruce Banner go to college?
- **A.** California Institute of Technology
- **B.** Massachusetts Institute of Technology
- **C.** Desert State University
- **D.** Princeton University

1582.

Doctor Strange's enemy and rival has long been the Ancient One's renegade student, Baron Mordo. Menacing though he is, Mordo has served under an even greater menace: the dread Dormammu, ruler of the Dark Dimension (shown at right), who for centuries has longed to conquer Earth.

Originally, Dormammu was a humanoid sorcerer from the dimension of the Faltine who transformed himself into pure mystical energy. As a result, though he wears a costume and retains a basic humanoid form, his head looks like a living, burning flame. Over the years, Dormammu has become the archenemy of Doctor Strange, who has repeatedly thwarted his attempts to add Earth to his conquests. But it was on Strange's first journey into Dormammu's realm that he met the great love of his life, the beautiful Clea, princess of the Dark Dimension, who eventually accompanied him back to Earth.

Which writer gave Clea her name?

- **A.** Stan Lee
- **B.** Roy Thomas
- **C.** Gary Friedrich
- **D.** Denny O'Neil

OBSESSED WITH MARVEL

1587. Which Marvel monster was also originally known as the Hulk?
A. Diablo
B. Xemnu the Titan
C. Taboo
D. Goom

1588. Which planet did the Metal Master come from?
A. A-Chiltar III
B. Astra
C. Vega Superior
D. Xeron

1589. Where did the original Ringmaster of Death appear?
A. *Captain America Comics*
B. *The Incredible Hulk*
C. *Marvel Mystery Comics*
D. *The Amazing Spider-Man*

1590. Who banished Tyrannus to Subterranea?
A. Merlin
B. King Arthur
C. The Roman Empire
D. The Deviants

1591. Where did the Leader first appear?
A. *Tales to Astonish* #60 (1964)
B. *Tales to Astonish* #62 (1964)
C. *Tales to Astonish* #63 (1964)
D. *The Incredible Hulk* #6 (1963)

1592. What was the former occupation of Silver Dagger?
A. Exorcist
B. Cardinal
C. Theologian
D. Sorcerer

1593. Who was the original creative team on *Doctor Strange*'s new series in 1974?
A. Steve Englehart and Frank Brunner
B. Steve Englehart and Gene Colan
C. Marv Wolfman and Gene Colan
D. Gardner Fox and Frank Brunner

1594. Which famous author did Doctor Strange encounter in Times Square on New Year's Eve?
A. Tom Wolfe
B. Stephen King
C. Stan Lee
D. Jonathan Lethem

1595. Who is *not* a member of the Witches in the series of the same name?
A. Jennifer Kale
B. The Scarlet Witch
C. Topaz
D. Satana

The Incredible Hulk

1596. Who or what is the Nameless One?
- **A.** One of a race of undersea monsters Namor fought
- **B.** Shuma-Gorath
- **C.** Leader of the other-dimensional monsters called Undying Ones
- **D.** Clea before her name was revealed

1597. Who starred in the backup series in the original *The Rampaging Hulk* (1977-1978)?
- **A.** Dominic Fortune
- **B.** Howard the Duck
- **C.** Moon Knight
- **D.** Ulysses Bloodstone

1598. To whom is Clea *not* related?
- **A.** Rintrah
- **B.** Dormammu
- **C.** Orini
- **D.** Umar

1599. How are Dormammu and Umar related?
- **A.** Father and daughter
- **B.** Brother and sister
- **C.** Cousins
- **D.** Son and mother

1600. How did Dormammu and Doctor Strange fight a duel in *Strange Tales* #140-141 (1966)?
- **A.** Hand-to-hand combat
- **B.** Rings of Raggadorr
- **C.** Crimson Bands of Cyttorak
- **D.** Pincers of Power

1601.

1602. Who first drew the Living Tribunal?
- **A.** Marie Severin
- **B.** Steve Ditko
- **C.** Bill Everett
- **D.** Dan Adkins

1603. What is Baron Mordo's middle name?
- **A.** Amadeus
- **B.** Vincent
- **C.** Karl
- **D.** Ludgate

1604. Where was the demon Zom imprisoned?
- **A.** An amphora
- **B.** A mystical cage
- **C.** An energy cube
- **D.** An underground cavern

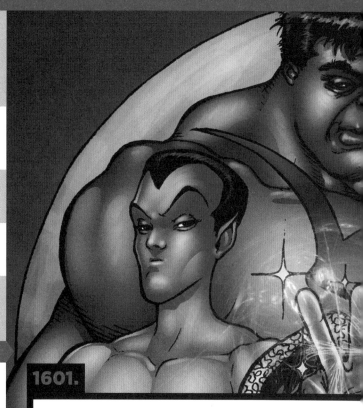

1601.

If the Avengers, Fantastic Four, and the X-Men are all Super Hero teams, then the Defenders were originally described as a nonteam. Conceived by writer Roy Thomas, the original Defenders were Doctor Strange, the Hulk, and the Sub-Mariner (shown above with the Silver Surfer)—three loners who banded together in emergencies to battle menaces to their world. There was no formal organization nor were there regular meetings; the Hulk and Namor resisted taking orders.

The Defenders first appeared in *Marvel Feature* #1 in 1971 and graduated to their own *The Defenders* comic

1605. How can the demon Zom be weakened?

A. Binding his hands

B. Preventing him from speaking spells

C. Severing his forelock

D. Blinding him

1606. Whom did the Hulk battle in the Avengers-Defenders War?

A. Iron Man

B. The Vision

C. Thor

D. Captain America

1607. Where was Dormammu reborn on Earth in *Doctor Strange* #6-8 (1975)?

A. The Grand Canyon

B. In a volcano

C. The San Andreas Fault

D. The temple of his worshippers

1608. What did the time-traveling sorcerer Sise-Neg finally become?

A. The magician Cagliostro

B. The first human being

C. The god Genesis

D. Eternity

1609. Who is Orini?

A. Dormammu's disciple

B. Umar's lover

C. Clea's father

D. All answers are correct

1610. What fate did Alpha the Ultimate Mutant mete out to Magneto in *The Defenders* #16 (1974)?

A. Turned to stone

B. Turned into a nonmutant human

C. Shrunken to miniature size

D. Turned into an infant

1611. Who was the mysterious assassin in writer Steve Gerber's run on *The Defenders*?

A. Richard Rider

B. An elf with a gun

C. One of the Bozos

D. The Foolkiller

1612. How was Dormammu finally defeated in "The End at Last" in *Strange Tales* #146 (1966)?

A. Bested in a duel by Doctor Strange

B. In a confrontation with Eternity

C. Betrayed by Umar

D. Overpowered by the horde of Mindless Ones

in 1972. The Silver Surfer also sometimes worked with the team, as did other heroes for brief stints. In time, the Defenders gained members who did not have their own series, notably Nighthawk, the former Squadron Sinister villain turned millionaire Super Hero. There was also Brunnhilda the Valkyrie, an Asgardian goddess whose spirit inhabited the body of a mortal woman before regaining her own, and later Hellcat, the Super Hero identity of Patsy Walker.

Which villain was in the first *The Defenders* story in *Marvel Feature* #1 (1971)?

A. Dormammu

B. Yandroth

C. Nebulon and the Squadron Sinister

D. The Nameless One

The Incredible Hulk

1613. Whose body did Brunnhilda the Valkyrie's spirit inhabit in early *The Defenders* stories?

A. Amora the Enchantress
B. Her original Asgardian body
C. Samantha Parrington
D. Barbara Norriss

1614. To which team did Nighthawk of the Defenders originally belong?

A. Squadron Sinister
B. Squadron Supreme
C. Redeemers
D. Avengers

1615. Who was *not* one of the Headmen?

A. Shrunken Bones
B. Thunder Head
C. Chondu the Mystic
D. Ruby Thursday

1616.

1617. Who is Dr. Arthur Nagan?

A. Asmodeus of the Sons of Satannish
B. Marduk of the Sons of Satannish
C. Gorilla-Man
D. Shrunken Bones

1618. Which Defender's brain was removed by Dr. Arthur Nagan?

A. Nighthawk
B. Doctor Strange
C. The Valkyrie
D. The Hulk

1619. Which series was concluded in the pages of *The Defenders*?

A. *Omega the Unknown*
B. *Shanna the She-Devil*
C. *The Claws of the Cat*
D. *The Eternals*

1620. Who headed the Bozos' Celestial Mind Control movement?

A. Lunatik
B. Ruby Thursday
C. Cyrus Black
D. Nebulon

1621. Who was the Red Guardian in *The Defenders*?

A. The Black Widow's husband, Alexi Shostakov
B. Dr. Tania Belinskaya
C. Soviet Super Hero of World War I
D. Josef Petkus

1616.

Though for more than three decades Patsy Walker (shown at right) has been best known as the Super Heroine Hellcat, her origins in comics are surprisingly different. She first appeared in 1944 in *Miss America Comics* #2, not as a Super Heroine but as the star of a teenage girls' comedy series. Patsy soon won her own *Patsy Walker* comic book in 1945, and it ran for 124 issues until December 1965. Al Jaffee wrote and drew most of the early stories, long before he became famous as a cartoonist for *MAD* magazine. Patsy also appeared in the spin-off comics *Patsy and Her Pals* and *Patsy and Hedy*. Patsy and Hedy first crossed over with the new Marvel Super Heroes of the 1960s in *Fantastic Four Annual* #3 (1965), which foreshadowed the unexpected twist that this comics heroine's life was to take.

What is the last name of Patsy's friend Hedy?

A. Watson
B. Collins
C. Wolfe
D. Fox

1613D 1614A 1615B 1616C 1617C 1618A 1619A 1620D 1621B

1622. Beyond the Defenders, which of the following super teams has Namor *not* been a member?

A. Avengers

B. Invaders

C. X-Men

D. Champions

1623. After the events of *Avengers Vs. X-Men*, Namor and Atlantis were in constant conflict with which kingdom?

A. Attilan

B. Wakanda

C. Latveria

D. Asgard

1624. During *Fear Itself*, who did *not* fight Attuma alongside Namor?

A. Doctor Strange

B. Silver Surfer

C. Hulk

D. She-Hulk (Lyra)

1625. Which member of the Illuminati did Namor state was the greatest man he knew?

A. Black Panther

B. Doctor Strange

C. Black Bolt

D. Himself

1626. Who was the sole survivor of Earth-4290001, which Namor destroyed?

A. Sun God

B. Jovian

C. The Rider

D. Doctor Spectrum

1627. After deeming the New Avengers incapable of saving the universe, Namor helped form what group?

A. The Cabal

B. Secret Defenders

C. Secret Avengers

D. The Illuminati

1628. Who left Namor to die on an alternate Earth during "Time Runs Out"?

A. Doctor Strange & Beast

B. Black Bolt & Black Panther

C. Captain America & Iron Man

D. Thanos & Doctor Doom

1629. Which team of super-powered characters seemingly beheaded Namor?

A. Frightful Four

B. Squadron Supreme

C. Masters of Evil

D. Defenders

The Incredible Hulk

1630. What is the name of Barbara Norriss's husband?

- **A.** Jim
- **B.** Jack
- **C.** John
- **D.** Joe

1631. Who was Patsy Walker's second husband?

- **A.** Kyle Richmond
- **B.** Daimon Hellstrom
- **C.** Jack Norriss
- **D.** Patsy never remarried

1632. Who is Buzz Baxter?

- **A.** Patsy Walker's first husband
- **B.** The Super Villain Mad-Dog
- **C.** Patsy Walker's high school sweetheart
- **D.** All answers are correct

1633. Whom did Patsy Walker visit in *The Defenders* #65 (1978)?

- **A.** Millie the Model
- **B.** Buzz Baxter
- **C.** Hedy Wolfe
- **D.** Mary Jane Watson

1634. Which member of Jennifer Walters's law firm is *not* named after a leading person in Marvel history?

- **A.** Goodman
- **B.** Holliway
- **C.** Lieber
- **D.** Kurtzberg

1635. How did the Leader (seemingly) die in *Tales to Astonish* #74 (1965)?

- **A.** He was overexposed to radiation
- **B.** His mind was overloading with knowledge from an alien device
- **C.** He perished in an atomic blast
- **D.** He was killed in combat with the Hulk

1636. Which subversive organization first appeared in *Tales to Astonish* #81 (1966)?

- **A.** Legion of the Living Lightning
- **B.** The M
- **C.** The Secret Empire
- **D.** The Sons of the Serpent

1637. Who or what was the Hulk-Killer in *Tales to Astonish* #86–87 (1966–1967)?

- **A.** Android created by the Leader
- **B.** The Abomination
- **C.** General "Thunderbolt" Ross's new anti-Hulk weapon
- **D.** Name for special agent of the Hulkbusters

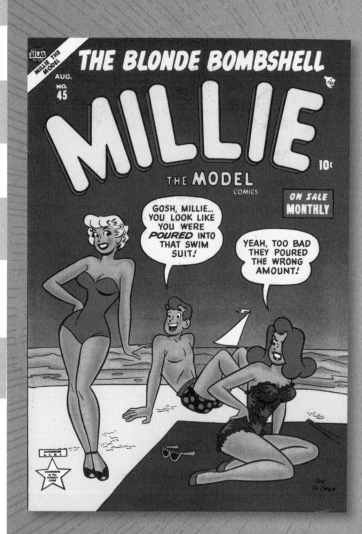

1638. Which omnipotent being confronted the Hulk in *Tales to Astonish* #89 (1967)?
- **A.** The Grandmaster
- **B.** The Watcher
- **C.** Galactus
- **D.** The Stranger

1639. What happened to the High Evolutionary in *Tales to Astonish* #96 (1967)?
- **A.** He devolved into a primitive life form
- **B.** He died in combat with renegade members of his New Men
- **C.** He tried unsuccessfully to evolve the Hulk into a higher being
- **D.** He evolved himself into a godlike being

1640. Who was Namor's second wife?
- **A.** Carrie Alexander
- **B.** Marrina
- **C.** Phoebe Marrs
- **D.** Jacqueline Trufaut

1641. Which monster did Namor fight in *Tales to Astonish* #71 (1965)?
- **A.** Seaweed Man
- **B.** Behemoth
- **C.** Lava Monster
- **D.** It, the Silent One

1642. Who attempted to usurp Atlantis's throne during Namor's initial "Quest" story in *Tales to Astonish*?
- **A.** Warlord Krang
- **B.** Byrrah
- **C.** Lord Seth
- **D.** Attuma

1643.

1644. Who was Millie the Model's niece, who starred in her own *Star Comic* in 1985-1986?
- **A.** Millicent
- **B.** Misty
- **C.** Chili
- **D.** Jill Jerold

1645. Who was a creator of the comic book about Millie the Model's niece?
- **A.** June Brigman
- **B.** Mary Wilshire
- **C.** Trina Robbins
- **D.** Amanda Conner

1643.

One of Marvel's longest-running series isn't a Super Hero comic at all. Millie Collins (shown at left) debuted in *Millie the Model* #1 in the winter of 1945.

Her series ran for 207 issues and twenty-eight years, not ending until December 1973. Although it was briefly an adventure series, *Millie* has usually been a humor comic.

The original *Millie* series spawned spin-offs: *A Date With Millie*, *Life With Millie*, *Mad About Millie*, and *Modeling With Millie*. Pioneering female comic book artist Ruth Atkinson illustrated the first issue of *Millie the Model* and may have been the character's creator. Dan DeCarlo drew *Millie* from 1949 to 1959, setting the visual style for the series. Stan Lee and artist Stan Goldberg then took over the series, even as Lee began co-creating the classic Marvel Super Heroes. After making occasional appearances in modern Marvel comics, including *The Defenders*, Millie returned to the spotlight in the new *Models, Inc.*

Who costars in *Models, Inc.*?

- **A.** Patsy Walker
- **B.** Mary Jane Watson
- **C.** Chili Storm
- **D.** All three

The Incredible Hulk

1646. Which god did the Hulk combat in *Tales to Astonish* #79 (1966)?
A. Hercules
B. Thor
C. Pluto
D. Loki

1647. Which Super Hero did Namor combat in *Tales to Astonish* #82 (1966)?
A. The Hulk
B. Iron Man
C. Captain America
D. Daredevil

1648. Who is Byrrah?
A. Namor's rival and cousin
B. Emperor Thakorr's stepson
C. Character created in the Golden Age
D. All answers are correct

1649. Which Super Hero did Dr. Walter Newell become?
A. Sharkskin
B. Triton
C. Stingray
D. Undertow

1650. What was Betty Dean's job when Namor first met her?
A. Policewoman
B. Olympic swimmer
C. Soldier
D. New York City mayor's aide

1651. What was Betty Dean's married name?
A. Alexander
B. Newell
C. Prentiss
D. Dean

1652. How did Betty Dean die?
A. Slain by Dr. Lemuel Dorcas in saving Namor's life
B. Old age
C. Cancer
D. Murdered by Tiger Shark

1653. How did Namor get amnesia before *Fantastic Four* #4 (1962)?
A. He recieved a severe head injury during destruction of Atlantean city
B. He had a traumatic shock when he witnessed the deaths of Thakorr and Fen
C. He was induced by Byrrah to rid himself of his rival for the throne
D. He was induced by Destiny's Helmet of Power

1660.

After Patsy Walker's career as the star of teenage girls' comics came to an end, Steve Englehart wrote her into the Beast's solo series in *Amazing Adventures*. Patsy was a now an adult and unhappily married to her high school sweetheart "Buzz" Baxter, a military officer and future criminal. Patsy befriended the Beast, and when the Beast joined the Avengers, a series Englehart also wrote, she followed him.

Tagging along with the Avengers on a mission, Patsy discovered a costume that amplified her athletic abilities. Donning the costume, she fulfilled her dream of becoming a Super Hero and named herself Hellcat (shown at left). Soon afterward, she joined the Defenders and became one of the team's mainstays for years. She married Daimon Hellstrom, and for a long time she was actually dead, but has since returned to life and starred in her own *Hellcat* miniseries (2000).

What was Hellcat's catchphrase?

A. "Cheese and crackers!"
B. "Oh my stars and garters!"
C. "Face front, true believer!"
D. "Face it, tiger, you just hit the jackpot!"

1654. What cosmic group did Doctor Strange lead during the "Time Runs Out" storyline?
A. Ivory Kings **C.** Black Swans
B. Black Priests **D.** Beyonders

1655. During *Secret Wars* (2015), what role did Doctor Strange play on Battleworld?
A. Sheriff **C.** Court Magician
B. Baron **D.** Demigod

1656. Who was the librarian from the Bronx who assisted Doctor Strange in his 2015 series?
A. Zelma **C.** Irma
B. Velma **D.** Norma

1657. What is the name of the creature made from pain and suffering that was locked in Doctor Strange's cellar?
A. Doctor Demonicus **C.** D'Spayre
B. Mister Misery **D.** N'Astirh

1658. During the "Last Days of Magic" storyline, who was hunting and killing heroes with magical powers?
A. Daimon Hellstrom **C.** Empirikul
B. Baron Mordo **D.** Mephisto

1659. Who was the magical protector of Mexico during "The Last Days of Magic"?
A. Talisman **C.** Doctor Voodoo
B. Monako **D.** Médico Místico

1660.

1661. What drinking establishment is a popular getaway for the Marvel Universe's magical heroes?
A. The Bar with No Name **C.** The Witch's Cauldron
B. The Quiet Room **D.** The Bar with No Doors

The Incredible Hulk

1662. What was the Missing Link in *The Incredible Hulk* #105 (1968)?

A. A being that is half-ape, half-man

B. A Sasquatch

C. An Abominable Snowman

D. A prehistoric man with super-powers

1663. Where did the Hulk travel to in *The Incredible Hulk* #109–110 (1968)?

A. Asgard

B. The Savage Land

C. The Soviet Union

D. Another planet

1664. Who or what was Umbu the Unliving in *The Incredible Hulk* #109–110 (1968)?

A. A gigantic mutant monster

B. A colossal alien robot

C. A Savage Land warrior with superhuman strength

D. An immense extraterrestrial warlord

1665. Who or what was the Galaxy Master in *The Incredible Hulk* #111–112 (1969)?

A. Creature that devours planets

B. Sentient cosmic entity that enslaves populations of planets

C. Monarch of a galactic empire

D. Galactus

1666. Who or what does Joe Timms become in *The Incredible Hulk* #121 (1969)?

A. The Glob

B. The Crawling Unknown

C. The Constrictor

D. The Inheritor

1667. Which Fantastic Four foe clashes with the Hulk in *The Incredible Hulk* #119–120 (1969)?

A. The Mad Thinker

B. The Monster from the Lost Lagoon

C. Psycho-Man

D. Maximus

1668.

1668.

Before there was Doctor Strange, Marvel had an earlier mystical hero, Doctor Druid (shown at right). In fact, with Doctor Druid's first appearance in *Amazing Adventures* #1, cover-dated June 1961, he became Marvel's first Super Hero of the 1960s, preceding the Fantastic Four (whose first issue came five months later).

Doctor Druid was originally called Doctor Droom. (His creators, Stan Lee and Jack Kirby, would within a year create their most famous villain, the similarly named Doctor Doom.) When Doctor Droom was revived in *The Incredible Hulk* #209–211 in 1977, he was renamed Doctor Druid. Writer Roger Stern added Doctor Druid to the Avengers in the 1980s, and British author Warren Ellis and artist Leonardo Manco made him the star of the miniseries *Druid* in 1995. Ultimately, Doctor Druid was killed by Hellstorm, but he was succeeded by his son, known simply as Druid.

What was Doctor Druid's full name?

A. Karl Amadeus Druid

B. Anthony Stewart Druid

C. Anthony Ludgate Druid

D. Stephen Ludgate Druid

1669. Who was the Night-Crawler in *The Incredible Hulk* #126 (1970)?

   A. Future member of the X-Men   **C.** One of the Undying Ones

   B. Monster later known as Dark-Crawler   **D.** One of the evil Inhumans

1670. Which legendary monster was the Hulk mistaken for in *The Incredible Hulk* #134 (1970)?

   A. The Golem   **C.** Sasquatch

   B. A Troll   **D.** Frankenstein's monster

1671. How did the Hulk change in *The Incredible Hulk* #130–131 (1970)?

   A. He reverts to a grey color   **C.** He and Banner split into separate entities

   B. He gains Banner's intellect   **D.** Banner's head is on The Hulk's body

1672. Who or what was Mogol in *The Incredible Hulk* #127 (1970)?

   A. A character who was destroyed by the Hulk   **C.** The Hulk's super-strong friend

   B. Robot created by Tyrannus   **D.** All answers are correct

1673. Which early twentieth-century costumed hero guest starred in *The Incredible Hulk* #135 (1971)?

   A. The original Union Jack   **C.** The Destroyer

   B. The Phantom Eagle   **D.** Captain America

1674. Who or what is Klaatu in *The Incredible Hulk* #136–137 (1971)?

   A. Immense monster in outer space   **C.** Demon from an alternate dimension

   B. Alien humanoid   **D.** Tyrannical leader of a foreign army

1675. What happened to Betty Ross in *The Incredible Hulk* #138 (1971)?

   A. She turned into glass   **C.** She became engaged to Glenn Talbot

   B. She went into a coma   **D.** She entered a convent

The Incredible Hulk

1676. What happened to the Hulk in *The Incredible Hulk* #123 (1970)?

A. He gained control over his transformations

B. He retained Banner's intellect and personality in Hulk form

C. Both A and B

D. He was put on trial

1677. Who is Psyklop?

A. Alternate Earth counterpart of Cyclops

B. Insectoid servant of the Dark Gods

C. The Space Parasite

D. Mythical cyclops that battled Namor and Hercules

1678. Who is Captain Cybor?

A. Modern pirate using advanced technology

B. Cyborg warrior

C. Leader of the Infraworlders

D. Cyborg starship captain who hunts Klaatu

1679. Who was Captain Cybor's first mate on his starship *Andromeda* in *The Incredible Hulk* #137?

A. The Abomination

B. The Hulk

C. Amphibion

D. Torgo

1680. What is K'ai?

A. Where Jarella reigned in the microverse

B. Mystic realm of Iron Fist's origin

C. Other-dimensional world ruled by Shazana

D. Princess of the Sagittarians

1681.

1682. Which real-life celebrity or celebrities appeared in *The Incredible Hulk* #142 (1971)?

A. Stan Lee

B. Author Tom Wolfe

C. Musician Alice Cooper

D. The rock band KISS

1683. Which enemy of the Fantastic Four combated the Hulk in *The Incredible Hulk* #143-144 (1971)?

A. Blastaar

B. Psycho-Man

C. Dragon Man

D. Doctor Doom

1681.

When Kang the Conqueror engaged in a competition with the all-powerful alien Grandmaster in *The Avengers* #69–70 (1969, issue 70 shown at right), the warlord from the future forced the Avengers to serve as his team of champions. The Grandmaster assembled his own team of super-powered players—Hyperion, Nighthawk, Doctor Spectrum, and the Whizzer—to become the Super Villains known as the Squadron Sinister. Roy Thomas, who wrote the story, subsequently introduced the Squadron Supreme, the Super Hero team of a parallel Earth, in *The Avengers* #85 and #86 (1971). This Squadron had its own heroic versions of Hyperion, Nighthawk, the Whizzer, and Doctor Spectrum, and many other members as well, including Power Princess, Amphibion, Lady Lark, the Golden Archer, and Tom Thumb. The Squadron Supreme continued to make guest appearances in series like *The Avengers* and *The Defenders*.

Which member of the Squadron Sinister reformed and joined the Defenders?

A. Hyperion

B. Doctor Spectrum

C. Nighthawk

D. The Whizzer

OBSESSED WITH MARVEL

1684. Who or what is the Shaper of Worlds?
A. A sentient Cosmic Cube
B. A Skrull with immense reality-shaping powers
C. One of the Celestials
D. An Elder of the Universe

1685. Who was the father of the Shaper's protégé Glorian?
A. Norman Osborn
B. Gregory Gideon
C. Wilson Fisk
D. "Thunderbolt" Ross

1686. How many siblings does Betty Ross have?
A. One
B. Two
C. Three
D. None

1687. What are Warthos?
A. The Hulk's alien allies in World War Hulk
B. Demonic beings serving Urthona
C. Giant creatures resembling pigs in K'ai
D. Sea monsters that Namor fought

1688. Who began writing The Incredible Hulk with issue #159 (1973)?
A. Bill Mantlo
B. Steve Englehart
C. Len Wein
D. Doug Moench

1689. Which writer of The Incredible Hulk first established that Bruce Banner suffered from multiple personality disorder?
A. Bill Mantlo
B. Len Wein
C. Peter David
D. Roger Stern

1690. Who was Captain Axis in The Incredible Hulk #155 (1972)?
A. Agent Axis under a new name
B. Nazi given super-powers by the Shaper
C. World War II Nazi agent with super-powers
D. Operative of the Red Skull

1691. Who is Xeron the Star-Slayer?
A. Energy harpooner who serves Captain Cybor
B. Member of the Creators in Doctor Strange #19–28 (1976–1978)
C. Ally of Stellaris in opposing the Celestials
D. Adversary of the Galaxy Master

The Incredible Hulk

1692. Who are Holi and Moli?
- **A.** Members of Clea's rebellion in the Dark Dimension
- **B.** Bereet's pets
- **C.** Members of K'ai's Pantheon of Sorcerers
- **D.** Members of the Bozos

1693. Why did Kang make a wager with the Grandmaster?
- **A.** To restore Princess Ravonna to life
- **B.** To gain mastery of time and space
- **C.** To destroy the Avengers
- **D.** Because both are compulsive gamblers

1694. Which incarnation of Kang is the enemy of the Squadron Supreme?
- **A.** Victor Timely
- **B.** Scarlet Centurion
- **C.** Immortus
- **D.** Pharaoh Rama-Tut

1695. Where did Captain Omen and his Infra-Worlders dwell?
- **A.** In the microverse
- **B.** In an alternate dimension
- **C.** In a world-sized spaceship
- **D.** In an immense submarine

1696. Who was Colonel Jack Armbruster?
- **A.** Navy officer who clashed with the Sub-Mariner in 1939
- **B.** General Ross's replacement hunting the Hulk
- **C.** Army officer who rescued General Ross from Russia
- **D.** S.H.I.E.L.D. operative in charge of Project: Greenskin

1697. Who returned from the dead in *The Incredible Hulk* #178 (1974)?
- **A.** The Gargoyle
- **B.** Major Glenn Talbot
- **C.** The Leader
- **D.** Adam Warlock

1698. Which X-Men foe did the Hulk combat in *The Incredible Hulk* #173–174 (1974)?
- **A.** The Cobalt Man
- **B.** Magneto
- **C.** The Blob
- **D.** The Maha Yogi

1699. Which alien menace returned in *The Incredible Hulk* #184 (1975)?
- **A.** Googam, Son of Goom
- **B.** Warlord Kaa the Shadow Alien
- **C.** The Space Parasite
- **D.** The Bi-Beast

1704.

Though they both appeared in *Strange Tales*, Brother Voodoo (shown at left) is a very different sort of sorcerer hero from Doctor Strange. Created by Roy Thomas and John Romita Sr., Brother Voodoo first appeared in comics form in *Strange Tales* #169 (1973) by Len Wein and Gene Colan. Brother Voodoo is Jericho Drumm, who worked in the United States as a psychiatrist. Jericho returned to his native Haiti on learning that his brother was dying, the victim of a voodoo priest who named himself after the god Damballah. Fulfilling his brother's dying wish, Jericho met with his brother's mentor, Papa Jambo, who taught him to become a houngan, or voodoo priest. Papa Jambo then raised the spirit of Jericho's deceased brother and joined it to Jericho's. Thus, Jericho Drumm became Brother Voodoo. Upon defeating Damballah, he became Haiti's most powerful voodoo priest. He can call upon his brother's spirit to increase his strength or to take mental possession of other people. Brother Voodoo is also known for making dramatic entrances by conjuring up smoke to the sound of beating drums. He has recently been renamed Doctor Voodoo.

What is the name of Jericho's brother?

A. Benjamin
B. Jeremiah
C. Joshua
D. Daniel

1700. Who was Lincoln Brickford?
A. Millionaire who dated Millie the Model
B. The Missing Link
C. One of Patsy Walker's pals
D. Secret leader of the Sons of the Serpent in *The Defenders*

1701. Who was Crackajack Jackson?
A. Elderly musician who befriended the Hulk
B. Father of criminal "Hammer" Jackson
C. Both A and B
D. None of these

1702. Who is Kropotkin the Great?
A. Sorcerer ally of Doctor Strange
B. Adversary of the She-Hulk
C. Stage magician in *The Incredible Hulk*
D. Poet friend of Dollar Bill in *The Defenders*

1703. What linked Hammer and Anvil together?
A. A telepathic connection
B. A chain from their days in a chain gang
C. An alien substance partially fused their bodies together
D. An alien chain that infused them with superhuman power

1704.

1705. Which voodoo master raised the dead villains called the X-Humed in *The Sensational She-Hulk* #34-35 (1991-1992)?
A. The Black Talon
B. Marie Laveau
C. Baron Samedi
D. Damballah

1706. What was particularly unusual about the Gremlin's talking monster Droog?
A. He spoke in riddles
B. He spoke in rhyme
C. He had an unusually extensive vocabulary
D. He spoke in a pseudo-Shakespearean manner

1707. Who is Isaac Christians?
A. Kyle Richmond's lawyer
B. Alternate identity of Arisen Tyrk
C. Father of the Mandrill
D. The Gargoyle of the Defenders

The Incredible Hulk

1708. Which X-Men foe took on the Hulk in *The Incredible Hulk* #194 (1975)?
- **A.** The Locust
- **B.** Kukulcan
- **C.** Lucifer
- **D.** Unus the Untouchable

1709. Which mystic aided the Hulk against the Maha Yogi in *The Incredible Hulk* #210–211 (1977)?
- **A.** Son of Satan
- **B.** Brother Voodoo
- **C.** Doctor Strange
- **D.** Doctor Druid

1710. Which seagoing villain clashed with the Hulk in *The Incredible Hulk* #219–220 (1978)?
- **A.** Captain Barracuda
- **B.** Captain Omen
- **C.** Commander Kraken
- **D.** Orka the Killer Whale

1711.

1712. In which series was Namorita apparently killed?
- **A.** *Namor the Sub-Mariner*
- **B.** *Thunderbolts*
- **C.** *Civil War*
- **D.** *The New Warriors*

1713. When did the original Human Torch first battle the Sub-Mariner?
- **A.** *The Human Torch* #5 (1941)
- **B.** *Marvel Mystery Comics* #8–10 (1940)
- **C.** *Sub-Mariner Comics* #23 (1947)
- **D.** *Marvel Mystery Comics* #17 (1941)

1714. Who endowed Tiger Shark with super-powers?
- **A.** Dr. Lemuel Dorcas
- **B.** Dr. Hydro
- **C.** Dr Henry Croft
- **D.** Dr. Walter Newell

1715. Who was Ikthon?
- **A.** High Priest of Atlantis
- **B.** Atlantis's Scientist Supreme
- **C.** Llyra's husband
- **D.** Officer in Atlantean navy

1716. Who officiated at the wedding of Namor and Dorma?
- **A.** Lord Vashti
- **B.** Father Neptune
- **C.** The blind elder Proteus
- **D.** The god Proteus

1711.

NOW LET'S SEE HOW TOUGH YOU ARE-- AGAINST *ME!*

The Hulk was so popular that the temptation to create a female counterpart of the character was too strong to resist. Although by this point Stan Lee had given up regularly writing comic books to become Marvel's publisher, he returned to co-create the She-Hulk with artist John Buscema in *The Savage She-Hulk* #1 (1980).

Los Angeles lawyer Jennifer Walters was Bruce Banner's introverted, somewhat mousy cousin. When she was shot by gangsters, Banner gave her a blood transfusion to save her life. His radioactive blood mutated Jennifer, who was genetically similar to Banner, into the She-Hulk (shown above). At first she was very much the female counterpart of the

IT'S A *GIRL!* BUT-- LOOK AT THE *SIZE* OF HER!

HER SKIN! IT- IT'S *GREEN!*

original Hulk. In her superhuman form she was taller, more powerfully built, had green skin and possessed vast superhuman strength. Her transformations were triggered by rage, like her cousin's, and initially the She-Hulk had a savage temperament. The original *The Savage She-Hulk* series lasted only twenty-five issues, but the character would achieve greater success later.

How many issues of *The Savage She-Hulk* did Stan Lee write?

A. Twelve
B. Ten
C. Two
D. One

1717. Which city did Namor and Triton team up to save in *Sub-Mariner* #2-3 (1968)?
A. Atlantis
B. Attilan
C. New York City
D. London

1718. How was Namorita apparently killed?
A. She was assassinated by Atlantean rebels
B. She died in hand-to-hand combat alongside New Warriors
C. She was executed for being an illegal clone
D. She was killed in an explosion caused by Nitro

1719. What is Jennifer Walters's middle name?
A. Susan
B. Ann
C. Renee
D. Barbara

1720. What is the name of Jennifer Walters's father?
A. Blake
B. Mark
C. Morris
D. Maurice

1721. Who was the mobster who attempted to have Jennifer Walters killed in *The Savage She-Hulk* #1 (1980)?
A. Caesar Cicero
B. Nick Trask
C. Silvermane
D. Nick Cloot

1722. Who led the Atlantean forces in the 1980s crossover story "Atlantis Attacks" in Marvel's 1989 annuals?
A. Attuma
B. Byrrah
C. Warlord Krang
D. Sub-Mariner

1723. Who is Karthon the Quester?
A. Atlantean warrior
B. Lemurian warrior
C. Alien explorer
D. Crew member for Captain Cybor

1724. Who was Naga?
A. Mad emperor of Lemuria
B. Tyrant with a serpentlike face and head
C. Wearer of the Serpent Crown
D. All answers are correct

The Incredible Hulk

1725. Who slew Naga?

A. Llyra

B. Karthon the Quester

C. The serpent god Set

D. Sub-Mariner

1726. What is Kamar-Taj?

A. Capital city of undersea Lemuria

B. Mystic realm of Iron Fist's origin

C. Birthplace of the Ancient One

D. Capital city of Jarella's kingdom

1727. What happened to the Ancient One upon his death?

A. He was reincarnated

B. His spirit took possession of a young student of sorcery

C. His spirit achieved nirvana

D. His spirit became "one with the universe"

1728. Who is Kaluu?

A. Sorcerer who studied alongside the Ancient One in their youth

B. Enemy of Doctor Strange

C. Mentor and ally of Doctor Strange

D. All answers are correct

1729. Who is Mr. Starkey?

A. Captain Barracuda's first mate

B. Captain Cybor's harpooner

C. One of Patsy Walker's high school teachers

D. Nebulon's alias as head of Celestial Mind Control

1730. Who were the People of the Mists in *Sub-Mariner* #16 (1969)?

A. Ghosts haunting wrecked ships

B. An isolated colony of Atlanteans

C. Seafarers of past centuries trapped in the Sargasso Sea

D. Red Raven's people

1731. Which mythical monster did Namor and Hercules *not* combat in *Sub-Mariner* #29 (1970)?

A. Scylla

B. Charybdis

C. The Hydra

D. Polyphemus the Cyclops

1732. By which name was the team of Hulk, Silver Surfer, and Sub-Mariner called in *Sub-Mariner* #34 (1971)?

A. Titans Three

B. The Order

C. The Giants

D. The Defenders

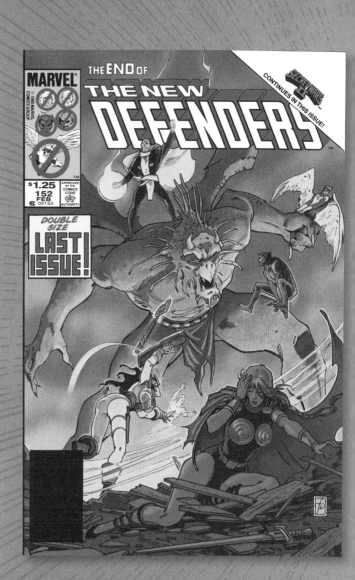

1738.

After Doctor Strange, the Hulk, Silver Surfer, and Sub-Mariner left the Defenders, the loosely knit nonteam was reorganized by Henry McCoy, the Beast, into a formal Super Hero team: the New Defenders. Among the new members were the Beast's fellow former X-Men, Angel, and Iceman. The New Defenders' head-quarters was the palatial mansion that Angel and his significant other, business executive Candy Southern, shared in the Rocky Mountains. Candy eventually became the New Defenders' leader in business matters (as opposed to combat). Other New Defenders included the Valkyrie, Moondragon, the Gargoyle, the mysterious Interloper, the assassin Manslaughter, the undersea warrior Andromeda, and the unearthly Cloud.

Writer J. M. DeMatteis began the reorganization of the Defenders, and Peter B. Gillis took over writing the series. The team came to an end in issue #152 (1986, shown at left) with a climactic battle against the Dragon of the Moon. But the team was not really gone; there was a short-lived third incarnation of the team, the Secret Defenders, and there have been several *Defenders* limited series since 2000.

Where was the New Defenders' mansion located?

A. Colorado
B. Utah
C. Arizona
D. New Mexico

1733. Where did Angel's Rocky Mountain mansion first appear?
A. *The Champions* #1 (1975)
C. *The Incredible Hulk Annual* #7 (1978)
B. *The X-Men* #1 (1963)
D. *The Uncanny X-Men* #129 (1980)

1734. What was Cloud's gender?
A. Male
C. Neither
B. Female
D. Either, depending on Cloud's choice at the time

1735. Who was Andromeda's father?
A. Attuma
C. Byrrah
B. Warlord Krang
D. Namor

1736. What is M.O.N.S.T.E.R.?
A. Subversive organization
C. League of early 1960s Marvel monsters
B. Mutant rights organization
D. Antimutant organization

1737. What was Cloud?
A. A sentient nebula in human form
C. A mutant with the ability to change from solid form to gas
B. An alien with the ability to take cloudlike form
D. A sentient star in human form

1738.

1739. What race did Interloper belong to?
A. The Asgardians
C. The Eternals
B. The Inhumans
D. The Deviants

1740. Who were the Hydro-Men?
A. Humans transformed into green, scaled humanoids
C. Humans given gills so they could breathe underwater
B. Atlanteans serving Dr. Hydro
D. Artificially created humanoids capable of breathing in or out of water

The Incredible Hulk

1741. Who was the creative team on *Tales of Atlantis* in *Sub-Mariner* #62–66 (1973)?
- **A.** Roy Thomas and Bill Everett
- **B.** Steve Gerber and Don Heck
- **C.** Steve Gerber and Howard Chaykin
- **D.** Roy Thomas and John Buscema

1742. Which Super Hero debuted in *Super Villain Team-Up* #5 (1976)?
- **A.** Stingray
- **B.** The Shroud
- **C.** Deathlok
- **D.** None of these

1743. Who was *not* one of the Secret Defenders?
- **A.** Darkhawk
- **B.** Deadpool
- **C.** Wolverine
- **D.** Cable

1744. Which character(s) co-starred in most issues of *Super Villain Team-Up*?
- **A.** Doctor Doom and Sub-Mariner
- **B.** Doctor Doom
- **C.** Sub-Mariner
- **D.** The Red Skull

1745. Which real-life figure appeared in *Super Villain Team-Up* #6–7 (1976)?
- **A.** Richard M. Nixon
- **B.** Dr. Henry Kissinger
- **C.** Leonid Brezhnev
- **D.** Mao Tse-Tung

1746. Which villains battled each other in *Super Villain Team-Up* #10–12 (1977)?
- **A.** Doctor Doom and Sub-Mariner
- **B.** Doctor Doom and Magneto
- **C.** Doctor Doom and the Red Skull
- **D.** Sub-Mariner and Magneto

1747. Which villains battled each other in *Super Villain Team-Up* #14 (1977)?
- **A.** Doctor Doom and Sub-Mariner
- **B.** Doctor Doom and the Red Skull
- **C.** Doctor Doom and Magneto
- **D.** Sub-Mariner and the Red Skull

1748. Which member of the Squadron Supreme was blinded?
- **A.** Hyperion
- **B.** Nighthawk
- **C.** Doctor Spectrum
- **D.** Power Princess

1749. Which member of the Squadron Supreme comes from Utopia Isle?
- **A.** Nuke
- **B.** Power Princess
- **C.** Amphibian
- **D.** Arcanna

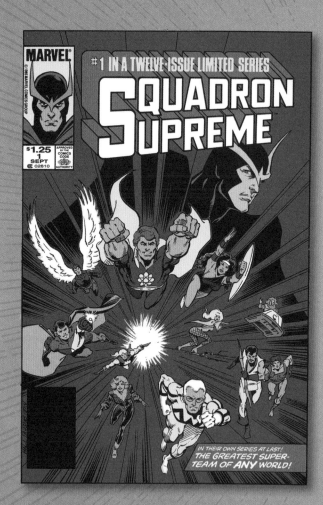

1754.

In 1986, the Squadron Supreme team won their own twelve-issue limited series (issue 1 shown at left), written by the late Marvel editor Mark Gruenwald, with art by Bob Hall, John Buscema, and Paul Ryan.

In the series, the America of a parallel Earth had been devastated by recent conflict. The Squadron Supreme decided that to save America they needed to take control of the nation and transform it into a utopia. The strongest dissenter was Kyle Richmond, alias Nighthawk, who had become president of the United States but had since resigned.

It was a saga about how even good men and women with the best intentions can turn democracy into a tyranny. So intent were they on their goal, the Squadron even rationalized brainwashing their enemies. In response, Nighthawk organized his Redeemers, a team of costumed heroes—and villains—to overthrow the Squadron's well-intentioned dictatorship. In the end, Nighthawk perished, but he proved triumphant, restoring freedom to his country and free will to its people.

Who was the first Squadron member to die in their series?

A. The Skrull
B. Nuke
C. Golden Archer
D. Tom Thumb

1750. What is unusual physically about Master Menace?
A. He is entirely hairless
B. His hair grows rapidly
C. His face is horribly scarred
D. Nothing

1751. Who was not an enemy of the Squadron Supreme's Nighthawk?
A. Remnant
B. The Rustler
C. The Mink
D. Pinball

1752. Which Squadron member died of cancer?
A. Nuke
B. Moonglow
C. Tom Thumb
D. The Shape

1753. Who was not a member of the Institute of Evil?
A. Doctor Decibel
B. Quagmire
C. Ape X
D. Inertia

1754.

1755. Who is Mark Milton?
A. The Whizzer
B. Doctor Spectrum
C. Hyperion
D. Golden Archer

1756. Who is not one of Arcanna's children?
A. Philip
B. Drusilla
C. Katrina
D. Benjamin

1757. What name was not used by James Dore Jr.?
A. Cap'n Hawk
B. American Eagle
C. Blue Eagle
D. Golden Eagle

1758. Who was not one of Nighthawk's Redeemers?
A. Lady Lark
B. Black Archer
C. Haywire
D. Redstone

1759. Which member of the Squadron Supreme was expelled for altering a colleague's mind?
A. Arcanna
B. Blue Eagle
C. Golden Archer
D. Tom Thumb

The Incredible Hulk

1760. Who is the Maestro?

A. Evil genius version of the Hulk in an alternate future

C. Sorcerer foe of Doctor Strange

B. Symphony conductor turned Super Villain

D. Fashion designer in *Models, Inc.*

1761. Where did the Keeper of the Comics Code appear before *The Sensational She-Hulk* #35 (1992)?

A. Bullpen Bulletins Page

C. *Not Brand ECCH*

B. *Crazy*

D. Nowhere

1762. Which Golden Age heroine was She-Hulk's friend Louise Mason?

A. Sun Girl

C. The Blonde Phantom

B. Miss America

D. The Silver Scorpion

1763. Who is Ulysses Solomon Archer?

A. Member of the Pantheon

C. Trucker hero of US-1

B. The Golden Archer

D. Member of the Hulkbusters

1764. Which classic Marvel monster menaced She-Hulk in *The Sensational She-Hulk* #31–33 (1991)?

A. Xemnu the Titan

C. Fin Fang Foom

B. Spragg the Living Hill

D. Gorgilla

1765. Which 1940s villain appeared as Professor Sanderson in *The Sensational She-Hulk* #29–30 (1991)?

A. Isbisa

C. Agent Axis

B. The Hyena

D. Future Man

1766. Who was Nick St. Christopher in *The Sensational She-Hulk* #7 and #8 (1989)?

A. Lawyer working for District Attorney Blake Tower

C. Assistant to Lexington Loopner

B. Attorney working with Jennifer Walters's father

D. Santa Claus

1767.

1768. Which of Howard the Duck's foes turned up in *The Sensational She-Hulk* #5 (1989)?

A. Doctor Bong

C. Le Beaver

B. Pro-Rata

D. The Kidney Lady

OBSESSED WITH MARVEL

1767.

Writer Roger Stern found the key to making the She-Hulk a successful character: instead of making her a rage-aholic like the original Hulk, Stern depicted her as a glamorous figure who reveled in having superhuman powers. Writer-artist John Byrne made her a substitute member of the Fantastic Four, using the exposure to further develop this new take on the She-Hulk's personality. Byrne also wrote and drew her brand-new comic book, *The Sensational She-Hulk*, which debuted in May 1989 (shown at right). In the brilliantly inventive comedy adventure series, Byrne pitted She-Hulk against some of the more absurd menaces from Marvel's past, such as the Toad Men from *The Incredible Hulk* #2 (1962). Byrne also allowed She-Hulk to "break the fourth wall," meaning she knew she was in a comic book and would talk to the reader and even complain to Byrne about the stories. Writer Dan Slott has successfully continued the mix of comedy and action in *She-Hulk* stories.

Who was the menace in John Byrne's first *The Sensational She-Hulk* issue?

A. The Headmen

B. Xemnu the Titan

C. The Ringmaster and the Circus of Crime

D. Doctor Angst and his associates

1769. Who was *not* one of the X-Humed?
- **A.** The Living Diamond
- **B.** Baron Heinrich Zemo
- **C.** The Changeling
- **D.** Black Bishop

1770. Which Giant-Man foe appeared in *The Sensational She-Hulk* #37 (1992)?
- **A.** The Magician
- **B.** The Porcupine
- **C.** The Living Eraser
- **D.** The Human Top

1771. Who is the Phantom Blonde?
- **A.** A mystery woman in *Models, Inc.*
- **B.** Louise Mason's daughter Wanda
- **C.** Louise Mason under a new name
- **D.** The Blonde Phantom's nemesis in the 1940s

1772. In which issue of *Strange Tales* does Doctor Strange *not* appear?
- **A.** #112 (1963)
- **B.** #113 (1963)
- **C.** #114 (1963)
- **D.** #115 (1963)

1773. Which member of the Riot Squad was "Thunderbolt" Ross?
- **A.** Hotshot
- **B.** Redeemer
- **C.** Rock
- **D.** Jailbait

1774. What relation is Matt Talbot to Glenn Talbot?
- **A.** Matt is Glenn's nephew
- **B.** Matt is Glenn's cousin
- **C.** Matt is Glenn's son
- **D.** Matt is Glenn's brother

1775. Who was drawn as the priest officiating at Rick Jones's wedding?
- **A.** Peter David
- **B.** Captain Mar-Vell
- **C.** Jack Kirby
- **D.** Stan Lee

1776. Who is *not* a member of the Headshop?
- **A.** Dead Head
- **B.** Headlok
- **C.** Headmistress
- **D.** Headgear

1777. What is distinctive about the Gulgol?
- **A.** It does not sleep
- **B.** It is said to be immune to magical attacks
- **C.** It is feared by Nightmare
- **D.** All answers are correct

The Incredible Hulk

1778. Who was Doctor Strange's love interest in the stories by Roger Stern and Marshall Rogers?
- **A.** Madeleine St. Germaine
- **B.** Sara Wolfe
- **C.** Morgana Blessing
- **D.** Victoria Bentley

1779. What is *not* the name of a Pantheon member?
- **A.** Agamemnon
- **B.** Clytemnestra
- **C.** Atalanta
- **D.** Delphi

1780. Who was Nadia Dornova?
- **A.** An actress
- **B.** The woman the Abomination loved
- **C.** Both A and B
- **D.** A Soviet spy

1781. Whom does the G'uranthic Guardian serve?
- **A.** Satannish
- **B.** Tiboro
- **C.** Nightmare
- **D.** Dormammu

1782. Who is Veritas?
- **A.** One of the Vishanti
- **B.** An Elder of the Universe
- **C.** The mystical entity embodying truth
- **D.** A member of Atlantean nobility

1783. Who was Lord of the Planets Perilous?
- **A.** Nebulos
- **B.** Tazza
- **C.** Yandroth
- **D.** Tiboro

1784.

1785. What is the name of Doctor Strange's sister?
- **A.** Denise
- **B.** Laura
- **C.** Laurel
- **D.** Donna

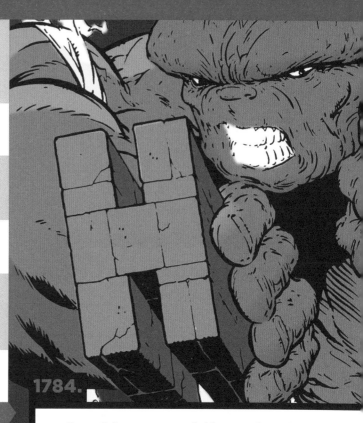

1784.

One of the most remarkable periods in the Hulk's history was the decade of stories written by Peter David, starting in 1987. Rather than writing the familiar, traditional version of the Hulk (shown above), David continually experimented with the character, repeatedly surprising and astonishing readers.

When David took over *The Incredible Hulk*, the character had reverted to the grey-skinned Hulk of the very first issue but smarter and more adult than the original version. David put this thuggish Hulk in a hat and suit and turned him into Mr. Fixit, a mob enforcer. Later, David turned the Hulk into a handsome green-skinned action hero who worked with

OBSESSED WITH MARVEL

1786. Who filled the Hulk's slot on the roster of the 2011 *Defenders* series?
- **A.** A-Bomb
- **B.** Red Hulk
- **C.** Red She-Hulk
- **D.** Totally Awesome Hulk

1787. Who did *not* join the Defenders in their 2011 series?
- **A.** Ant-Man
- **B.** Iron Fist
- **C.** Black Cat
- **D.** Nighthawk

1788. Which female warrior formed the new team featured in the 2013 title *Fearless Defenders*?
- **A.** Lady Sif
- **B.** Thor (Jane Foster)
- **C.** Valkyrie
- **D.** Thundra

1789. Who was *not* a member of the Fearless Defenders?
- **A.** Misty Knight
- **B.** Dani Moonstar
- **C.** Elsa Bloodstone
- **D.** Patsy Walker

1790. In the 2015 series *Patsy Walker A.K.A. Hellcat!*, what type of business does Patsy Walker start?
- **A.** Superhuman temp agency
- **B.** Acting school
- **C.** Talk radio station
- **D.** Coffee shop

1791. Which member of the most recent Squadron Supreme had previously served as an Avenger?
- **A.** Nighthawk
- **B.** Blur
- **C.** Doctor Spectrum
- **D.** Hyperion

1792. Which alternate universe did the Nighthawk from the 2016 *Squadron Supreme* series come from?
- **A.** Ultimate Universe
- **B.** Supreme Power
- **C.** New Universe
- **D.** Age of Apocalypse

the secret society known as the Pantheon. In the limited series *The Incredible Hulk: Future Imperfect* (1993), the Hulk visits an alternate future Earth ruled by an evil alternate version of himself, the Maestro. The stand-alone comic book *Incredible Hulk: The End* (2002) presents another alternate future in which the Hulk is the last man alive and is, each day, partially devoured by giant insects and then regenerates his body anew.

Where did the Hulk operate as Mr. Fixit?

- **A.** Chicago
- **B.** New York City
- **C.** Las Vegas
- **D.** Miami

The Incredible Hulk

1793. What was Dr. Charles Benton's name as the leader of the Sons of Satannish?

A. Phobos
B. Asmodeus
C. Marduk
D. Deimos

1794. Which talking animal(s) appeared in *The Incredible Hulk* #271 (1982)?

A. Howard the Duck
B. Super Rabbit
C. Rocket Raccoon
D. Ziggy Pig and Silly Seal

1795. Which real-life figure appeared in *Doctor Strange* #12 (1976)?

A. Jimmy Carter
B. Gerald Ford
C. Ronald Reagan
D. Richard M. Nixon

1796. What fate befell Doctor Strange in *Doctor Strange* #14 (1976)?

A. He allows Death itself to claim him
B. He loses his magical abilities
C. Dracula kills him and turns him into a vampire
D. He reverts to alcoholism

1797. Who is Mephista?

A. Mephisto's daughter
B. Mephisto's wife
C. Mephisto's sister
D. Mephisto in female form

1798. Who drew the *Rocket Raccoon* limited series (1985)?

A. John Byrne
B. Frank Brunner
C. Gene Colan
D. Mike Mignola

1799. What kind of animal is Rocket Raccoon's enemy Judson Jakes?

A. Toad
B. Rat
C. Mole
D. Badger

1800.

The alternate future Earth of the *Marvel 2099* line of comics had its own version of the Hulk (shown at right), created by writer Gerard Jones and artist Dwayne Turner. Instead of a genius nuclear scientist like Bruce Banner, Hulk 2099's human self is a movie studio executive named John Eisenhart. He tries to buy the movie rights to the story of the Knights of Banner, a cult that attempted to create a new Hulk through illegal gamma radiation experiments. When the Knights refuse, Eisenhart tells the police about the cult. This leads to a battle in which the police kill many of the Knights. His conscience awakened, Eisenhart tries to intervene on the Knights' side. But it's too late; one young Knight, Gawain, sets off gamma devices, and the radiation transforms Eisenhart into the Hulk of AD 2099.

In which issue did Hulk 2099 debut?

A. *Hulk 2099* #1 (1994)
B. *2099 Unlimited* #1 (1993)
C. *2099 Genesis* #1 (1996)
D. *2099 World of Tomorrow* #1 (1996)

1793B 1794C 1795D 1796C 1797A 1798D 1799C 1800B

1801. What was Glenn Talbot's rank at the time of his death?
- **A.** Colonel
- **B.** Major
- **C.** General
- **D.** None; he had been discharged

1802. Who was *not* one of the Rangers?
- **A.** Shooting Star
- **B.** Texas Twister
- **C.** Phantom Rider
- **D.** Two-Gun Kid

1803. Who was *not* one of They-Who-Wield-Power?
- **A.** Queen Kala
- **B.** Keeper of the Flame
- **C.** Prince Rey
- **D.** Tyrannus

1804. Who was *not* one of the Hulk-Hunters in *The Incredible Hulk* #269–270 (1982)?
- **A.** Dark-Crawler
- **B.** Space Parasite
- **C.** Torgo
- **D.** Amphibion

1805. Who is *not* one of the U-Foes?
- **A.** Piecemeal
- **B.** Vapor
- **C.** Ironclad
- **D.** Vector

1806. Who was *not* a member of the Triad?
- **A.** Glow
- **B.** Goblin
- **C.** Guardian
- **D.** Guardsman

1807. Who was *not* one of the Hulkbusters?
- **A.** Carolyn Parmenter
- **B.** Craig Saunders Jr.
- **C.** Dr. Katherine Waynesboro
- **D.** Samuel J. LaRoquette

The Incredible Hulk

1808. Who was the Evil One who fought the Hulk in *Tales to Astonish* #76–77 (1966)?

A. Dr. Konrad Zaxon
B. The Executioner
C. Tyrannus
D. The Leader

1809. What was Marlo Chandler's job when she first appeared?

A. Talk show hostess
B. Comic shop co-owner
C. Casino cocktail hostess
D. Aerobics instructor

1810. Who is *not* a member of the Pantheon?

A. Paris
B. Orestes
C. Prometheus
D. Ulysses

1811. Who is Dafydd ap Iowerth?

A. Sorcerer from Wales
B. Member of the Dragon Circle
C. Descendant of King Arthur
D. Both B and C

1812. Who is Baron Blood II?

A. Doctor Strange's brother Victor
B. Descendant of the original Baron Blood
C. Vampire imitating the original Baron Blood
D. Alias for Viscount Heinrich Krowler

1813. Who was Saru-San?

A. Mutant crustacean in *Sub-Mariner* #50 (1972)
B. Queen of the Sun in *Doctor Strange* #22 (1977)
C. Attuma's court jester in *Sub-Mariner* #4 (1968)
D. Wizard in microverse world in *The Incredible Hulk* #201 (1976)

1814. Who recreated Marvel monsters to fight the Hulk in *The Incredible Hulk Annual* #5 (1976)?

A. The High Evolutionary

B. Modok

C. The Leader

D. Xemnu the Titan

1815. Which Marvel monster was *not* recreated in *The Incredible Hulk Annual* #5 (1976)?

A. Googam, Son of Goom

B. Diablo

C. The Blip

D. Groot

1816. Which dimension does Tiboro rule?

A. The Quadriverse

B. The Moons of Munnopor

C. The Purple Dimension

D. The Sixth Dimension

1817. What was the name of Bruce Banner's college girlfriend in *The Incredible Hulk* #226 (1978)?

A. Betty

B. April

C. Sally

D. Jenny

1818.

1819. Who is Adam Qadmon?

A. Alias for Nebulon

B. Alias for Michael Korvac

C. Artificial man created by the Enclave

D. Another name for Eternity

1820. What was the Order?

A. The original Defenders under the mental control of Yandroth

B. A subversive organization opposed by the Pantheon

C. A cabal of evil sorcerers who opposed Doctor Strange

D. A religious group in undersea Atlantis

1818.

Some of the most extraordinary chapters in the Hulk's history took place in the "Planet Hulk" story arc in 2006 and the series *World War Hulk* in 2007 (issue 1 shown at left); Greg Pak was the principal writer for both. It began with the Illuminati, a secret society that included Reed Richards, Charles Xavier, and others. They trapped the Hulk aboard a spacecraft and sent it toward an uninhabited planet so he could no longer endanger anyone. Instead, the spaceship crashed on the inhabited planet Sakaar, where the Hulk became a gladiator, overthrew the Red King, the planet's ruler, and became the emperor of its warlike civilization. He married a woman named Caiera, who became pregnant.

But then the spacecraft, still located on the planet, exploded, killing Caiera and millions of others in its vicinity. Blaming the Illuminati, the vengeful Hulk returned to Earth and wreaked havoc. Finally, the Hulk discovered that his ally Miek had allowed followers of the Red King to cause the massacre on Sakaar. The Hulk reverted to human form and was imprisoned by S.H.I.E.L.D.

What is the name of the Hulk's son, who miraculously survived the massacre?

A. Skaar

B. Bruce Jr.

C. Omaka

D. Robert Jr.

The Incredible Hulk

CHAPTER SIX:

MARVEL KNIGHTS:
FROM DAREDEVIL TO THE PUNISHER

1821. What is Foggy Nelson's first name?
- **A.** Frederick
- **B.** Edward
- **C.** Francis
- **D.** Franklin

1822. In which section of New York City did Matt Murdock grow up?
- **A.** Lower East Side
- **B.** Queens
- **C.** Brooklyn
- **D.** Hell's Kitchen

1823. What is "Battling" Murdock's first name?
- **A.** Joseph
- **B.** Matthew (Sr.)
- **C.** Jonathan
- **D.** Jim

1824. Who turned out to be the Supreme Hydra in Jim Steranko's "Hydra" story line?
- **A.** Baron Strucker
- **B.** The Yellow Claw
- **C.** Anton Trojak
- **D.** Leslie Farrington

1825. Where did Matt Murdock go to college?
- **A.** Empire State University
- **B.** Columbia University
- **C.** Harvard University
- **D.** City University of New York

1826. What is an L.M.D.?
- **A.** Light Module Display
- **B.** Laser Manual Discharger
- **C.** Life Model Decoy
- **D.** Lethal Mechanized Dreadnaught

1827. Which Super Heroine became Daredevil's costar in issue #81 (1971) and became a title character starting with issue #92 (1972)?
- **A.** The Black Widow
- **B.** Elektra
- **C.** Shanna the She-Devil
- **D.** She-Hulk

OPPOSITE Daredevil, Punisher, Black Widow, Dagger, and Shang-Chi

1821D 1822D 1823C 1824A 1825B 1826C 1827A

1828. Who took over drawing *Daredevil* with issue #14 (1966)?
- **A.** Wally Wood
- **B.** John Romita Sr.
- **C.** Gene Colan
- **D.** Joe Orlando

1829. What are the Gladiator's principal weapons?
- **A.** Spear and shield
- **B.** Sword and shield
- **C.** Spinning discs on his wrists
- **D.** Scimitar and mace

1830. Who took over drawing *Daredevil* with issue #20 (1966)?
- **A.** Jack Kirby
- **B.** Wally Wood
- **C.** John Romita Sr.
- **D.** Gene Colan

1831. What does A.I.M. stand for?
- **A.** Advanced Idea Mechanics
- **B.** Advanced Idea Manufacturers
- **C.** Alternative Intelligence Makers
- **D.** Artificial Intelligence Machines

1832. What is the Hand?
- **A.** Criminal order of ninja
- **B.** Worshippers of the demon Beast
- **C.** Adversaries of the Chaste
- **D.** All answers are correct

1833. Which nemesis or nemeses of Thor battled Daredevil in *Daredevil* #30–32 (1967)?
- **A.** Mr. Hyde and the Cobra
- **B.** The Ringmaster and the Circus of Crime
- **C.** The Grey Gargoyle
- **D.** Thug Thatcher

1834.

1835. Which member of the Howling Commandos did *not* join S.H.I.E.L.D.?
- **A.** Eric Koenig
- **B.** Dino Manelli
- **C.** Gabe Jones
- **D.** Dum Dum Dugan

1834.

Boxer "Battling" Murdock was determined that his son Matt would have a better life than his own. He made Matt promise to study, but to use his fists when necessary. One day, young Matt pushed a blind man out of the path of an oncoming truck, and was blinded by the radioactive material the truck was carrying. The radiation also sharpened Matt's other senses to superhuman levels, and gave him a "radar sense" that compensated for his lack of sight.

When Battling Murdock refused to throw a fight, a crime boss called the Fixer had him killed. Though Matt became a lawyer, he also upheld the other part of his promise to his father and created another identity to avenge Battling Murdock's death. As the masked vigilante Daredevil, Matt fought his father's killers.

In this first story (shown at right), by co-creators Stan Lee and Bill Everett, Daredevil dressed in a black-and-yellow costume, but soon after he adopted the familiar red uniform he wears today. Who designed Daredevil's red costume?

- **A.** Jack Kirby
- **B.** John Romita Sr.
- **C.** Wally Wood
- **D.** Gene Colan

1836. Who killed Karen Page?
A. Elektra
B. Daredevil
C. The Kingpin
D. Bullseye

1837. Who created Bullseye?
A. Frank Miller and Roger McKenzie
B. Marv Wolfman and Bob Brown
C. Jim Shooter and Gil Kane
D. Frank Miller

1838. What other villain is known as the Fixer?
A. Mentallo's partner
B. Techno
C. Both A and B
D. The assassin who killed Peter Parker's parents

1839. What is the Purple Man's super-power?
A. Controls wills of others through pheromones
B. Has telepathic control of minds
C. Shape-shifts
D. Generates lights of different colors

1840. Who are the Daughters of the Dragon?
A. Worshippers of Shou-Lao
B. Leiko Wu and a team of female MI6 agents
C. Misty Knight and Colleen Wing
D. Female ninja serving Shang-Chi's father

1841. Who was the first Super Hero or Super Heroes to guest star in *Daredevil*?
A. Spider-Man
B. Captain America
C. Ka-Zar
D. Fantastic Four

1842. Which S.H.I.E.L.D. agent became infatuated with Elektra in *Elektra: Assassin* (1986–1987)?
A. Clay Quartermain
B. John Garrett
C. Alexander Pierce
D. Al MacKenzie

Marvel Knights

1843. What is Nightwing Restorations?
- **A.** Agency run by Black Jack Tarr
- **B.** Colleen Wing and Misty Knight's detective agency
- **C.** Jessica Jones's agency
- **D.** Jessica Drew and Lindsay McCabe's detective agency

1844. Who illustrated Frank Miller's *Elektra: Assassin* series (1986–1987)?
- **A.** Frank Miller
- **B.** David Mazzucchelli
- **C.** Bill Sienkiewicz
- **D.** Klaus Janson

1845. Who owns the bar in Hell's Kitchen that often appeared in *Daredevil*?
- **A.** Turk
- **B.** Josie
- **C.** Nick Manolis
- **D.** Eric Slaughter

1846. Who are Turk and Grotto?
- **A.** Minor criminals who repeatedly encounter Daredevil
- **B.** Shades and Comanche
- **C.** Underworld informers for Moon Knight
- **D.** Stiletto and Discus

1847. Who was Daredevil's mentor?
- **A.** Flame
- **B.** Star
- **C.** Stick
- **D.** Stone

1848. What happened to Matt Murdock's mother?
- **A.** She died
- **B.** She became a nun
- **C.** She remarried
- **D.** Unknown

1849. Who is responsible for revealing Daredevil's secret identity to the Kingpin?
- **A.** Ben Urich
- **B.** Elektra
- **C.** Foggy Nelson
- **D.** Karen Page

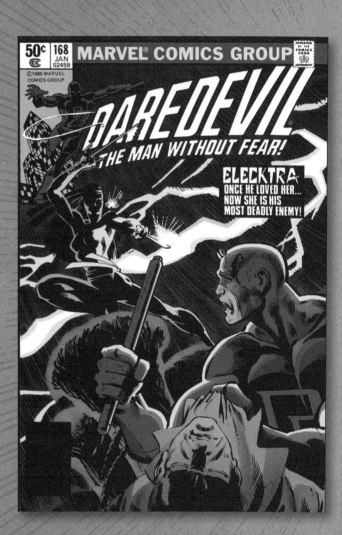

1854.

Starting in 1981, a new writer-artist named Frank Miller revolutionized the *Daredevil* series. Miller had previously drawn *Daredevil*, collaborating with writer Roger McKenzie, but with issue #168 (shown at left), Miller took over both writing and illustrating the comic. Miller brought new influences to *Daredevil*, including crime comics, film noir, Japanese manga, and the pioneering comic book work of Will Eisner.

Rather than pit Daredevil against conventional comics Super Villains, Miller made him a lone crusader against an empire of organized crime headed by Wilson Fisk, the Kingpin from *The Amazing Spider-Man*. Miller reworked Daredevil's enemy Bullseye into a chillingly psychopathic killer, and reshaped Daredevil, making him more passionate and willing to bend the rules. In *Daredevil* #168 Miller also introduced Elektra, Matt's college sweetheart, who was now a ninja assassin, sometimes Daredevil's ally and sometimes his adversary.

It was here in *Daredevil* that Miller's astonishing career as graphic novelist and filmmaker got its start. Who illustrated Frank Miller's "Daredevil: Born Again" (1986) story arc?

A. Frank Miller
B. David Mazzucchelli
C. John Buscema
D. Bill Sienkiewicz

1850. Who guest stars in *Daredevil* #16–17 (1966)?
A. Ka-Zar
B. The Black Panther
C. The Black Widow
D. Spider-Man

1851. Who was Roscoe Sweeney?
A. The Organizer
B. The Fixer
C. The Masked Marauder
D. Crime-Wave

1852. Which *Spider-Man* villain did Daredevil fight in *Daredevil* #2 (1964)?
A. Electro
B. Doctor Octopus
C. Mysterio
D. Kraven the Hunter

1853. Who is Zebediah Killgrave?
A. Blackwing
B. Death-Stalker
C. Mind-Wave
D. The Purple Man

1854.

1855. When did Daredevil get his red costume?
A. Issue #7 (1965)
B. Issue #8 (1965)
C. Issue #9 (1965)
D. Issue #10 (1964)

1856. Which hero did Daredevil battle in *Daredevil* #7 (1965)?
A. Ka-Zar
B. Captain America
C. Spider-Man
D. Sub-Mariner

1857. Who drew the cover and splash page of *Daredevil* #1 (1964)?
A. Joe Orlando
B. Wally Wood
C. Jack Kirby
D. Bill Everett

Marvel Knights

1858. Who is Wilbur Day?
- **A.** Leap-Frog
- **B.** Stilt-Man
- **C.** Bushwacker
- **D.** The Owl

1859. Which S.H.I.E.L.D. agent was *not* created by Jim Steranko?
- **A.** Countess Valentina Allegra de Fontaine
- **B.** Clay Quartermain
- **C.** The Gaff
- **D.** Jasper Sitwell

1860. Who was Scorpio?
- **A.** Nick Fury's brother Jake
- **B.** S.H.I.E.L.D. agent John Bronson
- **C.** Arnold Brown
- **D.** A Nick Fury L.M.D.

1861. How many issues of *Nick Fury, Agent of S.H.I.E.L.D.* did Jim Steranko write and draw?
- **A.** One
- **B.** Three
- **C.** Four
- **D.** Ten

1862.

1863. Who was *not* a member of the Unholy Three?
- **A.** Ape-Man
- **B.** Bird-Man
- **C.** Cat-Man
- **D.** Frog-Man

1864. Who was *not* a member of the Fellowship of Fear in *Daredevil* #6 (1965)?
- **A.** The Owl
- **B.** The Eel
- **C.** The Ox
- **D.** Mr. Fear

1865. Where did Daredevil travel in *Daredevil* #12-14 (1966)?
- **A.** France
- **B.** California
- **C.** Lichtenbad
- **D.** The Savage Land

1862.

In the 1960s, the tremendous success of James Bond inspired an entire superspy genre in popular culture. In creating their own super-spy series, Stan Lee and Jack Kirby gave the genre an inspired twist. Instead of copying the sophisticated Bond, they made their hero the middle-aged, street-smart Nick Fury—the hero of their World War II series *Sgt. Fury and His Howling Commandos*. Now a colonel assigned to the CIA and sporting an eye patch due to an old war injury, Fury was still recognizable as the feisty, plainspoken sergeant who had grown up on Manhattan's Lower East Side. The unlikely superspy was now in charge of the intelligence agency S.H.I.E.L.D., which was based in an enormous flying heli-carrier that was equipped with advanced technology supplied by Tony Stark. Fury, as S.H.I.E.L.D. director, led the battle against powerful subversive organizations, such as Hydra.

Starting in *Strange Tales* #135 (August 1965) before winning its own comic, *Nick Fury, Agent of S.H.I.E.L.D.* (issue 1 shown at right) reached its creative peak under writer-artist Jim Steranko, who combined brilliant visuals with dynamic cinematic storytelling.

What did the acronym S.H.I.E.L.D. originally stand for?

- **A.** Strategic Hazard Intervention, Espionage, and Logistics Directorate
- **B.** Supreme Headquarters International Espionage, and Law-Enforcement Division
- **C.** Strategic Homeland Intervention, Enforcement, and Logistics Division
- **D.** Strategic Homeland Intervention, Espionage, and Law-Enforcement Division

1866. Who created the art for *Daredevil* #12–13 (1966)?
- **A.** Jack Kirby and John Romita Sr.
- **B.** Wally Wood
- **C.** John Romita Sr.
- **D.** Jack Kirby and Bill Everett

1867. Who is Melvin Potter?
- **A.** One of the Fatboys
- **B.** The Gladiator
- **C.** One of the Wildboys
- **D.** The Tribune

1868. With which issue did Gene Colan end his original run drawing *Daredevil*?
- **A.** #50 (1969)
- **B.** #75 (1971)
- **C.** #100 (1973)
- **D.** #125 (1975)

1869. What was the Gladiator's profession apart from crime?
- **A.** Professional wrestler
- **B.** Costume shop owner
- **C.** Archaeologist
- **D.** Historian

1870. What was the name of the Punisher's wife?
- **A.** Lisa
- **B.** Louisa
- **C.** Barbara
- **D.** Maria

1871. In which branch of the armed services did Frank Castle serve?
- **A.** Army
- **B.** Marines
- **C.** Navy
- **D.** Air Force

1872. Who designed the Punisher's costume?
- **A.** Ross Andru
- **B.** John Romita Sr.
- **C.** Mike Zeck
- **D.** Gil Kane

Marvel Knights

1873. Which future Super Hero is the villain in *Daredevil* #62 (1970)?
- **A.** Stunt-Master
- **B.** Moon Knight
- **C.** The Punisher
- **D.** Nighthawk

1874. What name did the Punisher have when he was born?
- **A.** Frankie Villa
- **B.** Johnny Tower
- **C.** Frank Castle
- **D.** Francis Castiglione

1875. Who was the creative team on the first *The Punisher* limited series (1986)?
- **A.** Steven Grant and Mike Zeck
- **B.** Mike Baron and Klaus Janson
- **C.** Garth Ennis and Steve Dillon
- **D.** Gerry Conway and Ross Andru

1876. In which war did the Punisher serve?
- **A.** First Gulf War
- **B.** World War II
- **C.** Vietnam
- **D.** Korea

1877. For what career was Frank Castle studying before he entered the armed services?
- **A.** Priest
- **B.** Policeman
- **C.** Architect
- **D.** Doctor

1878. Where was Frank Castle born?
- **A.** New Jersey
- **B.** The Bronx
- **C.** Queens
- **D.** Brooklyn

1879. Where did Daredevil move to in the 1970s?
- **A.** Chicago
- **B.** San Francisco
- **C.** Boston
- **D.** Los Angeles

1880.

When writer Gerry Conway and artist Ross Andru introduced him in *The Amazing Spider-Man* #129 (1974), the Punisher (shown above) was a very different kind of hero for traditional Super Hero comics. War veteran Frank Castle was with his family when they stumbled across a gangland execution. The gangsters gunned down Castle's family, but Castle survived and became bent on vengeance. Castle renamed himself the Punisher and embarked on a one-man war against all criminals.

Customarily, Super Heroes did not kill their adversaries, but the Punisher was the first Marvel hero to defy that rule. Believing that the law let too many

OBSESSED WITH MARVEL

1881. Who was Death's-Head?
- **A.** A Hydra assassin
- **B.** Karen Page's father
- **C.** Foggy Nelson's father
- **D.** The Exterminator

1882. How is Mike Murdock related to Matt Murdock?
- **A.** Brother
- **B.** Uncle
- **C.** Matt Murdock posing as his brother
- **D.** Grandfather

1883. Who posed as Daredevil to convince the public he was *not* Matt Murdock?
- **A.** Bullseye
- **B.** Iron Fist
- **C.** Captain America
- **D.** The Punisher

1884. Who was Matt Murdock's secretary?
- **A.** Karen Page
- **B.** Becky Blake
- **C.** Both A and B
- **D.** Mary Walker

1885. Which of the following women did *not* date Matt Murdock?
- **A.** Glorianna O'Breen
- **B.** Natasha Romanova
- **C.** Heather Glenn
- **D.** Becky Blake

1886. Who unleashed the Death Spore?
- **A.** Hydra
- **B.** A.I.M.
- **C.** The Yellow Claw
- **D.** Dredmund Druid

1887. Who was Arnold Brown?
- **A.** Aide to the Kingpin
- **B.** Copperhead
- **C.** Imperial Hydra in original "Hydra" story arc
- **D.** Stunt-Master

criminals go free, the Punisher acted as judge, jury, and executioner.

Sometimes, as in Frank Miller's *Daredevil*, the Punisher is portrayed as a criminal himself who must be stopped; he has even been depicted as insane. But more often he has been portrayed as an antihero, bravely battling the worst of criminals, and has starred in as many as three monthly series simultaneously.

Where was the Punisher's family killed?

- **A.** Prospect Park, Brooklyn
- **B.** Little Italy, Manhattan
- **C.** Coney Island, Brooklyn
- **D.** Central Park, Manhattan

Marvel Knights

1888. What is true about the Yellow Claw in *Strange Tales* #163–167 (1967–1968)?

A. He was the son of the original Yellow Claw

C. He was the original Yellow Claw

B. He was a robot duplicate of the real Yellow Claw

D. He was a clone of the Yellow Claw

1889.

1890. Who did *not* work for Freelance Restorations?

A. Colleen Wing

C. Leiko Wu

B. Clive Reston

D. Black Jack Tarr

1891. Who is Rufus T. Hackstabber?

A. Eccentric client of Heroes for Hire

C. Witty cab driver ally of Shang-Chi

B. Cab driver identity of Moon Knight

D. Small-time criminal in Hell's Kitchen

1892. Who is Brynocki?

A. Robot created by Carlton Velcro

C. Cyborg villain in *Elektra: Assassin*

B. Robot created by the assassin Mordillo

D. Hydra assassin

1893. Who is Jake Gallows?

A. Alias for the Punisher

C. The Hangman

B. Punisher 2099

D. Hit man working for the Kingpin

1894. What was Pavane's trademark weapon?

A. Pistol

C. Whip

B. Sword

D. Crossbow

1895. Where did Nick Fury and Captain America combat the Yellow Claw's troops in "Project Blackout" in *Strange Tales* #160–161 (1967)?

A. The Statue of Liberty

C. Mount Rushmore

B. The U.S. Capitol Building

D. The Empire State Building

1889.

As Marvel greatly expanded its line of comics in the 1970s, the company delved into genres other than Super Hero sagas. With *Master of Kung Fu* (issue 19 shown at right), Marvel combined Asian martial arts with the style of classic adventure thrillers from the first half of the twentieth century.

The title character, Shang-Chi, is the son of an infamous Chinese criminal mastermind. While on assignment by his father to assassinate an old enemy, Dr. Petrie, Shang-Chi first meets his father's nemesis, Sir Denis Nayland Smith. The British intelligence agent opens Shang-Chi's eyes to his father's evil. Shang-Chi then works with Smith and his allies, both in opposing his father and in combating other master criminals.

Created by Steve Englehart and Jim Starlin in *Special Marvel Edition* #15 (1973), Shang-Chi reached his height in epic adventures with writer Doug Moench and artist Paul Gulacy in the *Master of Kung Fu* comic book.

What does Shang-Chi's name mean?

A. Seeker of serenity

B. Rising of the spirit

C. Master of martial arts

D. Son of the Emperor

1896. Which series was *not* published in the 1990s?
- **A.** *The Punisher*
- **B.** *Punisher War Journal*
- **C.** *Punisher War Zone*
- **D.** *The Punisher: Frank Castle*

1897. Who was Linus Lieberman?
- **A.** The Gaff
- **B.** Microchip
- **C.** Punisher 2099
- **D.** Mathemanic

1898. What is the name of Daredevil's mother?
- **A.** Trisha
- **B.** Colleen
- **C.** Maggie
- **D.** Maureen

1899. Who is Lynn Michaels?
- **A.** Diamonelle
- **B.** Lady Punisher
- **C.** New York City police detective
- **D.** All answers are correct

1900. What was the former Super Heroic identity of *Alias's* Jessica Jones?
- **A.** Ms. Marvel
- **B.** Jewel
- **C.** Marvel Woman
- **D.** Spider-Woman

1901. Who was the first female Hydra agent to appear in comics?
- **A.** The Viper
- **B.** Cassandra Romulus
- **C.** Laura Brown
- **D.** Madame Hydra

1902. What slows down Nick Fury's aging process?
- **A.** S.H.I.E.L.D. scientific secrets
- **B.** The Elixir Vitae
- **C.** The Super-Soldier serum
- **D.** The Infinity Formula

1903. Who was Coldfire?
- **A.** Moon Knight's brother Randall
- **B.** Luke Cage's brother James
- **C.** Nick Fury's brother Jake
- **D.** Moon Knight's sidekick Jeff Wilde

Marvel Knights

1904. Who is Joy Meachum?

- **A.** Harold Meachum's daughter
- **B.** Harold Meachum's wife
- **C.** Ward Meachum's wife
- **D.** Ward Meachum's daughter

1905. What happened in *The Punisher: Purgatory* (1998-1999)?

- **A.** The Punisher temporarily gained supernatural powers
- **B.** The Punisher was resurrected from the dead
- **C.** The Punisher fought in a war between angels and demons
- **D.** All answers are correct

1906.

1907. What was the name of Danny Rand's mother?

- **A.** Miranda
- **B.** Joy
- **C.** Heather
- **D.** Jennie

1908. Who or what is Death Sting?

- **A.** A weapon used by Baron Strucker
- **B.** A Hydra assassin
- **C.** Iron Fist's sister
- **D.** An enemy of Luke Cage

1909. Who was Lei Kung?

- **A.** Steel Serpent
- **B.** Iron Fist's mentor
- **C.** The Thunderer
- **D.** Both B and C

1910. How often does K'un-L'un normally appear on Earth?

- **A.** Once a year
- **B.** Every ten years
- **C.** Every five years
- **D.** On an irregular basis

1911. Who, wearing the guise of Iron Fist, was killed in *Power Man and Iron Fist* #125 (1986)?

- **A.** Danny Rand
- **B.** A H'ylthri double
- **C.** The Super Skrull
- **D.** An impostor serving Master Khan

1906.

American Wendell Rand once visited the mystical city of K'un-L'un, which only rarely appears on Earth. Years later, Wendell attempts to return to K'un-L'un with his wife, his nine-year-old son, Danny, and his business partner, Harold Meachum. But on the trip, the treacherous Meachum murders Wendell and wolves kill Danny's mother.

Danny is brought to K'un-L'un, where he is trained in the martial arts. At age nineteen he battles and kills the dragon Shou-Lao and plunges his fists into the dragon's heart. Thus, Danny gains the power of the "Iron Fist," enabling him to focus his chi (energy) into his fists, endowing them with superhuman force.

As Iron Fist, Danny returns to America, seeking vengeance for his father's death, but ultimately spares Meachum, who is killed by a different foe. Iron Fist goes on to become a Super Hero, first on his own and then working in partnership with Luke Cage.

Created by writer Roy Thomas and artist Gil Kane, Iron Fist debuted in *Marvel Premiere* #15 (1974, shown at right) before winning his own comic book. Who was the creative team on *Iron Fist* #1 in 1975?

- **A.** Roy Thomas and Gil Kane
- **B.** Doug Moench and Larry Hama
- **C.** Tony Isabella and Pat Broderick
- **D.** Chris Claremont and John Byrne

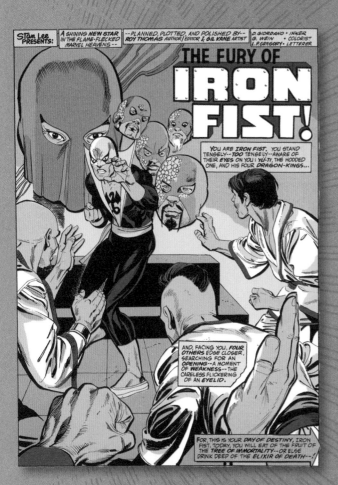

1912. Who is Steel Serpent?
- **A.** Son of Lei Kung
- **B.** Son of Yu-Ti
- **C.** Member of the Sons of the Tiger
- **D.** Shang-Chi's former friend Midnight

1913. For whom did Fritz von Voltzmann work?
- **A.** The Mandarin
- **B.** Carlton Velcro
- **C.** The Yellow Claw
- **D.** Baron Strucker

1914. Who killed Microchip?
- **A.** The Punisher
- **B.** Stonecutter
- **C.** Jigsaw
- **D.** Ma Gnucci

1915. Who was Jeryn Hogarth?
- **A.** The Black Spectre
- **B.** Head of S.H.I.E.L.D.'s ESP Division
- **C.** Doctor who gave Luke Cage his super-powers
- **D.** Lawyer behind Heroes for Hire

1916. Who is the August Personage in Jade?
- **A.** Shen Kuei
- **B.** Yu-Ti
- **C.** Lei Kung
- **D.** Master Khan

1917. What handicap does Daredevil suffer when he battles Mr. Hyde and the Cobra in issues #30–32 (1967)?
- **A.** Loss of his super-senses
- **B.** Deafness
- **C.** Crippled arm
- **D.** Crippled leg

1918. Which *Fantastic Four* villain did Daredevil battle in issues #35–36 (1967–1968)?
- **A.** The Wizard
- **B.** The Trapster
- **C.** The Sandman
- **D.** Doctor Doom

Marvel Knights

1919. How is the *Ultimate* version of Nick Fury *not* different from the original?
- **A.** He is African American
- **B.** He is a general
- **C.** He wears an eye patch
- **D.** He is not a World War II veteran

1920. Who was *not* an enemy of Luke Cage in his solo series?
- **A.** Chaka
- **B.** Shades and Comanche
- **C.** Piranha Jones
- **D.** Goldbug

1921. Where was Luke Cage born?
- **A.** Atlanta
- **B.** Harlem
- **C.** Philadelphia
- **D.** Alphabet City, Manhattan

1922. Who has *not* been one of the writers of *Runaways*?
- **A.** Brian Michael Bendis
- **B.** Terry Moore
- **C.** Joss Whedon
- **D.** Brian K. Vaughan

1923. What was Luke Cage framed and sent to prison for?
- **A.** Assault
- **B.** Burglary
- **C.** Heroin possession
- **D.** Murder

1924. Whom did Luke Cage marry?
- **A.** Harmony Young
- **B.** Dr. Claire Temple
- **C.** Misty Knight
- **D.** Jessica Jones

1925. Where was Luke Cage imprisoned?
- **A.** Seagate Prison
- **B.** Sing Sing
- **C.** The Raft
- **D.** The Vault

1926. What is the name of Luke Cage's daughter?
- **A.** Jessica
- **B.** Amanda
- **C.** Emma
- **D.** Danielle

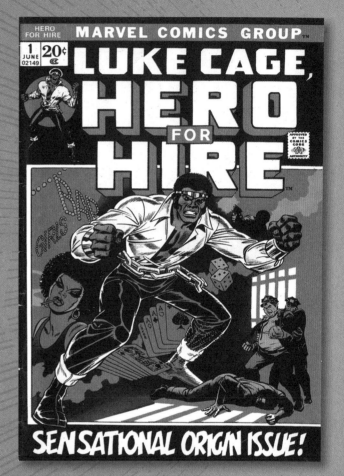

1929.

African American adventure heroes were a pop culture trend in the 1970s. Having already introduced one African American Super Hero, the Falcon, in *Captain America*, Marvel launched a new comic book series around another, *Luke Cage, Hero for Hire,* in 1972 (shown at left). His creators were writer Archie Goodwin and artist John Romita Sr.

Imprisoned for crimes he did not commit, the man who would become known as Cage volunteered for a medical experiment in order to win parole. Unexpectedly, the experimental treatment endowed him with superhuman strength and steel-hard skin. He escaped from prison and adopted the name Luke Cage, offering his services as a "hero for hire." Later, he dubbed himself Power Man, even defeating a similarly named Super Villain to win the right to the name. Cage soon after forged a partnership with the martial arts Super Hero Iron Fist, who became the co-star in *Power Man and Iron Fist.*

Where was Luke Cage's office?

- **A.** 42nd Street off Times Square
- **B.** Harlem
- **C.** Hell's Kitchen
- **D.** The Bronx

1927. Who was the film student who ran the Gem Theater beneath Luke Cage's office?
- **A.** John Ford
- **B.** Howard Hawks
- **C.** D. W. Griffith
- **D.** Frank Capra

1928. What continually frustrated Luke Cage at the Gem Theater?
- **A.** Noise from the audience
- **B.** A malfunctioning soda machine
- **C.** An annoying customer
- **D.** D. W.'s obsession with film history

1929.

1930. What does Doctor Doom do to Daredevil in *Daredevil* #37–38 (1968)?
- **A.** Shrinks him to miniature size
- **B.** Eliminates his radar sense
- **C.** Forces him to combat the Fantastic Four
- **D.** Switches bodies with him

1931. Who was Curtis Carr?
- **A.** Captain Hero
- **B.** Chemistro
- **C.** Morpheus
- **D.** Goldbug

1932. To what criminal organization do the parents of the Runaways belong?
- **A.** The Corporation
- **B.** The Pride
- **C.** The Order
- **D.** The Committee

1933. Who is *not* one of the Runaways?
- **A.** Karolina Dean
- **B.** Molly Hayes
- **C.** Alex Wilder
- **D.** Robert Markham

1934. For which criminal did Foggy Nelson's wife Debbie Harris once work?
- **A.** Crime-Wave
- **B.** The Organizer
- **C.** The Exterminator
- **D.** The Kingpin

Marvel Knights

1935. Which villain did the Exterminator later become?
- **A.** Bullet
- **B.** Bushwacker
- **C.** The Death-Stalker
- **D.** Bullseye

1936. Who was Willie Lincoln in *Daredevil* #47 (1968)?
- **A.** Blind Vietnam war veteran
- **B.** Lawyer opposing Matt Murdock in court
- **C.** Reporter for the *Daily Bugle*
- **D.** Henchman of Starr Saxon

1937. Who was Jonathan Powers?
- **A.** The Exterminator
- **B.** The Jester
- **C.** The Organizer
- **D.** Brother Brimstone

1938. Who was the original Mr. Fear?
- **A.** Larry Cranston
- **B.** Richard Raleigh
- **C.** Zoltan Drago
- **D.** Starr Saxon

1939.

1940. Where was Moon Knight born?
- **A.** San Diego
- **B.** Phoenix
- **C.** New York City
- **D.** Chicago

1941. What was the occupation of Marc Spector's father?
- **A.** Priest
- **B.** Rabbi
- **C.** Minister
- **D.** CIA agent

1942. What is Morpheus's power?
- **A.** He induces nightmares
- **B.** He can enter the Nightmare Dimension
- **C.** He puts victims into a sleeping trance
- **D.** He kills with his touch

1939.

Originally introduced as a villain in 1975, Moon Knight (shown above) quickly turned into a heroic and complex figure. A former boxer, Marine, CIA agent, and mercenary soldier, Marc Spector went to work for the terrorist leader Raoul Bushman, who planned to rob a pharaoh's tomb in Egypt. Horrified when Bushman killed archeologist Dr. Peter Alraune, Spector turned against him. When the terrorist left Spector in the desert to perish, Dr. Alraune's beautiful daughter Marlene placed the dying Spector before the tomb's statue of the moon god Khonshu. While Spector was fighting death, the god appeared to him in a vision, offering to save his

1943. Who is Jean-Paul DuChamp?

A. S.H.I.E.L.D. agent

C. European drug dealer and enemy of Cloak and Dagger

B. Moon Knight's pilot Frenchie

D. Vanessa Fisk's psychiatrist

1944. Which past Marvel writer shares the name of one of Moon Knight's alternate identities?

A. Don McGregor

C. Douglas Moench

B. Gerry Conway

D. Steven Grant

1945. Who is Dr. Noah Black?

A. Friend of Luke Cage

C. The criminal genetic engineer Centurius

B. Psychiatrist for Vanessa Fisk

D. The supernatural menace Centurius

1946. For which villain did the Unholy Three work in *Daredevil* #39–41 (1968)?

A. The Organizer

C. Count Nefaria

B. The Exterminator

D. The Kingpin

1947. Who is Jake Lockley?

A. One of the Runaways

C. New York cab driver

B. Alternate identity of Moon Knight

D. Both B and C

1948. Where does Daredevil battle the Jester on the cover of *Daredevil* #45 (1968)?

A. Times Square

C. Washington Square Park

B. The Empire State Building

D. The Statue of Liberty

life if he became Khonshu's champion. Spector agreed and thus became the costumed Super Hero Moon Knight, with Marlene as his confidante and lover.

Created by writer Doug Moench and artist Don Perlin, Moon Knight first won his own comic book in 1980, featuring tales by the classic creative team of Moench and artist Bill Sienkiewicz. In which other series did Moon Knight first appear?

A. *Power Man*
B. *Daredevil*
C. *The Rampaging Hulk*
D. *Werewolf By Night*

Marvel Knights

1949. During the acclaimed run by Mark Waid and Chris Samnee, Daredevil was disbarred and moved to which city?

　A. Los Angeles　　**C.** Portland

　B. San Francisco　　**D.** San Diego

1950. In which Marvel event did Daredevil lead The Hand from a temple in Hell's Kitchen?

　A. *Shadowland*　　**C.** *AXIS*

　B. *Fear Itself*　　**D.** *Secret Wars* (2015)

1951. When Daredevil returned to New York in his 2015 series, who became his sidekick?

　A. Echo　　**C.** White Tiger

　B. Power Man　　**D.** Blindspot

1952. Who once served as the nanny for the daughter of Luke Cage and Jessica Jones?

　A. Scarlet Witch　　**C.** H.E.R.B.I.E.

　B. Agatha Harkness　　**D.** Squirrel Girl

1953. Where did Luke Cage's team of Mighty Avengers make their headquarters?

　A. The Gem Theater　　**C.** Josie's Diner

　B. Avengers Mansion　　**D.** The Schaefer Theater

1954. Of which group has Luke Cage *not* served as the team leader?

　A. Thunderbolts　　**C.** New Avengers

　B. Mighty Avengers　　**D.** Fantastic Four

OBSESSED WITH MARVEL

1959.

The fearsome Cloak and Dagger (both shown at left) were originally two runaway teenagers. Tyrone Johnson was a seventeen-year-old African American. Tandy Bowen was a sixteen-year-old from a wealthy white family. They first met upon arrival in New York City, and the pair quickly bonded.

When some men offered Tandy a place to stay, Tyrone went along to protect her. He was right to be suspicious. The men forcibly subjected the teenagers to a new experimental form of synthetic heroin, but the drug activated their latent mutations. Tyrone became Cloak, an ominous figure who can open portals into the "Darkforce Dimension" and who feeds on the "light" (or life energies) of the victims he sends there. Tandy became Dagger, who creates daggers of "light" which drain victims of their energy. With their new powers, they became a team of vigilantes, focusing on fighting drug dealers.

Created by writer Bill Mantlo and artist Ed Hannigan, the characters Cloak and Dagger debuted in 1982. In which series did Cloak and Dagger first appear?

A. *The Amazing Spider-Man*
B. *Peter Parker, The Spectacular Spider-Man*
C. *Cloak and Dagger*
D. *The New Mutants*

1955. Where did Tyrone Johnson and Tandy Bowen first meet?
A. Port Authority Bus Terminal
C. The East Village
B. Times Square
D. Tribeca

1956. Which villain did Starr Saxon later become?
A. Mister Fear
C. Neither A nor B
B. Machinesmith
D. Both A and B

1957. Where is Tandy Bowen from?
A. Shaker Heights, Ohio
C. Chicago, Illinois
B. Columbus, Ohio
D. Philadelphia, Pennsylvania

1958. Who is Frank Farnum?
A. The Jester
C. The Masked Marauder
B. Speedball
D. Jigsaw

1959.

1960. Who is Count Bornag Royale?
A. Member of The M
C. Member of Hydra
B. Member of the Secret Empire
D. Member of A.I.M.

1961. What was *not* one of Baron Strucker's alternate identities?
A. Don Caballero
C. Anton Trojak
B. Emir Ali Bey
D. S.H.I.E.L.D. agent John Bronson

Marvel Knights

1962. Who was the Prime Mover?

- **A.** Daredevil's adversary Mr. Kline
- **B.** A robot playing a game with Doctor Doom in the *S.H.I.E.L.D.* series
- **C.** Member of System Crash
- **D.** An alien playing a game with Doctor Doom in the *S.H.I.E.L.D.* series

1963. What is Luke Cage's real name?

- **A.** Carl Lucas
- **B.** Luke Carter
- **C.** Charles Lucas
- **D.** Luke Charles

1964. Which crime family murdered Frank Castle's family?

- **A.** Cicero
- **B.** Nefaria
- **C.** Manfredi
- **D.** Costa

1965. Who is Orson Randall?

- **A.** Member of the Sons of the Tiger
- **B.** The first Iron Fist
- **C.** Danny Rand's predecessor as Iron Fist
- **D.** Captain Hero

1966. Who was Quan Yaozu?

- **A.** The August Personage in Jade
- **B.** The first Iron Fist
- **C.** Danny Rand's predecessor as Iron Fist
- **D.** Master Khan

1967. Who was Pickman during Jim Steranko's writer-artist run on *Nick Fury, Agent of S.H.I.E.L.D.*?

- **A.** Agent helping to track down Scorpio in issue 5 (1968)
- **B.** Nightclub comedian killed in issue 1 (1968)
- **C.** Caretaker of Castle Ravenlock in issue 3 (1968)
- **D.** Film director who encounters Nick Fury in issue 2 (1968)

1968.

1968.

In 1982, writer Tom DeFalco and artist Ron Frenz created the New Warriors, a fresh, young Super Hero team for a new decade. A new character, Night Thrasher (shown at right), who was a young African American corporate leader turned urban vigilante, formed the team. The other original members were all familiar faces from past Marvel series, including Richard Rider, alias Nova, who had his own comic in the 1970s; Angelica Jones, alias Firestar, a redheaded mutant who projected microwave energy; the Sub-Mariner's beautiful young cousin Namorita; Vance Astrovik, the new Marvel Boy, with his telekinetic powers; and Robbie Baldwin, the bouncing Speedball, who also previously starred in his own series.

The team met a sad end when most of its members were killed in an explosion caused by the villain Nitro, which would lead to the Super Heroes' civil war.

In which series did the New Warriors debut?

- **A.** *Marvel Comics Presents*
- **B.** *The New Warriors*
- **C.** *Thunderstrike*
- **D.** *Thor*

OBSESSED WITH MARVEL

1969. What type of energy can the new Power Man, Victor Alvarez, tap into?

- **A.** Chi
- **B.** Nuclear
- **C.** Solar
- **D.** Magic

1970. Which renowned animator wrote and drew the 2016 *CAGE!* limited series starring a retro Luke Cage?

- **A.** John Kricfalusi
- **B.** Genndy Tartakovsky
- **C.** Craig McCracken
- **D.** Pendleton Ward

1971. The original Night Thrasher returned to life in which comic book series?

- **A.** *New Warriors* (2014)
- **B.** *Contest of Champions* (2015)
- **C.** *Civil War: Choosing Sides* (2016)
- **D.** *Champions* (2016)

1972. Who served as the mentor for the new Power Man?

- **A.** Luke Cage
- **B.** Iron Fist
- **C.** White Tiger
- **D.** Dardevil

1973. Iron Fist once donned a white costume when he became the champion of which mystical entity?

- **A.** Agamotto
- **B.** Shuma-Gorath
- **C.** Cyttorak
- **D.** Dormammu

1974. In *Iron Fist: The Living Weapon*, what is the name of the next Iron Fist?

- **A.** Danielle
- **B.** Pei
- **C.** Brenda
- **D.** Fooh

1975. Where is Jessica Jones at the start of her self-titled 2016 series?

- **A.** In the future
- **B.** On vacation
- **C.** In prison
- **D.** In outer space

Marvel Knights

1976. What new identity did Speedball take in the Super Heroes' civil war?
- **A.** Asylum
- **B.** Darkling
- **C.** Penance
- **D.** Impulse

1977. Who is the second Night Thrasher?
- **A.** Dwayne Taylor's best friend
- **B.** Dwayne Taylor's illegitimate half-brother
- **C.** Dwayne Taylor's brother
- **D.** No relation to Dwayne Taylor

1978. What is the name of Foggy Nelson's younger sister?
- **A.** Jill
- **B.** Arlene
- **C.** Frances
- **D.** Candace

1979. Which museum do Mr. Hyde and the Cobra rob in *Daredevil* #61 (1970)?
- **A.** The American Museum of Natural History
- **B.** The Museum of Modern Art
- **C.** The Guggenheim Museum
- **D.** The Metropolitan Museum of Art

1980. Who was *not* one of the criminals whose abilities were transferred to the Masked Marauder's Tri-Man in *Daredevil* #22 (1966)?
- **A.** The Torpedo
- **B.** The Dancer
- **C.** The Mangler
- **D.** The Brain

1981.

1982. What happened to Daredevil's costume in *Daredevil* #5 (1964)?
- **A.** He switched to a red costume
- **B.** He lost his hood
- **C.** The "DD" emblem became "D"
- **D.** The "D" emblem became "DD"

1983. Who is Chastity McBryde?
- **A.** Femme fatale in *Master of Kung Fu*
- **B.** Former girlfriend of Matt Murdock
- **C.** S.H.I.E.L.D. agent in *Elektra: Assassin*
- **D.** Pretty Persuasions in *The New Warriors*

1981.

When Marvel writer Paul Jenkins and artist Jae Lee published *The Sentry* limited series (issue 1 shown above) as part of its *Marvel Knights* line in 2000, the story held that the Sentry was a forgotten Super Hero. Indeed, even the middle-aged Robert Reynolds had forgotten he once was the Sentry until the limited series began.

According to his backstory, the Sentry had started his super-heroic career before the origin of the Fantastic Four. He had been one of Marvel's most powerful Super Heroes, possessing extraordinary levels of super-strength, super-speed, and invulnerability;

1984. What team did the Punisher join alongside other skilled assassins like Deadpool and Elektra?

A. Thunderbolts   C. The Punishers

B. Mercs for Money   D. Sinister Syndicate

1985. Former Marine Rachel Alves-Cole worked with the Punisher after her family was gunned down where?

A. At her home   C. On a train

B. In Central Park   D. At her wedding

1986. During *Civil War II*, Elektra served as a field leader for which organization?

A. Hydra   C. S.H.I.E.L.D.

B. The Hand   D. The Yakuza

1987. With whom did Elektra share a relationship with when they were brainwashed prisoners in Pleasant Hill?

A. Baron Zemo   C. Bullseye

B. Kingpin   D. Absorbing Man

1988. Which character did not star in a new series launching from 2017's "Running with the Devil" story?

A. Elektra   C. Blindspot

B. Kingpin   D. Bullseye

1989. In his 2011 series, which of the following was *not* an alternate personality Moon Knight developed?

A. Wolverine   C. Spider-Man

B. Iron Man   D. Captain America

1990. What does Mr. Knight wear as a costume?

A. White business suit with mask   C. Bird skull mask

B. Hooded cape   D. Ancient Egyptian robes

he was also able to fly and to project immensely powerful energy. But the Sentry had a dark side, which manifested itself as "the Void." To safeguard the world from his other self, Reynolds erased virtually everyone's memory of the Sentry, including his own. He did so again at the end of *The Sentry* limited series, but the new story proved to be so popular that the character has returned in other various series.

Which team has the Sentry *not* joined?

A. Dark Avengers

B. Secret Avengers

C. Mighty Avengers

D. New Avengers

Marvel Knights

CHAPTER SEVEN:

HORROR HEROES:

FROM GHOST RIDER TO BLADE

1991. Who was the mother of Quincy Harker?
- **A.** Mina Murray
- **B.** Edith Harker
- **C.** Elizabeth Harker
- **D.** Lucy Westernra

1992. Who was Domini?
- **A.** Dracula's third wife
- **B.** Dracula's daughter
- **C.** Dracula's second wife
- **D.** An angel

1993. Who was Janus?
- **A.** Host of the Golden Angel
- **B.** Adversary of Dracula
- **C.** Son of Dracula
- **D.** All answers are correct

1994. Who started a Marvel comics adaptation of Bram Stoker's *Dracula* in the 1970s, but didn't finish it until the 2000s?
- **A.** Roy Thomas and John Buscema
- **B.** Len Wein and Bernie Wrightson
- **C.** Roy Thomas and Dick Giordano
- **D.** Marv Wolfman and Gene Colan

1995. What was Rachel van Helsing's preferred weapon?
- **A.** Wooden blade
- **B.** Crossbow
- **C.** Gun firing silver bullets
- **D.** Hammer and stake

1996. How did Quincy Harker die?
- **A.** He was bitten by Dracula
- **B.** He fell from a great height
- **C.** Of old age
- **D.** From the explosion of a bomb he set in Castle Dracula

1997. What was the Montesi Formula?
- **A.** Spell for creating vampires
- **B.** Means by which Dracula fathered a son
- **C.** Spell to destroy all vampires on Earth
- **D.** Chemical that turned Ted Sallis into Man-Thing

OPPOSITE Horror heroes from *Handbook: Horror* (2005)

1998. Who resurrected Dracula in *Tomb of Dracula* #1 (1972)?
- **A.** Clifton Graves
- **B.** Frank Drake
- **C.** Anton Lupescu
- **D.** Harold H. Harold

1999. Who is Aurora Rabinowitz?
- **A.** Member of Anton Lupescu's cult
- **B.** Howard the Duck's companion
- **C.** Secretary who befriended Quincy Harker's vampire hunters
- **D.** Lilith's human host

2000. Who did *not* write one of the first six issues of *Tomb of Dracula*?
- **A.** Gardner Fox
- **B.** Gerry Conway
- **C.** Marv Wolfman
- **D.** Archie Goodwin

2001. How old was Rachel van Helsing when Dracula killed her parents?
- **A.** Twenty-one
- **B.** Eighteen
- **C.** Nine
- **D.** An infant

2002. Who is Hannibal King?
- **A.** Author of horror fiction
- **B.** Vampire detective
- **C.** Sixteenth-century Puritan adventurer
- **D.** Exorcist

2003. What was the name of Quincy Harker's wife?
- **A.** Edith
- **B.** Elizabeth
- **C.** Agatha
- **D.** Abigail

2004. Who was Doctor Sun?
- **A.** Disembodied brain
- **B.** Adversary of Dracula
- **C.** Asian criminal mastermind
- **D.** All answers are correct

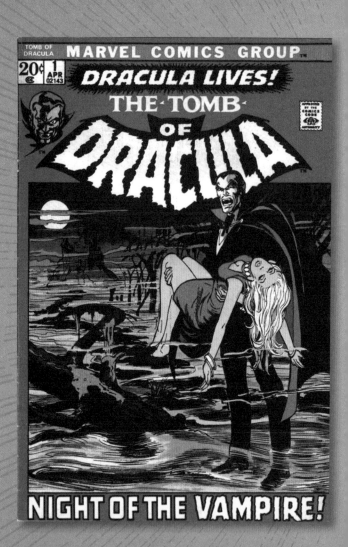

OBSESSED WITH MARVEL

2010.

In the early 1970s Marvel undertook a vast expansion of its line of comics and began to explore elements of classic horror stories. One of Marvel's first horror series was *Tomb of Dracula* (issue 1 shown at left); it was also considered one of the best. Its first issue was cover-dated April 1972, and it brought author Bram Stoker's vampires into the twentieth century. From its start, *Tomb* was drawn by Gene Colan, whose mastery of mood, atmosphere, and characterization made him perfect for the series. Except for the earliest issues, Colan teamed with writer Marv Wolfman and inker Tom Palmer in an outstanding creative partnership.

Tomb followed a team of vampire hunters, including Quincy Harker and Rachel Van Helsing, heirs of characters from Stoker's novel, and Dracula's own descendant Frank Drake. *Tomb's* greatest character was Dracula himself, a complex figure, both regal and ruthless, fearsome but admirable.

In which American city was much of the original run of *Tomb of Dracula* based?

A. New York City
B. Washington D.C.
C. Boston
D. Philadelphia

2005. Which of the following characters used the Montesi Formula?
A. Doctor Strange
B. Quincy Harker
C. Blade
D. Frank Drake

2006. In which series did monster hunter Ulysses Bloodstone's allies Brad Carter and P. D. Q. Werner first appear?
A. *The Incredible Hulk*
B. *Nick Fury, Agent of S.H.I.E.L.D.*
C. *Ka-Zar*
D. *Ghost Rider*

2007. Who was *not* a member of the Monster Hunters?
A. Makkari
B. Doctor Druid
C. Gilgamesh
D. Ulysses Bloodstone

2008. What is the name of Ulysses Bloodstone's daughter, who combats supernatural menaces?
A. Penelope Bloodstone
B. Elsa Bloodstone
C. Eve Bloodstone
D. Anna Bloodstone

2009. How long did Ulysses Bloodstone live?
A. Nearly a century
B. A millennium
C. 5,000 years
D. 10,000 years

2010.

2011. Who or what is Vlad Tepes?
A. Dracula's father
B. The first two parts of Dracula's full name
C. Dracula's true name
D. A historical monarch mistaken for Dracula

Horror Heroes

2012. What was Rachel Van Helsing's fate?
- **A.** Dracula turned her into a vampire
- **B.** Wolverine impaled her as a mercy killing
- **C.** First A, then B
- **D.** First B, then A

2013. Who is N'Kantu?
- **A.** Member of Blade's vampire hunters
- **B.** The Living Mummy
- **C.** Member of the Monster Hunters
- **D.** Voodoo priest in *Tales of The Zombie*

2014. Who is *not* a member of the Frankenstein family?
- **A.** Victoria
- **B.** Basil
- **C.** Eric
- **D.** Victor

2015. Who was *not* a member of the Legion of Monsters?
- **A.** Morbius the Living Vampire
- **B.** Werewolf by Night
- **C.** The Frankenstein Monster
- **D.** Ghost Rider (Johnny Blaze)

2016. Who was the first Marvel character known as the Ghost Rider?
- **A.** Nightmare
- **B.** Phantom Rider
- **C.** The Blazing Skull
- **D.** Death's-Head

2017. Who was the first supernatural Ghost Rider in the Marvel Universe?
- **A.** Johnny Blaze
- **B.** Noble Kale
- **C.** Pastor Kale
- **D.** Daniel Ketch

2018. Who was *not* a member of the Legion of Night?
- **A.** Jennifer Kale
- **B.** Angel O'Hara
- **C.** Martin Gold
- **D.** Dr. Katherine Reynolds

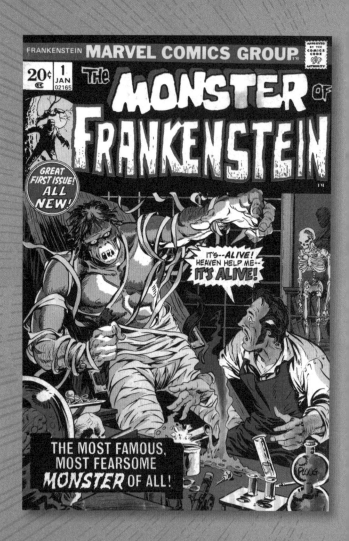

FRANKENSTEIN **MARVEL COMICS GROUP**

20¢ 1 JAN 02165

The **MONSTER** OF **FRANKENSTEIN**

GREAT FIRST ISSUE! ALL NEW!

IT'S--ALIVE! HEAVEN HELP ME-- IT'S ALIVE!

THE MOST FAMOUS, MOST FEARSOME **MONSTER** OF ALL!

2024.

Marvel's *The Monster of Frankenstein* began in 1973 with a four-issue adaptation of Mary Shelley's original 1818 novel (issue 1 shown at left). Gary Friedrich served as the writer and Mike Ploog as the artist. Stan Lee has long acknowledged that the 1931 film version of Frankenstein's Monster was one of the inspirations for the Hulk, so it was fitting that Marvel would create a series about the original. In addition to the Hulk, Marvel had also experimented with Frankenstein-inspired characters in *The X-Men* and *The Silver Surfer*. But rather than bringing readers the familiar lumbering, inarticulate version often presented on film, Marvel came up with a monster truer to Mary Shelley's concept: intelligent, articulate, and complex. Later issues did not live up to the initial adaptation's promise, but the Frankenstein Monster has remained part of the Marvel Universe, turning up in such unexpected places as *Iron Man*, *The Avengers*, *Bloodstone*, and *Marvel: The Lost Generation*.

Where did the Frankenstein Monster first appear in a Marvel comics story?

A. *The X-Men* #40 (1968)
B. *The Silver Surfer* #7 (1969)
C. *The Monster of Frankenstein* #1 (1973)
D. *Monsters Unleashed* #1 (1973)

2019. Who led the Howling Commandos of S.H.I.E.L.D. in their 2015 series?
A. Warwolf
B. Man-Thing
C. Dum Dum Dugan's LMD
D. Orrgo

2020. Who is Nina Price?
A. Vampire by Night
B. Jack Russell's niece
C. A Howling Commando
D. All answers are correct

2021. Which division of S.H.I.E.L.D. runs the Howling Commandos?
A. S.T.A.K.E.
B. S.W.O.R.D.
C. H.A.M.M.E.R.
D. A.R.M.O.R.

2022. Which classic S.H.I.E.L.D. agent was a zombie during his time on the new Howling Commandos?
A. Gabriel Jones
B. Rebel Ralston
C. Jasper Sitwell
D. Eric Koenig

2023. Which member of the Howling Commandos was introduced in the pages of *Superior Iron Man*?
A. Vampire by Night
B. Warwolf
C. Hit Monkey
D. Teen Abomination

2024.

2025. What member of the Howling Commandos went on to serve with the Mercs for Money?
A. Man-Thing
B. Hit-Monkey
C. Warwolf
D. Orrgo

Horror Heroes

2026. Which monster, using the name Adam, acts as ally to Elsa Bloodstone?

A. It, The Living Colossus
B. The Frankenstein Monster
C. The Living Mummy
D. The Golem

2027. Who was *not* a member of the Shock Troop in *Quasar*?

A. Doctor Druid
B. The Frankenstein Monster
C. The Living Mummy
D. Blazing Skull

2028.

2029. When did Jack Russell first become a werewolf?

A. The night of his twenty-first birthday
B. The night of his eighteenth birthday
C. The night before his twenty-first birthday
D. The night before his eighteenth birthday

2030. Where was Jack Russell born?

A. Los Angeles
B. Transylvania
C. Transia
D. Berkeley

2031. Who is Jack Russell's sister?

A. Lana
B. Lisa
C. Lissa
D. Laura

2032. What occupation does Jack Russell's friend Buck Cowan have?

A. Policeman
B. Actor
C. Writer
D. Detective

2033. What triggered Dan Ketch's initial transformation into Ghost Rider?

A. His hand was wet with the innocent blood of his wounded sister
B. He touched the gas cap of a mysterious motorcycle
C. Both A and B
D. He made a deal with Mephisto

2028.

In *Marvel Spotlight* #3 (1972), Marvel introduced contemporary werewolf Jack Russell in the series *Werewolf by Night* (shown at right), which soon graduated to its own comic. Editor Roy Thomas came up with the idea for a young werewolf, writer Gerry Conway and artist Mike Ploog worked on the original story, while Doug Moench wrote most of the issues of the original *Werewolf by Night* comic.

Although Jack Russell grew up and lived in Southern California, he inherited his ancestors' curse: for three nights in every lunar cycle, Russell is transformed into a savage werewolf.

What was Jack Russell's original name?

A. Jack Russell
B. Jacob Russoff
C. Yakov Russov
D. Jacob Russovich

2026B 2027B 2028B 2029D 2030B 2031C 2032C 2033C

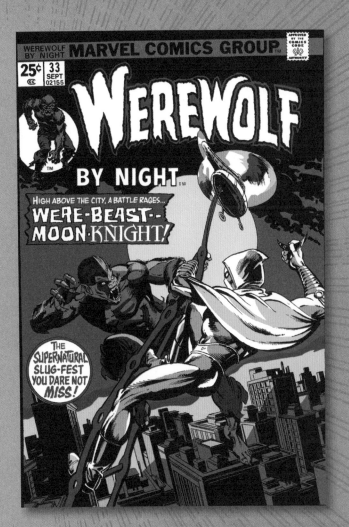

2034. Which enemy of the Werewolf by Night was a member of the Five Who Are All?

A. Moondark the Magician

B. Dr. Glitternight

C. Marduk Kurios

D. Morning Star

2035. Where was the Werewolf by Night sighted in *Code of Honor* #1 (1997)?

A. Rockefeller Center

B. Columbia University

C. The Bronx Zoo

D. Central Park

2036. What was the name of the demon who called himself Satan who turned Johnny Blaze into Ghost Rider?

A. Marduk Korios

B. Mephisto

C. Satannish

D. Thog the Nether-Spawn

2037. Who is the stepfather of the empath Topaz?

A. Swami Rihva

B. The sorcerer Taboo

C. Dr. Glitternight

D. Phillip Russell

2038. What is the name of Dan Ketch's sister?

A. Stacy

B. Barbara

C. Naomi

D. Jenny

2039. Which Ghost Rider enemy nearly killed Dan Ketch's sister?

A. Snowblind

B. Deathwatch

C. The Scarecrow

D. Zodiak

Horror Heroes

2040. Who was Michael Badilino?
- **A.** Vengeance
- **B.** Snowblind
- **C.** Deathwatch
- **D.** Blackout

2041. Where is Cypress Hills Cemetery located?
- **A.** Manhattan
- **B.** Brooklyn
- **C.** Queens
- **D.** New Jersey

2042. What was the name of Johnny Blaze's father?
- **A.** Craig Blaze
- **B.** Barton Blaze
- **C.** Crash Simpson
- **D.** Johnny Blaze does not know who his father was

2043.

2044. What is the name of John Blaze's wife?
- **A.** Emma
- **B.** Roxanne
- **C.** Naomi
- **D.** Mona

2045. How many children did John Blaze have?
- **A.** None
- **B.** Two
- **C.** Four
- **D.** Six

2046. What is the Ghost Rider's Penance Stare?
- **A.** Forces a victim to feel guilty for his sins
- **B.** Induces fear in his victims
- **C.** Compels a victim to confess his crimes
- **D.** Makes a wrongdoer feel all the pain he inflicted on his victims

2047. Who is Zero Cochrane?
- **A.** Vengeance 2099
- **B.** Doctor Neon
- **C.** Ghost Rider 2099
- **D.** Werewolf

2043.

Making a deal with the Devil never works out as one might hope. When Johnny Blaze learned that Crash Simpson, the stunt motorcyclist who raised him, was mortally ill, he made a deal with Satan (actually the demon lord Mephisto) to prevent Simpson's death. Mephisto abided by the letter of the bargain, but then allowed Simpson to die while performing a dangerous motorcycle stunt. Then Mephisto bonded Blaze's soul to the demon Zarathos, causing Blaze to transform into the Ghost Rider— a flaming skeleton who rode a motorcycle composed of "hellfire."

A LEGEND IS BORN!

2048. Where was Johnny Blaze born?

A. Long Beach, California
B. Waukegan, Illinois
C. Indianapolis, Indiana
D. Fresno, California

2049. How many cars was Crash Simpson trying to jump over on his motorcycle when he died?

A. Twelve
B. Twenty
C. Twenty-two
D. Twenty-five

2050. What are the Ghostworks?

A. Spectral adversaries of Ghost Rider
B. Part of the D/MONIX Corporation
C. Artificial intelligences in the alternate timeline of *Marvel 2099*
D. Investigators of supernatural phenomena

2051. What is Ghost Rider 2099?

A. A robot with human consciousness
B. A supernatural being
C. A human bonded to the demon Zarathos
D. A genetically engineered creature

2052. To which race did the Caretaker in *Ghost Rider* belong?

A. The Chaste
B. The Brood
C. The Blood
D. The Lilin

2053. Who is Drake Shannon?

A. The Water Wizard
B. The Orb
C. The Manticore
D. The Enforcer

Editor Roy Thomas, writer Gary Friedrich, and artist Mike Ploog all participated in devising the original Ghost Rider story, which appeared in *Marvel Spotlight* #5 (1973, shown above). Blaze was later succeeded as Ghost Rider by Dan Ketch, but more recently has resumed his Ghost Rider role.

What relation is John Blaze to Dan Ketch?

A. First cousin
B. Brother
C. Second cousin
D. Uncle

Horror Heroes

2054. What is the principal reason that the Orb always wears his eye-shaped helmet?
- **A.** To frighten his victims
- **B.** As a weapon
- **C.** His face was horribly disfigured
- **D.** For protection

2055. What powers does the Orb's helmet have?
- **A.** Fires laser blasts from its "pupil"
- **B.** Hypnotic abilities
- **C.** Both A and B
- **D.** None of these

2056. What is the name of Sleepwalker's realm?
- **A.** The Dream Dimension
- **B.** The Nightmare Realm
- **C.** The Mindscape
- **D.** The Dreaming

2057. Whose enemy was Doctor Vault?
- **A.** Morbius
- **B.** Werewolf by Night
- **C.** It, the Living Colossus
- **D.** Ghost Rider (Johnny Blaze)

2058. Who is Diane Cummings?
- **A.** Girlfriend of Jack Russell
- **B.** Faculty colleague of Daimon Hellstrom
- **C.** Wife of Dorian Delazny
- **D.** Bob O'Bryan's actress wife

2059.

2060. Who did *not* work at Delazny Studios?
- **A.** Bob O'Bryan
- **B.** Stunt-Master
- **C.** Johnny Blaze
- **D.** Simon Williams

2061. Who destroyed the Colossus's original stone body?
- **A.** The Kigor
- **B.** The Hulk
- **C.** The U.S. Army
- **D.** Doctor Vault

2059.

Just before the debut of the Fantastic Four in 1961, Marvel had specialized in stories about colossal monsters. In the 1970s, one such monster became the hero of his own series. In *Tales of Suspense* #14 (1961), sculptor Boris Petrovski constructed a hundred-foot-tall statue of a heroic figure as a protest against the totalitarian Soviet government. A member of the alien Kigor race transferred his mind into the statue, causing it to rampage through Moscow. In *Tales of Suspense* #20 (1961), the statue resided in Los Angeles, and the Kigors animated it again. This time they were defeated by Hollywood special-effects technician Bob O'Bryan. Starting in *Astonishing Tales* #21 (1973, shown at right), the statue, known as "It, the Living Colossus," now only thirty feet tall, was brought to life by the mind of Bob O'Bryan for a series of adventures. Though the original "It" was destroyed, duplicates have appeared in subsequent stories.

Who first drew the Colossus?

- **A.** Dick Ayers
- **B.** Bill Everett
- **C.** Jack Kirby
- **D.** Steve Ditko

OBSESSED WITH MARVEL

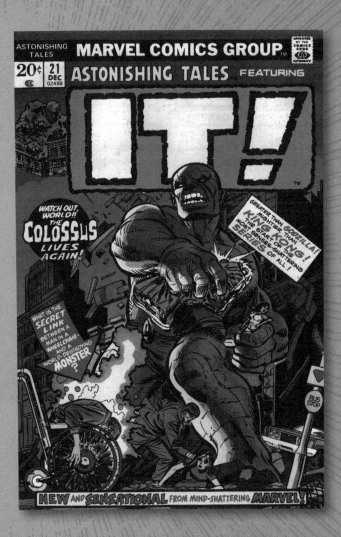

2062. What is the first name of Elsa Bloodstone's younger brother?

A. Ulysses   C. Bobby

B. Cullen   D. Declan

2063. In which series did the young Bloodstone make his first appearance?

A. *Avengers: The Initiative*   C. *Avengers Arena*

B. *Avengers Academy*   D. *Avengers Undercover*

2064. What does Elsa Bloodstone's younger brother do that she cannot?

A. Kill monsters   C. Turn into a monster

B. Talk to monsters   D. Control monsters

2065. Who was the Ghost Rider featured during the *Fear Itself* crossover?

A. Johnny Blaze   C. Alejandra Jones

B. Danny Ketch   D. Robbie Reyes

2066. Who was the Ghost Rider who starred in the 2014 series *All-New Ghost Rider*?

A. Johnny Blaze   C. Alejandra Jones

B. Danny Ketch   D. Robbie Reyes

2067. Robbie Reyes was possessed by which spirit?

A. Zarathos   C. Mephisto

B. Eli Morrow   D. Noble Kale

2068. What secret installation does S.T.A.K.E. use as their headquarters?

A. Area 51   C. Area 13

B. Area 52   D. Area 666

Horror Heroes

2069. Which organization opposed the elder Bloodstone?
A. The Hellfire Helix
C. The Conclave
B. The Conspiracy
D. The Secret Empire

2070. Who is Stacy Dolan?
A. New York City police detective
C. Both A and B
B. Dan Ketch's girlfriend
D. None of these

2071. What relation is the new Caretaker in *Ghost Rider* to the original Caretaker?
A. Son
C. Daughter
B. Granddaughter
D. Grandson

2072. Who is Martin Gold?
A. Cast member in *The Golem*
C. Angel O'Hara's boyfriend
B. Disc jockey ally of Man-Thing
D. Winky Man in *Howard the Duck*

2073. Who created the Living Mummy?
A. Len Wein and John Buscema
C. Steve Gerber and Rich Buckler
B. Roy Thomas and Gray Morrow
D. Mike Friedrich and Tony DeZuniga

2074. Who is the mentor of sorceress Jennifer Kale?
A. Joshua Kale
C. Dakimh the Enchanter
B. Modred the Mystic
D. Zhered-Na

2075. To whom is Jennifer Kale *not* related?
A. Dan Ketch
C. John Blaze
B. Topaz
D. Noble Kale

2076.

2077. Where was Ted Sallis born?
A. Omaha, Nebraska
C. St. Louis, Missouri
B. Cambridge, Massachusetts
D. Citrusville, Florida

2076.

In the Florida Everglades, biochemist Dr. Theodore "Ted" Sallis was working on a secret government project, not suspecting that the woman he loved, Ellen Brandt, had betrayed him to the subversive organization of scientists known as A.I.M. Sallis escaped into the swamp and injected himself with the only sample of his serum in order to keep it out of criminal hands. The serum combined with the swamp's mystical energies to transform Sallis into a massive creature called the Man-Thing (shown at right). Though possessing only dim traces of his human intellect and memories, the Man-Thing is an empath, sensing and responding to human emotions. Stan Lee, Roy Thomas, Gerry Conway, and artist Gray Morrow all collaborated in creating Man-Thing in *Savage Tales* #1 (1971). But the writer most associated with the character is the late Steve Gerber, whose Man-Thing stories paved the way for adult supernatural comics series at Marvel.

What was the original intent for Sallis's formula?

A. Endow people with psychic abilities
B. Accelerate the growth of plants
C. Cure diseases
D. Recreate the Super-Soldier serum

OBSESSED WITH MARVEL

2078. What emotion causes someone to burn at the Man-Thing's touch?
- **A.** Rage
- **B.** Fear
- **C.** Hatred
- **D.** Despair

2079. Who was Franklin Armstrong Schist?
- **A.** Enemy of Man-Thing
- **B.** Seeker of the Fountain of Youth
- **C.** Amoral businessman
- **D.** All answers are correct

2080. What was Richard Rory's occupation?
- **A.** Musician
- **B.** Radio disc jockey
- **C.** Novelist
- **D.** Advertising copywriter

2081. Which Man-Thing story featured ad man Brian Lazarus?
- **A.** "The Kid's Night Out"
- **B.** "Song-Cry of the Living Dead Man"
- **C.** "A Candle for Saint-Cloud"
- **D.** "Night of the Laughing Dead"

2082. Who was Ross G. Everbest?
- **A.** Winky-Man
- **B.** The original Foolkiller
- **C.** The Space Turnip
- **D.** Bellboy who aided Le Beaver

2083. What was the profession of Darrel Daniel, whose soul was put on trial in Man-Thing's swamp?
- **A.** Artist
- **B.** Actor
- **C.** Clown
- **D.** Writer

2084. Who is Korrek?
- **A.** Member of the Lilin
- **B.** One of the Gargoyles of Stonus Five
- **C.** Other-dimensional barbarian warrior ally of Man-Thing
- **D.** Member of the Entropists

Horror Heroes

2085. Who was the original captain of the pirate ship *The Serpent's Crown*, whose crew is cursed never to die?

A. Maura Hawke

B. Captain Jedediah Fate

C. Maura Spinner

D. Khordes the satyr

2086. Who was Zhered-Na?

A. Mentor of Dakimh

B. Lookalike for Jennifer Kale

C. Sorceress of ancient Atlantis

D. All answers are correct

2087. What is the name of the second caretaker in *Ghost Rider* who succeeded the original in 2008?

A. Marie

B. Louise

C. Sara

D. Elaine

2088. How does the title character of *Terror Inc.* take on the abilities of others?

A. Absorbs them telepathically

B. Replaces his body parts with theirs

C. Duplicates their DNA

D. Switches bodies with them

2089. In which series did the Terror first appear?

A. *Terror Inc.*

B. *St. George*

C. *Doctor Zero*

D. *Ghost Rider*

2090. Which artist first drew Howard the Duck?

A. Frank Brunner

B. Val Mayerik

C. Gene Colan

D. John Buscema

2091. What was the original job that Howard the Duck's companion Beverly Switzler held?

A. Artists' life model

B. Accountant

C. Political campaign worker

D. Rock musician

2092. Who was *not* one of Dr. Angst's allies against Howard the Duck?
- **A.** The Spanker
- **B.** Winky-Man
- **C.** Black Hole
- **D.** Sitting Bullseye

2093. Which political party ran Howard the Duck's campaign for President?
- **A.** The All-Night Party
- **B.** Mad Genius Associates
- **C.** The New Populist Party
- **D.** S.O.O.F.I.

2094. Who successfully sabotaged Howard the Duck's presidential campaign?
- **A.** Bzzk'Joh
- **B.** Le Beaver
- **C.** Doctor Bong
- **D.** Reverend Joon Moon Yuc

2095. Who has turned Howard the Duck into a human and a mouse?
- **A.** The High Evolutionary
- **B.** Doctor Bong
- **C.** Sersi
- **D.** Doctor Strange

2096.

2097. Who was the first menace that Howard the Duck battled in Cleveland?
- **A.** Garko the Man-Frog
- **B.** Bessie the Hellcow
- **C.** Pro-Rata the Cosmic Accountant
- **D.** The Space Turnip

2098. Who is *not* one of Howard the Duck's friends?
- **A.** Jennifer Kale
- **B.** Paul Same
- **C.** The Kidney Lady
- **D.** Winda Wester

2099. Where did Howard the Duck have his showdown with Le Beaver?
- **A.** The White House lawn
- **B.** Convention hall in New York City
- **C.** Niagara Falls
- **D.** Cleveland

2096.

In the course of Thog the Nether-Spawn's scheme to conquer the multiverse, beings from disparate alternate realities appeared at the Nexus of All Realities in *Adventure Into Fear* #19 (1973). Among them was a feisty, bad-tempered but likable talking duck called Howard. Readers immediately took to Howard, who soon returned in his own stories, first in *Giant-Size Man-Thing*, and then in his own *Howard the Duck* (issue 8 shown at left) comic book. Howard was superbly illustrated first by Frank Brunner and then by Gene Colan. But the man most responsible for Howard's success was his creator, the late Steve Gerber, who turned the series into a brilliant work of satire—not only parodying comics, but also popular culture, American society, and politics. Most famously, Gerber had Howard the Duck run for president in 1976 on the slogan "Get down, America!"

In which city does Howard the Duck live?

- **A.** Boston
- **B.** Cleveland
- **C.** Los Angeles
- **D.** Hoboken

Horror Heroes

2100. Which of Doctor Bong's hands was severed and replaced with a metal ball?

A. Left

B. Right

C. Both

D. Neither

2101. Which real-life rock star or stars appeared in the original *Howard the Duck* series?

A. The Grateful Dead

B. Alice Cooper

C. Paul McCartney

D. KISS

2102. How is Lee Switzler related to Beverly?

A. Father

B. Brother

C. Uncle

D. Nephew

2103. How was Howard the Duck's presidential campaign wrecked?

A. A court declared that a duck from another world could not run for president

B. Howard was framed for embezzling money from his campaign

C. A fake photo of Howard taking a bubble bath with Beverly was leaked

D. An actual photo of Howard taking a bubble bath with Beverly was leaked

2104. Who once married Beverly Switzler?

A. Howard the Duck

B. G. Q. Studley

C. Dreyfuss Gultch

D. Doctor Bong

2105. Who is Rick Sheridan?

A. Actor at Delazny Studios

B. Boyfriend of Elsa Bloodstone

C. Secret identity of Sleepwalker

D. Human host of Sleepwalker

2106. Who is *not* one of Sleepwalker's enemies?

A. Bookworm

B. Lullaby

C. Dreamqueen

D. Cobweb

2107.

Simon Garth, the title character of Marvel's 1970s black-and-white magazine *Tales of the Zombie*, actually first appeared in a story called "Zombie!" in *Menace* #5 (1953). *Tales of the Zombie* #1 (1973, shown at right) not only reprinted that classic tale, but provided a prequel—written by Roy Thomas and Steve Gerber, and illustrated by John Buscema and Tom Palmer—that gave the Zombie an origin.

When wealthy New Orleans businessman Simon Garth fired his gardener Gyps, Gyps took revenge by abducting Garth and turning him over to voodoo cultists. The priestess of the cult, Layla, turned out to be Garth's secretary, who was in love with him. She was unable to prevent Gyps from killing Garth, and Gyps forced her to resurrect Garth as the Zombie. Although Garth in Zombie form was laid to rest in the next to last issue, the Zombie has subsequently been resurrected.

Who co-created Simon Garth, the Zombie?

A. Stan Lee and Joe Maneely

B. Stan Lee and Bill Everett

C. Stan Lee and Jerry Robinson

D. Stan Lee and John Romita Sr.

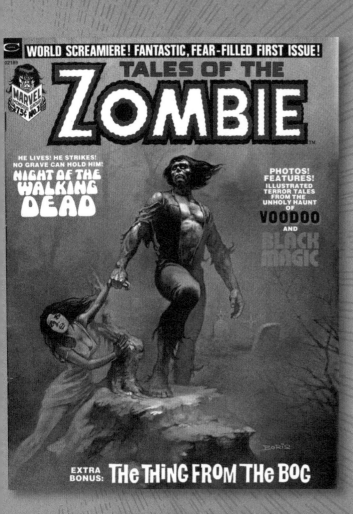

2108. Who is Jacob Goldstein?

A. Member of Dracula's search party for the Chimera

B. Distant ancestor of Jack Russell

C. The Blue Bullet

D. The Golem of the 1940s in *The Invaders*

2109. Who is Professor Abraham Adamson?

A. Archaeologist who discovered the Living Mummy

B. Man whose life force animated the Golem in *Strange Tales*

C. Member of the Legion of Night

D. Teacher of Victor Frankenstein

2110. For how many issues did *Tales of the Zombie* run?

A. Eight

B. Ten

C. Twelve

D. Twenty

2111. What is the name of Simon Garth's daughter?

A. Debbie

B. Donna

C. Alison

D. Meredith

2112. After the black-and-white series *Tales of the Zombie* ended, in which color comics series did Simon Garth return?

A. *The Avengers*

B. *Brother Voodoo*

C. *Daredevil*

D. *Doctor Strange*

2113. Where was Simon Garth born?

A. Haiti

B. Little Rock, Arkansas

C. Birmingham, Alabama

D. New Orleans, Louisiana

2114. In which business did Simon Garth make his fortune?

A. Banking

B. Real estate

C. Coffee

D. Cotton

Horror Heroes

2115. Who is Lester Verde?
- **A.** Roulette
- **B.** Zodiak
- **C.** Doctor Bong
- **D.** Stunt-Master

2116. What is Sominus?
- **A.** Other-dimensional realm
- **B.** Realm of Thog the Nether-Spawn
- **C.** Dimension of the N'Garai demons of Korrek
- **D.** The Nightmare dimension

2117. Who is Alyssa Conover?
- **A.** Girlfriend of Richard Rory
- **B.** Member of H.E.A.R.T.
- **C.** Rick Sheridan's girlfriend in *Sleepwalker*
- **D.** Angel O'Hara's best friend

2118. Who was the first vampire?
- **A.** Nosferatu
- **B.** Nimrod
- **C.** Torgo
- **D.** Varnae

2119. How are Rebecca and Jason Adamson related to Abraham Adamson in *The Golem*?
- **A.** They are his children
- **B.** They are his grandchildren
- **C.** They are his niece and nephew
- **D.** They are his parents

2120. What does the word *EMETH* on the Golem's forehead mean?
- **A.** Life
- **B.** Power
- **C.** Truth
- **D.** Justice

2121. Who turned Dracula into a vampire?
- **A.** Mephisto
- **B.** Turac
- **C.** Lianda
- **D.** Varnae

2124.

As part of the wave of action heroes in the 1970s, Blade made his first appearance in *Tomb of Dracula* #10 (1973, shown above). Created by writer Marv Wolfman and artist Gene Colan, Blade took his name from his trademark weapons, the wooden blades he used to hunt Dracula and other vampires. When Blade's mother was about to give birth to him, a doctor arrived who proved to be a vampire named Deacon Frost. As she gave birth to Blade, Frost killed her, but

2122. Who was Dracula's first wife?
- **A.** Elianne
- **B.** Zofia
- **C.** Maria
- **D.** Lianda

2123. Who was Dracula's second wife?
- **A.** Cristina
- **B.** Zofia
- **C.** Maria
- **D.** Gretchen

2124.

2125. Who was *not* a member of the Nightstalkers?
- **A.** Rachel Van Helsing
- **B.** Frank Drake
- **C.** Blade
- **D.** Hannibal King

2126. In which comics series did the first solo *Blade* story appear?
- **A.** *Dracula Lives*
- **B.** *Vampire Tales*
- **C.** *Haunt of Horror*
- **D.** *Monsters Unleashed*

2127. Who was *not* a member of the Darkhold Redeemers?
- **A.** Sam Buchanan
- **B.** Louise Hastings
- **C.** Sheila Whittier
- **D.** Victoria Montesi

2128. Who wrote the book of evil magic called the Darkhold?
- **A.** Satannish
- **B.** Chthon
- **C.** Mephisto
- **D.** Marduk Korios

2129. What form do the benign gods of Therea take?
- **A.** Cats
- **B.** Dogs
- **C.** Humanoids
- **D.** Squidlike

the vampire was driven off before he could attack the newborn as well. As a result of the circumstances of his birth, Blade gained various powers, including an immunity to vampire bites. A longtime supporting character in *Tomb of Dracula*, Blade finally won his own first comic book series in 1994.

What is Blade's real name?

- **A.** Jamal Afari
- **B.** Eric Brooks
- **C.** Orji Jones
- **D.** Jonas Cray

Horror Heroes

2130. Where is the demon fight club held in the criminal nation of Bagalia?
- **A.** Mephisticuffs
- **B.** The Hole
- **C.** Constrictor's Snakepit
- **D.** Massacrer Casino

2131. What classic Marvel demon has a home in Bagalia's Helltown district?
- **A.** Mephisto
- **B.** Daimon Hellstrom
- **C.** Satana
- **D.** Zarathos

2132. Who helped bring Doctor Voodoo back to life during the *AXIS* crossover?
- **A.** Scarlet Witch
- **B.** Doctor Strange
- **C.** Doctor Doom
- **D.** Red Onslaught

2133. Where did Morbius the Living Vampire call home in his 2013 series?
- **A.** Brownsville
- **B.** Greenpoint
- **C.** Brooklyn
- **D.** Queens

2134. Which classic Marvel monster starred in a 2017 series written by horror legend R.L. Stine?
- **A.** Werewolf by Night
- **B.** Ghost Rider
- **C.** Morbius
- **D.** Man-Thing

2135. What was the name of Marvel's major monster crossover event in early 2017?
- **A.** *Monsters Return!*
- **B.** *Monsters Unleashed!*
- **C.** *Monsters Attack!*
- **D.** *Monsters United!*

2136. What object prevents the unwanted use of the young Bloodstone's powers?
- **A.** A bloodgem ring
- **B.** An ancient scepter
- **C.** An enchanted coin
- **D.** A cursed dagger

2137.

In the early 1970s, Marvel decided to see how far it could go toward depicting a vampire within a comics code that prohibited supernatural characters. In *Amazing Spider-Man* #101 (1971), writer Roy Thomas and artist Gil Kane created Morbius the Living Vampire (shown above). Morbius was not a true supernatural vampire, but rather owed his origin to science fiction. Attempting to cure himself of a blood disease, Dr. Michael Morbius conducted experiments with vampire bats that backfired, turning him into a superhuman creature that needed to attack and bite victims for their blood to survive. Since Morbius's vampirism was not supernatural, the Comics Code Authority had no problem with it.

OBSESSED WITH MARVEL

2138. What shape is the birthmark on Daimon Hellstrom's chest?
- **A.** Triangle
- **B.** Circle
- **C.** Pentagram
- **D.** Inverted cross

2139. When Morbius went on trial, who was his defense attorney?
- **A.** He defended himself
- **B.** Jennifer Walters
- **C.** Foggy Nelson
- **D.** Matthew Murdock

2140. In which subject does Michael Morbius hold a Ph.D.?
- **A.** Chemistry
- **B.** Physiology
- **C.** Biology
- **D.** Biochemistry

2141. Who is *not* one of the Foolkillers?
- **A.** Mike Trace
- **B.** Runyan Moody
- **C.** Greg Salinger
- **D.** Kurt Gerhardt

2142. Who is Simon Stroud?
- **A.** CIA agent who hunted Morbius
- **B.** Government agent out to capture Sleepwalker
- **C.** The Enforcer
- **D.** Film director ally of the original Bloodstone

2143. Who was Martine Bancroft?
- **A.** Girlfriend of Zero Cochrane
- **B.** Michael Morbius's fiancée
- **C.** Actress at Delazny Studios
- **D.** Voodoo sorceress based in New Orleans

2144. What power does Morbius share with supernatural vampires?
- **A.** Hypnotic ability
- **B.** Ability to turn into a bat
- **C.** Ability to transform into mist
- **D.** Ability to mentally control certain animals

2145. Which opera's premiere performance did Dracula attend, as shown in *Thor* #333 (1983)?
- **A.** *Tannhauser*
- **B.** *Don Giovanni*
- **C.** *The Tales of Hoffmann*
- **D.** *The Flying Dutchman*

(The code was soon amended, permitting Marvel to portray true vampires like Dracula.) Originally an antagonist for Spider-Man, Morbius later appeared in his own stories in *Adventure Into Fear, Vampire Tales,* and eventually his own *Morbius* comic. Morbius has best been portrayed as a reluctant vampire, ridden by guilt over his compulsion to attack victims, and desperately seeking a cure for his condition.

During Morbius's first meeting with Spider-Man, what was unusual about the latter?

- **A.** He had lost his spider-sense
- **B.** He had grown four extra arms
- **C.** He had lost his spider-powers
- **D.** He had grown organic web-shooters

Horror Heroes

2146. Who is the Black Rose?
- **A.** Dr. Katherine Reynolds
- **B.** Roxanne Blaze
- **C.** Elsa Bloodstone
- **D.** Martine Bancroft

2147. Who is *not* one of the Three-Who-Are-All in *Werewolf by Night*?
- **A.** Fire-Eyes
- **B.** Burning Snake
- **C.** Goat Child
- **D.** The Hooded One

2148. Which alien race created modern werewolves?
- **A.** Celestials
- **B.** Fortisquians
- **C.** The Arcturans
- **D.** The Nuwali

2149. What is the true name of the demon who called himself Satan and fathered Daimon Hellstrom?
- **A.** Asmodeus
- **B.** Satannish
- **C.** Marduk Kurios
- **D.** Mephisto

2150. Who allegedly was Yah, whom Howard the Duck meets in Steve Gerber's final Howard story?
- **A.** A barroom philosopher
- **B.** God
- **C.** The Devil
- **D.** Steve Gerber himself

2151.

2152. Who is Charles Barnabus?
- **A.** Vampire
- **B.** Executor of the Bloodstone estate
- **C.** Elsa Bloodstone's ally against Dracula
- **D.** All answers are correct

2153. In which state was Greentown—Daimon Hellstrom's birthplace—located?
- **A.** Connecticut
- **B.** Massachusetts
- **C.** New York
- **D.** Maine

2151.

When Daimon Hellstrom first appeared in *Ghost Rider* #1 (1973), he called himself the Son of Satan, and indeed his father was a demon who called himself Satan and who mated with a mortal woman. Satan and his mate also had a daughter, Satana, who starred in her own comics stories in the 1970s. Daimon Hellstrom rebelled against his demonic heritage and became an exorcist, battling against his father's demonic kind. Besides his human soul, Hellstrom also possessed a Darksoul that granted him supernatural powers. He could project magical energy called soulfire from his trident made of netheranium. Created by writer Gary Friedrich and artist Tom Sutton, Hellstrom later married Patsy Walker, alias of the Super Heroine Hellcat. In the 1990s, in the series *Hellstorm: Prince Of Lies* (primarily written by Warren Ellis), the Son of Satan renamed himself Hellstorm, slew his father, and succeeded him as ruler of a hell-like dimension.

Who was Daimon Hellstrom's mother?

- **A.** Minerva Bannister
- **B.** Katherine Reynolds
- **C.** Victoria Wingate
- **D.** Victoria Bentley

2154. What was Daimon Hellstrom's academic specialty, apart from demonology?
A. Psychology
B. Anthropology
C. Theology
D. Archaeology

2155. Where was Daimon Hellstrom first based in the *Son of Satan* series?
A. Salem, Massachusetts
B. St. Louis, Missouri
C. Washington D.C.
D. New Haven, Connecticut

2156. What kind of supernatural being is Satana?
A. Demon
B. Sorceress
C. Succubus
D. Vampiress

2157. Who is Mildred Horowitz?
A. Would-be detective who met Hodiah Twist
B. Head of S.O.O.F.I.
C. Leader of rock band with which the future Doctor Bong performed
D. The Kidney Lady

2158. When was Dracula first mentioned in a Marvel Universe story?
A. *The X-Men* (first series) #40 (1968)
B. *The Amazing Spider-Man* #101 (1971)
C. *Fantastic Four* #30 (1964)
D. *Tomb of Dracula* #1 (1972)

2159. Which detective modeled himself after Sherlock Holmes and investigated cases involving the supernatural?
A. Hodiah Twist
B. Conrad Jeavons
C. Teddy Durance
D. Jeffrey Winters

2160. Which writer co-created the Holmes-like detective in *Vampire Tales* #2 (1973)?
A. Roy Thomas
B. Steve Gerber
C. Don McGregor
D. Doug Moench

Horror Heroes

CHAPTER EIGHT:

COSMIC CHARACTERS:
FROM SILVER SURFER TO CAPTAIN MARVEL

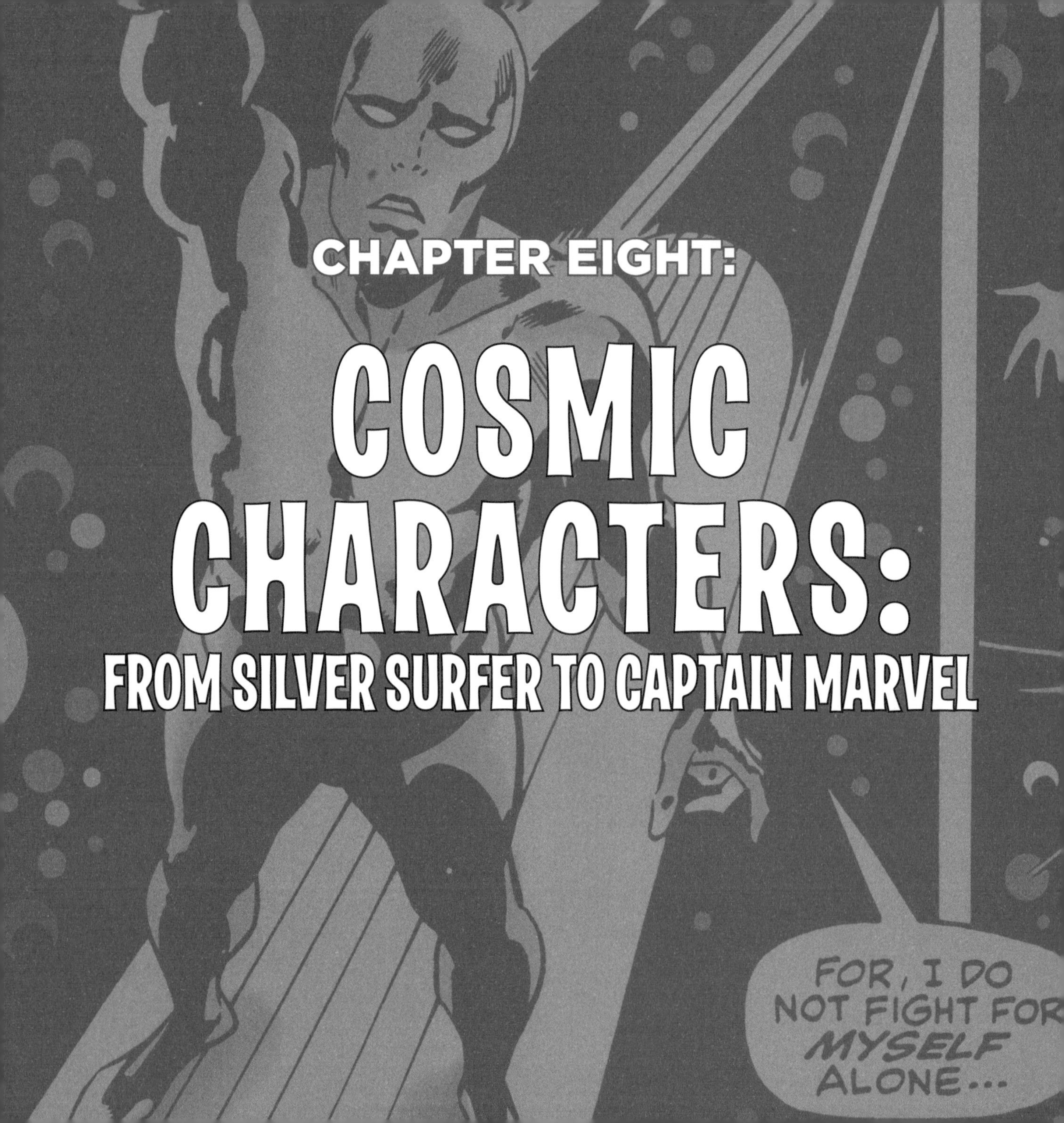

2161. What is the name of the Silver Surfer's true love on Zenn-La?
A. S'Byll
C. Ardina
B. Andarr Bal
D. Shalla Bal

2162. Who is the demon who has long sought to capture the Silver Surfer's soul?
A. Mephisto
C. Thog
B. Satannish
D. Zarathos

2163. Who is Thanos's brother?
A. A'Lars
C. Eros
B. Chronos
D. Uranus

2164. Who was *not* a member of the Infinity Watch?
A. Gamora
C. Drax the Destroyer
B. Pip the Troll
D. Jack of Hearts

2165. Who is Jack Hart?
A. Major Victory
C. Star-Lord
B. Jack of Hearts
D. Quasar

2166. Who is *not* one of the Elders of the Universe?
A. The Grandmaster
C. The Runner
B. The Contemplator
D. The Stranger

2167. Which alien race did the Silver Surfer combat in issue 2 (1968) of his original series?
A. The Enslavers
C. The Badoon
B. The Skrulls
D. The Kree

2168. Which Super Hero did the Silver Surfer battle in issue #4 (1969) of his original series?

A. "Him" (Adam Warlock)

B. The Hulk

C. Thor

D. The Thing

2169.

2170. With which artist did writer Steve Englehart team up on *Silver Surfer* in the 1980s?

A. Frank Brunner

B. Ron Lim

C. Marshall Rogers

D. Al Milgrom

2171. How many issues of the original *Silver Surfer* series did Jack Kirby draw?

A. None

B. One

C. Two

D. Ten

2172. With whom did Stan Lee collaborate on the first *Silver Surfer* graphic novel in 1978?

A. John Romita Sr.

B. John Buscema

C. Jack Kirby

D. Gene Colan

2173. With which famed cartoonist did Stan Lee collaborate on *Silver Surfer: Parable* in 1988?

A. Jack Kirby

B. Moebius

C. Hugo Pratt

D. Osama Tezuka

2174. How did the Silver Surfer finally get past Galactus's barrier around Earth?

A. Galactus removed the barrier

B. He traveled on a spaceship without his board

C. He teleported

D. He went through a space warp

2169.

After Stan Lee and Jack Kirby introduced him in *Fantastic Four* #48 (1966), the Silver Surfer became so popular with readers that in 1968 he won his own comic book series (issue 1 shown at right). In its first issue, Lee and artist John Buscema revealed that the Surfer had once been an ordinary humanoid living in the world of Zenn-La among an advanced civilization. So peaceful and idyllic was Zenn-La that he longed for a life of adventure. Galactus came to Zenn-La intent on consuming the planet. The future Silver Surfer offered to become Galactus's herald if he would spare Zenn-La from destruction. Galactus agreed, transforming him into a silver-skinned superhuman and giving him the cosmic surfboard to ride. Though the initial series lasted only eighteen issues, the Silver Surfer has continued to appear—in his own series, and as a guest star in other comics—ever since.

What is the Silver Surfer's real name?

A. Jartran Radd

B. Norrin Radd

C. Fennan Radd

D. Norrin Konn

2175. Who created Battleworld in *Marvel Super Heroes Secret Wars* (1984–1985)?
- **A.** Galactus
- **B.** The Grandmaster
- **C.** The Stranger
- **D.** The Beyonder

2176. What is Eros's name as a Super Hero?
- **A.** Ganymede
- **B.** Starfox
- **C.** Xenith
- **D.** Legacy

2177. Who is Heather Douglas?
- **A.** Moondragon
- **B.** Sundragon
- **C.** Ikaris's companion
- **D.** Girlfriend of Rick Jones in *Captain Marvel*

2178. Which race founded the colony on the planet Uranus?
- **A.** The Kree
- **B.** Eternals
- **C.** Inhumans
- **D.** Fortisquians

2179. What was the Beyonder's motivation in coming to Earth in *Secret Wars II* (1985–1986)?
- **A.** To conquer the world
- **B.** To learn the nature of desire
- **C.** To be worshipped
- **D.** To judge humanity's worthiness to survive

2180. Who was known as Hollywood in *Guardians of the Galaxy*?
- **A.** Alison Blaire
- **B.** Simon Williams
- **C.** Mojo
- **D.** Bereet

2181. Which cosmic hero once carried Captain America's shield?
- **A.** Star-Lord
- **B.** Quasar
- **C.** Major Victory
- **D.** Jack Flag

Cosmic Characters

2182. Who was Legacy?

A. Marvel Boy

B. Creator of the Legacy Virus

C. Captain Mar-Vell's son

D. Major Vance Astro

2183. Who was Genis-Vell's mother?

A. Una

B. Moondragon

C. Elysius

D. Carol Danvers

2184. With which character did Captain Mar-Vell switch places between Earth and the Negative Zone?

A. Walter Lawson

B. Carol Danvers

C. Yon-Rogg

D. Rick Jones

2185. With whom was Captain Mar-Vell in love in his original series?

A. Carol Danvers

B. Una

C. Elysius

D. Lou-Ann Savannah

2186.

2187. Captain Mar-Vell is a member of the white Kree race. What color skin do other Kree, such as Ronan, have?

A. Green

B. Blue

C. Purple

D. Red

2188. Who was Dr. Walter Lawson?

A. Scientist who aided the Silver Surfer

B. Scientist impersonated by Captain Mar-Vell

C. False identity created by Captain Mar-Vell

D. False identity used by Maelstrom

THE MARVEL COMI

"THE GO

CAP

MAR

2186.

After the Fantastic Four had bested both their robot Sentry and Ronan the Accuser, the alien Kree Empire sent a spy mission to Earth. The Kree war hero Captain Mar-Vell infiltrated the American space program, posing as one of its scientists. But Mar-Vell found himself going into action on Earth against threats like a revived Kree Sentry robot and the Super-Skrull. Becoming known on Earth as Captain Marvel, he began sympathizing with the humans who were his supposed enemies. Created

GROUP PRESENTS...
...ING OF
...TAIN
...VEL!"

by Stan Lee and Gene Colan in *Marvel Super-Heroes* #12 (1967, shown above), Captain Marvel quickly gained his own series. He memorably met his end in Jim Starlin's landmark 1982 graphic novel *The Death of Captain Marvel*. Since his demise, other heroes have taken the name Captain Marvel, including Mar-Vell's son Genis-Vell, who starred in his own *Captain Marvel* series. How did Mar-Vell die?

A. He perished in the Negative Zone's explosive area

B. He was slain in combat

C. He died of cancer

D. He was sacrificed to Mistress Death by Thanos

2189. After *Civil War II*, the modern Guardians of the Galaxy found themselves stranded on which planet?
A. Chitauri-Prime
B. Moord
C. Mars
D. Earth

2190. Which member of the Guardians gained temporary cosmic powers from the Black Vortex?
A. Star-Lord
B. Gamora
C. Drax
D. Rocket

2191. Which Earth hero has *not* been a member of the Guardians of the Galaxy?
A. Iron Man
B. Captain Marvel
C. Spider-Man
D. The Thing

2192. Who did the Guardians of the Galaxy ally with in the first arc of 2015's *Guardians Team-Up* series?
A. Nova
B. Avengers
C. X-Men
D. Thanos

2193. Which member of the Guardians headlined their very first solo comic series in late 2016?
A. Star-Lord
B. Drax
C. Groot
D. Gamora

2194. When the modern Guardians disbanded, who briefly replaced them as protectors of the universe?
A. Annihilators
B. Space Knights
C. Star Masters
D. Starjammers

Cosmic Characters

2195. What relation is Drax the Destroyer to Moondragon?
A. Ex-lover
C. Brother
B. Father
D. No relation

2196. Which team did Carol Danvers join as Binary?
A. Starjammers
C. Cosmic Commandos
B. Avengers
D. Starmasters

2197. Who hired Carol Danvers to edit *Woman* magazine?
A. Michael Rossi
C. Barney Bushkin
B. J. Jonah Jameson
D. Arabella Jones

2198.

2199. Where was Carol Danvers born?
A. Philadelphia
C. Orlando
B. Boston
D. San Diego

2200. Which physical problem did Ms. Marvel suffer from?
A. Drug addiction
C. Alcoholism
B. Heart disease
D. Diabetes

2201. Who designed Ms. Marvel's black costume in *Ms. Marvel* #20 (1978)?
A. John Romita Sr.
C. Dave Cockrum
B. John Buscema
D. Jim Mooney

2202. Which X-Men villain did Ms. Marvel combat in *Ms. Marvel* #6 (1977)?
A. Unus the Untouchable
C. The Cobalt Man
B. Grotesk
D. Sauron

2203. Which X-Men villain debuted in *Ms. Marvel* #9 (1977)?
A. Warhawk
C. Caliban
B. Arcade
D. Deathbird

2198.

Carol Danvers was introduced in *Marvel Super-Heroes* #13 (1968)—by writer Roy Thomas and artist Gene Colan—as the young head of security at Cape Canaveral. It was there that she first encountered the Kree warrior Captain Mar-Vell. His enemy Colonel Yon-Rogg abducted Danvers, knowing Mar-Vell would go to her rescue. In the ensuing battle, a Kree device called the Psyche-Magnitron exploded, giving Danvers a combined human and Kree genetic structure. Endowed with super-powers, Carol Danvers became the Super Heroine Ms. Marvel starting in *Ms. Marvel* #1 (1977, shown above) and eventually joined the Avengers. In battle with Ms.

2204. Which X-Men villain debuted in *Ms. Marvel* #16 (1978)?
- **A.** The White Queen
- **B.** The Shadow King
- **C.** Mystique
- **D.** Mister Sinister

2205. What were "the People" in *Ms. Marvel* #20–21 (1978)?
- **A.** Alien humanoids
- **B.** A Native American tribe
- **C.** Sentient lizards
- **D.** A community of mutants

2206. What is the name of Carol Danvers's father?
- **A.** Jim
- **B.** Fred
- **C.** Joe
- **D.** Henry

2207. What sound does Bug make due to a tough membrane in his throat?
- **A.** Wheet!
- **B.** Waugh!
- **C.** Snik!
- **D.** Tik!

2208. Who is Major Victory?
- **A.** Descendant of Steve Rogers
- **B.** Cyborg created by the Ryker brothers
- **C.** Major Vance Astro
- **D.** Jack Flag

2209. Which of these heroes had a sentient spacecraft named *Ship*?
- **A.** Quasar
- **B.** Star-Lord
- **C.** The thirty-first-century Guardians of the Galaxy
- **D.** Monark Starstalker

2210. Which writer co-created the original Star-Lord in *Marvel Preview* #4 (1976)?
- **A.** Doug Moench
- **B.** Roy Thomas
- **C.** Steve Englehart
- **D.** Chris Claremont

Marvel, the mutant Rogue, who later joined the X-Men, supposedly absorbed her super-powers permanently, but Danvers later gained cosmic powers and adopted the name Binary. Those powers faded away, but Danvers retained her Ms. Marvel powers, eventually reassuming that name as well, and has played prominent roles in different incarnations of the Avengers.

Which other Super Heroine has used the name Ms. Marvel?

- **A.** Jean Grey
- **B.** Rachel Summers
- **C.** Valeria Richards
- **D.** Sharon Ventura

Cosmic Characters

2211. Who has *not* been a member of the twenty-first-century Guardians of the Galaxy?
- **A.** Mantis
- **B.** Silver Surfer
- **C.** Adam Warlock
- **D.** Bug

2212. Who is the counterpart of the Guardians' Vance Astro on Earth-616?
- **A.** Star-Lord
- **B.** Jack Flag
- **C.** Justice
- **D.** Nova

2213. Where was Vance Astrovik born?
- **A.** Hoboken, New Jersey
- **B.** Saugerties, New York
- **C.** Woodstock, New York
- **D.** Mamaroneck, New York

2214. What super-power does Major Vance Astro possess?
- **A.** Super-strength
- **B.** Psychokinesis
- **C.** Telepathy
- **D.** Discharges bioelectric energy

2215. Who is Aleta?
- **A.** Starhawk's wife
- **B.** Starhawk's foster sister
- **C.** Both A and B
- **D.** Neither A nor B

2216. What is Martinex's super-power?
- **A.** Creating crystalline forms
- **B.** Projecting heat
- **C.** Projecting cold
- **D.** Projecting heat and cold

2217. From which race on Earth were Martinex's ancestors?
- **A.** African
- **B.** Asian
- **C.** Caucasian
- **D.** Latino

2218. Who was *not* a member of the Galactic Guardians?
- **A.** Replica
- **B.** Talon
- **C.** Phoenix IX
- **D.** Mainframe

OBSESSED WITH MARVEL

2219. What is unusual about Yondu's arrows?

A. They're composed of pure energy

B. They're controlled by sound

C. They're controlled by light

D. They're controlled mentally

2220. To which race did Talon belong in the original *Guardians of the Galaxy*?

A. Inhumans

B. Eternals

C. Deviants

D. Werewolves

2221. What metal was used in the bodysuit Vance Astro wore to prevent his thousand-year-old body from decaying?

A. Adamantium

B. Titanium

C. Copper

D. Vibranium

2222. What are the Stark?

A. Thirty-first-century decendants of Tony Stark in *Guardians of the Galaxy*

B. Employees of Stark Industries in AD 2020 in *Machine Man 2020*

C. Future warrior society using Tony Stark's technology in *Guardians of the Galaxy*

D. Robots based on Tony Stark's designs in AD 2020 in *Machine Man 2020*

2223.

2224. In which series did Jack Flag first appear?

A. *Nick Fury, Agent of S.H.I.E.L.D.*

B. *Civil War*

C. *Captain America*

D. *Guardians of the Galaxy*

2225. Who or what is Cosmo?

A. Talking animal that debuted in *Rocket Raccoon* miniseries

B. Eccentric alien friend of Comet Man

C. Middle name of Quasar (Wendell Vaughn)

D. Dog with human intelligence who works with the new Guardians of the Galaxy

---

2223.

In the thirty-first century of an alternate future, a reptilian alien race called the Badoon conquered the Earth and its colonized planets. A band of freedom fighters arose, known as the Guardians of the Galaxy, created by writer Arnold Drake and artist Gene Colan in *Marvel Super Heroes* # 18 (1969). Their leader was Major Vance Astro, a twentieth-century astronaut who survived through suspended animation. His cohorts included the super-strong Charlie-27 from Jupiter; Martinex, a crystalline humanoid from Pluto; and Yondu, an archer from Beta Centauri. Later they were joined by Nikki, a girl from Mercury with flame for hair, and the mysterious superhuman mutant Starhawk (shown at left). Steve Gerber wrote their adventures in *Marvel Presents* and Jim Valentino wrote and drew the 1980s *Guardians of the Galaxy* comic. In 2008, the writing team of Dan Abnett and Andy Lanning introduced a new version of the Guardians of the Galaxy, uniting a number of Marvel's cosmic characters.

Which character organized the Abnett/Lanning Guardians of the Galaxy?

A. Adam Warlock

B. Star-Lord

C. Rocket Raccoon

D. Bug

Cosmic Characters

2226. Who created Groot in the new *Guardians of the Galaxy*?
- **A.** Stan Lee, Jack Kirby, and Dick Ayers
- **B.** Dan Abnett and Andy Lanning
- **C.** Larry Lieber and Steve Ditko
- **D.** Jim Valentino

2227. What is Makkari's primary super-power?
- **A.** Has intuitive genius at designing machinery
- **B.** Able to alter his own physical appearance
- **C.** Able to psionically rearrange matter
- **D.** Has super-speed

2228. What is Sersi's primary super-power?
- **A.** Animating inanimate objects
- **B.** Casting illusions
- **C.** Influencing the emotions of others
- **D.** Psionically rearranging matter

2229.

2230. What job did Sersi hold in Neil Gaiman's *Eternals* series?
- **A.** Actress
- **B.** Musician
- **C.** Event planner
- **D.** Dancer

2231. In which city did the Dreaming Celestial once stand?
- **A.** San Francisco
- **B.** New York City
- **C.** London
- **D.** Los Angeles

2232. Who is Ransak the Reject?
- **A.** Defective robot in *Machine Man*
- **B.** Deviant rejected for looking human
- **C.** Renegade Kree in *Captain Marvel*
- **D.** Operative of Thanos

2233. In *The Avengers*, what name did the Eternal call the Forgotten One?
- **A.** Hercules
- **B.** Gilgamesh
- **C.** Samson
- **D.** Beowulf

2229.

Jack Kirby created, wrote, and drew his last great series, *The Eternals*, starting in 1976. Colossal, armored "space gods" called the Celestials had experimented on humanity's ancestors, creating the Eternals, a race of immortal superhumans whom humanity once believed to be gods and mythic heroes. The Celestials had also created the Deviants, a race of grotesque beings who were once thought to be demons and devils. Now the Celestials had returned to observe humanity for fifty years. If they found the human race unworthy, the Celestials would destroy it. Meanwhile, the Eternals and Deviants reemerged to interact with modern-day humans. Although *The Eternals* (issue 7 shown at right) lasted only nineteen issues, it was revived for a twelve-issue limited series in the 1980s, and recently for a new series written by Neil Gaiman and illustrated by John Romita Jr.

Which member of the Celestials was the judge of humanity in the original series?

- **A.** Gammenon
- **B.** Arishem
- **C.** One Above All
- **D.** The Dreaming Celestial

OBSESSED WITH MARVEL

2234. What is the name of the Deviants' nation?

A. Pangea
B. Lemuria
C. Attilan
D. Olympia

2235. Who is Lord Ghaur?

A. Martian Overlord in *Killraven*
B. Monarch of the Badoon in *Guardians of the Galaxy*
C. Deviant high priest
D. Deviant warlord

2236. Which Host of the Celestials came to Earth in *Eternals* #1 (1976)?

A. First
B. Third
C. Fourth
D. Fifth

2237. Which of the Eternals inspired Shakespeare's creation of Puck in *A Midsummer Night's Dream*?

A. Druig
B. Sersi
C. Sprite
D. Makkari

2238. Which of the Deviants is the former lover of Thena of the Eternals?

A. Ransak the Reject
B. Ghaur
C. Brother Tode
D. Kro

2239. In which mountains did the Celestials land in *Eternals* #1 (1976)?

A. Alps
B. Andes
C. Himalayas
D. Olympus mountain range, Greece

2240. Who rules the Eternals in the Kirby and Gaiman limited series?

A. Valkin
B. Thena
C. Zuras
D. Ikaris

2241. Who or what is Karkas?

A. Eternal
B. Servant of Mistress Death
C. Deviant mutate
D. Deviant

Cosmic Characters

2242. In which series did the Celestials declare their judgment on humanity?

A. *The Eternals* (1970s series)
B. *The Eternals* (1980s series)
C. *Thor*
D. *The Eternals* (2000s series)

2243. Who is *not* one of the Olympian Eternals?

A. Zuras
B. Thena
C. Ikaris
D. Makkari

2244. What is the Uni-Mind?

A. Advanced computer in *Guardians of the Galaxy*
B. Collective being formed by Eternals merging together
C. Leader of Martians in *Killraven*
D. Leader of the Fourth Host of the Celestials

2245. What was the Eternal Kingo Sunen's profession in the twentieth century?

A. Assassin
B. Movie actor
C. Martial arts teacher
D. Samurai

2246.

2247. Who was *not* a member of Nextwave?

A. Elsa Bloodstone
B. Tabitha "Boom Boom" Smith
C. Comet Man
D. Machine Man

2248. Who is Sunset Bain?

A. CEO of Baintronics
B. Tony Stark's classmate
C. Madame Menace
D. All answers are correct

2249. Who is Christopher Powell?

A. Darkhawk
B. Comet Man
C. Killraven
D. Star-Lord

2246.

In 1976, Jack Kirby began writing and drawing a Marvel comic book series based on the film *2001: A Space Odyssey*. In issue #8 (1977), Kirby introduced X-51, an experimental robot with a capacity for independent thought who was treated by his creator as a son. When his creator was killed, X-51 escaped, only to be hunted by the army. But X-51's goal was to become part of human society, and he even adopted a human identity, Aaron Stack. Although Marvel lost the rights to *2001: A Space Odyssey*, X-51 continued in his own series, titled *Machine Man* (issue 1 shown at right). Kirby wrote and drew the first nine issues, and when the series was later revived, it was drawn by another Marvel pioneer, Steve Ditko. Writer Tom DeFalco and artists Herb Trimpe and Barry Windsor-Smith collaborated on a *Machine Man* limited series set in the year 2020 of an alternate future.

What was the name of X-51's creator and parent figure?

A. Gears Garvin
B. Dr. Abel Stack
C. Peter Spaulding
D. Curtiss Jackson

2242C 2243C 2244B 2245B 2246B 2247C 2248D 2249A

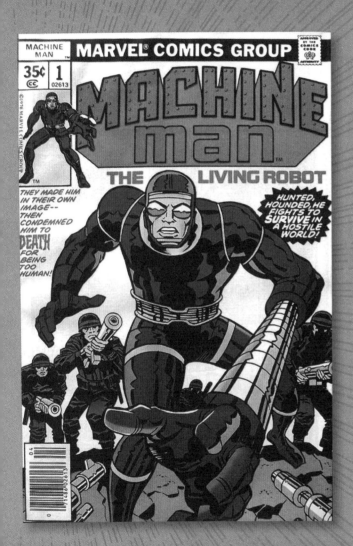

2250. Which member of the original Guardians of the Galaxy sported a new look in 2014's *Guardians 3000*?

A. Charlie-27

B. Martinex

C. Vance Astro

D. Nikki

2251. Which member of the Guardians changed genders once again in 2014's *Guardians 3000*?

A. Charlie-27

B. Starhawk

C. Martinex

D. Yondu

2252. What was the name of the human who joined the team in *Guardians 3000*?

A. Drake Colan

B. Geena Drake

C. Arnold Colan

D. Gene Arnold

2253. Which time period was *not* represented in the roster for *Guardians of Infinity*?

A. Circa 1000 BC

B. Circa 1000 AD

C. Circa 2000 AD

D. Circa 3000 AD

2254. Which modern Guardians of the Galaxy member was *not* a part of the Guardians of Infinity team?

A. Drax

B. Star-Lord

C. Groot

D. Rocket

2255. Who was the leader of the Guardians team from the distant past in *Guardians of Infinity*?

A. Skytower

B. Stella Nega

C. Aerolith

D. Astrolabe

2256. Who led the Newcomers against the Guardians of Infinity?

A. Hermetikus

B. Al-Hasan

C. The Colonizer

D. Martinex

Cosmic Characters

2257. Who wrote and drew the 1980s *Eternals* limited series?
- **A.** Walter Simonson and Sal Buscema
- **B.** Walter Simonson
- **C.** Peter B. Gillis and Sal Buscema
- **D.** Peter B. Gillis, Walter Simonson, and Sal Buscema

2258. What was the Doomsday Man in *The Silver Surfer* #13 (1970)?
- **A.** Robot
- **B.** Creation of Victor Frankenstein's descendant
- **C.** Alien from an alternate future
- **D.** Monster serving the Badoon

2259. Who was the menace in the final issue of the Silver Surfer's original series?
- **A.** Mephisto
- **B.** Maximus and the evil Inhumans
- **C.** The Stranger
- **D.** Galactus

2260. Which alien race was ruled by Empress S'Byll?
- **A.** Contraxians
- **B.** Kree
- **C.** Shi'ar
- **D.** Skrulls

2261. What was the team of superhumans based on Xandar called?
- **A.** Champions of Xandar
- **B.** Defenders of Xandar
- **C.** Avengers of Xandar
- **D.** Spaceknights of Xandar

2262.

2263. Who was *not* one of Richard Rider's high school friends?
- **A.** Bernie Dillon
- **B.** Steve "Headset" Rubino
- **C.** Ginger Jaye
- **D.** Roger "Caps" Cooper

2264. Who is *not* a member of Charles Rider's immediate family?
- **A.** Richard
- **B.** Gloria
- **C.** Robert
- **D.** Laura

2262.

In an attempt to introduce a new teenage Marvel Super Hero in the tradition of the early Spider-Man, writer Marv Wolfman and artist John Buscema created the first issue of *The Man Called Nova* (1976, shown above). When the alien pirate Xorr destroyed the planet Xandar, Rhomann Dey was the last surviving member of its Nova Corps of warriors. But he would not survive for long. The dying Dey followed Xorr to Earth, and then bequeathed his powers to a human at random. That human was Richard Rider, a high

2265. Who took over as Nova when Rich Rider was presumed dead?
- **A.** Sam Alexander
- **B.** Frankie Raye
- **C.** Mile Morales
- **D.** Peter Quill

2266. In his 2013 series, from whom did the new Nova get his helmet?
- **A.** Rich Rider
- **B.** A dying alien
- **C.** His father
- **D.** Star-Lord

2267. Who was Jesse Alexander?
- **A.** Father of Sam
- **B.** A Black Nova
- **C.** A school janitor
- **D.** All answers are correct

2268. Of which team has a Nova *not* officially been a member?
- **A.** Champions
- **B.** Guardians of the Galaxy
- **C.** Avengers
- **D.** New Warriors

2269. Which version of Nova headlined the character's 2016 series?
- **A.** Sam Alexander
- **B.** Richard Rider
- **C.** Both A & B
- **D.** None of the above

2270. What was the Black Vortex?
- **A.** A cursed lake
- **B.** A black hole
- **C.** A magic mirror
- **D.** A cosmic deity

2271. Which team of Earth heroes became Captain Marvel's support team in outer space?
- **A.** Defenders
- **B.** Excalibur
- **C.** Alpha Flight
- **D.** Force Works

2272. Who became the new Quasar during the events of *Avengers: Standoff*?
- **A.** Neutron
- **B.** Wendell Vaughan
- **C.** Phyla-Vell
- **D.** Avril Kincaid

school student in Long Island, New York, who thus became the Super Hero Nova the Human Rocket (and soon bested Xorr). Not only did Nova possess superhuman strength, but he could fly through the air at super-speed. Nova was also a founding member of the New Warriors but luckily was not present when most of the team perished in an explosion in Connecticut. What other superhuman is known as Nova?

- **A.** Brandy Clark
- **B.** Frankie Raye
- **C.** "Her"
- **D.** Tanya Belinskya

Cosmic Characters

2273. Combined with his alien genes from his mother, what gave Jack of Hearts his superhuman powers?

A. Terrigen mist
B. Zero fluid
C. Cyborg parts
D. Mutation from radiation

2274. In which series did the heroes of Earth combat the Goddess?

A. *Infinity Crusade* (1993)
B. *Infinity Gauntlet* (1991)
C. *Infinity Abyss* (2002)
D. *Infinity War* (1992)

2275. In which series did the abstract being Master Hate first appear with Mistress Love?

A. *The Thanos Quest* (1990)
B. *Infinity Gauntlet* (1991)
C. *Warlock and the Infinity Watch* (1992-1995)
D. *Quasar* (1989-1994)

2276. Who was *not* a member of the Starmasters in the miniseries of the same name?

A. Silver Surfer
B. Sundragon
C. Morfex
D. Beta Ray Bill

2277. Who is *not* one of the Seven Friendless?

A. Ego
B. Entropy
C. Epiphany
D. Empathy

2278. Which character from another Marvel series became a member of Power Pack?

A. Artie Maddicks
B. Illyana Rasputin
C. Franklin Richards
D. Kitty Pryde

2279.

Marvel's youngest Super Hero team is comprised of the Power children—Alex, Jack, Julie, and Katie (shown at right). The team was created by writer Louise Simonson and artist June Brigman in *Power Pack* #1 (1984). The children's father, Dr. James Power, invented a converter that derived energy from antimatter. Aelfyre Whitemane, a member of the alien race of Kymellians, sought to warn Dr. Power about the device's dangers. But members of another alien race, the Snarks, mortally wounded Aelfyre Whitemane and abducted Dr. Power and his wife. Dying, Whitey (as the children called Whitemane) endowed the Power children with various super-powers. The children then thwarted the Snarks, destroying the converter and rescuing their parents. The kids continued to act as Super Heroes, calling themselves Power Pack. Initially, Alex called himself Gee, Jack was known as Mass Master, Julie was Lightspeed, and Katie was Energizer, although their names and powers would subsequently change.

What is the birth order of the Power children from oldest to youngest?

A. Alex, Julie, Jack, Katie
B. Julie, Alex, Jack, Katie
C. Jack, Julie, Alex, Katie
D. Alex, Katie, Julie, Jack

2280. What is the name of Power Pack's "smartship"?
- **A.** Sunday
- **B.** Wednesday
- **C.** Friday
- **D.** Saturday

2281. What is the name of the Power children's mother?
- **A.** Margaret
- **B.** June
- **C.** Ann
- **D.** Louise

2282. Who was the Bogeyman?
- **A.** A Snark
- **B.** A Morlock
- **C.** Dr. Power's boss
- **D.** Mrs. Power's boss

2283. How old was Katie Power when she first became super-powered?
- **A.** Two
- **B.** Three
- **C.** Four
- **D.** Five

2284. Which member of Power Pack was known as Starstreak?
- **A.** Julie
- **B.** Alex
- **C.** Katie
- **D.** Julie and Katie

2285. Which member of Power Pack once possessed all the children's powers as Powerpax?
- **A.** Jack
- **B.** Katie
- **C.** Alex
- **D.** Julie

2286. Who is Tattletale?
- **A.** Katie Power
- **B.** Kofi Whitemane
- **C.** Franklin Richards
- **D.** Jack Power

2287. Which Hollywood figure or figures co-created Comet Man?
- **A.** Kevin Smith
- **B.** Bill Mumy and Miguel Ferrer
- **C.** Joss Whedon
- **D.** J. Michael Straczynski

Cosmic Characters

2288. From which alien race does Comet Man's friend Max come?
 A. Axi-Tun
 B. Pegasusians
 C. Fortisquians
 D. Contraxians

2289. Who co-created Darkhawk with artist Mike Manley?
 A. Fabian Nicieza
 B. Scott Lobdell
 C. Danny Fingeroth
 D. Tom DeFalco

2290. Who is *not* a member of the Loners?
 A. Darkhawk
 B. Ricochet
 C. Dazzler
 D. Turbo

2291. Who created Monark Starstalker in *Marvel Premiere* #36 (1976)?
 A. Howard Chaykin
 B. Jim Starlin
 C. Archie Goodwin and Walter Simonson
 D. Marv Wolfman and Dave Cockrum

2292. Which writer co-created *The Sword in The Star* from *Marvel Preview* #4 (1976)?
 A. Doug Moench
 B. Steve Gerber
 C. Bill Mantlo
 D. Don McGregor

2293. Which member of the Shi'ar Imperial Guard was once known as Quasar?
 A. Impulse
 B. Neutron
 C. Electron
 D. Starbolt

2294.

2295. Where were Wendell Vaughn's headquarters?
 A. Four Freedoms Plaza
 B. The Baxter Building
 C. The Chrysler Building
 D. The Flatiron Building

2294.

Wendell Vaughn, the hero known as Quasar (shown above), was created by writers Roy Thomas and Don Glut and artist John Buscema. He originally appeared in *Incredible Hulk* #234 (1979) as a member of the S.H.I.E.L.D. Super-Agents. Vaughn wore wristbands from the planet Uranus that the Super Villain Crusader had once used to manipulate energy. The Crusader had falsely claimed to be the 1950s hero Marvel Boy, and so Vaughn called himself Marvel Man, then later changed his name to Quasar. But Vaughn found his true destiny in *Quasar* #1 (1989), the start of his own sixty-issue

OBSESSED WITH MARVEL

2296. Who or what is Epoch?
- **A.** Member of the Seven Friendless
- **B.** Son of Eon
- **C.** Daughter of Eon
- **D.** Servant of Immortus

2297. What was the name of Wendell Vaughn's father?
- **A.** Gilbert
- **B.** Myron
- **C.** Mark
- **D.** Gardner

2298. Which Super Villain became Anomaly?
- **A.** Maelstrom
- **B.** Skeletron
- **C.** Erishkigel
- **D.** Thanos

2299. Which abstract being became the patron of Quasar?
- **A.** Eternity
- **B.** Infinity
- **C.** The Living Tribunal
- **D.** Master Order

2300. Who was Kayla Ballantine?
- **A.** Quasar's girlfriend
- **B.** Wendell Vaughn's secretary
- **C.** Former possessor of the Starbrand
- **D.** All answers are correct

2301. What is the name of Quasar's sister?
- **A.** Gayle
- **B.** Catherine
- **C.** Sara
- **D.** Norma

2302. Who was Buried Alien in *Quasar* #17 (1990)?
- **A.** Blue Marvel
- **B.** The super-speedster called Fastforward
- **C.** Unbeing
- **D.** Kid Reaper

2303. Which abstract being did Maelstrom serve?
- **A.** Oblivion
- **B.** Mistress Death
- **C.** Lord Chaos
- **D.** Entropy

series written by the late Mark Gruenwald. Traveling to Uranus, Quasar encountered the cosmic entity Eon, who appointed him to be Protector of the Universe, succeeding the deceased Captain Mar-Vell. Quasar's wristbands allowed him to tap into energy from the Quantum Zone. Seemingly killed by Annihilus, Quasar has since returned as a being composed of quantum energy. What is Wendell Vaughn's middle name?

- **A.** Michael
- **B.** Elvis
- **C.** John
- **D.** Mark

Cosmic Characters

2304. Who was *not* one of the Weird Sisters allied with Maelstrom?

A. Beauty

B. Charm

C. Truth

D. Love

2305. Who was *not* a prisoner on the Stranger's planet in *Quasar* #14–16 (1990)?

A. Jakar

B. Votan

C. Ego-Prime

D. Krakoa the Living Island

2306. Who is Peter Quill?

A. Captain Atlas

B. Count Abyss

C. Foolkiller II in *Omega*

D. Star-Lord

2307.

2308. Who was Senator Kyle Munson?

A. Politician who was impersonated by the Man-Beast

B. Senator who declared the Silver Surfer to be a menace

C. Adversary of X-51 in *Machine Man* series

D. Ally of Zuras in *The Eternals*

2309. To which alien race did Jack of Hearts's mother belong?

A. Contraxians

B. Kree

C. Fomalhauti

D. Pegasusians

2310. Who was Thanos's mother?

A. Hecate

B. Elysius

C. Sui-San

D. Matriarch of the Universal Church of Truth

2311. Who was Fooferah?

A. Starship crew member in *Rocket Raccoon*

B. Superfast rabbit in the Runner's race in *Quasar*

C. Superfast bird in the Runner's race in *Quasar*

D. Alien coyote in the Runner's race in *Quasar*

2307.

Created by writer–artist Jim Starlin in *Iron Man* #55 (1973), Thanos (shown above) has been one of the greatest villains in the Marvel Universe. The son of Mentor, ruler of Saturn's moon Titan, Thanos wiped out millions of the denizens of Titan. Later, Thanos fell in love with Mistress Death, the "abstract being" who incarnates the concept of mortality. In hopes of pleasing her, Thanos plans to commit universal genocide, exterminating all life in the cosmos. His schemes were thwarted by the Avengers, Captain

2312. On which planet was Peter Quill elected King?
A. Chandilar
C. Spartax
B. Titan
D. Skrullos

2313. What cosmic villain is known as the "Destroyer of Destroyers"?
A. Yotat
C. J'Son
B. Hala
D. Kindun

2314. In which alternate universe did Star-Lord, Drax, and Nova trap themselves in order to defeat Thanos?
A. Weirdworld
C. Otherworld
B. The Cancerverse
D. The Dark Dimension

2315. Who was the last Kree Accuser who sought revenge for the destruction of her homeworld?
A. Ronan
C. Nebula
B. Minerva
D. Hala

2316. After losing the throne, Peter Quill's father took what villainous identity?
A. Mr. Knife
C. Yotat
B. Ego
D. Death's Head

2317. What is the name of Thanos's secret Inhuman son?
A. Thane
C. Flint
B. Grid
D. Iso

2318. What was revealed about Thanos in the first issue of his 2016 series?
A. He is now a hero
C. He is married
B. He is dying
D. He is a clone

Mar-Vell, and Adam Warlock. Yet Thanos later allied himself with Warlock and other heroes in opposing such menaces as Warlock's alternate selves, the Magus and the Goddess. Which side Thanos will take in future cosmic conflicts remains to be seen.

Of which race are the gods of Titan such as Mentor and Thanos an offshoot?

A. Gods of Olympus
B. Eternals
C. Asgardians
D. Inhumans

Cosmic Characters

2319. Which Earth are the original Guardians of the Galaxy from?
- **A.** Earth-689
- **B.** Earth-691
- **C.** Earth-238
- **D.** Earth-311

2320. Who is Krugarr?
- **A.** Dictator of the Axi-Tun
- **B.** Empress of the Snarks
- **C.** Pope of the Universal Church of Truth
- **D.** Sorcerer Supreme in the Earth-691 timeline of the *Guardians* series

2321. Who is Dr. Samuel Holden?
- **A.** Companion of Sersi
- **B.** Human who once became part of the Uni-Mind
- **C.** Professor at City College, New York
- **D.** All answers are correct

2322. Where did Dr. Daniel Damian first appear?
- **A.** The *Eternals* #1 (1976)
- **B.** *Fantastic Four* #64 (1967)
- **C.** *Fantastic Four* #65 (1967)
- **D.** None of these

2323.

The most enigmatic series in Marvel history was aptly titled *Omega the Unknown*. The title character was a superhuman alien adult, apparently the last survivor of his race, who escaped from robotlike creatures (shown at right) and journeyed to earth. But arguably the leading character of *Omega* was really a young, precociously intelligent boy named James-Michael Starling, who one day discovered that his supposed parents were actually robots. Both James-Michael and Omega—both of whom could project energy blasts from their hands—went to live in Manhattan's run-down Hell's Kitchen neighborhood. Created by writers Steve Gerber and Mary Skrenes and artist Jim Mooney, *Omega* debuted in 1976 but lasted only ten issues. Writer Steven Grant later resolved the Omega story line in *Defenders*, but we may never know how the late Steve Gerber intended to explain the mysteries of *Omega*, a series which still haunts its admirers. Which major novelist wrote his own comics version of *Omega the Unknown*, published from 2007 into 2008?

- **A.** Jonathan Lethem
- **B.** Michael Chabon
- **C.** Stephen King
- **D.** Neil Gaiman

2324. What was the job of James-Michael Starling's friend Amber Grant?
- **A.** Nurse
- **B.** Reporter for the *Daily Bugle*
- **C.** Artists' life model
- **D.** Freelance photographer for the *Daily Bugle*

2325. Where was Omega the Unknown shot dead?
- **A.** Las Vegas
- **B.** New York City
- **C.** Los Angeles
- **D.** Citrusville, Florida

2326. Which codename did Monica Rambeau use during her time with the Ultimates?

A. Captain Marvel

B. Pulsar

C. Photon

D. Spectrum

2327. Which member of the Ultimates has the power to smash through dimensional barriers?

A. America Chavez

B. Blue Marvel

C. Spectrum

D. Captain Marvel

2328. From where did the Ultimates rescue Anti-Man, the nemesis of the Blue Marvel?

A. The Superflow

B. Exo-Space

C. The Negative Zone

D. Battleworld

2329. Where did the Ultimates make their headquarters?

A. The Triskelion

B. Wakanda

C. Alpha Flight Space Station

D. The Blue Area of the Moon

2330. Who was the human companion of the Silver Surfer in his 2014 series?

A. Rick Jones

B. Dawn Greenwood

C. Alicia Masters

D. Frankie Raye

Cosmic Characters

CHAPTER NINE

MARVEL TIME:
FROM BLACK KNIGHT TO KILLRAVEN

2331. What is Baron Strucker's first name?
- **A.** Ernst
- **B.** Wolfgang
- **C.** Werner
- **D.** Fritz

2332. Whose battle cry was "Okay, Axis, here we come!"?
- **A.** Sgt. Fury and his Howling Commandos
- **B.** The Invaders
- **C.** The 1940s Young Allies
- **D.** The Kid Commandos

2333. Which fellow member of the Liberty Legion did Miss America marry?
- **A.** The Thin Man
- **B.** The Blue Diamond
- **C.** The Whizzer
- **D.** The Patriot

2334. Who created the original Marvel Boy of the 1940s?
- **A.** Bill Everett
- **B.** Bob Oksner
- **C.** Joe Simon and Jack Kirby
- **D.** Stan Lee and Jack Kirby

2335. Who has *not* been known as Marvel Boy?
- **A.** Martin Burns
- **B.** Vance Astrovik
- **C.** Jeff Mace
- **D.** Robert Grayson

2336. Which writer co-created the title character of the 2000 *Marvel Boy* miniseries with artist J. G. Jones?
- A. Garth Ennis
- B. Mark Millar
- C. Grant Morrison
- D. Warren Ellis

2337. To which race does the Marvel Boy of the 2000 miniseries belong?
- **A.** Titanian Eternals
- **B.** Kree
- **C.** Inhumans
- **D.** Uranian Eternals

2338. Who created the 1930s adventurer Dominic Fortune?
A. Len Wein and Dave Cockrum
B. Doug Moench and Paul Gulacy
C. Howard Chaykin
D. Archie Goodwin and Al Williamson

2339. Who was Bob Frank?
A. Captain Daring
B. The Black Marvel
C. The Whizzer
D. The Patriot

2340. What was the name of the modern heroic Black Knight's original winged horse?
A. Valinor
B. Aragorn
C. Pegasus
D. Legolas

2341. How did the Patriot die?
A. He was murdered by the Red Skull
B. Of cancer
C. Of old age
D. He was shot by an assassin

2342.

2343. Who is Sabbath Raven?
A. Killraven's father
B. Killraven's wife
C. Dominic Fortune's girlfriend
D. Killraven's sister

2344. In which war did the members of Freedom's Five fight?
A. World War II
B. World War I
C. American Revolution
D. War of the Worlds

2345. Where was Miss America born?
A. Concord, Massachusetts
B. Philadelphia, Pennsylvania
C. Washington D.C.
D. Boston, Massachusetts

2346. Who or what was Horace Grabsheid?
A. Golden Age Timely Comics artist
B. The Blue Bullet
C. Real name of Marvel Boy's father
D. Real name of Dr. Reinstein of Super-Soldier Project

2342.

In 1955, the Super Hero genre had virtually disappeared from comics. But writer-editor Stan Lee and artist Joe Maneely combined elements of the Super Hero story with the swashbuckler to create Marvel's original Black Knight in *Black Knight* #1 (1955, issue 3 shown at right). A member of King Arthur's court, Sir Percy of Scandia pretended to prefer music to combat. But secretly Sir Percy was the Black Knight, Arthur's greatest champion against such foes as Mordred and Morgan Le Fey. In the 1960s, Marvel introduced two of Sir Percy's descendants: Nathan Garrett, a villainous Black Knight, and Dane Whitman, the present-day heroic Black Knight.

From what did Merlin forge the Black Knight's Ebony Blade?

A. Uru metal
B. Enchanted steel
C. Meteorite
D. Wakandan vibranium

OBSESSED WITH MARVEL

2347. Which major event caused serious damage to Marvel's space-time continuum?
- **A.** *Age of Ultron*
- **B.** *Fear Itself*
- **C.** *Avengers Vs. X-Men*
- **D.** *Infinity*

2348. Who was the future Captain America introduced in *Ultron Forever*?
- **A.** Ian Rogers
- **B.** Franklin Richards
- **C.** Danielle Cage
- **D.** Alex Power

2349. Which Avenger traveled through time to kidnap Kang's infant self, igniting Kang War One?
- **A.** Iron Man
- **B.** Hercules
- **C.** Vision
- **D.** Thor

2350. In an alternate future, whose child did not serve on the Next Avengers?
- **A.** Captain America and Black Widow
- **B.** Black Panther and Storm
- **C.** Hawkeye and Mockingbird
- **D.** Vision and Scarlet Witch

2351. Who was *not* a member of the secret team of heroes featured in *Avengers 1959*?
- **A.** Nick Fury
- **B.** Ulysses Bloodstone
- **C.** Namor
- **D.** Dominic Fortune

2352. Who served with Logan and Sabretooth on a pre-Xavier team in 2012's *First X-Men*?
- **A.** Cyclops
- **B.** Emma Frost
- **C.** Holo
- **D.** Deadpool

2353. Who was *not* a member of the forgotten 1970s team of Mighty Avengers?
- **A.** Blade
- **B.** Kaluu
- **C.** Blue Marvel
- **D.** Luke Cage

2354. During *Original Sin*, who was revealed to have died in the 1960s and replaced by a Life Model Decoy?
- **A.** Dum Dum Dugan
- **B.** Phil Coulson
- **C.** Maria Hill
- **D.** Nick Fury

Marvel Time

2355. How did the Yellow Claw prefer that his name be translated?

- **A.** Golden Claw
- **B.** Golden Talon
- **C.** Golden Fist
- **D.** Golden Hand

2356. What is the real name of the Yellow Claw's right-hand man, Fritz von Voltzmann?

- **A.** Werner von Krimm
- **B.** Karl von Horstbaden
- **C.** Franz Gerhardt
- **D.** Colonel Wolfgang von Krantz

2357. What reason did the Yellow Claw give in *Agents of Atlas* for his many clashes with Jimmy Woo?

- **A.** He claimed he was destined to rule the world
- **B.** He accused Woo of being a pawn of capitalist America
- **C.** He was testing Woo to prove his worth to succeed him as khan
- **D.** He held personal hatred for Woo for daring to oppose him

2358. Who is Mr. Lao?

- **A.** A god
- **B.** A dragon
- **C.** A sorcerer
- **D.** Human executive in the Atlas Foundation

2359. Who created Silly Seal and Ziggy Pig?

- **A.** Stan Lee and Jack Binder
- **B.** Al Jaffee
- **C.** Ernie Hart
- **D.** Vince Fago

2360. Who is smarter, Ziggy Pig or Silly Seal?

- **A.** Silly
- **B.** Ziggy
- **C.** They are equally stupid
- **D.** They are equally clever

2361. Who co-created Jack Frost of the Liberty Legion?

- **A.** France Herron
- **B.** Otto Binder
- **C.** Stan Lee
- **D.** Klaus Nordling

2362. Who is the original Baron Blood?

- **A.** Doctor Strange's brother
- **B.** Vampire nephew of Union Jack I
- **C.** Vampire brother of Union Jack I
- **D.** Grandnephew of Union Jack I

2363. Who refused to rescue the third Phantom Rider from a lethal fall?
- **A.** Caleb Hammer
- **B.** Mockingbird
- **C.** Hawkeye
- **D.** The Rawhide Kid

2364. Who was Flaming Star?
- **A.** Leader of the Skull-Men in *The Blazing Skull*
- **B.** Native American who gave the first Phantom Rider his costume
- **C.** Shaman of the Small-Folk in *Devil Dinosaur*
- **D.** Wizard of the lost civilization of Kalahia in *The Thin Man*

2365.

2366. Who was the original 3-D Man?
- **A.** Chuck Chandler
- **B.** Delroy Garrett
- **C.** Hal Chandler
- **D.** Chuck and Hal Chandler

2367. Who was Plan Chu?
- **A.** Adversary of the Invaders
- **B.** Original leader of Hydra overthrown by Baron Strucker
- **C.** Jimmy Woo's name as the Yellow Claw's successor
- **D.** The Yellow Claw's real name

2368. Who is the principal villain in *The Invaders* #19-21 (1977)?
- **A.** The Red Skull
- **B.** Agent Axis
- **C.** Adolf Hitler
- **D.** Iron Cross

2369. Who is the Venus of *Agents of Atlas*?
- **A.** Mutant with psionic ability to influence emotions
- **B.** Human Super Heroine modeling herself after the goddess Venus
- **C.** One of the Sirens of myth
- **D.** Olympian goddess of love

2365.

By the late 1940s, Super Heroes had lost their popularity with readers, and Marvel successfully turned to another genre, the Western. Kid Colt, Marvel's longest-running Western hero, debuted in *Kid Colt, Outlaw* #1 (1948), and his series continued to 1979. The Rawhide Kid first appeared in *Rawhide Kid* #1 (1955), but it was Stan Lee and Jack Kirby who revamped the character into the classic version in *Rawhide Kid* #17 (1960). Similarly, Lee and Kirby created a new version of the Two-Gun Kid in *Two-Gun Kid* #60 (1962): he was now lawyer Matt Hawk, who secretly became a masked gunfighter. The strangest of Marvel's Western heroes was the original Ghost Rider, later known as Phantom Rider, who posed as an avenging ghost. Created by writers Roy Thomas and Gary Friedrich and artist Dick Ayers, he debuted in *Ghost Rider* #1 (1967). Which writer guest starred all four Western heroes in *The Avengers* #142 (1975, shown at left)?

- **A.** Roy Thomas
- **B.** Gerry Conway
- **C.** Steve Englehart
- **D.** Roger Stern

Marvel Time

2370. Which of the following describes one of the three versions of the character known as Gorilla-Man?

A. M'Baku

B. Member of the High Evolutionary's New Men

C. Member of the Headmen

D. Member of the Unholy Three

2371. Which jungle hero has guest starred in *Agents of Atlas*?

A. Original Ka-Zar

B. The Black Panther's father T'Chaka

C. Shanna the She-Devil

D. Jann of the Jungle

2372. In which series did the group that later became the Agents of Atlas previously appear?

A. *Avengers Forever*

B. *What If?*

C. Both A and B

D. Neither A nor B

2373. What is the real name of the original Gorilla-Man of the 1950s?

A. Ken Hale

B. Jeff Mace

C. Arthur Nagan

D. Franz Radzik

2374. Who was *not* one of the Kid Commandos?

A. Bucky

B. Human Top

C. Spitfire

D. Golden Girl

2375. Whose parents were Fred and Nora?

A. Bucky

B. Toro

C. Human Top

D. Nick Fury

2376.

2377. Who is Gwenny Lou Sabuki?

A. Jimmy Woo's girlfriend

B. Sun Girl

C. Golden Girl (*The Invaders*)

D. Golden Girl (Timely Comics version)

2378. Which Marvel character is summoned by Hitler as an ally in *The Invaders* #32 (1978)?

A. Apocalypse

B. Dormammu

C. Thor

D. Loki

2376.

According to *What If?* #9 (1978), back in 1958 FBI agent Jimmy Woo first organized a team known as the Agents of Atlas (inspired by Atlas Comics, Marvel's name at the time) because his nemesis, the Yellow Claw, had kidnapped a major political figure. Joining the team were Marvel Boy (the 1950s version); Venus; the original Gorilla-Man; and M-11, the Human Robot. The team rescued the Claw's captive but later disbanded. Then in 2006 came the limited series *Agents of Atlas* (issue 1 shown above), written by Jeff Parker and drawn by Leonard Kirk. Woo, now a S.H.I.E.L.D. agent, reunited the team, which

2379. Which Western hero traveled from the nineteenth century into the twentieth century to work alongside Hawkeye and the Avengers?

A. The Rawhide Kid
B. The Ringo Kid
C. Kid Colt
D. Two-Gun Kid

2380. Which Marvel hero has the same name that the Phantom Rider originally had?

A. Ghost Rider
B. The Punisher
C. The Spirit of Vengeance
D. Terror

2381. Which Western hero was raised by Ben Bart of the Texas Rangers?

A. Rawhide Kid
B. The Outlaw Kid
C. Two-Gun Kid
D. Kid Colt

2382. Why was Kid Colt considered an outlaw?

A. He shot a man in self-defense
B. He shot his foster father's murderers
C. He killed his father's murderer
D. He was formerly a member of a gang of bank robbers

2383. How did the Yellow Claw (apparently) meet his end in *Agents of Atlas*?

A. He was murdered by his rival
B. He was killed in combat with Jimmy Woo
C. He was swallowed by a dragon
D. Extreme old age

2384. What is Kid Colt's first name?

A. Ben
B. Lance
C. Blaine
D. Johnny

2385. Which name has been given as the Rawhide Kid's real name?

A. Johnny Clay
B. Johnny Bart
C. Both A and B
D. Neither A nor B

2386. Which Western hero rode a horse named Steel?

A. The Outlaw Kid
B. Reno Jones
C. Kid Cassidy
D. Kid Colt

now also included the Sub-Mariner's cousin Namora. Together they battled the Yellow Claw's Atlas Foundation. The Claw named Woo as his successor and apparently committed suicide. Woo and his Agents of Atlas determined to use the Atlas Foundation to fight for justice.

Who did the Claw kidnap in 1958?

A. Vice President Richard M. Nixon
B. Senator John F. Kennedy
C. President Dwight Eisenhower
D. President Harry S. Truman

Marvel Time

2387. Which of the following best describes Kid Colt when he was a member of the 2000 version of the Young Allies?

A. Alien Kymellian

B. Descendant of original Kid Colt

C. Part human, part Kymellian

D. Modern cowboy who models himself after Kid Colt

2388. Where did Matthew Hawk get his education?

A. Princeton University

B. Columbia University

C. Yale University

D. Harvard University

2389. Which Western hero rode a horse named Apache?

A. The Apache Kid

B. The Rawhide Kid

C. Arizona Annie

D. Red Wolf

2390. How did the Phantom Rider convince people he was a ghost?

A. He faked his own death

B. He wore a phosphorescent costume

C. He learned mystical spells from an American Indian shaman

D. He possessed mental ability to cast illusions

2391. Where was the Two-Gun Kid based?

A. Tombstone, California

B. Tombstone, New Mexico

C. Tombstone, Arizona

D. Tombstone, Texas

2392. Who was the original Phantom Rider?

A. Lincoln Slade

B. Reno Jones

C. Hamilton Slade

D. Carter Slade

2393. Who is the heroic Phantom Rider who lives in the twenty-first century?

A. Carter Slade

B. Hamilton Slade

C. Lincoln Slade

D. Reno Jones

2394. To which team does the twenty-first-century Phantom Rider belong?

A. Outlaws

B. Rangers

C. Four Horsemen of the Apocalypse

D. Nightstalkers

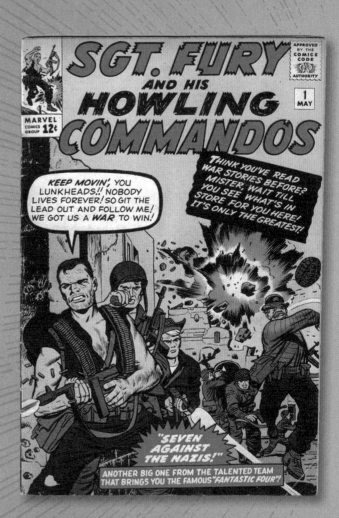

2399.

Stan Lee and Jack Kirby—having already revitalized the Super Hero genre with series such as *Fantastic Four*—proved they could keep creating winners when they launched the war comic *Sgt. Fury and His Howling Commandos* #1 (1963, shown at left). Set during World War II, the series starred the indomitable Sgt. Nick Fury who headed a special unit of U.S. Rangers known unofficially as the Howling Commandos. Fury's right-hand man was Corporal "Dum Dum" Dugan, a brawny Irish American with a trademark red mustache and derby. Also in the unit: Gabe Jones, Marvel's first African American hero; and Izzy Cohen, Marvel's first explicitly Jewish hero. Other Howlers included young "Junior" Juniper, German defector Eric Koenig, Italian American movie star Dino Manelli, Englishman Percy Pinkerton, and Southerner "Reb" Ralston.

Which member of the Howlers was killed in the fourth issue?

A. Eric Koenig
B. Izzy Cohen
C. Junior Juniper
D. Pinky Pinkerton

2395. For whom did the Western hero Caleb Hammer work?
- **A.** Federal government
- **B.** Pinkerton's Detective Agency
- **C.** No one; he was a gun for hire
- **D.** Texas Rangers

2396. Which writer co-created Caleb Hammer?
- **A.** Gary Friedrich
- **B.** Peter B. Gillis
- **C.** Don McGregor
- **D.** Steve Englehart

2397. Who wrote the series *Blaze of Glory* (2000) that reunited Marvel's Western characters?
- **A.** John Ostrander
- **B.** Tom DeFalco
- **C.** Ron Zimmermann
- **D.** Jimmy Palmiotti

2398. What was the Howling Commandos' battle cry?
- **A.** "Hawk-a-a-a!"
- **B.** "Wahoo!"
- **C.** "Yahoo!"
- **D.** "It's clobbering time!"

2399.

2400. Who was Lady Pamela Hawley?
- **A.** Spitfire in *The Invaders*
- **B.** Nick Fury's deceased girlfriend
- **C.** Nick Fury's wife
- **D.** Wife of Union Jack I

2401. To which officer did Sgt. Nick Fury report?
- **A.** Sam Sawyer
- **B.** Simon Savage
- **C.** Colonel Krag
- **D.** General Argyle Fist

2402. What job did Reb Ralston hold after leaving the military?
- **A.** Truck driver
- **B.** Newspaper owner
- **C.** U.S. senator
- **D.** Corporate executive

2403. Whom did Captain Simon Savage encounter in issues #2-4 (1968) of *Captain Savage and His Leatherneck Raiders*?
- **A.** The Hand
- **B.** Baron Strucker and Hydra
- **C.** The Red Skull
- **D.** The Yellow Claw

Marvel Time

2404. Who first succeeded Jack Kirby as the principal artist on *Sgt. Fury*?
- **A.** John Severin
- **B.** Dick Ayers
- **C.** Marie Severin
- **D.** Doug Wildey

2405. What was Sam Sawyer's nickname?
- **A.** Sad
- **B.** Happy
- **C.** Angry
- **D.** The Old Man

2406. What musical instrument did Gabe Jones play?
- **A.** Trombone
- **B.** Bugle
- **C.** Drums
- **D.** Piano

2407. In which war did the Howling Commandos *not* serve?
- **A.** World War II
- **B.** Korea
- **C.** Vietnam
- **D.** First Gulf War

2408. In which nation did Hydra originate?
- **A.** Germany
- **B.** Greece
- **C.** China
- **D.** Japan

2409. What job did Percy Pinkerton hold after leaving the military?
- **A.** Manager of a pub in London
- **B.** Author
- **C.** Manager of a Playboy-style gentleman's club
- **D.** Mercenary leader

2410.

2411. Which of the following is *not* one of the real names of the 1940s Young Allies?
- **A.** Geoffrey Worthington Vandergill
- **B.** Henry Tinkle
- **C.** Pat O'Toole
- **D.** Washington Carver Jones

2412. Whose sidekick was Boom Boom Brown?
- **A.** Rawhide Kid
- **B.** Two-Gun Kid
- **C.** Kid Colt
- **D.** The Gunhawks

2410.

In creating the Invaders, writer Roy Thomas and legendary comic strip artist Frank Robbins were filling a gap that Marvel had left open in the early 1940s, when it was still called Timely Comics. Its leading Super Heroes had not formed into a team until the All Winners Squad in *All Winners Comics* #19, in 1946. Thomas and Robbins thought, what if Timely Comics' greatest Super Hero stars had joined forces against the Axis powers—Germany, Italy, and Japan—during World War II? In *Giant-Size Invaders* #1 (1975, shown at right), Captain America, his sidekick Bucky, the original Human Torch and his partner, Toro, and the Sub-Mariner teamed up to fight the Axis powers in their own territory before the armies of America, Britain, and their allies could mount full-scale invasions. Thomas later revived lesser-known Timely Super Heroes to form the Liberty Legion, a team to battle enemy agents on the home front.

Who suggested the formation of the Invaders in *Giant-Size Invaders* #1 (1975)?

- **A.** Franklin Delano Roosevelt
- **B.** General Dwight Eisenhower
- **C.** Captain America
- **D.** Winston Churchill

OBSESSED WITH MARVEL

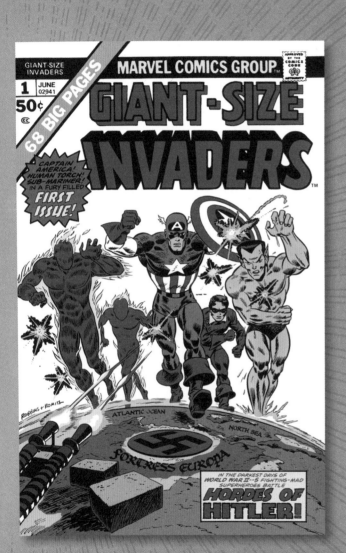

2413. Whom did the Patriot marry?
- **A.** Elizabeth Barstow
- **B.** Betty Dean
- **C.** Betsy Ross
- **D.** No one

2414. Which Golden Age character was *not* co-created by Stan Lee?
- **A.** The Blonde Phantom
- **B.** The 1940s Vision
- **C.** Father Time
- **D.** The Witness

2415. Who was *not* a member of the Liberty Legion?
- **A.** The Patriot
- **B.** The Blue Diamond
- **C.** The Fin
- **D.** The Red Raven

2416. What is the name of Nick Fury's sister?
- **A.** Katherine
- **B.** Laura
- **C.** Maria
- **D.** Dawn

2417. Who was the original Union Jack?
- **A.** John Falsworth
- **B.** Montgomery Falsworth
- **C.** Brian Falsworth
- **D.** Roger Aubrey

2418. In which war did the first Union Jack fight?
- **A.** World War II
- **B.** Second Boer War
- **C.** World War I
- **D.** None of these

2419. Which Super Heroine did Jacqueline Falsworth become?
- **A.** Silver Scorpion
- **B.** Spitfire
- **C.** Sun Girl
- **D.** Blonde Phantom

2420. Who was U-Man?
- **A.** Member of the First Line
- **B.** Cyborg soldier in *Deathlok*
- **C.** Robot created by Baron Heinrich Zemo
- **D.** Atlantean Super Villain working with Nazis

Marvel Time

2421. Who was Willie Lohmer?
- **A.** Master Man
- **B.** Iron Cross
- **C.** Agent Axis
- **D.** Nazi agent working with the Crusaders

2422. Who was *not* a member of Freedom's Five?
- **A.** Crimson Cavalier
- **B.** Ghost Girl
- **C.** Sir Steel
- **D.** Phantom Eagle

2423. Who was *not* one of the Crusaders?
- **A.** Spirit of '76
- **B.** Tommy Lightning
- **C.** Warrior Woman
- **D.** Dyna-Mite

2424. Who was the original Destroyer in the 1940s comics?
- **A.** Brian Falsworth
- **B.** Keen Marlow
- **C.** Jack Castle
- **D.** Roger Aubrey

2425. How did the Whizzer obtain his super-powers?
- **A.** By inhaling "heavy water"
- **B.** Through a transfusion of mongoose blood
- **C.** Through a cobra bite
- **D.** Through a mongoose bite

2426. How many issues did *Red Raven Comics* last?
- **A.** One
- **B.** Six
- **C.** Ten
- **D.** Twelve

2427. Who created the Red Raven?
- **A.** Otto Binder and Al Gabriele
- **B.** Joe Simon and Jack Kirby
- **C.** Joe Simon and Louis Cazeneuve
- **D.** Stan Lee and Al Gabriele

2428. Of which race were Red Raven's Bird-People an offshoot?
- **A.** Shi'ar
- **B.** Inhumans
- **C.** Deviants
- **D.** Eternals

2429. Where did Red Raven's Bird-People live?
- **A.** Floating island in the sky
- **B.** An alternate dimension
- **C.** A hidden city atop a mountain in Europe
- **D.** An uncharted island in the Bermuda Triangle

2430. Who was Jamie Jacobs?
- **A.** The Golem of World War II
- **B.** The Super Hero Fiery Mask
- **C.** The second Phantom Rider
- **D.** The Black Marvel

2431. Who was the cyborg Siege in *Deathlok*?
- **A.** Jeff Mace
- **B.** Jack Castle
- **C.** Patrick Carney
- **D.** John Kelly

2432.

Deathlok (shown at left), created by artist Rich Buckler and writer Doug Moench, first appeared in *Astonishing Tales* #25 (1974). In the future of an alternate timeline, Colonel Luther Manning was mortally injured by a concussion bomb. The Ryker brothers, Simon and Harlan, had Manning converted into a cyborg warrior called Deathlok, who was part man and part machine. Deathlok overcame his programming and rebelled against Simon Ryker, who intended to use cyborg soldiers to conquer the world.

Sixteen years after his creation, a new Deathlok was introduced into the mainstream Marvel Universe set in the present day. Instead of Luther Manning, the mortal behind the warrior was named Michael Collins. Created by writers Dwayne McDuffie and Gregory Wright and artist Jackson Guice, the Collins Deathlok debuted in *Deathlok* #1 (1990). S.H.I.E.L.D. agent Jack Truman became yet another Deathlok cyborg in the 1999–2000 *Deathlok* limited series.

In what year, in the alternate timeline, was Luther Manning resurrected as Deathlok?

- **A.** 2099
- **B.** 1985
- **C.** 1990
- **D.** 2020

2433. By what name was the original Deathlok also known?
- **A.** The Annihilator
- **B.** The Obliterator
- **C.** The Destroyer
- **D.** The Demolisher

2434. On which alternate Earth did the Luther Manning Deathlok originate?
- **A.** Earth-5311
- **B.** Earth-4935
- **C.** Earth-7484
- **D.** Earth-4263

2435. Who is Dr. Bruce Dickson?
- **A.** The Patriot
- **B.** The Blue Blade
- **C.** The Thin Man
- **D.** The Black Marvel

2436. Who is Madeline Joyce?
- **A.** The Silver Scorpion
- **B.** The Blonde Phantom
- **C.** The 1940s Black Widow
- **D.** Miss America

2437. What other leading character was created by Rich Buckler?
- **A.** Gabriel, Devil Hunter
- **B.** Devil-Slayer
- **C.** Son of Satan
- **D.** Terror, Inc.

Marvel Time

2438. Who was Elton R. Morrow?
A. Captain Wings
B. The Blue Diamond
C. The Black Marvel
D. Phantom Reporter

2439. Whose adversary was Toughy Cat?
A. Slapstick
B. The Blonde Phantom
C. Ziggy Pig and Silly Seal
D. Super Rabbit

2440. Who was Dr. Robert Paine?
A. Captain Wonder
B. The Black Fox
C. Dynamic Man
D. Phantom Reporter

2441. To whom was the hippie Super Hero Captain Hip married?
A. Pixie
B. Sunshine
C. Rapunzel
D. Firefall

2442. About how long can Chuck Chandler exist as a three-dimensional being?
A. One hour
B. Three hours
C. Twenty-four hours
D. Three days

2443. What was Chuck Chandler's occupation before becoming the 3-D Man?
A. Test pilot
B. Secret agent
C. Soldier
D. Scientist

2444.

2445. Who were the 3-D Man's principal adversaries in the 1950s?
A. Communist agents
B. Hydra
C. Political witch-hunters
D. The Skrulls

2446. Who else besides the *Lost Generation* hero is known as the Black Fox?
A. Villain from *Strange Tales Annual* #2 (1963)
B. Female adversary of Luke Cage
C. New Man serving the Man-Beast
D. Elderly jewel thief in *Spider-Man*

2444.

In H. G. Wells's classic 1898 science-fiction novel *The War of the Worlds*, Martians invade the Earth in an ultimately unsuccessful attempt at conquest. In *Amazing Adventures* #18 (1973), writers Roy Thomas and Gerry Conway and artist–co-plotter Neal Adams created a sequel to Wells's saga, Marvel's own *War of the Worlds* series. In an alternate future over a century since the events in Wells's novel, the Martians return to Earth. This time, they succeed in taking over the planet. Under Martian rule, an orphaned boy grows up to become the gladiator known as Killraven

2447. Who is Eric Simon Payne?
- **A.** Devil-Slayer
- **B.** The Patriot
- **C.** The Thunderer
- **D.** Captain Terror

2448. Which Golden Age heroes are *not* members of The Twelve in the series of that name?
- **A.** The original Black Widow and Mr. E
- **B.** The Challenger and the Thunderer
- **C.** The Fiery Mask and the Laughing Mask
- **D.** The Witness and Rockman

2449. Which member of the Lost Generation of Marvel heroes was an Eternal?
- **A.** Pixie
- **B.** Major Mercury
- **C.** Both A and B
- **D.** Oxbow

2450. What was the name of Killraven's mother?
- **A.** Mary
- **B.** Martha
- **C.** Marsha
- **D.** Maureen

2451. Who was Grok?
- **A.** Clone of Volcana Ash's husband
- **B.** Clone of Carmilla Frost's father
- **C.** Carmilla Frost's mutated brother
- **D.** Clone of Mint Julep's brother

2452. In which year did the Martians' second invasion of Earth occur in the *Killraven* series?
- **A.** 2100
- **B.** 2025
- **C.** 2001
- **D.** 1999

2453. Who was *not* a member of Killraven's Freemen?
- **A.** Volcana Ash
- **B.** Hawk
- **C.** M'Shulla Scott
- **D.** Old Skull

2454. Who or what was Mourning Prey?
- **A.** Hunter in *Devil Dinosaur*
- **B.** Native American in *Red Wolf*
- **C.** Insectlike mutant in *Killraven*
- **D.** Outlaw in *Killraven*

(shown above). Breaking free from the alien rulers, Killraven becomes the leader of the Freemen, a band of freedom fighters determined to overthrow the Martians. The series was soon renamed *Killraven* and reached its creative heights under writer Don McGregor and artist P. Craig Russell.

What is Killraven's real name?

- **A.** Joshua Raven
- **B.** Donald Raven
- **C.** Jonathan Raven
- **D.** Kevin Raven

Marvel Time

2455. Which artist co-created the Whizzer?
- **A.** Al Avison
- **B.** Syd Shores
- **C.** Klaus Nordling
- **D.** Jack Kirby

2456. What is the Beat Street Club?
- **A.** Coffeehouse hangout of Captain Hip
- **B.** Clubhouse in *Ziggy Pig and Silly Seal*
- **C.** Coffee shop in *3-D Man*
- **D.** Headquarters of the Fallen Angels

2457. Who is Super Nazi?
- **A.** Superhuman enemy of the Invaders
- **B.** Original name of Master Man
- **C.** Human adversary of Captain America
- **D.** Pig enemy of Super Rabbit

2458. Who did *not* guest star in *Marvel: The Lost Generation*, set before the Fantastic Four's origin?
- **A.** Ikaris
- **B.** Doctor Strange
- **C.** Nick Fury
- **D.** Thor

2459. How does Super Rabbit gain his super-powers?
- **A.** By drinking a secret potion
- **B.** By rubbing his magic ring
- **C.** By reciting a secret formula
- **D.** By shouting a magic word

2460. When did Super Rabbit debut?
- **A.** 1930
- **B.** 1940
- **C.** 1943
- **D.** 1963

2461. Who is the enemy of Dr. Yesterday?
- **A.** Slapstick
- **B.** Super Rabbit
- **C.** Deathlok
- **D.** Killraven

2462. What can Devil-Slayer do with his shadow cloak?

A. Open portals to other dimensions

B. Cause it to obey his mental commands

C. Teleport over limited distances

D. All answers are correct

2463. Who created Citizen V and the Blue Diamond?

A. Bill Everett

B. Stan Lee and Jack Binder

C. Joe Simon and Jack Kirby

D. Ben Thompson

2464. Who did *not* join the Fallen Angels?

A. Siryn and Warlock

B. Boom Boom and Sunspot

C. Magik and Magma

D. Ariel and Chance

2465. On which alternate earth did Devil Dinosaur originate?

A. Earth-82432

B. Earth-78411

C. Earth-148611

D. Earth-7414

2466. Which X-Men villain organized the group that became the Fallen Angels?

A. Mystique

B. Nanny

C. Vanisher

D. Mister Sinister

2467.

2468. Which writer co-created the Fallen Angels?

A. Louise Simonson

B. Terry Austin

C. Ann Nocenti

D. Jo Duffy

2469. What are Bill and Don, the cybernetically enhanced pets of Gomi of the Fallen Angels?

A. Lobsters

B. Monkeys

C. Cats

D. Turtles

2467.

In a primeval world, a brutal tribe of early humans called the Killer-Folk captured a young dinosaur that looked like a Tyrannosaurus rex, and attempted to kill him with fire. Instead, Moon-Boy, a young, fur-covered humanoid of the Small-Folk, set the dinosaur free. Devil, as he called the dinosaur, had not escaped unscathed; the fire had permanently turned his hide bright red. Devil Dinosaur, a surprisingly intelligent beast, was grateful and loyal to Moon-Boy, and they became inseparable companions. Debuting in *Devil Dinosaur* #1 (1978, shown at left), Devil and Moon-Boy were created by Jack Kirby. The series lasted merely nine issues; nonetheless, Devil Dinosaur has had a cult following and continues to appear. Though Kirby intended *Devil Dinosaur* to be set in prehistoric times on Earth, Marvel later established that Devil and Moon-Boy were from an alternate Earth in the present day.

To which Super Hero team did Devil Dinosaur and Moon-Boy once belong?

A. Guardians of the Galaxy

B. Fin Fang Four

C. Fallen Angels

D. Defenders

2470. Who was Timely Comics' original Black Widow?
- **A.** Agent of Satan
- **B.** Former Nazi agent
- **C.** Russian spy battling Nazis
- **D.** Woman detective avenging her dead husband

2471. How did the Blue Diamond gain his diamond-hard skin, which gave him super-strength and near-invulnerability?
- **A.** Mutation
- **B.** Experiments to create a super-soldier
- **C.** Diamond fragments embedded in his body
- **D.** Mystical transformation

2472. How did Miss America gain super-powers?
- **A.** She was injected with a Super-Soldier serum
- **B.** She was endowed with powers by the spirit of Uncle Sam
- **C.** She tampered with an experimental device that was hit by lightning
- **D.** A lightning bolt hit her

2473. What were Miss America's super-powers?
- **A.** Flight
- **B.** Super-strength
- **C.** Both A and B
- **D.** Super-speed

2474. Who is Elizabeth Barstow?
- **A.** Ghost Girl
- **B.** The Silver Scorpion
- **C.** The Blonde Phantom
- **D.** The 1940s Black Widow

2475. Who is Mark Anthony Todd?
- **A.** The Black Marvel
- **B.** The Blazing Skull
- **C.** The Patriot
- **D.** The Red Raven

2476.

2476.

One of Marvel's greatest comics miniseries, *Marvels*, retold the history of Super Heroes from the late 1930s into the early 1970s from the point of view of photojournalist Phil Sheldon. First published in 1994, *Marvels* was the breakthrough project for its two creators, writer Kurt Busiek and artist Alex Ross. Ross's painted artwork succeeded in combining a sense of the fantastic with a heightened photorealism, vividly bringing the classic Marvel characters—the "Marvels"—to life. In the course of *Marvels*, Sheldon witnessed the debut of the original Human Torch and became a war correspondent covering the new

OBSESSED WITH MARVEL

Super Heroes' battles against the Nazis. A great supporter of Super Heroes, decades later Sheldon was present at the wedding of Reed Richards and Susan Storm, and also for the first appearance of Galactus on Earth. But upon witnessing Spider-Man's failure to save the life of Gwen Stacy, Sheldon became disillusioned with the Marvels he once idolized.

Who created the 2009 sequel, *Marvels: Eye of the Camera* (shown above)?

A. Kurt Busiek and Alex Ross
B. Jim Krueger and Alex Ross
C. Mark Waid and Alex Ross
D. Kurt Busiek, Roger Stern, and Jay Anacleto

2477. What is Electroplasm?
A. Living unstable molecules composing Slapstick's body
B. Energy force that animated Timely's robot hero Electro
C. Power source for the 1950s Atlas Communist villain Electro
D. Organic power source for M-11, the Human Robot

2478. How did Captain Hip and Sunshine acquire their super-powers?
A. Experimental psychedelic drugs
B. CIA experiments
C. Mutation
D. They had no actual super-powers

2479. Which hero did *not* survive after the defeat of the Skrull invaders in *Marvel: The Lost Generation* #12 (2000)?
A. Black Fox
B. Major Mercury
C. Pixie
D. Yankee Clipper

2480. What is the name of Phil Sheldon's wife?
A. Beth
B. Doris
C. Jennie
D. Maggie

2481. Who was the original Citizen V?
A. J. J. Watkins
B. Dallas Riordan
C. Paulette Brazee
D. John Watkins

2482. What is the name of the mutant girl whom Phil Sheldon aided in *Marvels*?
A. Maggie
B. Ann
C. Carol
D. Valerie

2483. What ailment struck Phil Sheldon in *Marvels: Eye of the Camera*?
A. Cancer
B. Heart disease
C. Blindness
D. Alzheimer's disease

2484. Whom did Phil Sheldon meet in the final panels of *Marvels* (1994)?
A. Alex Power
B. Frank Castle
C. Dan Ketch
D. Kitty Pryde

Marvel Time

2485. From which century did Dr. Cassandra Locke travel in *Lost Generation*?
    A. twenty-second   **C.** twenty-seventh
    B. twenty-fifth   **D.** thirtieth

2486. Who was Ruth McCrae?
    A. Rebound   **C.** Firefall
    B. Rapunzel   **D.** Gadfly

2487. Where did Dr. Robert Paine teach?
    A. Empire State University   **C.** Northeastern University
    B. Northwestern University   **D.** University of Chicago

2488. What was the name of Black Fox's beloved who was killed by Nocturne?
    A. Martha   **C.** Marian
    B. Mary   **D.** Miriam

2489. Which member of the First Line originated in comics as the Eternal Brain?
    A. Reflex   **C.** Flatiron
    B. Walkabout   **D.** Yeti

2490. Who created the comedy character Powerhouse Pepper, who appeared in the 1940s in *Timely Comics*?
    A. Dan DeCarlo   **C.** Harvey Kurtzman
    B. Al Jaffee   **D.** Basil Wolverton

2491. Who was once believed to have killed Professor William Carmody?
    A. Nocturne   **C.** The Deviants
    B. The Skrulls   **D.** None of these

2492. What did Pixie's "pixie dust" do?
    A. Paralyze her adversaries   **C.** Levitate people and objects
    B. Shrink people and objects   **D.** Temporarily turn people to stone

2493. What was Nightingale's super-power in *Lost Generation*?
    A. Powerful vibrations of voice   **C.** Healing
    B. Flight   **D.** Telepathy

OBSESSED WITH MARVEL

2494. What was the connection between the Templar and the Squire in *Lost Generation*?

A. Teacher and student
C. Older and younger brothers
B. Father and son
D. Uncle and nephew

2495. When Mr. Justice was a boy, whose sidekick was he?

A. The Patriot
C. The Spirit of '76
B. Black Fox
D. Yankee Clipper

2496. What was the secret of Effigy, a member of the First Line?

A. He was a Soviet double agent
C. He was a mutant
B. He was a U.S. agent spying on the First Line
D. He was a Skrull

2497.

2497.

By the year 2000, over half a century had passed since the start of Marvel's Golden Age. With their 2000–2001 series *Marvel: The Lost Generation* (issue 1 shown at left), writer Roger Stern and artist John Byrne chronicled an untold history of Super Heroes between World War II and the debut of the Fantastic Four. Most of the featured Super Heroes belonged to the team called the First Line (shown at left), including the original Black Fox, Effigy, Flatiron, Major Mercury, Mr. Justice, Oxbow, Pixie, and Walkabout. The majority were ultimately killed thwarting an invasion by the alien Skrulls, so America was without Super Heroes when the Fantastic Four made their debut, launching the Marvel Age of Comics.

What was atypical about the publication of *Marvel: The Lost Generation*?

A. It was published every two weeks
B. It was published from issue #12 to #1, with stories in reverse chronological order
C. It was published as a series of three four-issue miniseries
D. It was published on a weekly basis

2498. Who is Jeff Mace?

A. The Yankee Clipper
C. The Spirit of '76
B. The Patriot
D. Mr. Justice

2499. Which Western hero's real last name was Liebowicz?

A. Kid Cassidy
C. The Black Rider
B. Two-Gun Kid
D. The Rawhide Kid

2500. Who is Waffles?

A. Friend of Slapstick
C. Supporting character in *Ziggy Pig and Silly Seal*
B. Secret identity of Super Rabbit
D. Supporting character in *Two-Gun Kid*

Marvel Time

ABOUT THE AUTHORS

Peter Sanderson has co-written and authored ten books on Marvel Comics, including *The Marvel Vault*, *The Marvel Encyclopedia*, and multiple volumes of *The Official Handbook of the Marvel Universe*. He lives in New York City.

Marc Sumerak is an Eisner and Harvey Award nominated writer and editor whose work has been seen in countless publications from Marvel Comics for nearly two decades. He is the author of Marvel's *Avengers Armory* and Marvel's *Guardians of the Galaxy: Rocket's Guide* for Scholastic. Marc lives in Cleveland, Ohio, where he continues to write an endless stream of comics, books, and video games. Find out more at www.sumerak.com.